CALL TO ARMS

STEWART BINNIE

First Edition
Copyright 2016 Stewart Binnie
All rights reserved

All characters in this publication, with the exception of prominent politicians and soldiers of the day, are fictitious and any resemblance to real persons, living or dead, is purely coincidental.

AUTHOR'S NOTE

When Europe went to war in 1914, the British Expeditionary Force comprised six regular divisions. The French Army mobilised sixty two infantry divisions and the German Army fielded eighty seven.

The British Army relied on volunteers and by the end of 1915, the number of men under arms had risen to over two and a half million. Nonetheless, the size of the army was still inadequate and the flood of volunteers had diminished as a result of the demands of the war economy and the scale of the casualties.

When the Government introduced military conscription in January 1916, single men between the ages of eighteen and forty one were required to register for military service. This was soon extended to married men and the age limit was raised. Those seeking to avoid enlistment on grounds of ill-health, occupation, personal belief or family obligations were subject to the scrutiny of military tribunals.

Claimants found to have no valid grounds for exemption were offered the choice of enlistment, manual labour under military or Home Office supervision or imprisonment involving recurring sentences with hard labour.

Sixteen thousand men, eligible for military service, objected to conscription. Many agreed to perform non-combatant duties but some 'absolutists' refused to undertake compulsory service of any kind, often spending three years or more in prison. Seventy three died in prison or after release as a result of the effect of hard labour on their physical and mental health.

By November 1918, the British Empire had four million men under arms and had suffered almost nine hundred thousand casualties. Two million men had been wounded.

Two hundred and fifty thousand recruits were under age at the time of their enlistment.

ABOUT THE AUTHOR

Stewart Binnie's first novel *Across The Water* was published by Secker and Warburg in 1979. His recently completed novel, *Call to Arms*, the story of a Quaker family in the Great War, has been in the making for twenty years, and is the first of several, historical and contemporary works, he intends to write.

Stewart's professional life began in publishing and included stints as an editor in the college department of McGraw Hill, group sales director at WHS Distributors and five years as Managing Director of Hatchards, during which time that business grew from a single store in Piccadilly to a chain of thirty branches.

The growth of Hatchards led to career in private equity, initially at Schroder Ventures and Schroders, and thereafter to the leadership of a succession of private equity-backed businesses, largely in the fashion industry. They included ten years as chairman of Aurora Fashions, the holding company of brands such as Oasis, Warehouse, Karen Millen and Coast, and as the chairman of other retail businesses. His most recent appointment was that of chairman and CEO of Jaeger. His private equity activities have also included periods as chairman of Helicon Publishing Group and a director of Cassell plc.

Stewart was a director of the Edinburgh International Festival for six years and was on the board of the Traverse Theatre, Scotland's leading new writing theatre, for four years. Stewart now writes for publication on a full-time basis.

To Carol, Duncan and Madeleine

PART I

April 1916

CHAPTER 1

The town hall stood on a gentle slope, a thoroughfare alive with traffic. Red motor buses with tumbling staircases spilt passengers from open decks or jostled carts and bicycles as they stuttered down the road. *Maples Carpets*, one declared; *New Zealand Butter*, said another as hats, caps and boaters mingled on its steps. The Gothic building with its canopied doorway, tall windows and clock tower remained unmoved, its fluttering flags its only hint of grandeur. The war had given the flags a lease of life. They had seemed to flutter more vigorously since the outbreak of hostilities. Behind them, rows of terraced houses, lines of smoking chimneys pressed upward from a river that turned and twisted as it flowed, an artery that lined by wharves and warehouses, surged towards the sea.

The town hall door was firmly closed, the pavement thronged with visitors. Workmen queued haphazardly, smoking, ragging each other in loud, persistent voices designed to mask their apprehension. Many had removed their caps in anticipation of their appearance before the tribunal. The employers formed a group apart, in sombre suits, high collars and black, top hats, watch chains glinting in the sun, vexed that the days of cheap, plentiful labour were gone forever, destroyed by an army unmindful of their needs.

Robert edged along the crowded pavement, his sister at his side, bemused to find so many claimants there. It seemed that applicants from every walk of life sought exemption from conscription. He looked about him nervously, the bravado with which he had left the house giving way to feelings more in keeping with his uncertain future. He had been teaching at Swarthmore, a Quaker college in Pennsylvania, when war had been declared in August 1914 and hadn't witnessed the patriotic fervour, the rush to enlist of the early months of the war

"Surprised to see so many people?" Alice asked. "Well, don't be. The days of the eager volunteer are behind us.

"That's hardly surprising when the casualty lists are so long."

"It's not only that. The employers are digging in their heels. They've realised how much profit's to be made from supplying the army's needs. Suddenly, every occupation is vital to the war effort, no matter how obscure."

"So am I wasting my time?" Robert asked, hinting at the uncertainty he had been at such pains to conceal from his family.

Alice inhaled the aroma of hops from the nearby brewery. The brewery yard had been a makeshift parade ground in the early months of the war. It had led to many ribald comments by tired volunteers as they marched, wheeled and sloped their arms before the brewery walls.

She shrugged, smiling at her brother fondly. It was good to have him back after his long absence. It would be so cruel if he was conscripted soon. She said, "Who knows? The tribunals aren't courts of law - far from it."

"They're required to uphold the law. That must count for something – even at a time like this?"

"They don't hear evidence or call witnesses. You present your case to them and they consider it. That's about it, really. They have many prejudices, their judgements are uneven and they have more work than they can handle. The law's ambiguous as well, or at least many of the tribunal members think it is. Some of them haven't read the Act."

Robert refused to be discouraged. He felt his case was strong. He was more than willing to support the war effort, providing that he wasn't conscripted or subject to military supervision. Nonetheless, he wasn't looking forward to airing his beliefs. It wasn't that he thought they didn't bear scrutiny or that his intentions contradicted them. He was embarrassed to proclaim them for fear of sounding pompous or self-righteous. Beliefs in his view were a private thing, best kept out of sight.

He had hardly unpacked his trunk before his conscription papers had arrived and he had been compelled to decide about his future. He had intended to join the Friends' Ambulance Unit, as many of his circle had in the early months of the war, but the introduction of conscription had put paid to any element of choice. Now he had to justify his unwillingness to enlist to a group of strangers. He wasn't troubled by the prospect of their animosity. What he feared most was that he might be thought a shirker or a coward.

Alice gave him an encouraging smile as they parted at the door before climbing the steps to the public gallery, filled with a sense of foreboding. She wondered why he had come back from America. She had advised him to stay away, knowing that he would never agree to serve in the army. She had predicted that if he declined to enlist, on the grounds that he was a practicing Quaker and an avowed pacifist, the outcome might be imprisonment for the duration of the war. She hoped his views wouldn't lead him into danger and that he would prove equal to the challenges he faced. She had still to find an empty seat in the public gallery when the first applicant was called.

Five tribunal members: a chairman, a retired major, a clergyman and two lay members lined the bench, surrounded by forms and papers. Their self-confidence suggested that they and others like them had always run the country and knew what was best for it.

The major rocked gently as the chairman made the introductions, his knuckles white against his face. He wore a pristine uniform; medals clung to his chest like brightly coloured insects, a triangle of ribbons pointing to his head. He stared at the rows of faces, alert for opposition, suspicious of their presence. He viewed everyone who came before them as a potential recruit. There was a big push coming shortly. It was an ill-kept secret. Every man available was required for victory. His blazing eyes said unequivocally: "I'd be there, by God, given half the chance."

Alice attempted to disturb his concentration by staring at him but his eyes scythed through the sea of faces, intent on intimidating those present. She had heard his platitudes before. He harangued the applicants for exemption in parade-ground tones, an old man urging mindless sacrifice on others' hapless sons whilst he stayed gloriously immune.

The first applicant was painfully shy. He stood silently before the bench, a nervous youth, head bowed, stealing surreptitious glances at his family in the public gallery.

"What's your name?" the chairman asked, without looking up.

The applicant gave his name, address and occupation. The tribunal members could barely hear his halting words.

"What are your grounds for exemption?"

"My family needs me, sir."

The youth looked up at his mother in the public gallery, a withered, untidy woman, flanked by two young children, one of whom, a girl, clung to her fearfully.

"Why's that?"

"My sister's sick and can't be left alone, sir. She needs somebody with her all the time. My brother can't look after her. He's too young. I work and help to care for her."

"What about your father?"

"Dead, sir. Killed in France last year."

Whilst the chairman was avuncular but irresolute, the major spoke with great authority of the father's wishes for his son, as if he'd known him when he was alive and was familiar with his views. When the youth informed him of the doctor's bills and the unpaid rent, he claimed his army pay would suffice to meet their needs.

The tribunal members conferred briefly before rejecting the application. The youth's face showed only quiet resignation. He would not have troubled them, had his mother not insisted. She sobbed quietly, alarmed for her young children, fearing what might befall her son.

Alice witnessed his dismissal with dismay. If someone so young and vulnerable, merited no consideration, what hope was there for Robert?

The succeeding applicants were neither bashful nor tongue tied, nor willing to accede to the tribunal's uneven judgement without a show of protest. The avalanche of claims was evidence that the mounting death toll had not gone unobserved. The tribunal members began to panic at the variety of excuses offered. They doubted the obscure activities claiming exemption were vital for the war effort and yet the employers demanding their support and understanding were worthy citizens like them. Even the major was chastened, certain that the army was the victim of a vast conspiracy.

Robert's entry afforded welcome respite from the procession of excuses. Here was an instance of blank refusal that everyone could understand. The major's eyes narrowed determinedly as Robert rose to his feet, fumbling in his waistcoat pocket for the piece of paper he had lost.

Noting his confusion, Alice could not resist a smile. How many lectures had he given without his lecture notes? He was known for his absent mindedness. However, once on his feet, his mind was crystal clear. He could speak unprompted for hours on subjects dear to him. She only hoped that he would focus on the purpose of his visit and not be provoked into airing his views on the war.

The major looked Robert up and down, affronted by his vigorous, good health. He saw a tall man with broad shoulders, thick red hair brushed back from his brow, a splash of freckles on his cheeks and lively blue eyes that seemed out of place amid the drabness of the chamber. He had read his biography with unconcealed distaste. Thirty two years old, a university professor, no doubt ready to employ deft phrases to mask his cowardice. Squaring his shoulders, fingering his ribbons, he prepared to ensure that Robert fulfilled his obligations to his country.

The chairman asked, "What are your grounds for exemption?"

"I'm applying on grounds of conscience."

The chairman's eyes betrayed a faint unease. He repeated Robert's assertion in a tone of gentle reprimand, making him seem more wilful than his words deserved.

"Your objection's the result of religious belief?"

Robert shook his head. "My objection's prompted by my personal beliefs."

The chairman frowned, not liking the distinction Robert was at pains to make. He preferred to put people into categories. It helped him to cope with the avalanche of claims. He feared that Robert was going to be vexatious and was troubled by the prospect of his obduracy.

"What about your duty to your country?"

"The dictates of conscience outweigh those of employer, church or state."

"Whatever the circumstances?"

"That must be the case, if we're to live as individuals, responsible to God and to each other for what we do and say."

They had agreed that Robert would rely on the long-established Quaker tradition of non-violence and opposition to military service.

For generations, their family's behaviour had accorded with the pacifist principles of their seventeenth century forebears. Though Robert would never be persuaded to bear arms, there was other useful work that he could undertake if he was relieved of the obligation to wear a uniform and was not subject to the military imperatives.

The major's face was distorted by a mocking, almost gleeful smile. Confident he had Robert's measure, he said, "I think you'd best serve the country by engaging with the enemy."

The chairman fell back into his chair, resigned to conceding the floor to his military colleague. He hoped his intervention would be brief. He regarded his prominence and that of others like him as one of the war's more unfortunate consequences.

"What's this conscience you talk of?" the major asked, a vexed look on his face. "Enlisted men don't have a conscience? Is that what you're suggesting? You think your beliefs superior to theirs?"

"Not superior - but different, yes."

The major's indignation mounted. "They're volunteers - fighting for their country willingly. Many of them will pay for their commitment with their lives. Their consciences dictate that they protect their homes and families. What makes you feel differently? Can't you see our country's at risk?"

Robert found it difficult to articulate his feelings before a hostile audience. Enlisting under any circumstances was contrary to everything he believed in. He and the major inhabited different, separate worlds. What did the military and pacifist traditions have in common beyond their preoccupation with war? The former saw war as in the nature of things, unavoidable, a contest that had to be fought, with its heroes and villains, its prizes of treasure and territory. The latter saw war as a failure, evidence of men's inability to live in peace with each other, resulting in grief and hardship, vaulting from one generation to the next, nothing learnt. Conflict had prompted his study of history, his reflections on the causes of war, but even as he had turned the pages of his books and advanced his theories, the world had erupted again, commencing without warning the greatest conflict of all.

He said, "I think the war's a monumental folly foisted on the country by inept diplomacy; it's a tragedy no amount of strident patriotism can mask. I feel that all I can do is to help others to live with its consequences and wait for it to pass."

Three journalists tucked away in the corner of the chamber stirred like cats, alerted by Robert's stern defiance. They were tired of hearing about sheet metal workers, tanners, carpenters and mechanics unable to be spared by their employers. Someone declining to enlist by reason of choice was worthy of a story. Their handwriting began to populate the virgin paper before them on the table.

The clergyman was also stimulated by Robert's defiance. He was a tall, gangly man with unruly white hair, given to casting despairing glances round the room. He found the proceedings trying and wished he was elsewhere but Robert's references to God had transformed his features. Religion was solely his affair. He had made that clear to everyone.

"You're a Quaker, aren't you?"

"I belong to the Society of Friends - as do all the members of my family."

"Well, I know Quakers who've enlisted," the clergyman said with an air of triumph. He exchanged a knowing look with the major.

"That's hardly surprising. The Society doesn't have a single viewpoint. Some members enlisted at the outset. Others attempted to help, as I'm trying to do, in ways short of military service whilst some declared their outright opposition to the war and determined to campaign for peace."

"Your refusal to enlist's a matter of personal preference?"

"I'm certainly not trying to represent the views of any religious organisation. I'm here to declare my opposition to conscription and to ask leave to serve my country in other, useful ways."

The clergyman leaned across the table and said loudly, "Shall your brethren go to war and you shall sit here?"

Numbers, Chapter thirty two. Robert had often heard the Bible's words on his father's lips. Wisely, he concealed his knowledge, lapsing into silence as the clergyman continued.

"The church believes you have a duty to defend your country and that the war is just. Its chaplains are in the line, comforting the wounded and the dying, ensuring that the casualties receive a decent Christian burial."

"I've nothing but admiration for their efforts."

"So why don't you follow their example then and stop wasting our time?" the major demanded.

Robert ignored his intervention. His focus was the clergyman and his suggestion that his position wasn't a Christian one.

"The Society of Friends embraces many viewpoints. That's inevitable when it dispenses with the need for any interlocutor between man and God. The problem with the church's stance is that it cuts the ground from under individual dissent. It denies the fact that everyone's entitled to act in accordance with the dictates of his conscience and his understanding of Christ's teaching, regardless of what the church says on the matter."

The clergyman raised his hands in despair, saying, "That's a recipe for moral anarchy," and sank back into his seat.

The major decided on another charge, believing wrongly that a breakthrough beckoned.

"What would you do if the Hun was at the door? Would you fight to save your family or attempt to shield it with your precious conscience?"

"The Hun isn't at the door."

"He soon will be if it's left to the likes of you."

Robert looked across to Alice. Her face was masked by the hat of the woman in front of her. How would she have responded to this most predictable and difficult of questions? Unable to consult her, he offered the major a question of his own, fearing even as he did so that the tribunal members might think he was trying to be clever.

"Suppose I was carrying dispatches on which the fate of an army depended and saw that my family was in danger. What should I do? Should I stop and help them or attend to my duties?"

"Your duty would be to your dispatches."

"Then, for purposes of this discussion, consider me to be carrying dispatches."

"What's that supposed to mean?"

"I believe there are higher goals than the preservation of one's safety or the security of one's family. I'm not prepared to enlist under any circumstances."

There was a brief pause whilst each side waited for the other to speak. Mindful of the queue of claimants, the chairman prepared to begin his summation. He had barely collected his thoughts when one of the lay members began to speak.

"Would you reject an offer of conditional exemption if it was offered to you?"

"No, providing I wasn't required to enlist."

His interrogator made no attempt to mask his scepticism. He regarded himself as the only member of the tribunal to have Robert's measure.

"Many of your kind have said they'll do nothing to support the war."

"I'm not an absolutist. I've been working with my parents to help the families of the casualties, many of whom are facing great hardship. I can help in many ways if I'm free to do so."

The chairman said, "This tribunal doesn't grant absolute exemption. It has neither the power nor the inclination to do so."

"I've studied the Act and believe the tribunal can grant absolute exemption if it choses to."

The major said, "We haven't granted absolute exemption to anyone whose work doesn't make it imperative."

"Stand down whilst we confer," the chairman said, "this case has already taken up too much time."

Robert rose, grateful that their scrutiny was over. He felt that he had failed to do justice to his cause. It had been foolish to suppose that the tribunal would ignore popular feeling. Conditional exemption, even if granted to him, might bear a heavy price.

The chairman consulted with his colleagues, concealing his views until each of them had commented on Robert's case. Heads bowed, faces stern, they spoke in fierce whispers. The major spoke the longest, the effort of restraint colouring his features. The others exchanged covert glances, smiles and gestures as they sought consensus. The chairman watched them, paused to swoop when a verdict neared. His head lifted triumphantly as the discussion drew to a close. He urged Robert to stand to receive the verdict, writing notes as he spoke.

He said, "The Tribunal grants you exemption, conditional on your joining the Non-Combatant Corps for the duration of the war."

Struggling to hide his disappointment, Robert asked, "What are your grounds for refusing absolute exemption?"

The chairman said, "We aren't required to give reasons for our verdict." He began to gather up his papers, eager to move on.

"May I appeal?"

"It has to be lodged within seven days."

"How can I appeal if I don't know the grounds for your verdict?"

"The Appeal Tribunal will inform you of our views."

Robert strode from the chamber. The hearing had lasted fifteen minutes. Alice was waiting for him on the pavement outside. She looked chastened by what she had heard. When Robert saw her standing there, waiting eagerly, he rushed across to her and said, "I was never going to gain absolute exemption, was I?"

"Few people do, except on grounds of employment. I keep thinking of that poor youth, the one with the widowed mother. He was surely a deserving cause?"

"There must something we can do to help him."

Before Alice could reply, a young woman came up to them and handed Robert a leaflet, thrusting it into his hand when he hesitated to take it. He thanked her and paused to read it, a frown on his face, before handing it to Alice.

It said, "Free tickets to Berlin via Boulogne and Havre for adventurous young men."

CHAPTER 2

The family gathered for the morning reading as Alice removed the breakfast dishes from the long oak table. Robert arranged the dining chairs down one side of the room whilst his father rang the bell that summoned everyone. The maids filed in obediently, cook leading with the rolling gait characteristic of her middle years whilst the kitchen maid, an elfin figure, brought up the rear, eyes darting nervously as she took her place. Louise read the hymn in a clear, even voice whilst her husband followed with a chapter from the scriptures. Twice, he stopped to clear his throat before persisting manfully, ignoring his wife's anxious glances. Alice sat by the window, her face latticed by the early morning sunlight, her eyes following the tall flowers that swayed gently in the wind whilst Michael, her younger brother, fidgeted uncomfortably, staring at the floor. When the brief service was over and everyone was about to leave the room, he jumped to his feet and said loudly, "I have something to tell you."

Everybody stared at him anxiously. He was due to leave for boarding school in York later that day. Now, his strident voice intruded on their pious thoughts.

"What is it?" his father asked, unnerved by the sudden interruption.

He assumed it was an issue relating to Michael's schooling, always a vexed question at the beginning of term. He began to shepherd everyone towards the door but Michael stood his ground, determined to retain the initiative now that he had their attention.

He said, "I'd prefer to speak to everyone, if you don't mind."

"Go ahead then," his father said, fighting his anxiety. "What have you been up to?"

"I'm not going back to school."

"That's why you haven't done your packing," his mother said.

"I'm not going back," repeated Michael, his frustration mounting.

"Whether or not you go back to school isn't your decision," his father said, struggling to control his indignation." Turning to the others, he said, "Do any of you know what's going on?"

"I can't go back. It isn't possible," Michael said, with no small satisfaction.

Robert intervened on his behalf. "You'd better hear him out." His expression made it clear that Michael's news was not about to please his family.

Michael said, "I've enlisted in the East Surrey Regiment. I start my training tomorrow." He added with a hint of pride. "I'll be going to France in three month's time."

Alice said, "It usually takes longer than that," but no one was inclined to debate the point with her.

Now the moment was upon him, Michael felt the words he had rehearsed so carefully did scant justice to the situation. He wanted to ensure, though it was hardly necessary, that his family grasped the enormity of his decision. He had been contemplating it for months but only now, when a further term at school beckoned, had he been moved to act. He looked to Robert for support but his brother's face was a blank mask, betraying nothing. Robert had learnt of his intentions the previous evening. He had tried to talk him out of it for the sake of the family only to discover that it was too late to intervene.

"Of all the times to choose." Alice spoke without rancour but her disappointment was obvious. "Last week, Robert and I were at the Wandsworth Tribunal, trying to make them understand that we're committed pacifists who want no active part in the war."

"I thought I spoke for everyone here when I gave my evidence," said Robert. "I hadn't realised we were divided on the issue."

"You never asked me for my views," said Michael.

His preference had been to steal away but Robert had urged him to face his parents, to explain his reasons for enlisting, for rejecting everything they valued. Now he was glad that he had stayed. He felt exultant, beyond remorse, now the news was out, ready to face the full weight of his father's indignation, his mother's anxious pleas.

His family considered his words in silence, a silence that grew in weight and stature until it seemed to fill the room. Then everyone began to speak at once until he was overpowered by the number and persistence of their questions.

"I'm only doing what everyone else is doing," he kept repeating until there was nothing else to say.

He turned and left the room, leaving them to contemplate his stark betrayal of everything they cherished. Despite two years of war, the pressure to conform, they were still a pacifist household, loyal to their beliefs, and Michael's words and actions, the first breech in their defences, had left them reeling.

"He's picked an unfortunate time to turn his back on us," Bennett said as Michael retreated down the hall. He stared at Robert expectantly but Robert was reluctant to be drawn. He lowered the chair that he was carrying and sat astride it, his arms around its back and said, "I don't think we should criticise him for his timing. The more important question is why he's chosen to do it."

"Well, whatever his reasons, he seems very committed to them," Alice said, "I doubt that we'll persuade him to change his mind."

"We'll see about that," her father said, with more conviction than he felt.

"He's just a boy," protested Louise, believing that he had acted on impulse and might yet be persuaded to have a change of heart.

"He must have lied about his age."

"There's lots his age and younger at the front; the army has few scruples in these matters."

"Well, we'll have to think of something," Louise said, looking at her husband expectantly, "we can't just let him go."

"I don't think we have any choice. If he's signed his attestation papers, he's committed to enlisting."

"Well, he has," said Robert. "He made sure of that before he told us anything, so there's nothing we can do."

~

Bennett lay back in his study chair and vainly tried to order his thoughts. His study, which lay at the front of the house, overlooking the street and common, was his workplace and sanctuary. Through the open window he could hear the sounds of the village: an engine shunting at the station, the clank of couplings, the hiss of steam; the murmuring of the swiftly flowing brook; the rooks gathering in the trees; the cries of children playing on the green. Now, as he regarded the paintings, the rows of books, the stuffed animals, the pipe racks and the large globe in the corner of the room, he wondered what had prompted Michael's brave, defiant words. Why had his family's example failed to bind him to their cause?

He had taken Michael's allegiance for granted, mistaking his long silences, the unanswered letters for affirmation of their views. He ought to have recognised that no one, especially his younger son with his taste for adventure, was immune to the effects of the war's intoxicating brew. Its fire had consumed young and old alike, immune to class, creed or occupation. Quakers, no less than others, had struggled with its hold.

Some had urged the abandonment of the traditional testimony against war. He recalled the Yearly Meeting of a year ago, the challenge and uncertainty prompted by the conflict. The majority had confirmed its cherished peace principles but had failed to deal with those already in uniform. Whilst most of those of military age had resisted the thought of alternative service, the Meeting had felt obliged to leave the matter to the individuals affected.

His opposition to the war had never wavered. Hatred of war was deeply ingrained in his consciousness. When he was younger he had been a fierce critic of the Boer War, viewing it as a contemptible adventure born of greed and pride. The actions of the British Army at the time had filled him with a sense of outrage that still lingered. He was only too aware that the war now raging was infinitely more painful. In the eighteen nineties, it had been only too easy to support the underdog against a bullying Crown, The present conflict involved a brutal stalemate that favoured neither side. Nor was it a minor skirmish in some far-flung land, magnified beyond its merits by an eager press; the hundreds of thousands dying now were civilians in everything but name. He might condemn the Government at every opportunity but the actions of the Germans gave little grounds for sympathy and he recognised the difficulty involved in disengagement when neither side had gained the upper hand.

The thought of Michael's defiance filled him with despair. Michael was eighteen years old, still a child in many ways, eight years younger than his sister Alice. His arrival had been a miracle, bewildering after many fruitless years. Indulged, protected, he had grown up an enigma, outwardly compliant but inwardly aloof, adored and yet curiously indifferent to the affections of his parents, resistant to their earnest, pious ways. Now the feared rebellion had arrived, he was at a loss for words. He felt compelled to act but was uncertain what to do. He knew only that the war that had consumed him for so long had, unexpectedly, ensnared his younger son.

~

Louise tapped lightly on the study door. There was no reply at first and then a muffled voice invited her to enter. She pushed against the door, driven by a sense of desperation that refused to let her go.

Her husband was sprawled in the armchair by the fireplace, an open newspaper on his lap. A pall of smoke hovered above his head; his half-closed eyes peered out from behind his reading glasses. He rose politely from his chair, smiling wanly, and then fell back, as though the effort was too much for him. Louise sat down before the fire, stabbed the dying embers with the poker and turned to face her husband.

She was a tall, long-limbed woman; her posture reflected the strictures of an upbringing that had made her conscious of her height. Her hair, once black, was greying and her striking features bore the traces of the years, but when she smiled her face lit up, alive with charm; in sorrow, she assumed the woeful look of a disconcerted child.

Her husband watched her warily, no sign of welcome on his anxious face. He glanced at the clock on the mantelpiece, its persistent rhythm filling him with a sense of urgency. He said, "When I spoke to him about his plans, he was very evasive."

"Yet you did nothing?" Louise's voice betrayed her disappointment.

Bennett tugged nervously at his beard, crossed his sprawling legs and reached for the pipe that lay smouldering but neglected on the table by his chair. Noticing Louise's look of disapproval, he puffed on it without enthusiasm and returned it to the table.

"I don't see what I could have done. Could I have changed his mind... even had I known his intentions?"

Louise shrugged doubtfully. There had been a time when their children were compliant, mindful of their parents' wishes but now they were adults with minds of their own and any lingering influence they had over them had been shattered by a war that recognised no boundaries. She gazed intently at the hearth as a cinder flared, licking briefly at the smouldering coals. When she spoke she scarcely recognised her voice. It issued from somewhere deep inside her, a distant cry alive with fear and pain.

"He isn't old enough to enlist. He's still six months short of his eighteenth birthday."

"Many of them lie about their age. It's a measure of their eagerness, their desire to sacrifice themselves, even as others find excuses to remain at home."

"Alice says there are boys of fourteen and fifteen at the front."

"I'm sure they're sent home if they're that young. I can't think they'd be much use to anyone."

"Everyone's welcome if they can be trained to fire a rifle or thrust a bayonet."

She recalled the volunteers camped in Richmond Park in the early days of the war, the fervour with which they thrust their gleaming bayonets into bags of straw.

Her husband said, "We've failed in some way, haven't we? There's no other explanation for his conduct. Why would he turn his back on everything we hold dear?"

"Oh, I don't think we should blame ourselves."

Louise looked at him expectantly. She was not concerned with explanations any longer, with who was right or wrong. Nor was she prepared to have her husband wheel out his guilt for inspection when there was work to be done. When he tried to avoid her gaze, her eyes followed his tenaciously.

"We can stop him if we want to."

"How are we going to do that when he's so resolute? You heard what he said. His training starts in three day's time."

"We can contact the War Office. When they know he's under age, they'll have to send him home."

"You wouldn't do that, would you, for a matter of six months?"

"Why wouldn't I? He's my son. I don't believe the war's a cause worth dying for, any more than you do. He has no business there, when we're opposed to war in all its forms."

"You wouldn't bring him back against his will though, would you? He'd hate you for the rest of his life and still enlist as soon as he could."

Louise understood what she was asking but her face betrayed no hint of hesitation. Michael's safety was her paramount concern. She was certain that he meant well, that he had no wish to hurt his parents or go against their wishes. He was simply another boy drawn to the conflict by a misplaced sense of duty, a need for excitement and the desire to stand with his contemporaries. He was only exceptional insofar as his parents were pacifists and avowed opponents of the war.

Bennett gazed into the fire, lips pursed tightly, before twisting in his chair as if a knife had been thrust into his side. He said, "I'm not going to attempt to interfere with his plans. I couldn't bring myself to do it. You heard what he said this morning. He's enlisted. That's the long and short of it. There's nothing we can do.

"He's only a boy. He doesn't know what he's doing."

Louise struggled to fight back her tears. When her husband rose from his seat to comfort her, she waved him back indignantly.

"Man, boy, what's the difference?" he muttered angrily as he fell back into his chair. "He'll discover manhood soon enough in France. He's convinced his place is at the front. I won't attempt to thwart him if that's what he believes."

"He'll die. They all die. Don't you care about him?"

Louise reached across for the newspaper that lay at Bennett's feet. Several of the pages fluttered to the floor as she sought the one she needed.

"There you are."

She struck the page with the back of her hand and waved it angrily in front of her husband's face.

"Column upon column of casualties. That's what being a soldier means. That's the reality of war. You depart these shores, an eager youth, with high hopes, a sense of duty, the conviction you'll be spared and you end up in a long column of names, ringed in black. Behind every name lies a grieving mother who allowed her son to go and a desolate father who clapped him on the back and urged him to do his duty."

"Of course, I care about him. He's our youngest child. But I won't betray him. I won't go behind his back if I can't persuade him to see reason. Our opposition won't make any difference. He'd find some way of getting there; they always do."

"Make him wait until he's old enough."

Louise clutched her husband's arm. Her fingers gripped his flesh with unexpected force. "The war might be over soon. He might not get another chance to go." When he remained silent, she added despairingly, "I can't understand why you haven't moved heaven and earth to stop him. It's almost as if you're proud of his enlistment."

The truth was that she understood only too well. He was the victim of his own unbending principles. The supremacy of conscience was the cornerstone of his faith, his bequest to all his children. His was a world in which sincerity made anything forgivable. Though Michael's precipitate action flew in the face of everything they had taught him, he was immune to his father's wrath because he believed he was doing the right thing. She no longer cared for principles. She would sacrifice them all to save Michael from the guns. She had held too many weeping mothers in her arms to have any illusions about what his going meant and knew the rhetoric of politicians and the assurances of generals would never halt the carnage.

CHAPTER 3

Robert was walking down the stairs, cup of tea in hand, when the letter came. He heard the gate bang, the postman's tread along the garden path and the noise of letters falling on the mat. He quickly riffled through the bundle, discarding those of little interest. He tore open the War Office envelope and shook its contents loose. The message it contained was brief: following his failure to appeal against the verdict of the Wandsworth Tribunal, he was deemed to have enlisted. He had been assigned to the Eastern Non-Combatant Corps and any failure to report to the barracks forthwith would result in his arrest.

Later that morning as he and Alice strolled together to the village shops, past the pond where children paddled in the shallows on sultry summer days and horses stooped to drink their fill as they rested from their labours, the letter was uppermost in their thoughts. Though inevitable in view of the Tribunal's verdict, he had still been surprised to see its baldly stated choice. Conscription might be familiar to the French and Germans, the backbone of their continental armies, but compulsion was alien to the England he had left behind. He found it difficult to believe that he had become a soldier in spite of his intentions.

They paused before the village inn with its shuttered windows and its fading sign, its forge and stables where the smell of ale, horses and molten metal mingled in the air. They sauntered past the butcher's, its frontage draped with carcasses, the ironmongery where rows of pans and buckets glinted in the sunlight and stopped at the railway bridge to watch the passing trains. They ambled through the narrow streets that led back to the pond, pausing to retrieve a ball that bobbed elusively on the surface of the water, urged on by a group of boys who pulled and fought each other. Filing through the trees to the common, they searched until they found a glade, a clearing concealed by trees and bushes and flung themselves upon the grass.

Alice sat upright, outwardly composed, her face serene, struggling to mask her feelings of trepidation, the uncertainty she felt. What was going to happen to her family now that her brothers were about to go their separate ways and her parents were divided? She had hoped that Robert's return from America would give rise to a renaissance. Instead, the family's unity was shattered, their views in disarray. Her loyalties lay with Robert. She had urged him to resist conscription and must help him bear the consequences of his refusal to enlist but she was also moved by Michael's bold commitment. She only wished her parents were united and would give a clear lead.

She recognised that she had lived a charmed life, that she had never grieved for anyone, had not experienced the loss of family or friends. Witnessing others' pain as she assisted her mother with her work, she realised how helpless one became in the face of grief. The weight of loss was hard to bear and impossible to share. She could only contemplate the trials awaiting them and hope that she'd be strong.

She turned to Robert and said, "I didn't think it would ever come to this, did you?"

Robert gazed at the tall horse chestnut tree that marked the northern boundary of the clearing. They had always thought of it as their secret hiding place. The tree still bore the scars of their childhood games: initials, hearts with arrows through them and cryptic messages. Its branches towered above them, the sunlight on the leaves weaving complex patterns on the grass. Robert thought of the events that it had witnessed and wished for their return.

He said, "I thought it was inevitable after the tribunal. Until then, I was able to think otherwise, to convince myself that some form of compromise might be possible."

"What sort of compromise?"

"I thought I might escape the army's clutches if I undertook some useful work on behalf of those affected by the war."

"Well, now you know better, don't you?"

Robert winced at Alice's directness, her desire to get to the heart of things. She had always been that way. Obfuscation was a skill denied to her. She spoke without fear or hesitation or regard for the consequences of her words. He inclined to silence, requiring time to sift the evidence before making known his views.

She sat beside him on the grass, toes peeping from beneath her skirt, fingers playing with her hair. Even now, she wasn't convinced her brother really understood what he was in for. You could never be sure with Robert. His self-assuredness was misleading. For all his intellect and education, he could be unworldly, bestowing on others without discrimination the same good intentions, the affable benevolence he offered to the world. She felt it was incumbent on those closest to him, and on her especially, to spell out the likely consequences of his actions.

Robert affected a nonchalance that failed to mask his apprehension and said, "Well, we know what happens next, don't we?"

"We do, Alice said, without hesitation. "You'll fail to attend the barracks and they'll come for you." She paused to contemplate the prospect of Robert being arrested. It scarcely seemed possible that any member of her family could fall foul of the law. "There'll be an appearance before a magistrate and imprisonment. After that? Who knows?"

She looked her brother in the eye, wondering why he sought to hide his feelings from her. He had always been protective of her, regarding her as someone to be shepherded through life. There again, he was so wrapped up in his own world, always engaged in scholarly pursuits, that he could appear insensitive to others' feelings. Those who knew him well recognised him as a man whose heart was filled with kindness, who cared greatly for the needs of others but lacked the means for its expression.

He said, "The army doesn't know what to do with a cadre of objectors that challenges its jurisdiction. Though we didn't mean to, we've thrown a spanner in the works."

He watched his sister with affection. She looked tired and flustered. Her fingers tugged nervously at the hem of her dress. Her long dark hair, neatly tied behind her head, emphasised her slender shoulders. She shared her mother's striking features but in miniature, bringing a new delicacy to what was written boldly on Louise's face, reminding him of a garden bird, expectant, quick of movement, alert for predators. He wanted to put his arm around her, hold her tightly, urge her not to worry but held back, relying on her love and understanding to reveal his feelings for her.

Her life had been a curious one, full of early promise and yet disappointing, lacking the success she craved but had never openly acknowledged. She had followed in his footsteps, graduating from London University in 1909, the Coronation Year, when bonfires were lit on every hillside and there were parties in the streets. In pride of place in Bennett's study was a photograph: Alice in gown and mortar board, her parents proud and smiling at her side. The single mindedness of study gone, she had appeared to flounder. She had taught in a school only to find that she had little appetite for the rigours of the classroom. She had worked as a journalist until thrown off course by a love affair with a fellow journalist that had ended badly. She had moved back home temporarily and once there had stuck fast, acting as her father's secretary, working with her mother with victims of the war, knowing she had opened her wings but had failed to fly.

She said, "The Government thinks it's acted fairly, that it's made an effort to accommodate your opposition to conscription by offering you non-combatant duties."

"But I'm still required to enlist."

"They won't be shifted on the matter of conscription."

"Well, it's left me stranded. If I enlisted as a non-combatant, I'd have to spend my time digging ditches or paving roads or whatever duties the army conjures up to keep me occupied. Their so-called 'alternative service' is a form of punishment, dressed up in weasel words."

"I think you'd be good at digging ditches. You're built for it… It would give your eyes a rest."

She wondered what was going to happen to him. He had always been her hero and mentor. She hung upon his every word. They had corresponded all the time that he had been away. Now she wanted him to raise his standard, shout his defiance of the Government from the rooftops, but felt obliged to temper her support for fear of the consequences.

"The Tribunal was a revelation, wasn't it? Whatever happened to the avalanche of volunteers? No wonder the Government is worried. The reasons conjured up to avoid enlistment were extraordinary. Suddenly, every job imaginable is vital to the war effort and no one can be spared."

Robert recalled the major's ill-concealed aggression. His reaction was a sign of things to come. He wished he could summon up cold anger but all he felt was a grim foreboding, a nagging anxiety at the trials awaiting him. What would prison be like? He had absolutely no idea. He only knew that he was ill-equipped to leave his orderly life.

"Do you ever wish you hadn't come back?" Alice asked. "You must have been tempted to stay at Swarthmore for the duration of the war, free from all of this, able to pursue your writing and teaching, without anybody interfering or telling you what to do?"

Robert was quick to reply but his eyes avoided hers, his words merely echoing what he'd said before. "Two years away was long enough. We belong together at a time like this. I also felt I ought to do something, that it wasn't right to sit the war out with impunity. Everyone forgets that I care about my country and recognise my obligations to it."

"But you must have seen conscription coming? We all warned you that it was on the way and what it might mean for somebody in your position."

"I'd hoped to join the Friends' Ambulance Unit."

"Many Friends have left it, claiming it's been subsumed into the Royal Army Medical Corps."

"Well, it couldn't charge round northern France for ever, doing only what it chose to do. When it started, the medical services were in crisis. Now they're better organised and everyone's much clearer about what is needed. Anyway, it isn't on offer to me now I've been conscripted."

Alice looked at him suspiciously. The words he spoke were laudable but there was something missing, some issue she couldn't quite put her finger on that had persuaded him to leave his post. It was unusual for Robert to be guarded with her. The matter must be serious. She wanted him to share it with her so that they were confidants again.

She said, "Did something happen at the college? Why did you come back to this?"

~

"Oh, there you are," said Michael, as he burst into the clearing and threw himself down on the grass beside them. "I've been looking for you everywhere. I should have known I'd find you here."

Robert welcomed his brother's' arrival with a broad sweep of his arms. "What are you doing here? Shouldn't you be packing?"

"My training starts tomorrow but I'll be at home for weeks."

Robert said, "We'll see who leaves first; it might be me at this rate."

"Why? Have you heard from them?" Michael stared intently at his brother, trying to read the situation, to anticipate what might happen next.

"A letter came this morning, I'm deemed to have enlisted."

He patted his pockets, searching for the letter. Alice and Michael exchanged a covert smile at his confusion.

"It's in your back pocket," Alice said, "I saw you put it there."

Robert extracted the crumpled letter and handed it to Michael. He took it eagerly and scanned its sentences before handing it back.

"What are you going to do?"

"What can I do? They'll come for me soon enough. I'll be arrested and charged and events will take their course."

He tried to impress his younger brother with his nonchalance but the words didn't come out right. Alice noted his anxiety. It was gnawing at him, persistent but unseen, biting into his self-confidence, destroying his usual robust, good humour, as he came to grips with the nature of the challenge facing him. Michael could scarcely contain his excitement. He looked at them in turn, twisting and turning, eyes alight, face flushed. He reminded Alice of a boy about to go on his first school journey, leaving his anxious parents on the station platform, mindful only of the great adventure that lay ahead. She wondered how anyone could have two such different brothers: Robert, large, broad shouldered, untidy, vague; Michael, small, dark, impatient and orderly. Although Michael was about to join an infantry regiment, she felt strangely confident that he would thrive there whereas the prospect of Robert''s imprisonment filled her misgivings.

Michael said, "You don't have to go to prison, do you? There must be some way round it?"

"I think it's gone too far for that."

"You could become a teacher. They're exempt – at least mine were."

"I'm not going to resort to anything like that."

"Then, you'll have volunteered – no less than I've volunteered to join the army."

"You make me sound like a martyr."

"He thinks you're playing into the hands of those who want to punish you," Alice said.

"Why not become a non-combatant? That's what I'd do if I were in your shoes."

"I don't think you would," Robert said, a look of scepticism on his face. "You're as obstinate as the rest of us. Anyway, I'm not going to join the army in any guise. I tried to make that clear."

Michael shrugged and looked away. He and the rest of the family spoke different languages, employing the same words for different purposes, their high-flown rhetoric contrasting with his down-to-earth practicality. Though he loved and respected his brother, in the matter of the war he was convinced that he was wrong. He believed that Robert's refusal to enlist was only possible because people like him chose to fight for King and Country.

Alice said, "You condemn us by your eagerness to fight."

Michael stared at the ground, tracing patterns in the dust with his thumb and forefinger, causing armies of ants to scurry back and forth across the changing landscape in a flurry of activity.

"That wasn't my intention."

"That's how it seems."

"Someone has to go, otherwise we'd be defenceless."

Alice paused to watch a brightly coloured jay as it swaggered on a mound of earth, fragments of a worm dangling from its mouth.

"I wish you weren't so enthusiastic. It seems that every generation is seduced by war."

"Now we've come this far, we can't turn back."

Michael was eager to abandon rhetoric and argument in favour of actions likely to demonstrate his resolve. There was no malice in his haste, no rejection of his family or their views, just bewilderment at their conclusions and an inability to cope with their incessant, moral struggle. Robert's letter from the War Office was the signal to depart.

He said, with a hint of pride, "Father has agreed that I can go. He said he won't try to prevent it, in spite of my being under age."

Alice felt her brother's words betrayed little understanding of the agony and heartache that had accompanied that decision.

Robert wished he possessed his brother's capacity to ignore the facts, to put aside all argument and follow where his emotions chose to lead him. The robust intellect, the carefully cultivated scepticism, that had propelled him through school and university to a professorship was as much a burden as it was a virtue. It encouraged him to examine every decision he was called upon to make, to look at it from every side and angle. The process rendered him remote from life so that others thought him cold and indecisive.

He wondered about Michael's relish for the task to come. His mission was to kill as many Germans as he could, many of them conscripts, little older than himself. He was proposing to embark on an unequal struggle against barbed wire, machine guns and artillery. If dying for one's country had ever been a noble cause, it was surely misplaced on the Western Front.

"What about you? What are your plans now?" Michael said to Alice, believing that her life also was about to change.

"I'm going to work at the No-Conscription Fellowship."

"What's that?" Michael asked suspiciously.

"I want to help those resisting conscription. Keeping track of them, recording where they are and what is happening to them would be no small thing."

"No, it wouldn't," said Robert, finding a degree of comfort in the thought that support might be available to him and others like him.

Michael reached into the pocket of his trousers and drew out a packet of cigarettes. He offered them first to Alice and then to Robert, though neither of them had ever smoked in his presence. Robert surprised her by accepting one. He lit it and puffed on it uncertainly, purporting to enjoy it, whilst Michael lay back on the grass inhaling deeply, ignoring his sister's disapproval.

When Robert had finished his cigarette, he stood up abruptly and ground the stub beneath his foot, brushed his trousers with deliberate care and ran his fingers through his hair. His hair ignored his efforts to reorder it, tumbling back across his face as soon as he withdrew his hand. Above his head, a line of clouds slipped across the sky, obscuring the sun that had embraced them as they lay upon the grass, flooding with dark shadows the clearing they claimed as theirs. He observed a figure on the winding path between the trees: a nanny, stout and neat, heading to the station. A small boy staggered after her, wails issuing from his contorted face. She turned and urged him to go faster but he remained unmoved until, despairing at their lack of progress, she swept him up into her arms and his plaintive cries gave way to sobs of gratitude.

He offered Alice a helping hand, looming over her, lifting her with ease, plucking the grass from her sleeve, whilst Michael hovered round them, wanting to be helpful but unsure what to do. They stood together awkwardly, as if posing for a photograph, aware that the countdown to their final moments together had begun.

Alice said to Robert, "I'm very proud of you, you know that don't you? I'll do everything possible to support your opposition to conscription."

She placed her hand on his shoulders as she slipped her shoes back on. He felt solid, immoveable and she was grateful for his strength. He pulled her to him, held her tightly and kissed her lightly on the cheek.

"And me? Are you proud of me as well?"

Michael spoke light-heartedly, a faint smile upon his face, but behind his words lay an intensity that was inescapable.

"I think you're very brave. I recognise that you have every right to follow your conscience and do what it demands of you. I'll always love you and watch over you as best I can. We're still a family and will remain so even though our views divide us."

"I couldn't agree more," Robert said.

"That's good enough for me."

Michael embraced his sister, holding her to him for what seemed to her an age, knowing he would always remember their last day together, the moment of their parting.

Robert stretched out his hand. Michael shook it vigorously, embarrassed by Robert's solemnity but grateful for his blessing. For all his bravado and enthusiasm, it was no small thing to turn his back on his family. Alice watched them cautiously, aghast at the parting in prospect. She felt their earnest handshakes, the kisses on her cheek, had destroyed a period of amnesty in which those she held most dear had escaped the war. She had always known it had to end but regretted it had come when Michael was so young and Robert newly back in London.

Together, they walked back to the house, weaving through the trees and bushes, along the winding paths familiar since childhood, across the wooden footbridge that arched above the stream, until within sight of the house they cherished, with its tall windows and ivy-covered walls, the home that each of them had found so hard to leave. Whilst the others lingered, Michael strode ahead, throwing back the gate, marching up the path, eyes darting right and left, absorbing everything, preparing to transport its memory with him to the front. Robert could only envy his eagerness and wish that it was not his lot to swim against so strong a tide. Michael's certainty meant that he could be no less committed to his chosen path than his younger brother.

Three days later, whilst Michael was queuing at the Quartermaster's store for his boots and uniform, two policemen arrested Robert, escorting him to Hammersmith Police Station. There, in a damp and airless cell that smelt of urine, he awaited his appearance in front of the magistrate, before being fined five pounds, to be deducted from his army pay, and transferred to the army camp at Harwich.

In the offices of the No-Conscription Fellowship, Alice wrote Robert's name, address and other details on an index card. There, it took its place in a box of cards, ready to record every detail of her brother's fate at the army's hands.

PART II

June, 1916

CHAPTER 4

They left Felixstowe before dawn, shadowy figures in the grey half-light, marching through glistening streets, over rain-kissed cobbles, in the manner of soldiers yet a ragged band, naked of possessions. The station was deserted, its café closed; newspapers stood in forlorn piles, rocks uncovered by the tide. The train was standing at the platform, doors flung open, waiting on the locomotive that inched along the track towards it, wheels creaking, steam hissing from beneath its cab. Robert gazed dejectedly from the platform, imagining the weeping families, khaki throngs and loud farewells that might have been his valediction. He had never thought to depart for France, still less to leave in such a manner. His dismay increased when the carriages jolted, the wheels of the locomotive spun on the slippery track and the train crept forward. It weaved across the points beyond the platform, whistling half-heartedly as it passed the signal box, its couplings groaning, the chill, white dawn sliding past the window, their escorts' watchful faces sole witness to their exodus.

"Well, that's that," Robert thought as dawn revealed a quilt of fields and hedgerows, chimneys smoking peacefully, tall trees, rich canopies, bushes blanketed with dew, a watery sun. "They're making an example of us. Why else would they spirit us away?"

He gazed at his companions. Their faces, though familiar, told him little of their thoughts. Their expressions were patient, stoical, their eyes focused on the images that rushed past the window as they waited on events to reveal their destination.

As the train skirted London, labouring through endless suburbs stirring into life, he wondered at the stealth suggested by their route. It was a hopeful sign, perhaps, an indication of unease on the army's part. The billowing smoke from the locomotive shrouded the brightly polished tracks. Stations, a blur of names and shapes hurried past the window; signals rose and fell obediently as they gathered speed. Later, their pace slowed as they neared the sea. There, crowded troop trains waited patiently, heads craning from their windows whilst others rattled northwards empty, ready to collect more men and deliver them to the waiting ships.

They had argued frequently as the miles slipped by, knowing they must act if they were to save themselves, but unsure what to do. There was no knowing what might happen to them. Wild rumours heightened their uncertainty, enhanced by the malign spirit of the camp.

"What are we going to do?" asked Taylor, one of the most vocal of their number. "We must do something to escape the army's clutches."

Robert wondered what he had in mind. He knew only that Taylor had a view on everything. The source of his self-confidence lay in the belief that his love of God set him apart from other men. It was his compensation for a troubled marriage, the reward for a virtuous existence. He felt that his beliefs made him distinctive and that without them he would be unremarkable, a man, who expecting much, had achieved little in the eyes of the world.

"What can we do?" Levine asked, "events will have to take their course." He didn't suggest what that course might be but his dour expression left Robert in little doubt that he feared the worst.

Levine was a bookseller and pamphleteer who loved to air his revolutionary views in Robert's presence. The source of his modest living was a shop filled to overflowing with books and pamphlets about politics. Each day, he sat patiently behind the desk that, cluttered with letters, catalogues and stock cards, served as both an office and a counter, pausing only in his reading to jot down an arresting thought or sentence or to dash off a letter to the authors, journalist and politicians with whom he engaged in a long and fruitless correspondence on matters of the day.

Robert's concern was to find a way to publicise their predicament. He was convinced that public recognition of their plight was their only hope of freedom. He produced a scruffy piece of paper from the pocket of his jacket and a worn-down pencil he had managed to retain in spite of many searches. He said, "I'm going to write a note saying who we are and spelling out what's happened to us."

Unmoved by Robert's declaration, Levine said, "What are you going to do with it when you've written it?"

Robert listened to the panting locomotive, the steady rhythm of its wheels on the burnished tracks. Standing between the seats in the crowded compartment, his face pressed against the window, the passing scenery was a jumble of shapes and images that served only to confuse him, compounding an anxiety about their intended destination that grew worse with every mile that passed.

When the train slowed at a station, he decided that the time had come to act. He forced open the window of their compartment and tossed out the note he had written so painstakingly. It seemed a meagre thing as it pirouetted above the platform, laden with their hopes. Robert craned his head to see if anyone had stooped to pick it up but the train hurried on, picking up speed again, and obscuring his view. Nonetheless, he felt that he had done something, that he had acted in their interests in spite of Levine's pessimism, his belief that the note was nothing more than an empty gesture.

"Even if the note's found and handed in to someone who understands its origins, no good will come of it," Levine insisted. "The fact is that no one cares about us. Why should they? They think that we're shirkers or cowards and deserve the army's worst."

Robert didn't share his gloom. "There's no harm in trying," he said when his turn came to occupy a seat. "We have a right to be treated with respect, no matter what our views."

The others nodded eagerly though they recognised their hopes were likely to be dashed. They knew that they could transform their prospects at any time if they chose to. All they had to do was to agree to wear a uniform and perform whatever tasks were asked of them but knowing how easy it was to step back from the brink was of little comfort to them. The army's malevolence had wrought a solidarity in their ranks. Now anyone abandoning his stance would have to recognise that any change of heart on his part had let the others down.

Southampton was a mass of troops, horses, supplies, artillery, and vehicles. Soldiers stood beneath the swinging cranes and gantries or on the decks of the ships that crowded the grey water, smoke idling from their funnels. Robert wondered who controlled the patient men, the restless horses, the silent, brooding guns. He then perceived an order, a rhythm, an industry that bore everything forward, emptying the lines of trains, loading the patient ships until they were filled to overflowing. The objectors scarcely merited a glance from the sweating stevedores, the weary clerks, the harassed officers as they mounted the gangplank of their ship. Robert watched with consternation as the vessel filled with troops, feeling like another apprehensive soldier destined for the front.

They were surprised to find their few belongings waiting for them. Their presence was a sign that their misdemeanours had been forgiven, that they would have a chance to start afresh in France. Robert thought the timing of the gesture cleverly contrived. He had never felt so isolated.

The preparations going on around him mocked their sensibilities, making their actions deserving of contempt and ridicule.

He thought of his last meeting with Michael, and wondered at his whereabouts. Was he waiting on the tide? He searched the rows of soldiers for Michael's features until the mass of khaki swam before his eyes. He pictured him in uniform, grey eyes squinting from beneath his helmet, wearing the mocking, quizzical look he effected when with strangers. Twice he thought he saw him and, his spirits lifting, waived in recognition but there was no response. The features he had mistakenly identified were merely Michael's memory painted on another's face.

The ship departed silently, shuddering as it turned, intimidated by the open sea, the escorts waiting there. There were soldiers everywhere. Robert feared the ship would sink beneath the weight of bodies. Factory workers, farm hands, shop assistants, clerks and drivers in tightly knit groups; they came from every walk of life, enmeshed in packs and rifles, struggling to light cigarettes, shouting to each other in the wind. Some of them he failed to understand. Their dialects were like a foreign tongue. Others spoke in the familiar accent of the London tradesman. The officers were a class apart, distinguished by their peaked caps, leather riding boots, neatly-pressed jodhpurs and Sam Browns'. Some of the soldiers were boisterous; they joked and sang; others were morose and thoughtful, unattached to any group. The veterans of Ypres and Loos recalled the fighting there in the vernacular of the trenches, their accounts laced with phrases borrowed from their officers. The newcomers listened to their stories, the anecdotes they heard painting vividly the confusion that was battle, not with bold strokes of the brush but with deft touches that transformed a monolith into groups of comrades so that a victory became a bombardment endured, an advance survived.

On the open sea, a heavy swell began to take its toll. Green, taut faces scrambled for the rail or queued fretfully for latrines filled with vomit. Robert stood apart, relishing the wind that whipped his face, breathing greedily, cleansing his lungs of the prison's foul air. He recalled the claustrophobic cells and shivered at their memory.

He heard a group of soldiers laugh uproariously and turned towards them. Amidst the sea of khaki, stood Hick's portly figure, a victim of the camp at Harwich, conspicuous in his civilian clothes. A music hall performer, he strutted up and down the deck, an officer's cap jammed over his eyes, a swagger stick beneath his arm, bellowing orders at the top of his voice in clumsy imitation of Sergeant Bulmer. The soldiers laughed and cheered as he portrayed the sergeant's efforts to make them drill at Harwich. Hicks had fought a long and bitter duel with him. Bulmer had been fooled by his affability into thinking he was likely to be cowed.

Robert had no need of Hick's caricature to remind him of the sergeant's ways. His cheek still bore the imprint of his blow. He recalled the uniform that Bulmer had thrown at his feet when he had refused to wear it. It had lain there awkwardly, symbolic of the gulf between them, as the sergeant bellowed into his face, breathing heavily. When Robert had remained motionless, the sergeant's commands had become a tirade. "Put it on, damn you, put it on," he had ordered repeatedly, and when Robert shook his head, he had clenched his fists and his feet had performed a jig as he struggled to contain his wrath.

"Look," Robert had said, in a last desperate effort to retrieve the situation, "I can't wear a uniform. It would be the first irretrievable step to becoming a soldier and I'm not prepared to take it. I'm here because I refused to enlist."

His cheek had taken the full force of the sergeant's fist. Staggering from the blow, he had been about to fall when arms grasped him, holding him upright. Through a blur of colours, he saw Bulmer turn on his heel, anxious to distance himself from his misdemeanour. "You're a soldier whether you like or not.," he called over his shoulder. "You'll obey orders soon enough, like the rest of them."

That had been Robert's tenth day at Harwich, another in a new and brutal universe he hadn't known existed. The objectors had occupied a cell buried in the bowels of the Napoleonic redoubt that overlooked the town and harbour, immune to the sunlight that played upon the camp, cloaked in a deep mantle of unmoving air. It had been devoid of furniture save for a small sheet of iron that, protruding from the wall, had served as a seat, table and shelf. During the day Robert had sat on his roughly folded jacket; at night, he wrapped his overcoat around him on the rough, stone floor.

They had remained standing on the square whilst the camp went about its business. The queue of conscripts at the Quartermaster's store had been unending. They waited patiently for their uniforms, boots and weapons. The line had moved forward without pause or comment, the conscripts too intent on their housekeeping to note the duel on the square. The objectors' uniforms had remained untouched. They had seemed to acquire a life of their own. Robert would have been unsurprised if one of them had enveloped him, forcing his arms into its sleeves, his legs into its trousers. He thought them capable of joining the conscripts drilling on the square, of performing steps and pirouettes with the same ill-fitting grace. It scarcely mattered who occupied them. They only required a living, breathing body around which to drape themselves and the assurance that their owner would obey orders with alacrity.

When Hicks saw Robert, he waved him forward, urging the soldiers to make a passage for him. Robert hastened to his side, an appreciative smile upon his face. Hick's persistent good humour had served them well in the confines of the cells. He had never once been cowed by the conditions.

"That was some performance - even the officers enjoyed it."

"Some of them are very young and conscious of their dignity."

"They are, aren't they?"

Their youth was the first thing Robert had noticed about them. Michael was surely not the only one who had lied about his age.

"It didn't stop them laughing though. Nor me. I thought you had him to a tee."

"Oh, good," said Hicks, "there's nothing I like better than a good review. I always used to scour the papers for any mention of my name."

"You must wish you were on the stage again?"

"I'd be a very busy man."

London's music halls, theatres and clubs were filled to overflowing, besieged by a population eager for any pleasure that kept the war at bay. The nature of the fare had changed. The theatres Hicks had abandoned in such disgust had been recruiting halls for the army. Now, the flag waving of the early months of the war had given way to a new escapism. The returning soldiers, their friends and families, were united in wanting nothing that reminded them of the trenches. Unfortunately, it had come too late for Hicks. With no employer, he had been a ready candidate for the conscription he opposed.

They watched the restless waters of the Channel slip beneath the hull. Two destroyers rode the waves beside them, guns bristling reassuringly, their sloping funnels scrawling plumes of smoke across an empty sky. The scene filled Robert with a sudden joy, a pleasure he had not experienced since the time of his arrest. He resolved to draw upon its memory in the days to come.

They were joined at the rail by Clapham, a bespectacled and earnest journalist who articulated the views of the working man, moving easily across the divides of class and language. Not for him the blinkered chauvinism of the popular press. He had sought to part the veil of censorship, to write the inconvenient truths he believed the conduct of the war required in defiance of the Defence of the Realm Act, the strength of popular feeling and the disapproval of the publishers. His determination to address the issues had cost him his employment. When conscription came he felt that he had no alternative but to resist its pull.

He said, "Men like Sergeant Bulmer shouldn't be underestimated. Their efforts oil the wheels of war. Without their dedication, none of this would be possible."

"They're instruments of a larger folly," Robert claimed.

"The mark on your face tells a different story."

The purple patch on Robert's cheek, the half-closed eye were undiminished. Robert relied on the observations of his friends to remind him of his changed appearance.

He surveyed the crowded deck, the flotilla of ships. "I hadn't really grasped the scale of the conflict before."

"I wish I were free to write about it."

Clapham felt it was the cruellest blow, to witness events that were so momentous and be denied the opportunity to tell the world. He was forever marshalling scenes and events in his mind even though he had no platform beyond the ears of his companions.

Robert looked at the crowded deck, the groups of soldiers huddled there. They were largely volunteers swept to France on the tide of sentiment that had seen so many abandon work and family in their eagerness to serve. He wondered how many still retained their enthusiasm. He had expected them to be hostile to objectors and the absence of animosity had taken him by surprise. He felt like a boxer who, having climbed into the ring with malevolent intentions, had found himself confronting a friendly, outstretched hand. They had asked him many questions, listening respectfully to everything he had to say, reserving their distaste for those at home loudest in their patriotism, for contractors grown fat on wartime profiteering and for the petty tyrants of the training camps. Even amongst the officers, those most loyal of men, the idealism of the heady, early days had given way to a dour resolve. Shipping the objectors to France against their will had given them a new status. No one who had defied the army in such a blatant way or shown themselves prepared to risk their lives for the cause that they believed in could be called a coward.

"If I'd had your guts a year ago, I probably wouldn't be here now," a taciturn corporal had said to Robert as they tried to light their cigarettes in the brisk, sea breeze. He looked Robert up and down, inhaling deeply, intrigued by his presence. Fingering the sleeve of his jacket, he said "I'm surprised you're still wearing this. I would have thought they'd have had it off your back by now."

"They tried to remove it."

Robert pointed to his bruised cheek. "That's what got me this."

"Hit you, did they?"

"Others fared much worse."

Robert told him of the objector made to stagger round the camp for hours weighed down by shot and pack until his legs gave way and spoke of someone beaten with sticks and sandbags who had refused to cry out.

"There's more of that to come. They can do things to you at the front that they can't do elsewhere."

"How old are you?" Robert asked, preferring not to think about what the army had in store for them.

The corporal smiled knowingly. Old men as well as young lied about their age. His wary eyes regarded Robert unblinkingly. When they came to part, he possessed a grip of iron.

He said, "Let me give you some advice. Your best chance of getting back to Blighty in one piece is to refuse to do *anything*. Once you acknowledge their authority, you'll be at their mercy. Then they'll shoot you soon as look at you, if you don't do what you're told."

The corporal had given Robert a packet of Capstan and a box of Swan Vestas. Robert had accepted them willingly, grateful to have something to share with the others. He felt compelled to grasp at every pleasure like any soldier. None of them, himself included, knew if they were coming back.

The ship rounded the harbour at dusk, a dark shadow on the restless water. The destroyers had already turned for home. He glimpsed the quay between the rows of heads at the rail, heard the rattle of the chains, the clank of shunting wagons, the shouts of stevedores and the persistent cries of seagulls. He saw a horse dangling from a sling above the dock, kicking helplessly. Troops formed up on the quayside. Officers bellowed orders. Hands waved in recognition or clasped in swift farewell. Robert felt the spell of France envelope him: the surge of optimism, the taste of fear, the ill-controlled excitement that was the lot of anybody buoyed up by promises of victory. Then, as the soldiers marched away in step, arms swinging, weighed down by pack and rifle, his optimism faded. His mind returned to the corporal's warning, the trials that lay ahead.

CHAPTER 5

Mr Bennett had never believed in miracles; his convictions were much too down to earth for that. But in the matter of the note and its discovery, divine intervention was not to be dismissed. How else could a scruffy piece of paper thrown from the window of a speeding train have reached his daughter at the No-Conscription Fellowship? Was that not a miracle? How else would he have had the opportunity to intercede on behalf of those in France? Shaking his head in wonderment, he crossed the study floor and stood longingly before the rack of pipes. He was forbidden to smoke by all his doctors; it was the only advice they could all be relied upon to give. Moreover, he rarely had the opportunity to enjoy a pipe or cigarette in peace. Louise did not even need to scold or threaten him. The knowledge of her disapproval ruined any chance of pleasure. She allowed him one cigarette a day; every evening, after dinner, she dispatched him to his study with a disapproving air. Now, as he reached up for the nearest pipe, a heavy, curving Meerschaum and sucked briefly on its blackened stem, he promised himself that when the war was over, he would smoke openly and unashamedly by way of celebration.

His opposition to the war had intensified since Michael's enlistment. He still recalled the shock of seeing him in uniform. It made little difference that he had declined to become a subaltern, viewing a position in the ranks as a sign of his sincerity. He had broken with a family tradition of opposition to war going back centuries and had done so abruptly and determinedly.

He had hated him at first for his defiance. Then, his anger had given way to a period of doubt, to a time of wondering whether his son's behaviour resulted from his own inflexibility. He knew that when it came to issues of principle, he was immoveable, convinced that God's teaching could not be abandoned when circumstances made it inconvenient.

Robert's abduction had been the final straw. Robert and him were as one on the subject of the war. The only difference was their ages. Robert was eligible for conscription; he was gloriously immune. Now he was resolved to save him even though the weapons available to him were few in number and time was of the essence. For the first time in his life he was prepared to acknowledge his obscurity. He was not an important or influential politician. He had never frequented the committee rooms where power dwelt and deals were struck. He had to rely on others' rhetoric and influence, equipping them to argue and to bargain on his son's behalf. It had been no easy matter to make sure his views were heard. He was only too aware of how difficult it was for the government to control the vast bureaucracy that the war had spawned. It was evident in the contradictory statements issuing from Whitehall. Tales were legion of the struggles between the Cabinet and the generals that it ostensibly controlled. Yet, strangely, he had felt equal to the challenge. In spite of the war, he still had faith in Britain's robust democracy, a faith resulting from membership of that liberal, non-conformist network whose influence exceeded the numbers it could muster. Moreover, censorship had not diminished the impact of publicity. It was only necessary to create sufficient fuss, to distract the Cabinet from its principal concerns, for outcomes to be changed. He had set to work determinedly, working with others of like mind. He had employed letters, speeches, visits until the plight of Robert and others was a matter for discussion in the House of Commons. He had succeeded in placing their predicament on the national agenda but their fate was no clearer now than when his efforts had begun. The publicity resulting from his labours had proved a two-edged sword. The intervention of the Cabinet had made the military more determined that events in France should run their course. Unless he found a means to tip the balance in their favour, there was every possibility that the objectors would be tried and executed in spite of all his efforts.

The thought of their jeopardy brought him to his feet. He began to pace his study, oblivious to the chiming of the grandfather clock in the hall, the voices in the kitchen. If only he could find some way to cross to France, to visit the camp where Robert and the others were being held against their will. His presence would remind the army of the nation's scrutiny and offer some slight hope to the reluctant conscripts in their midst. He wasn't sure that any good would come of it or how he would contrive to engineer a visit but saw it as their only hope.

CHAPTER 6

They had seen the men tied up against the barbed wire fence that marked the perimeter of the camp but it was only when they were sentenced to Field Punishment No 1 and were required to share their fate that they learnt the punishment was known as 'crucifixion'.

"It's just the thing for you," a sergeant had said to Robert, without a trace or irony. "Arms outstretched, above your shoulders, tied up tight. We do it properly in this camp. No token efforts here. It'll make you wish that you hadn't defied us."

"It won't make any difference," Robert had replied, as he recalled the sweating soldiers, eyes dull with pain, hanging from the wire, unmoving save to try to shift their weight, ease their aching limbs and shield their faces from the sun.

"We'll see," the sergeant said. "You won't enjoy it, that's for sure. Who knows? It might make you think again."

Now, Robert was in agony. It wasn't his aching limbs, the lacerations of the rope, the pounding headache that troubled him. It was the sunburn that he'd suffered. His face and arms were badly burned. He had been awake throughout the night, attempting to sleep without touching his face or lying on his arms. The prospect of another morning in the hot sun filled him with foreboding. He needed to obtain one of the few places under the tree with the towering canopy that anchored the corner of the camp and provided welcome shade for those secured within its shadow.

His companions were sympathetic and had done what they could do to protect him. Levine had acquired a long sleeve shirt for him and Hicks had secured a cap to shield his face but he still hoped for a place in the shade. When he had raised the possibility with one of the NCOs, he had laughed in his face. His request would make it more likely that he would be positioned in the sun again.

"Leave it to me, I'll get you some shade," Castlereagh asserted when he left the cell, though how he was going to do this he declined to say, leaving Robert to conclude that he would have engineer his own good fortune.

Castlereagh was their self-appointed leader. The quintessential public school man, tall and upright, with the easy effort of command assumed so effortlessly by young men of his class, he addressed everyone with the same cold eye, jutting jaw and loud, assertive voice, rewarding their respect with a generous smile and a brisk 'well-done'. Robert had been astounded to discover him in their midst. He properly belonged in the line or on the General Staff.

His presence might have been unwelcome in other circumstances. His boundless self-confidence, his righteous indignation when ignored, the certainty that everyone would follow where he chose to lead might have been irritating in other circumstances but in the struggle to resist the camp's encroachment, his attitude had been invaluable. It was too easy to sink into self-pity, to wonder at the wisdom of continued opposition. His value lay in his tireless efforts to employ to good effect the time that hung so heavily on everybody's hands.

Robert tried to time his exit so that he would be one of the last to go to the wire. Previously, those tethered last had been favoured with a position beneath the tree. This time, their captors started at the other end and by the time he neared the fence, the best places had been taken, the guards pushing and shoving everyone into position without regard for their needs. Robert marvelled at the enthusiasm with which they carried out their orders. They clearly resented the civilians in their midst.

"He needs to be in the shade," Castlereagh said to the young officer supervising their punishment. He pointed to Robert's reddened face, the blisters on his nose.

"He'll go where he's put," the officer said with no great show of interest, "it's all the same to me." He motioned a guard to take Robert's arm. "He can't wear that either," he said, pointing at the cap that Robert had pulled down over his eyes. "He'll be tied up bare-headed like the rest."

"Well, no, he won't," Castlereagh said defiantly. "We've talked it over and we don't think it's fair that he should have to suffer in this way. Why not place him beneath the tree and let him wear his cap. Where's the harm in that? Can't you see how much he's suffering. Why add to his distress?"

The officer hesitated. He was young and inexperienced and didn't want to cause a fuss but he couldn't allow prisoners to decide things for themselves, even these strange people newly out from Blighty who refused to parade or wear a uniform and were neither one thing or the other.

The corporal holding Robert by his sunburnt arm attempted to take matters into his own hands but Robert stood his ground. He was already feeling faint from the heat and lack of sleep. He wasn't sure quite how he was going to weather another morning on the wire when the sun was at its height.

"We decide who goes where," the corporal said with vehemence. He pointed to the position on the wire that he had in mind for Robert. "You can either walk there on your own or the lads will carry you. It's up to you. Now, move yourself before it all turns nasty."

"No, he isn't," Castlereagh contradicted, "he's going there."

He pointed to a gap beneath the tree and started forward, intent on occupying it on Robert's behalf. When a soldier stepped forward to block his way, Castlereagh shouted, "No one move. Sit down where you are." Turning to the officer, he said, "No one here's going anywhere until this is sorted out."

To Robert's surprise, the objectors sat down as one. It was the first time they had attempted to assert themselves since their reluctance to parade had brought them to the camp. It felt good to express their will. They were tired of the harsh conditions, the disregard in which they were held. They welcomed an opportunity to further Robert's cause.

The guards gathered round them, preparing to haul them off. Prisoners were frequently dragged to and from the wire. Some of them were too weak to get there on their own or had to be helped back to the cells when their punishment was over. Sentences were implemented without regard for the condition of the prisoners. Rarely was anyone excused unless their life was at risk.

The officer regarded the scene with consternation. He wasn't in the camp by accident. His battalion commander had engineered his transfer from the line in the belief that he was about to break down. His duties were intended to keep him safe from harm. He had been told that, if he did well, everyone would view his new posting as just another of the army's whims. He didn't want anyone to make a fuss or draw attention to their plight. Nor did he care who went where. He wasn't a bully like so many of the others. He just wanted everyone to be in their rightful place before the CO began his daily inspection. If things got out of hand, he might find himself in the line again which was the thing he feared most.

In an effort to avert a confrontation, he said, "It's too late to start again." He added, without conviction, knowing that tomorrow he had duties elsewhere, "We'll try a different way the next time."

Castlereagh was unmoved. He sensed weakness in the officer's attempts at conciliation and was determined to exploit it. He was still standing. The other objectors had sat down on the spot, as he had required of them, the look on their faces declaring that they would have to be carried to the wire if they didn't get their way.

Robert could only marvel at their solidarity. They had acted together previously, defying orders that compromised their unwillingness to join the army or participate in its activities but they had never acted on behalf of any individual before. He was delighted by their support and hoped it wouldn't lead to violence. He decided that if there was any sign of that, he would walk to the wire without protest and take up a position in the sun. Meanwhile, he sat cross-legged on the ground, a resolute expression on his face, his sunburnt arm smarting from the corporal's grasp.

The guards waited on the order to move the protesters, relishing the prospect of confrontation. The officer remained reluctant to let them loose on the prisoners. Though he felt the prisoners could be relied upon to offer no resistance, their recalcitrance meant that they would have to be dragged to the wire. There was an unwelcome ambiguity about their status and he didn't quite know how to treat them. Were they in the army or weren't they? They didn't look as though they were. They still wore civilian clothes and refused to drill. What would happen if one of them was hurt? He wouldn't be able to rely on the usual platitudes to explain away the casualties.

Conscious that an inspection was imminent, he shouted with all the authority he could muster, "Tie him up in the shade." He pointed at Robert with a look of contempt on his face. "Put the rest of them where you like. Tie them good and tight. They'll soon do what we ask them after a few days on the wire."

The objectors were trussed up against the wire, arms outstretched above their shoulders. Robert's face was pushed against the barbs. He could scarcely move or breathe. Stretching was impossible and he had cramp in his leg, adding to his agony. Painful though his position was, he had escaped the sun. Castlereagh was tied up next to him, a look of triumph on his face as he was thrust up against the wire. Separate, they were exposed and vulnerable. Together, they had a power denied to them as individuals. He didn't doubt there would be other opportunities for collective protest before their time was up.

Three days later, when their punishment was over, they were released from their irons and allowed to sit on the grass outside their cell to eat their breakfast. They ate greedily, uncoiling like reptiles in the sun as they eased their limbs. The soldiers guarding them seemed more benign, as though their prisoners had unwittingly taken a test and met its requirements. Castlereagh was exultant. He felt that they had asserted themselves to good effect. The optimists began to hope that the army had relented. Perhaps word had come from England and preparations were under way for their return? Their expectations increased when they were ordered to parade with the other prisoners and no attempt was made to make them don uniforms or to make them drill.

They moved stiffly across the square to the appointed place, their hearts beating faster at the prospect of an end to their uncertainty. Only when they saw the unrelenting face of the CO did their doubts begin to surface. He confirmed their worst fears as soon as he began to speak. Because of their intransigence, four of the objectors were to be immediately subject to a full field court martial. Castlereagh was amongst the prisoners chosen. His similarity with the strutting, young staff officers who visited the camp, the outrage occasioned by his defiance, made his selection inevitable. Robert's inclusion was the price of his special treatment on the wire. No one established the basis on which the others were selected. Castlereagh's anger at the army's actions was matched by his surprise that Robert, whose conduct had been exemplary, was amongst those nominated to test the proposition that objectors to conscription could be subject to a field court martial for disobeying lawful orders.

CHAPTER 7

Louise had never imagined that she would have reason to defy her husband or the courage to do so. She had always bowed to his wishes, even when she disagreed with him because she felt it was her duty as a wife. But now her son's life was in jeopardy, questions of duty and loyalty could wait. She addressed the envelope, knowing that she would only rest easy when it had been posted. In her haste, she neglected to seal it. It rested on the garden table, framed by the sunlight, testament to her determination to do her utmost for her son.

She had barely completed the task when Alice appeared. Had she seen the letter, Louise wondered, as Alice waved from the top of the garden? She seemed unmindful of the confusion prompted by her presence. She strolled down the lawn, weaving idly between the trees, her hands behind her back, her face averted from the sunlight.

"Well, any news?" Louise asked as Alice removed her hat, adjusted the pins that held her hair in place and drew a chair up to the table.

Alice shook her head and a lock of hair detached itself from the pin that held it and tumbled across her face. She swept it away with an impatient gesture of the hand.

"That might be no bad thing?" Louise looked expectantly at Alice. "It means the army doesn't know what to do, that Robert's fate is unresolved."

Alice's scepticism was obvious. The truth had been the first casualty of Robert's abduction. None of them spoke openly of their thoughts or feelings any more. They merely hastened to console each other, their views concealed behind a brittle confidence.

"Father's very worried, though he does his best to hide it from us," she said, looking irritated. "I wish he'd be frank with us. Men are so boring at times like this. They treat us like children. They're always trying to protect us, to shield us from the truth when we want to know everything that they know so that we can decide things for ourselves."

Louise winced at her words. She was also guilty of putting on a brave face, of pretending that life would soon return to normal even though it had changed for ever. It was her way of coping with the shock of Robert's arrest, the blow of Michael's enlistment. She wondered if Alice understood the depth of her despair.

"He's trying his best, you know," she said, wanting to be loyal in spite of the letter. When she criticised others, she always did it obliquely, preferring to damn them with faint praise. For the most part, she tried not to judge others' actions, knowing that the world was an imperfect place and that life was difficult.

She viewed the garden with distaste. The heat had imposed a silence upon it, a languor punctuated only by the insects that darted busily between the flowers, the leaves that whispered overhead. Normally, she took great delight in it, liking nothing better than to prowl its borders, trowel in hand, planting and pruning but now she had no appetite for its careful symmetry, its tapestry of colours, its cultured shrubs and hedges. Her pleasure had been destroyed by her concern for her sons, by their impotence in the face of the army's power. She almost welcomed the tiresome shortages, the lack of servants and the restrictions of a war economy. Coping with them as best she could helped assuage her guilt at being safe and free.

She said, "The army will have to bring them home eventually. It can't continue to defy the government, not now they're known to be in France."

Alice waved her hands in consternation. "They're capable of anything. Mr Asquith claims that Robert and the others are still in England. Lord Derby insists that they're in France and that they'll be shot for disobedience. Who's telling the truth? As long as the Government's divided, the Army can do as it pleases."

Louise lapsed into silence. Whilst Bennett had sprung into action at the news of Robert's abduction, she had retreated into herself, her brave face concealing her belief that the world had become an uninviting place. It was a far cry from her Herculean efforts in the early months of the war.

Before the war, she had been a political activist. Much to Bennett's consternation, she had joined Mrs Fawcett's National Union of Women's Suffrage Societies, contributing to *Common Cause* and actively campaigning for the enfranchisement of women. She had protested fiercely at the laws condemning suffragettes to continual imprisonment and had been arrested during the protest over their introduction. When the war came, she had been shocked at the speed with which the suffragettes had become the mouthpiece of the British army. She still recalled with horror Mrs Pankhurst's claim that "to give one's life for one's country, for a great cause, is a splendid thing." She had always believed rights for women, internationalism and pacifism to be inextricably linked. The involvement of women in the mainstream of political life was to be the prelude to a kinder, saner world. Therein lay their claim to an independent voice. It was a rude shock to see suffragettes become the army's recruiting sergeants. Their bellicosity had thrown her into turmoil. Did women share men's flaws and had only been denied the opportunity for their full expression by a lack of opportunity? If that was the case, it was better to remain in the obscurity of the nursery and kitchen than to change one's nature. Disillusioned, she had determined to confine herself to helping those who suffered as a consequence of the war.

When conscription reached the statute book, she realised that the strength and dedication that everyone had admired had only been made possible by her immunity to the ravages of the war. Robert's conscription, arrest and imprisonment had destroyed her equanimity. Michael's decision to enlist had been a further blow. Perhaps if she had shared her contemporaries' belief that King and Country was a cause worth dying for, she would have felt differently. In the event, the possibility of their untimely deaths consumed her. She continued to help and comfort others but with a heavy heart. She had become another mother fearful for her sons' safety.

"Who were you writing to?" Alice asked.

Louise's correspondence was legendary, embracing a vast network of Quaker families in both the old world and the new.

Her mother started abruptly, waving briefly at a bee that hovered by her hat. Her hand fluttered in the air before retreating to her bag.

She said, "No one in particular," and shrugged dismissively, knowing that her air of injured innocence would prove a poor defence against her daughter's scrutiny.

Alice gazed at her suspiciously. Her mother was a woman without guile. She retained an air of innocence everyone remarked upon, a freshness unperturbed by the rigours of the world. Now her face was troubled, her expression petulant, as she snatched her bag from the table.

Alice said, "I didn't mean to pry," and rose from the table, disconcerted by her mother's troubled gaze. Seeing that her mother was about to speak, she sat down again, waiting on her words.

Louise sighed heavily, leaning forward in her chair. She looked around uneasily. Satisfied that no one was within earshot, she said reluctantly, "I've written to the War Office about Michael."

"Saying what?" Alice asked, though she knew precisely what her mother had in mind.

"To alert them to the fact that he's six months under age and asking them to send him home."

"Do you think they mind how old he is?"

"The Military Service Act is quite clear on the matter."

"That's as may be, but the Army doesn't care one way or the other."

"If it's brought to their attention, they have to act."

"Have you told father what you intend to do?"

"I haven't told anyone but you. Least of all, have I told your father. I pleaded with him to stop Michael going but he wouldn't do it."

"You resolved to take matters into your own hands?"

"Is that so unreasonable?"

Alice gazed at her mother in astonishment. Her hand fluttered to her throat and her fingers began to fuss with the necklace that hung there. Her mother acting in defiance of her father's wishes was entirely without precedent.

Louise said; "Your father said that Michael was old enough to make up his own mind. He claimed that he and Robert had done everything they could to dissuade him from enlisting but, if he was absolutely determined to go, he would do it with their blessing. I could hardly believe my ears."

Alice was confounded by the discovery of a rift between her parents when the need for love and understanding had never been greater. Worst of all, it seemed that they had ceased to discuss things openly. Louise purported to agree with Bennett even as resentment smouldered deep inside her. Even Robert's jeopardy had failed to unite them.

"You know you won't save him, don't you? He's about to leave for France. The army wants everyone it can get for the big push."

Louise remained silent, her striking face distorted by concern. Alice thought the last few months had aged her precipitately, converting youth into old age, without reference to the years between. When Louise spoke again, it was more in sorrow than in anger.

"Robert's abduction was the final straw. What right do they have to treat him like that when he's merely acting in accordance with his conscience? Something broke inside me when I heard the news. I felt I had to try to save Michael whilst there was still time. I wanted to make certain one of them would be spared."

Alice reached across the table and took her mother's hand; it was cold in spite of the sun. The letter hadn't gone; there was still an opportunity to divert her from a course of action that would serve no purpose other than to alienate her from her husband and her son.

She said, "I know you're acting for the best but you still ought to speak to father. He has a right to be consulted before the letter goes."

"But he'll try to stop me. I know he will. He'll say that Michael is entitled to act in accordance with his conscience, no less than you or Robert."

"But isn't that the case?"

"I can't tell you how tired I am of listening to people talk about duty and honour, when I see only mothers grieving for their sons and husbands. The only duty I accept now, in this world gone mad, is a mother's duty to keep her children safe from harm."

"But we're not children any more."

Alice rose from the table. She was always on the move, never still, as if being still meant wasting precious time. Since Robert's abduction, her restlessness had worsened. She was to be seen striding restlessly about the house, vexed at his disappearance and her inability to help him.

"What about Michael? Has he got no say in this? He's determined to join the army, convinced that it's his duty. He won't be grateful if you thwart him."

"But he's only a boy. He doesn't know his own mind. I'm only trying to do what's best for him."

Alice said, "I can't help but think that the War Office is overflowing with letters from anxious relatives. There's nothing we can do to postpone Michael's enlistment. What matters is that we stay united as a family, in spite of our differences, and support each other."

The truth was that she didn't know what she wanted any more. Why shouldn't they risk their lives for their beliefs? Wasn't that what everyone was doing whom the war had in its grasp? Their actions were foolish yet admirable. She hoped they wouldn't pay too dearly for their impetuosity.

Louise pushed her chair aside and rose to her feet. She struggled to hold back the tears that threatened to betray her feelings. When she was sure of her composure, she reached out for Alice, grateful that one of her children was immune from the war's pull. Alice held her mother tightly and then, her arm around her waist, led her back to the house, knowing that she would do nothing to prevent her posting the letter.

Bennett joined them in the house, his long face pale and stern beneath his beard, all bustle and self-importance, swollen with the news he had to tell them. Doctor Meyer, the well-known Baptist minister and evangelist, had engineered a meeting with Lord Kitchener, the Minister of War, and had been asked by the Minister, who was concerned for the objectors' welfare, to visit those who had been been abducted to the front. Lord Kitchener was an opponent of conscription, believing that a volunteer army was more likely to defeat the enemy. Now, after questions in Parliament and the lobbying of the No-Conscription Fellowship, he had felt compelled to act and Doctor Meyer, his chosen emissary, had asked Bennett to accompany him on his visit. Bennett could only speculate as to what would come of it, but the opportunity to meet Robert and his companions was not to be missed. Louise hung upon his every word, wanting to believe in his purposeful ambition whilst Alice, though delighted that his efforts had borne fruit, almost hated him for kindling hope's deceptive flame in her mother's breast, thinking his optimism born of misplaced vanity, a determination to believe in their immunity in spite of the forces ranged against them.

Later in the solitude of her room, she relived the day's events, gazing from the window out across the common to where the willows dipped and swayed above the stream that bubbled into life beyond the empty road. An old man dozed on a bench, awaking with a start each time his head fell forward. Three boys played 'tag' among the grasses, chasing after each other, shouting in high-pitched voices, lost to the demands of their game. She looked across at the polo ground, deserted save for the handful of ageing gardeners who fought to keep the weeds at bay. She watched the sun as it sank below the trees, painting their foliage in a golden hue and thought about the war, wondering how long it would have to continue before only the young and old remained.

CHAPTER 8

Robert woke to the sound of guns. He glimpsed flashes of light and heard, above the wind and the mounting bustle of the camp, the crack of field guns, the faint 'whoof' of mortars and the blast of high explosive, the unwelcome chorus mocking his puny efforts at resistance.

He sprang to his feet when the guards came for them, grateful that the waiting that had so weighed down on him was over. He stood nervously outside the cell, hands rigid at his side, shifting from one foot to the other. When the order came to march, he stepped forward with the others, hobbling on his stiffened limbs, determined to represent their cause with all the vigour he could muster.

They followed four soldiers with rifles and fixed bayonets to the hut that occupied a corner of the camp. The soldiers' faces wore a new solemnity. Outside the hut, two men tugged wearily on the ropes that trailed from the flagpole, attempting to unfurl the flag left tangled by the previous night's storm. Robert watched them warily, too preoccupied to find amusement in their labours. A group of soldiers and an NCO clustered by the door of the hut, talking quietly. He heard one of them say, "There ought to be some other way. It isn't right to do them in." He noted the words of sympathy and was grateful for them though the tidings they contained were ominous.

Inside the hut, four pairs of highly polished boots protruded from beneath a low table, heels planted firmly on the bare boards. The table was strewn with papers, bundles of documents neatly tied with ribbons, and copies of The Manual of Military Law. Robert stared at their audience suspiciously, surprised to find their protest the focus of so much effort, whilst feeling slightly guilty at the trouble he had caused. Behind the heaps of papers sat four officers, silent and unmoving as the prisoners took their places. Robert noted the insignia on the shoulders of their tunics: the two diamond shaped pips below a crown of a colonel on the tunic of the court president and the three stars of a captain worn by his companion. The two stars and one star of a lieutenant and a second lieutenant adorned the uniforms of the younger men.

He was struck by the appearance and demeanour of the captain, a man about his own age. His face was weathered, his features handsome, his expression wearied as he toyed with his pencil. He glanced up briefly at the prisoners but otherwise showed little interest in their presence. The colonel, by contrast, examined them intently as they took their seats. Robert attempted to gauge his mood, his attitude towards them but his face was impassive, his hands clasped together tightly on the table. The subaltern was nervous, his hands shook as he reached for his papers. Robert supposed that this was his first court martial and that he had little idea what to expect. The task was unenviable for somebody so young. He thought back to the tribunal, the words he might have uttered there and how he had been destined to enlist no matter what he said. He wondered if his words now would have any greater effect, for they were surely guilty of the crimes assigned to them. The four men before him might be judge and jury, but he was still determined to put his case to them as best he could. Even to see an expression of sympathy on their faces, a look of understanding in their eyes would be a kind of victory.

The sentries took their places by the door, eyes alert, as if fearing the prisoners might make a run for it if events didn't go their way. The colonel introduced the members of the court, the prosecuting counsel, the defending counsel and the legally qualified court martial officer. The witnesses sat off to the side, their faces solemn, weighed down by the information they were due to impart. The colonel announced the date and type of trial, the name of the officers present and the task before them, speaking so loudly that Robert wondered if he was hard of hearing. The prisoners' details were read out: their unit, rank and service number and the charges brought against them. Each of them was accused of disobeying the lawful command of a senior officer whilst in the field. There was no reference to the myriad, minor offences that they had committed on their way to the camp.

The drill sergeant whom they had defied was called upon to give his evidence. On the parade ground, he was a tyrant, his voice a lash across the shoulders of the prisoners. Everyone was cowed by the stentorian commands, the biting sarcasm that issued from his lips. Now, he stumbled over every word, though the case he had to make could not have been more plain. Abandoning the parade ground had emasculated him. He reminded Robert of a fish, newly landed, flapping uselessly on the quay's dry stones. Questioned by the prosecutor, he stumbled through his evidence. The colonel sat poised to intervene, making the sergeant still more nervous, until his words became a garbled stream.

"That's enough," the colonel said to everyone's relief, his expression conveying to the prisoners that their misdemeanours were worse than he had feared. He turned to the defending officer with a look of expectation, wondering what defence he might conjure up when their guilt was so plain.

The defending officer was no less mystified. He had questioned each of the defendants in turn, hoping vainly for some plea that he could enter in mitigation of their conduct but all of them had freely admitted their defiance and appeared to be intent on prompting the army to do its worst.

He said, "The defendants have no excuse to offer for their conduct. They agree that they defied the sergeant's orders and that they were lawful ones. They also understand that they're in the field and subject to its regulations and what that might mean for them by way of punishment."

"How would they behave now, knowing what lies in store for them?" asked the colonel. "Would they behave any differently? Are they more inclined to obey lawful orders than they were before?"

"I think I can speak for all of us," Castlereagh claimed, "when I say that we would do the same thing again."

The defending officer shrugged hopelessly. He began to speak, thought better of it and lapsed into silence. He could scarcely countenance that the defendants wouldn't try their utmost to mitigate their conduct.

The colonel was also surprised, though the court papers had catalogued a raft of misdemeanours. He turned to the defendants and asked them outright if anyone had anything to say in their defence. He could think of no excuse for their conduct but felt that they should be given every opportunity to justify their behaviour.

Robert was the first to speak.

"Ah, Professor Bennett," said the colonel, "I thought we might hear from you. You have something to say in mitigation of your conduct? If so, now's the time to say it." He looked at Robert expectantly, hoping that at least one of them would see sense.

Robert was startled by the use of his title. No one had used it since his return to England. Now the moment was upon him, he felt there was little useful he could say. It seemed to him that their only hope of salvation lay in some procedural shortcoming.

He said, "I would like to ask if the court is properly constituted."

"Why would it not be?"

"Are the officers present sufficiently senior to rule upon our case? Is a lieutenant colonel, a captain and two lieutenants sufficient for such grave allegations?"

The colonel looked disconcerted. He had asked the same question. The court had been put together at very short notice.

He turned expectantly to the court officer who said confidently, "It would have been more usual to have a major present but the presence of a captain is perfectly consistent with the requirements of the Military Manual. So, yes, the court is properly constituted, even for an offence that might carry the death sentence."

Robert said, "We've no wish to justify our conduct. We don't think we've done anything wrong. However, we do have an issue with the Army's behaviour and our appearance here today."

"What about it?"

The colonel knew he had no reason to fear Robert's testimony but was intimidated by the resolute look on his face, his carefully calibrated sense of outrage. He was aware that he was a university professor, a historian by all accounts, and might yet have a trick up his sleeve.

"I would like to know why we've been denied proper legal representation."

The colonel was taken aback. He had been told that the matter was settled. He said, "But you have the defending officer." He looked across at the officer who had spoken up on behalf of the accused. He was sitting at the table, a resigned look on his face. He had warned them not to challenge the court's jurisdiction. The colonel said: "The defending officer can hardly be blamed if you choose to offer no defence."

Robert smiled apologetically. "I'm talking of civilian representation. We asked that a barrister be sent out from England to act on our behalf. We even gave you names to choose from but the request was rejected."

"Well, of course, it was," the colonel offered confidently, "this isn't a civilian case." He leaned forward across the desk, his expression a scowl. "You know the arguments as well as I do. They hardly bear repeating. You are deemed to have enlisted under the terms of the Military Service Act. That being the case, your conduct falls within our jurisdiction. You are therefore guilty under military law if you disobeyed the lawful command of a senior officer. You don't need me to tell you," he added for good measure, "how unfortunate that could be for you."

Robert shook his head vigorously. "The Act required us to enlist unless given exemption by a tribunal. We declined to enlist and failed to gain exemption. We're therefore liable to prosecution under the terms of the Act. However, as you well know, there's no provision in the Act for our forcible removal from England or even for thinking that we have committed a military offence."

The colonel was unmoved. "In the eyes of the law, you're a soldier whether you care to be or not."

The defending officer rose to intervene. He saw no virtue in open defiance and had said so repeatedly. He had recommended that they recognise the court's jurisdiction, admit the offences, offer up their beliefs in mitigation of their conduct and hope for a lenient sentence. That meant anything other than the death sentence. None of the defendants, even Robert, whom he had found the most helpful, appeared to have grasped how seriously the army viewed their conduct and how close to the death sentence they were.

Before he could speak, Robert said, "We insist that we're returned to England immediately for prosecution in the civil courts."

The colonel shook his head. "You're deemed to have enlisted and fall within our mandate and that's the end of the matter. As for your being in France?" He hesitated at this point, less sure of his ground, before concluding, with more confidence than he felt, "The army's entitled to send you wherever it chooses, as is the case with any conscript."

"It wasn't military law that brought us here. It was malice, an unreasoning desire to punish us for failing to obey orders. No one else from the Non-Combatant Corps has ended up here."

Having shown little interest hitherto, the captain, groaned loudly. The sound was sudden and unexpected. Even he seemed surprised. He had been ordered to attend the day's proceedings even though his battalion was about to go back into the line. Why they had chosen him he had never discovered but here he was, witnessing this dialogue of the deaf, whilst his company moved up without him. He could never reconcile himself to the lack of urgency behind the lines. Every time he came out, he entered a world which seemed to mock the dangers afflicting those in the forward positions. It was though the soldiers in the trenches were forgotten, the enemy they faced a vague and distant threat. Now whilst they played charades with this group of cranks, his company was occupying its sector, preparing to attack. What was the point of this court martial? What was it supposed to achieve? It was obvious that the defendants would never serve, even if they were dragged into the line. They were pacifists. Why anyone would be a pacifist was quite beyond him. It was a contemptible stance, a luxury only made possible by the efforts of people like him, people who served gladly and willingly, prepared to sacrifice their lives for their country. But however deplorable their views, the objectors obviously felt strongly about them and were even prepared to die for them. So why bring them here? They properly belonged in prison in England like the defendant had claimed.

Robert fell silent, expecting the captain to give voice to the resentment he felt, but he said nothing, outwardly composed but angry, biting his tongue, in an effort to appear impartial and to confine himself to the facts. Everyone was bemused by his strange intervention but Robert saw its significance immediately. It was the voice of the dying, distilled into one brief cry of protest. He was devastated by the insight. It was a reminder, in the shadow of the firing squad, that other men no less sincere, had taken a very different view.

"Have you finished?" the colonel asked. He made it clear that he thought he should do so by reaching again for his papers.

"I've nothing more to add," Robert said with alacrity. The captain resumed his silent vigil, seemingly disinterested once more.

Clapham waved his right to speak with a quick shake of his head. He had told Robert earlier that he intended to say nothing. He didn't see the point of dragging out the proceedings when the army's mind was already made up.

"It mightn't be," Robert had said. "There might still be room for manoeuvre, even now."

"I don't think so," Clapham had said, "why else would they have brought us here? Our fate will be decided in Whitehall, not here in this camp."

Castlereagh was determined to make the court martial the occasion for a spirited rebuttal of their treatment. Whilst it was inevitable that he should seek to unburden himself after weeks of frustration, the officers could hardly fail to resent the flow of invective directed at them. The colonel's face took on a look of martyrdom, a combination of polite scepticism and mounting disbelief. The captain rocked back in his chair, his face colouring noticeably as he stifled the urge to reply. He directed a look of implacable hostility at Castlereagh.

The colonel said wearily: "I must remind you that we're here to hear the evidence and to effect a judgement on your conduct. How you got here, your previous behaviour, your beliefs and politics have no bearing on this case."

The word politics seemed to hang in the air, anathema in a soldier's world, conjuring up images of indecision and compromise and interference in the conduct of the war.

If Castlereagh's assertions were unhelpful, Taylor contrived to make a bad situation worse. He rose to his feet, a tall emaciated man, pinched and humourless, a pale stripe above his lip where a moustache had flourished once. He spoke slowly and emphatically as he did in every circumstance. Robert always wanted to finish his sentences for him. To the astonishment of the court, he visited the wrath of God upon its officers. He even likened the colonel to Pontius Pilate in respect of his indifference to their plight. Robert thought it was a striking metaphor but one unlikely to help their cause. Taylor's shrill words left him in no doubt that he was badly scared.

The comparison outraged the colonel who was trying his best to be fair. Did the man think he liked doing this? Someone had to preside over the court martial and he had been chosen, as he always was when there was dirty work to be done, because he was thought to be a safe pair of hands.

"How dare you speak to me like that?" he asserted, rising from his seat, before sinking back into his place again, determined to bring the proceedings to a swift conclusion.

~

"Well, what do you make of that?" the colonel asked after the prisoners had left the room. He leaned back in his chair, arms folded, glad to see the back of them.

He hated courts martial and had only been persuaded to preside because the general had been unwilling to take no for an answer. He always felt that the need to resort to military law was a sign of failure and that a commanding officer's presence and example should be sufficient to inspire the men. As for bad apples, and there were always some, the best battalion commanders had their ways of dealing with them, without resort to the Military Manual or the lawyers who blurred the distinction between right and wrong. However, the objectors were different. He could see that. They were a queer lot, there was no denying it, such strong opinions and such divergent views. The only thing they had in common was their unwillingness to serve. He was entirely at a loss to understand their reasoning but for him, it was different. The war had rescued him from obscurity. It was a chance to avail himself of opportunities denied to him in peacetime, and he was grateful for its presence.

He said, "I think we can agree that they're guilty, as they've made no effort to deny the charges against them. Furthermore, they're all in this together. What holds for one of them, holds for them all. What we have to decide now is their sentence. So, who would like to go first?"

He looked expectantly at the subaltern. The convention was that the junior officer declared his views first. That way, no one could accuse him of having been influenced by the more senior officers. He felt sorry for Griffiths. Barely twenty years old by the looks of him with probably not much more than a year in the line. This court martial was certainly his first. It was a big responsibility for such a young man.

If Griffiths thought so, he gave no sign of it. The Military Manual was on the desk in front of him, a slip of paper indicating the relevant page. He opened it quickly and said without hesitation, "It's the death penalty. That's what it says here."

Though the colonel winced at his directness, he couldn't fault his reasoning. He knew what the manual had to say on the matter. The question was whether the circumstances were such as to justify a departure from its provisions and whether some nuance couldn't be brought into play to achieve an outcome acceptable to both sides.

If such things were possible, they had eluded the lieutenant.

"Death, I'm afraid, sir," he said with a show of regret that the colonel found unconvincing. A political answer, he thought. He wants to be seen to do the right thing, to express a view that won't hurt his prospects.

He turned expectantly to the captain, looking to him for a considered view, one that would reflect the complexity of the matter. For the death sentence to prevail, they had to be unanimous. He hoped the captain would spare him the necessity of exercising the decisive vote.

He said, "Well, Captain Fielding, what do you think? Death, in your view?"

"They've done field punishment – that's made no difference."

"No, we're not going to persuade them to cooperate, whatever we do."

The captain looked out of sorts and had done since the proceedings began. He clearly had no appetite for this sort of thing but then few of them had. There was something else bothering him, something unrelated to the court's judgement. Some issue back in the line probably or news from home that he hadn't liked. The captain had said, earlier on, that he was about to go up again, and hadn't looked too happy about it. He was probably all geared up for it and resented being held back. There again, he might have had some premonition that things were not going to go well and had the wind up. It happened to everybody at times, especially if their last show had been a bad one. Well, he hoped he wasn't going to let his misgivings affect his judgement. He had to be above all of that when lives were at stake.

The captain understood the need for detachment well enough but was struggling to achieve it. He had taken against the prisoners. There was no denying it. He hadn't had an issue with the first one. He at least had shown some recognition that there was a war on and, having tried and failed to challenge the court's jurisdiction, had possessed the sense to keep quiet thereafter. But the others had irritated him hugely with their pomposity, their obliviousness to the larger issues at stake.

"It's death, for me, I suppose. That's what the regulations say. Besides, they've had their chance…"

Though he spoke with assurance, his eyes betrayed an uncertainty that belied his words. The colonel waited, saying nothing, thinking that the captain might yet qualify his judgement but when he looked at him expectantly, he shook his head, making clear that he had nothing else to say.

"He's leaving it to me," the colonel thought. "He knows that if I vote against the death penalty, everyone will have to revisit their verdict. He wants me to decide whether we ought to be lenient."

He thought about the prisoners and how badly their words had supported their cause. It would be very easy to allow resentment at their accusations to colour his judgement but he wasn't about to do that. He was also aware of the signals coming down from on high. Nothing that could be regarded as interference in the deliberations of the court. The brass were too subtle for that. But there was undoubtedly a feeling abroad that discipline needed to be tightened up, that the courts had been lenient of late and that the presence of the objectors afforded an opportunity to remind everyone that there was no room for magnanimity.

"Well, two can play at that game," concluded the colonel.

He was not about to override the views of the others. Only the captain had betrayed the slightest doubts about demanding the death penalty. Nor was he going to go out on a limb by ignoring the hints and suggestions that had come his way. He intended to make sure that the High Command had the last word and knew of only one way to do that.

He said, "I vote for death, as well. The prisoners have been sentenced to death. The court will deliver its verdict and then the matter is out of its hands."

With that he rose from his seat and thanked all the officers present for their help with a firm shake of the hand. When he saw that the captain had gone deathly white, he patted him on the shoulder.

"Don't worry. I'm sure we've acted properly."

"Well, I hope so," the captain said, regretting his decision.

CHAPTER 9

Frank Taylor's conversion began with a poster on the window of an empty shop, its dire warning and its promise of eternal life. He didn't recall what propelled him into the mission hall but knew as soon as the words of the hymn faded and the preacher took the stage that his words were meant for him. His excitement mounted as the sermon reached its climax. He longed for the forgiveness of the silent waters beneath the stage. He watched spellbound as the others filed past him, heads bowed, hands raised in supplication as the curtains were drawn back until, plucked from the audience by an unseen hand, he had found himself amongst them, shivering with trepidation as he pledged his life to God. Being an Christian had been strange at first, carrying the label, fashioning his life after the promises he'd made. He began by being euphoric, wanting to shout his status from the rooftops, to inform everyone, even strangers, of his new beginning. But when he saw their scepticism, he realised he must combine with others of like mind if he was to prosper and became a determined, earnest Christian, respected for his views. Every Sunday saw him seated in the front pew of the undistinguished hall where his congregation gathered, Bible in hand, echoing the preacher's words. When the hymns were sung, his voice was the loudest. He guided the collection boxes up and down the rows. If children in the congregation were inattentive, he stilled their whispers with a disapproving stare. He tried to live in accordance with Christ's teaching and when others thought him pompous or self-righteous, he was unconcerned. He read his Bible incessantly, believing it the word of God and boasted he had read no other book since the age of twenty. When he waited for the workmen's trains that took him to the city, he carried it beneath his arm; on balmy days he read it in the park as he ate his lunch and he scrutinised its contents before he went to sleep each night. When members of the congregation solicited his advice, he urged them to employ it as their companion and guide.

He refused to enlist, arguing that an unwillingness to bear arms was central to his faith and purported to welcome martyrdom. The trepidation prompted by the court martial was profoundly disturbing. It mattered little that everyone feared the consequences of their refusal to obey orders. The others didn't share his expectations or believe themselves invulnerable. "If I've received the gift of eternal life, what is there to fear?" he asked himself repeatedly, even as his consternation mounted, resisting all his prayers.

His uncertainty directed him to others, as if by showing them the route to salvation, he might restore his faith but when he looked for converts, it seemed that everyone was spoken for. Few of the objectors were weak or vacillating men. Only Robert was prepared to speak of his desire for a certainty greater than that afforded by mere strength of character but Robert had always recoiled from the loud, proclaiming kind of Christianity that saw its task as saving others' souls.

"You can't afford to hesitate when you're in such danger," Taylor said to him, his eyes alive with fervour. "You can't call yourself a Christian unless you believe that Jesus was the Son of God."

Following the court martial, Robert began to share Taylor's sense of urgency, needing a clear view of his beliefs, a map by which to travel, but Taylor's intervention served only to deny him that elusive harmony from which a deeper insight might emerge.

Castlereagh's view was that certainty was born of opposition and that the actions of the army would suffice to make them resolute.

Robert said, "I'm tired of being tolerant, of always seeing other's points of view. I want to have the certainty of believing that I'm right."

But even as he spoke, he recognised that he was doomed to suffer unrestricted vision. It was what he had always striven for but it made life very hard as they waited for the verdict of the court.

Taylor pursued him with a manic vigour when the trial was past. Robert hid amongst his fellow prisoners as best he could, ever mindful of the watching figure. Finally, in desperation, he challenged his fitness to prevail.

Taylor was not unduly worried, thinking it only a matter of time before Robert turned to him for help. He had seen the same resistance melt away in other troubled souls and knew that no one could predict when the Lord's will would prevail. Robert was a case quite different from others he had known. He came from Christian parents but was free of all indoctrination. He claimed to believe in God and yet showed no obvious signs of devotion. He listened to his entreaties but was unmoved by them, neither meeting them with stern contempt nor embracing them wholeheartedly.

Robert grew adept at resisting Taylor's pleas. He challenged his assumptions, forcing him to examine his beliefs. Taylor was unused to such vigorous ripostes, untested as he was against so well-informed a foe. When he challenged Robert, his own beliefs began to crumble until he found himself addressing questions he had long ignored.

Robert was waiting in the queue to wash, attempting to ignore the brackish water, the scum of soap, the rusting razors and the impatient, shoving prisoners when Taylor rushed towards him, a wild expression on his face. When Robert attempted to ignore him, he grasped his arm and and said loudly, "It's gone; somebody's taken it; I can't find it anywhere."

The strain of waiting on their sentence was testing everyone. No one seemed responsible for them or knew what was going to happen. The attempts to make them wear a uniform, drill on the square or participate in the onerous duties inflicted on other prisoners had ceased, leaving them free to make what they could of their circumstances.

"What's gone?"

"My Bible's disappeared."

Taylor raised his arm despairingly, oblivious to the grunts of protest from the other prisoners waiting in the queue.

His Bible had seemed as much a part of his person as his arm or leg. It was astonishing that he had retained it for so long. No one else had managed to keep their personal possessions. Robert put it down to the fact that his captors had decided that relieving him of it was more trouble than it was worth. It had proved to have its uses when they were deprived of books and newspapers. Taylor allowed others to read it beneath his watchful eye and their brief, religious services relied upon its presence.

"Where do you think you left it?"

Taylor pointed to the latrines, the queue of prisoners waiting patiently.

"You took it in there with you?"

"I left it on the grass outside the door."

"In full view of everyone?"

"No one would steal a Bible?"

"They'll steal anything in here."

The camp was full of thieves. Anything left unattended was sure to disappear. It was part of the art of survival. Not that there was much to steal. Food was the principal target. It was likely to be whisked away at any time, to be shared out haphazardly or fought over by the prisoners.

"I thought you might know where it is."

"Why would I know?" Robert asked

Taylor looked at him accusingly. "You've tried to undermine my faith in every way …"

"I've done nothing other than defend myself against your preaching," but even as he spoke, Robert knew the words weren't true. He had challenged Taylor's faith, resenting his fundamentalism, viewing it as an anvil on which to shape his own beliefs.

"I don't know where your Bible is."

"How can I survive the filth and degradation of this place without its words of comfort?" Taylor pointed at the camp's buildings, the empty square, the makeshift cells. "How can I face the future without the scriptures at my side?"

Everyone was watching them: objectors, prisoners, guards, expecting another of the fits of violence so frequent in the camps but Robert placed his hand on Taylor's arm, the simple gesture calming him, and said, "Wait here 'till I've finished and then we'll go and look for it."

Taylor waited as each prisoner splashed the tepid water on his face and took his turn with the rusting razor, Robert watched him from the corner of his eye. His aggression had given way to a poverty of spirit obvious to someone who had spent so many hours in his presence. His sorrowful expression filled him with remorse. He wouldn't have challenged his beliefs or made light of their circumstances if time had not weighed on his hands.

They made an effort to locate the missing Bible but it was a hopeless task. There was nowhere to conceal it. Perhaps one of the guards had removed it or a prisoner had stolen it in the hope of trading it for food or cigarettes? More likely, it had been dismembered and its pages put to uses Robert dared not mention. Taylor grew even more dejected when they failed to find it. He couldn't bear to think of it in disrespectful hands.

Clapham said unhelpfully, "He's your responsibility. I don't know what you've done to him but only you can calm him down."

Robert wanted only to bring the episode to a swift conclusion.

"I don't know what makes you think I can help him. I'm the least suitable person imaginable. I spend my whole time arguing with him. I'm probably the reason for his collapse."

"Well, you didn't steal his Bible."

"It's a miracle he got it this far. I only wish that we could find it. Its disappearance is the final straw."

"He's convinced himself that you have insights that will help restore his faith.."

"I've got nothing more to offer than the belief that we might be saved and the certainty that what we're doing is right and probably worth dying for."

"Let's hope it doesn't come to that."

Clapham's sentiments remained firmly lodged in Robert's mind. Taylor's beliefs had proved brittle when tested by their circumstances. His determination to persuade others of his views had been an effort to convince himself.

"I'll do what I can to put his mind at rest. But it won't be easy, his whole life has been based on the premise that he was uniquely close to God."

Clapham said, "He won't find God in here."

The bickering of the guns over the horizon intensified as he spoke. Theirs was a quiet sector, though the preparations they had witnessed on the passage north suggested that was about to change. But even in the absence of an offensive, the sparring continued: bombardments, raids and sorties, intended to establish the strength and disposition of the enemy.

Robert said, "The prospect of death has made old men of us."

He urged Taylor to live from day to day. He said his crisis was an opportunity for him to build a new and robust faith and Taylor ceased to agitate, to inflict his views on others, leaving Robert to believe that his efforts to assist him had met with some success.

He was aided in his efforts by unexpected news.

He became aware of persistent attempts to diminish the squalor of the camp, of frequent inspections, of the unexplained attention of officers and guards.

"What's going on?" he asked. "Why this sudden activity?"

"Visitors from England," Castlereagh said. "That can only mean one thing. Our supporters have discovered our whereabouts and have come to save us."

Everyone clapped and shouted when they heard the news.

"This surely means we're going home," Clapham said, eyes dancing with excitement. "The army can hardly execute us in full view of the world."

Robert doubted that the army would release its hold on them easily. The passage to the front had opened his eyes to the true nature of its power. He saw little reason for believing that a High Command immune to the loss of life on the grand scale would be intimidated by visitors from England but wisely kept his counsel. The prospect of a visit had restored their hopes of freedom and that was benefit enough.

CHAPTER 10

The faces of the soldiers gathered on the square gave no hint of pleasure. They had turned out spick and span before for cursory inspections by senior officers and visitors. They knew they were just another aspect of the pomp and ritual that governed every aspect of the war. The objectors could scarcely conceal their excitement. For them, the visit represented the resumption of their links with another, saner world that might yet protect them from the army's wrath. They stood patiently in their dishevelled civilian clothes amidst the lines of soldiers, united in the hope that the unexpected visit might unlock the door to freedom.

They waited under the watchful eyes of NCOs for two long hours, talking in hushed voices, wary and impatient. The appointed hour came and went. The prisoners shrugged indifferently, grateful to be spared a day's fatigues. The objectors fought to hide their disappointment and nursed their fading hopes.

When at last they came; two small patches of colour amidst a sea of khaki, weaving haphazardly towards them, making for the group of huts and buildings that housed the cookhouse, mess and workshop, they passed the rusting appendage that was the objectors' home without a backward glance. The khaki escort surrounded them whichever way they turned. Nothing met their eye without a word of explanation. When they moved, their escort followed them, shepherding them to the appointed places, shielding from their curious gaze the worst features of the camp.

The group was led by Major Wilberforce, the camp's CO. His barrel chest advanced towards the line; one hand rose and fell with stiff precision, the other gripped the swagger stick beneath his arm. He never looked back, confident that everyone was following in his wake. Robert had spoken to him only once. On arriving at the camp, he had been paraded before the major with the other objectors. He recalled his look of bewilderment when he observed their civilian clothes and was told of their refusal to obey orders. He had looked at each of them in turn, shaking his head and saying: "You'll find out soon enough what happens to objectors here." Thereafter he had left others to deal with them as best they could. Now, as he eased his way along the line, noting an irregularity of dress or a posture that displeased him, his tired eyes missed nothing. He could tell who was intimidated by his harsh regime and who disregarded it. He knew that everyone hated the camp's petty regulations and menu of reprisals, but hated the prospect of the line still more. That was the nature of his hold over them. Malingerers or criminals: he didn't really care. His purpose was to punish them for their misdemeanours and send them back into the line.

Robert scrutinised the visitors' uneven progress, snatching glimpses of them as they passed between the lines. One of them in coat and hat was wilting in the heat. He glanced at the prisoners, eyes darting up and down the lines as if in search of something. There was something familiar about the tall, stooping figure, hands locked behind his back, the fulsome beard, the loping, wolf-like stride. How often he had run by his father's side, trying to match his stride, a small child hoping to be swung aloft. He felt the blood rush to his face as the procession moved fitfully towards him. The familiar figure was no figment of a tortured mind. His father had contrived to visit them. Their eyes met briefly. A nod of recognition passed between them before the group moved on, leaving Robert to judge whether his father's presence gave sufficient grounds for hope.

He wondered later why he hadn't stepped forward with some word of greeting but his father's step had never faltered. His demeanour had discouraged any sign of recognition. Robert accepted that was how it had to be. His efforts were on behalf of everyone. He could not be seen to favour any individual if his presence was to save them from the firing squad.

The others were remorseful and perplexed. The visit, so timely in its incidence, had raised their hopes and dashed them. They had longed for a dialogue, a chance to evidence their suffering and had been disappointed.

That night, as Robert slept, his father's image rose up to greet him. He stood next to him, a tall, familiar figure, arms outstretched, but Robert couldn't bring himself to take his hand or ask for his assistance. When, at last, they spoke, lips moving rapidly, the silence was unbroken. Though inhabiting each other's lives, they were unable to communicate their thoughts and feelings.

He woke with a sense of failure and lay, shifting uncomfortably, confused by his dreams, attempting to assimilate the previous day's events.

Castlereagh, curled up in the corner, said, "Robert, are you awake?"

Robert attempted to distinguish his features in the twilight, unnerved by the disembodied voice that spoke his name. It might have been his father speaking, so vivid was his dream.

"That's our last chance gone, isn't it?" Castlereagh whispered fiercely, his voice so low that Robert wondered if his words were meant for him. Many prisoners conducted fractured conversations with themselves.

"I watched you as they came towards us. You started forward, thought better of it and did nothing. Why didn't you speak out? Why didn't any of us? We watched them walk away without doing anything to help ourselves. We should have spoken up whilst we had the chance."

"There was nothing we could have done. At least, they know we're here. They've seen us with their own eyes. They know what we're up against. Now it's up to them."

He said nothing about his father. He had managed to visit them, an astonishing achievement, but what more could he do? The army was powerful; the front was its demesne. Knowing of his father's presence would merely raise the hopes of everyone when there were scant grounds for believing that anything had changed.

~

"They're coming back," Hicks reported, as they ate their breakfast sprawled carelessly upon the grass, wrestling as they always did with what to eat and what to save for later. "We'll be allowed to talk to them."

He spoke excitedly, full of everything he had overheard. He said that two of them would be allowed to have a conversation with their visitors, free of supervision. It was up to them to choose their representatives.

"So who's to go?" asked Castlereigh, "and what are they to say?" His tone suggested that he expected to be one of those selected.

He failed to get his way. Everybody wanted an opportunity to press the case for freedom. Some were worried about their families and what had befallen them. Castlereigh didn't have a family dependent on his meagre pay. He had not been rudely separated from his children. His home wasn't under threat because the rent had gone unpaid or a malevolent landlord had cast his family on the street. They were still trying to decide who to choose to represent them when Robert said, "I want to go."

He rarely put himself forward. He preferred to hear the views of others. The virtue of listening had been impressed upon him as a child.

Castlereigh was disconcerted by his intervention. He thought him content to let him take the lead in matters that affected them.

"Why you?" he asked.

Robert hesitated before replying, conscious of the eyes upon him. He didn't want to be seen to be exploiting his father's presence. He knew he could rely on him to do his best for all of them. Nor was he certain his father would welcome his appearance. He might think it ungenerous of him to put his own needs first.

He said, "One of them's my father. He's been active on our behalf since we were forcibly enlisted."

Everyone was taken aback by the disclosure. They didn't know what to make of it. "He'll make our case with vigour?" asked Castlereigh, mindful of Robert's circumspection on matters of concern to him.

"I would have thought his presence here was evidence enough of his effectiveness."

Castlereigh said, "There're many different viewpoints here and it's important they be heard." There was a murmur of agreement from the others present.

"We have a common interest in avoiding the firing squad."

Robert knew his father would be franker with him present. He was also desperate to see him. It might be his last opportunity to speak to him or to any member of his family. Castlereigh would have to control his wilfulness.

Castlereigh looked to the others for guidance, but their focus was on Robert. Robert noted their earnest glances, their needs and expectations. He hoped they wouldn't be disappointed with the outcome. Gaining access to the camps was one thing, changing the intentions of the High Command was another. There was an inevitability about the firing squad; there had been since they came to France. They had been treated harshly in England but their lives had never been in danger. It was a different matter when the army reigned supreme. Their only hope was that the High Command would decide that their execution wasn't worth the trouble. That was what his father would rely upon, employing reasoned argument until the army tired of him and foisted the objectors on to somebody else.

He said, "I want Clapham with me. The army might prove reluctant to execute so public a critic of the war."

Clapham feigned reluctance but was eager to attend. Enforced idleness had made him irritable and restless. He missed the opportunity to write. It was how he made sense of the world. To be making history and to be denied the opportunity to write about it was a cruel fate.

He said, "I was blacklisted for my lack of patriotism."

"The prospect of your execution will bring journalists rushing to your side."

"Well, I hope you're right," said Clapham, cheered by the thought that his notoriety might prove to be the means of their salvation.

There had been few signs of solidarity when he had criticised the conduct of the war. He had been condemned as unpatriotic and hounded from office but it was easy to forget that back in England, there were other siren voices struggling to be heard.

They were still discussing tactics when the soldiers came for them.

"Well, who's it to be?" demanded the officer in charge.

When Robert and Clapham stepped forward, he looked at them suspiciously before urging them forward with an impatient wave of his hand.

He marched them across the square at the double, wondering why they merited such trouble. He thought of all the prisoners that had passed through the camp: every kind of miscreant from abject coward to hardened criminal. None of them had received so much attention. This lot clearly had important friends.

"One thing," he said when they reached the hut. "You can say whatever you like in there. No one'll try to stop you." He pointed to the door, the sentry standing there, his face expressionless. "But, by this time tomorrow, your visitors will be back in London, going about their business whilst you'll still be here, under our control. I wouldn't make a fuss, if I were you. Otherwise, the firing squad might happen sooner than you think."

Robert gave him a wintry look. The same thought had occurred to him. His father's visit might engineer their safe return to England and an appearance before the civil courts. There again, it might accelerate their punishment, persuading the authorities to act quickly, whilst there was still time.

CHAPTER 11

Mr Bennett and Dr Meyer could not have been more different. Their belief in God and the forms of worship they favoured were poles apart. Dr Meyer was a founder of chapels and the author of innumerable books and pamphlets. He was a fiery preacher who toured the country to proclaim the gospels. He was a scourge of prostitution, drinking and public vice and a thorn in the side of every local authority he thought to be lax in such matters.

Bennett's only claim to office was membership of a committee set up by the Society of Friends to facilitate prison visits and he had no appetite for evangelicalism, believing that it was for the individual to find his own route to God. Nonetheless, there existed between the two men a bond of respect that had grown through the years. They delighted in debating their beliefs, heard each other's views with respect and happily diverged, convinced that the Heaven that would receive them when their lives were over would accommodate all men of good intent.

The day after the parade they found themselves in a hut awaiting a delegation of the objectors. Dr Meyer's task was to write a report for the Minister. Writing was not an issue for him. His ability to write with consummate ease was evidenced by the avalanche of books published in his name. He felt less sure of his ground with respect to the wide variety of views represented by the prisoners. His was a view of the world in which right and wrong were clearly demarcated. The route to God was clear to him if not to others. However, he knew that Bennett had skills denied to him, not least his persistent belief in the good of others. People opened their hearts to him, confident there would be no recriminations. It made him a good investigator, a ready means of access to men of varied views.

"Do you think that we'll meet Robert?" Dr Meyer asked his friend.

Though Bennett gave a watery smile, there was no concealing his excitement at the prospect of meeting his son. It had been so long since they had spoken and so much had occurred since their last encounter. He was not sure if he could bear being denied the opportunity to meet him after all the trouble he had taken. The chance to exchange a word or two was all he asked for. If things went badly wrong, they might never meet again. He put aside the thought, telling himself that no good would come of speculation but waiting for the door to open, he scarcely dared look up.

He was delighted to find that Robert was one of the objectors admitted to the interview. He and Clapham were seated in the centre of the room, opposite the visitors. Dr Meyer made the introductions and outlined the purpose of the visit. When the soldiers showed signs of lingering, the minister looked at them expectantly. They departed reluctantly. Once outside the door, their footsteps ceased. The group inside lowered their voices, fearing to be overheard.

Robert and his father spoke cautiously, each struggling to contain the emotion they felt at meeting in such circumstances. Bennett was reluctant to release his son's hand when he shook it. Robert found it hard to meet his gaze.

"Hello, Robert," Bennett said. "I'm pleased to see you looking well."

Robert noted a slight tremor in his voice but if his father was shocked at his appearance he gave no sign of it, save for a wariness, at odds with his usual frank appraisal.

"This is Clapham, a journalist. His frank views have landed him in France."

"I know of him and think highly of his work."

Clapham looked pleased. It was a long time since anyone had said a good word about him. He assured himself that he would always have an audience, however unpopular his views, but being unnoticed and unsung, writing for a world without discernment, was dispiriting,.

Father and son evaluated each other as they resumed their seats. Bennett looked tired and drawn but had changed his clothes and was dressed more appropriately. It was barely ten o'clock and the hut was warm but neither visitor had removed their jacket or loosened their collars. Bennett's face was heavily bearded, the dark hair that masked his chin tapering into its customary point. His eyes shone with their usual disconcerting intensity. He placed his hands neatly into his lap and sat upright in his chair. Dr Meyer was clean shaven and restless. A handsome, charismatic man, he looked strangely out of sorts in their small group. Robert suspected that he had not been keen to come to France but the call of the Minister of War, the fact that some of his flock were in danger and Bennett's insistence, had propelled him forward. He seemed shocked by what he had seen of the camp and the extent of the preparations for the new offensive. His demeanour filled Robert with little confidence about their prospects.

"Did you have trouble finding us?" Robert asked. "We thought no one knew we were here."

"The War Office knew," said Dr Meyer.

Bennett said, "The note you threw out of the train window was the first clue as to your whereabouts."

Robert looked at him with incredulity. He had never imagined that anyone would find it, still less that they would read it and make sense of its terse plea.

"It reached the House of Commons and prompted questions about your whereabouts," said Dr Meyer.

"Alice has it now," Bennett added, pride in his voice. "It's part of her growing collection of messages at the No-Conscription Fellowship."

Dr Meyer said, "She's doing a good job. They all are. Without their efforts, we'd have no idea what was going on."

"You know we've been tried and are awaiting sentence?"

"We certainly do."

Dr Meyer looked across at Bennett, seeking confirmation of his swift assertion. Bennett nodded in agreement. The look that passed between them offered few clues as to their feelings on the matter.

"We pleaded guilty," Robert said. When his father looked disconcerted, he asked, "What else could we do? We had repeatedly disobeyed the lawful commands of senior officers. We challenged their right to put us on trial but, as you might imagine, that didn't get us very far.."

"I don't suppose it did," said Dr Meyer.

Bennett leant forward in his chair, elbows on his knees, an earnest look upon his face. "Dr Meyer and I are to report to the Minister on the conditions under which you're being held. That would suggest that the War Office and the army are not entirely at one in the matter."

"That's good," Clapham declared.

"Well, possibly, it could go either way."

There were times when Robert wished his father was less candid. He was certainly not about to offer up the optimistic tidings that he had hoped for. He was grateful that he had chosen to attend the interview. He would have the opportunity to inject more grounds for hope in the message he took back.

Dr Meyer looked closely at the two objectors, relieved to find in their demeanour no obvious distress. He was an optimist by nature. It was the source of his boundless energy, his desire to improve the world. But in the matter of the army, he was out his depth. He could denounce the iniquities of the situation but when it came to the practicalities of changing them, he was unsure of his ground. The objectors were a difficult lot. Their defiance was driven by many different impulses. Some were earnest Christians like himself, attached to one of the minorities opposed to military service, but others were Godless, trade unionists and socialists or worse, for whom he felt little sympathy. Nonetheless, he couldn't sit idly by whilst sincere, well-meaning men were persecuted for their beliefs. That was going too far.

"We shouldn't read too much into your presence, then?"

Clapham spoke carelessly but the question had him on the edge of his seat. Behind the cool demeanour was a deeply anxious man.

Bennett said, "The army did everything they could to stop us coming here and even when the details of the visit had been agreed, they tried to prevent us from meeting you in private." He looked across at the door and said with a faint smile, "If, indeed, we are meeting you in private."

He continued, "Two years of war have curtailed the power of the civilian authorities. The army resists any attempt by the Government to encroach on its conduct of the war, in spite of its failure to make progress."

"Or because of it?" said Robert.

"It wanted conscription in order to build an army of truly continental proportions, notwithstanding the number of men already under arms. But conscription has proved a mixed blessing. Since the Act was introduced, more men have gained exemption from military service than have been compelled to enlist."

"Do they want to make an example of us?"

"Certain influential men in the War Office are of the view it would be helpful."

"They've been malevolent from the first. Not that we've made it difficult for them. We've consistently refused to do what they've asked of us."

"They want to punish you, but there's more to it than that. They hope to demonstrate to the politicians who are seeking to restrain them that they'll brook no interference in their conduct of the war."

"There's also the impact of your presence on the men in France," Dr Meyer added. "Nothing that implies that orders are open to question or that sacrifice isn't inevitable can be tolerated here."

"What happens next?" Clapham asked

He feared that they had been allowed visitors because they were about to die. Yet, he was grateful for their presence, no matter what the reason. It helped to know that a connection still existed to the world outside.

Bennett didn't know whether to cheer them up, sow false optimism, leave them with a legacy of hope, as was his inclination, or prepare them for the worst. He elected to steer a middle course.

"They can hardly hold a field court martial and declare you innocent but I doubt they've decided your sentence yet."

He listened to the commotion outside: the tramp of feet, the bark of orders, steps fading into the distance. Why was there so much drilling? Was a battalion that paraded well more effective? He must ask Michael when he saw him. He doubted it made any difference but was wholly ignorant of the army's ways.

"They wouldn't dare execute us, would they?" Clapham asked, sounding far from confident they'd be spared.

"Dr Meyer's report will describe the conditions under which you're being held, the punishments to which you've been subjected and will emphasise the danger you're in. We'll brief journalists who are sympathetic to your situation and petition the Government. That's being organised, as we speak. We'll also make sure there are further questions in the House of Commons about the army's intentions towards you."

"Where does the Government stand in all this? Robert asked. "You've spoken about the High Command, the War Ministry and House of Commons. What about the Cabinet? What are their intentions?"

Bennett looked disconcerted. He only knew what little Alice had told him of the activities of the No-Conscription Fellowship and its overtures to the Prime Minister. He was aware of the many claims that had issued from the lips of Government ministers since the time of their arrest. The truth was that there was no single viewpoint. The objectors were sailing in uncharted waters and might yet fetch upon the rocks.

He said, "I've spoken to Mr Lloyd George."

Robert was impressed. He was long familiar with his father's prodigious energy when committed to a cause but hadn't realised that his political connections were so extensive. Having decided that Minister of Munitions was a potential ally, his father had no doubt pursued him, hoping to win him over to their cause.

"Was he helpful?"

"Not in the least. He's abandoned his former radicalism. He's dedicated to the successful prosecution of the war by all the means at his disposal."

"He was the architect of conscription," said Clapham.

"I thought he might have some interest in mitigating the consequences of his policies. I pointed out it was hardly in the national interest to persecute those who had declined to enlist on grounds of conscience but he wasn't persuaded. Quite the opposite, I thought. He saw some virtue in hounding objectors when recruitment was flagging."

"Why's he so against us?" Robert asked.

"Perhaps, you remind him of how far he's travelled in the pursuit of power?"

Bennett had found the Minister greatly distracted by the burdens of office. It had been hardly surprising given the many challenges posed by the conflict. The war was not going well. The casualties were mounting. There were shortages of munitions and supplies. New strategies and tactics were required. There were rifts between the Government and the High Command over the conduct of the war. A new offensive was about to begin, the nature and timing of which was the result of an unhappy compromise between Britain and its ally, France. It was little wonder that he looked tired and preoccupied. Yet, he was still the man to whom the country looked for victory. It had merely added to his disappointment that this towering figure, though willing to devote thirty minutes to his concerns, had been unsympathetic. It made it more likely that the High Command would be given a free hand in deciding the objectors' fate.

"I wouldn't be surprised if the Government were to fall soon," said Dr Meyer, speaking confidentially. "The House no longer splits on party lines. The war has resulted in a sea of factions, each vying for power and influence."

"Which means," said Bennett, leaning back perilously on his chair, "that we can't offer you any certainty about the future. But we're optimistic, aren't we?" He turned to Dr Meyer.

"Yes, very optimistic."

Robert, having spent a lifetime observing his father's moods and expressions, found his assurances unconvincing. Nonetheless, he thought it better to accept them at face value. He wondered what his father might have said had they been alone.

Bennett said, "I would urge you to remember, whenever you incline to despair, that Britain's still a vigorous democracy. That hasn't changed. It can only be helpful that the whole country knows of your presence in France and is aware that you were brought here against your will. Whatever happens to you will take place in full view of the world and those responsible for it will be held to account. That'll make anyone think twice about harming you."

He fell back into his seat, exhausted by the effort to conceal his emotions. He scrutinised Robert surreptitiously, attempting to gauge the impact of his words. What a change three months had wrought in him. He had urged him to postpone his return, knowing of the impending Act and its likely consequences for someone of his age and beliefs but his warnings had been ignored. Why had he come back when there was a ready explanation for his absence? Many of his friends had asked him that question. But those who had questioned Robert's motives didn't understand the family's traditions. He had abandoned his teaching post, leaving behind a job he loved, because he believed that it was the right thing to do. He could only applaud his decision - he hoped he would have done the same in the circumstances. But though he had known that resisting conscription would bear a price, he had never believed that the army would go to such trouble to intimidate and punish those who opposed it. Now he had seen the camps for himself, the lengths to which the army was prepared to go, he feared his efforts might be insufficient to save him.

"Now we have work to do," he said, taking out his watch and noting the time with some anxiety. "Tell us what we need to know for our report. How've you fared at the army's hands?"

Clapham related their story, speaking quickly. He spoke matter-of-factly, drawing on his descriptive powers, but though his words were measured, there was no concealing his dismay at all that had befallen them. Robert added little, knowing that the picture Clapham painted with such skill spoke for itself.

Bennett listened in amazement. He could scarcely credit that an unwillingness to enlist could have led to such a catalogue of abuse and intimidation. There again, it had to be seen in the context of the camps, the carnage elsewhere. He had encountered a world of unimaginable violence that had few rules borrowed from civilian life.

There was a commotion outside the door, the sound of voices. The escort had returned to take them to the cells. They looked at each other, unsure what to do now the time had come to part. Bennett, willing to do anything to prolong their stay, said, "Is there anything you need? If so, you'd better tell us now."

He spoke to Robert directly, as if the others were no longer present. He wondered when he would see him again, what he could do to keep him safe. He noted that he had lost weight, that his face was careworn. His eyes, always so alert, so intensely blue, had dulled. His hand shook and his voice possessed a tremor that was new. Yet, he was undefeated. That was something to be grateful for. He retained a look of defiance, of quiet determination and was still capable of a ready smile. He sat upright in his chair, shoulders back, chest prominent, not slumped, defeated like Clapham. Seeing him, he was filled with an immense pride that he had gone to such lengths to assert his beliefs. He could only marvel at his fortitude and pray for his safety.

He turned to Clapham with a look of concern and said, "What about the others? What can we do to help them, other than to say that we've seen the conditions in which they're being held and are working with others to get them home again?"

"Please tell our families we're alive and well and look forward to returning home when the army's tired of us."

Clapham looked at each visitor in turn, the tall bearded chaplain with the fierce expression and the renowned preacher with his cheerful demeanour which the conditions of the camp had failed to extinguish. Two less similar men it would have been hard to find but together they had found their way to France, had made contact with them and by virtue of their presence had given everyone new grounds for hope. He wondered if they grasped how much it meant to them to know that they had supporters. They had been friendless for so long that they were inclined to forget that others opposed the war. The trade unions had expressed their misgivings. Certain sections of the press had voiced their concerns about the conduct of the war and politicians in Parliament and elsewhere were challenging the army's hegemony. For now, only a stone or two had come loose but in time their efforts might prompt an avalanche.

"Go back to England and continue the good work on our behalf," Clapham concluded, attempting to sound untroubled and confident, "and if your efforts fail to prevent the army from doing its worst, rest assured that we'll always be grateful for your support."

"Oh, we're not done yet," Dr Meyer said, a look of determination on his face.

It would be easy to underestimate Dr Meyer, thought Robert. Behind the genial expression lay a steely resolve. Nothing less would have got him this far. Armed with his experience of France, he would be a formidable advocate on their behalf. He wondered whether they had done justice to the deprivation and punishment that had been their reward: the fatigues with pack and shot, the crucifixions, the overcrowded cells and the starvation diet. But their visitors weren't there to change the army's ways. Their task was to return them to the jurisdiction of the civil courts. He recalled one of Dr Meyer's sermons in Lambeth, his unrelenting focus on the power of the Gospels and the recollection reminded him that he had a request to make.

"There's something we need." Robert could hear their escort forming up outside the door and loud voices calling to each other.

"We can't give you anything," said Dr Meyer, with a dismissive wave of his hand. "We arrived with clothes and food, and other things we thought you'd need, but they took them away, marvelling at our naivety, and said they'd be waiting for us when we returned to the ship."

Robert had eyes only for his father's briefcase. It sat on the chair beside him, black leather, worn at the corners, fading initials embossed on its front.

"What do you want?"

"We need a Bible - to replace the one we've lost."

Bennett was surprised by the request. Robert's diffidence towards organised religion had long troubled him. He found his views diffuse, though he had wisely kept his counsel, knowing that if Robert was to grow closer to God, it would be in the manner and at the time of his choosing. The thought that his son had turned to the scriptures for comfort was welcome news.

"You've managed all this time without one?"

"We had one but it was stolen."

"Have mine," Bennett said, though he would not have parted with it readily in other circumstances. His Bible had been his father's and his father's before that. He had hoped that one day it would be Robert's and that he would put it to good use. He liked to think of it being handed down from one generation to the next, a companion to all.

"They won't allow it," Dr Meyer warned. "You know what they said to us."

"How can a Bible cause offence?"

Bennett extracted the black, leather bound Bible from his briefcase, its pages tipped in gold. A scarlet ribbon marked the chapter he had read the previous evening. He handed it to Robert as if presenting him with an award. "Here, take this with my blessing. It would have come to you eventually. What better time to give it to you?"

Robert was unsure how to respond. He hadn't anticipated his father would produce the family Bible. He didn't want to be responsible for it in his present circumstances. He was about to explain this to his father when the door of the hut swung back to reveal their escort. Their stern countenances confirmed that they had to come to return them to their cells.

Robert and his father embraced. The others shook hands. Dr Meyer started to deliver some parting words but Bennett warned him off with a touch on his arm, believing that no good would come of pious sentiments or expressions of regret. The objectors were in the army's hands. He could only watch them leave, noting Robert's upright bearing, his forthright expression, with a measure of pride and pray that the army would prove magnanimous to someone whose only misdemeanour was to act according to his principles. He wondered whether he would ever see him again. There was no way of knowing. He could only wait and hope. The court martial had reached a verdict and passed a sentence which would be reviewed by the High Command. Then, an order would be given that would pass down the hierarchy until it reached the camp where the prisoners were held.

CHAPTER 12

The waiting soldiers formed three sides of a square. Gone was the easy banter, the quick asides frequent at such gatherings. There was a sullen silence that hung heavily in the air like an early morning mist before the sun disperses it. Faces craned for better vantage or exchanged uneasy glances. The officers stood on a makeshift platform on the fourth side of the square. In the centre of their band was Major Wilberforce, his expression sombre, his eyes masked by his cap. He held a sheaf of papers in his hand. He glanced down at them repeatedly, waiting for everyone to settle down before starting the proceedings.

To the prisoners, the walk to the square, though short, had seemed interminable. The worn, damp grass beneath their feet was treacherous for those weakened by hunger and lack of exercise. Castlereagh, anxious to get on, slipped on the damp earth, falling awkwardly. When hands reached out to steady him, he shook them off, denying weakness with a derisory smile. Robert was propelled by a mechanism he barely understood. Unfailing steps conveyed him forward though his mind struggled to slow his wilful limbs. He could hear the sound of his clothing rubbing against his body as he walked and the whispered asides amongst the waiting soldiers meant for their neighbours. He was conscious of the eyes focused on his face. The stares alighted on his skin, as lightly as a lover's fingertips, alert for signs of fear. There was no longer any consolation in knowing that others shared his plight, no comfort in the glances of his friends, in exchanging a tight-lipped smile, a nod of recognition with those he knew so well.

Major Wilberforce waited patiently as a silence descended on the gathering. He looked round slowly, examining the orderly ranks, his fellow-officers, the objectors conspicuous in their civilian clothes, waiting on his words. His eyes dwelt on the prisoners, noting their demeanour, seeking signs of trepidation. Some of them avoided his stare. Others affected an unconvincing nonchalance. A few were openly defiant, challenging him to do his worst but he was not fooled by their veneers. He knew that inwardly they trembled, whatever mask they chose to shield them from his scrutiny. He had announced death sentences before. They were frequent in the camps. He knew that the objectors hung upon his every word. It was the culmination of their journey through France, the consequence of their defiance. He felt no pity for them. He wanted them to suffer, to experience what the troops felt when the whistles blew and they clambered out of the trenches to almost certain death. What were they after all but cowards and shirkers? Their obstinacy, their high-minded wilfulness, was an affront to the diligent and committed soldier on whom the prosecution of the war depended. He waited interminably, or so it seemed to those dependent on his words. Only when he could procrastinate no longer, did he begin to speak.

Robert was summoned first.

"Attention."

He started at the loud command, as if it were meant for someone else.

"Prisoner, advance four paces, quick march."

He stepped forward as instructed but declined to march, moving in the manner of his choosing, a curious bear-like shuffle towards the spot indicated. His legs refused to budge initially. He thought his escort might have to drag him forward, hold him upright whilst his sentence was read out. He stood there, a look of bewilderment on his face, desperate to please, as if his conduct in the next few minutes might have some bearing on his fate, his gaze fixed on the piece of paper in the major's hand. He trembled slightly as he waited, perspiring visibly, hands rigid at his side.

The major stood unmoving as Robert approached. Robert was struck at how well-turned out he was. His boots gleamed. His puttees were immaculate and bound tightly. His uniform fell in neat folds across his body. His appearance was in stark contrast to that of the filthy, skeletal figures of the camp. He searched his fleshy features for clues as to his message. No blemish, hair or wrinkle escaped his scrutiny. He doubted he had ever gazed at another human being with such intensity. The Colonel remained indifferent to his glances, looking only at the paper, red tabs in the corner, held tightly in his hand.

Robert noted the red tabs as he began to speak. His stomach lurched at the sight of them. He knew what their presence meant; an officer had warned him to look out for them. It meant that it was all up with them, that their worst fears had been realised..

Wanting to conduct himself with dignity, he prayed silently as he waited on the major's words.

"Please God, help me to resist this last humiliation with all the equanimity and fortitude You've bestowed on me so far."

The major read out his misdemeanour – refusing to obey the lawful command of a senior officer in the field zone - his voice rising and falling, curiously high-pitched for a man of his corpulence, issuing from his lips as if circumnavigating an impediment to the flow of air somewhere deep inside him.

Then, eventually, it came, the vital, last crescendo. "The sentence of the court is to suffer death by being shot…"

Though straining to hear the major's words, Robert could scarcely take them in. He had anticipated the moment so often that now it was upon him, he was overwhelmed by it. He was on the outside looking in, watching a drama unfold, spectator rather than participant.

How long did the major wait before pronouncing his rider? To the solemn officers, the unmoving ranks of soldiers, it was but a moment. To Robert it seemed like an age. He was convinced that he had been forgotten and that the announcement of his sentence had concluded the proceedings.

The major continued pointedly, "The sentence has been confirmed by the Commander-in Chief."

Shock acceded to the terror it had held at bay. Robert had imagined himself prepared for martyrdom, reconciled to a violent end at the army's hands, but when the fatal confirmation tumbled from the colonel's lips, he realised that his vibrant hope, his robust attitude, had been an affectation. He had left the shallows, swept headlong into a raging sea whose icy waters embraced him eagerly, catching at his throat, entangling his limbs, preventing thought or movement as they tossed him to and fro. The sudden, unexpected glimpse of death invoked long neglected thoughts from the dark well of his childhood fears, thoughts whose roots lay outside the realm of reason, determined voices that thrust all hope aside. They mocked his parents' faith, the teaching of the church, insisting that death was surely nothing but the opposite of life, a void beyond all pain and joy. He glimpsed his lifeless body, prostrate on the ground, a corpse amidst a pool of blood, prey to men's enquiring glances. Suppose his last, destructive glimpse of life was forever his companion? Death was only tolerable at the time and in the manner of his choosing. No one should possess the power to wrest life from his grasp.

He recalled his final months in America, the circumstances of his departure, his decision to leave. Mary's face loomed up before him: two heads on the pillow, noses touching, eyes darting furiously as their lips came together. Why had he abandoned her when he had known that back in England, conscription awaited him? He had told his parents that he felt it was his duty to return but that was only half the story when his obligations to his students, his fellow teachers, the college they attended, had provided sufficient grounds for him to stay. He had put them aside in his anxiety to leave, placing his head into the lion's mouth when there was no need for it, in a vain attempt to atone for his misdeeds. Now he was about to pay the price for the mistake that had brought him home, more quickly and decisively than he had ever imagined.

The major looked around with obvious satisfaction before his eyes returned, devoid of compassion, to the lonely figure before him. He noted that he sought to make a good impression, even as his body trembled, when form no longer mattered, pretending the harsh words had left him unperturbed. He watched him carefully before his satisfaction gave way to frustration. There was a look of disappointment on his face as he said reluctantly, "It was afterwards commuted by him to one of penal servitude for ten years." He vainly attempted to give the impression that there was more to come, though it was clear that he had delivered his message.

Robert remained motionless for fear of jeopardising his reprieve by some thoughtless word or gesture but when the major dismissed him, his joy was boundless. He turned towards his comrades, his face alive with hope. In the time the major had taken to draw breath, he had been tethered to a stake, blindfolded, had heard the rifles load and felt the impact of the bullets. Now he was alive and unharmed. He was not a man who had just received ten years' penal servitude. He was a man who had unexpectedly been given the gift of life.

The major watched him turn and go. There was a new spring in Robert's step, a robustness previously concealed. He felt no magnanimity towards him, only resentment at his reprieve. He had not anticipated that the army would flinch from doing its duty. Why should Robert be spared when enlisted men, some deserving their fate, others innocent of nothing more than shattered nerves, were taken out and shot at dawn? The politicians had interfered again. He was sure of it. No good would come of their intervention when so many were called upon to die and did so without protest.

He sentenced each of the objectors in turn, his resentment increasing as the numbers mounted. The prisoners watched him warily. No one could be quite sure that some quirk of the military code would not prompt him to treat him differently. Everyone suffered the same sentence with its cruel delays, the churlish reprieve. Denied the advantage of surprise, he emphasised the length of every sentence, determined to impress upon his victims the years that lay ahead. But his breath was wasted, his warnings of no account. He was a hanging judge who had removed his black cap unexpectedly and begrudgingly shown mercy. The onlookers grasped the harshness of the sentences. Those who knew the camps and prisons cringed at their implications but the prisoners remained gloriously immune to their uninviting future.

By the time the sentencing was over, a brisk wind had sprung up, unnoticed, tugging at the sleeves of the departing soldiers, nudging the creaking buildings and chasing the flotsam of the cookhouse stores across the crowded square. The escort started up abruptly; rifles rose and fell, the lines of onlookers dispersed, ragamuffin witnesses, chattering excitedly. The short walk to the cells seemed endless, each step an awful effort. Robert's left eye twitched uncontrollably; he struggled to overcome it and to arrest his shaking hands. Hicks dragged his feet as if he wore chains around his ankles. Taylor trembled visibly, his sparse body shivering. Castlereagh held his head high, striding out, arms swinging briskly but it was all for show, a performance, unrelated to his feelings, a mask intended to conceal his horror at what had taken place.

The next day, they contemplated the implications of their sentence. They were vague about its details; they had been given no indication of when and where it might begin. They remained in limbo, spared the interminable fatigues and punishments but lacking any of the comforts or distractions that made life bearable. Their consolation was their reprieve and each others' company. There had grown up amongst them a rare spirit, a sense of perils shared. Robert was to look back on his last days in France as a time enriched by sympathetic companions, tribulations overcome and the optimism resulting from the knowledge that they had survived the army's worst.

Only Taylor seemed shattered by the experience. His faith had proved an inadequate barrier to the fear of death. He thought himself a coward and when Robert tried to reason with him, proved inconsolable.

"Why be ashamed?" Robert asked. "I died a thousand deaths out there on that square. We were convinced we were going to die. What could be more human than to be afraid? You'll always retain your frailty, whatever you believe in."

Taylor nodded in agreement and his spirits lifted for a time. He attempted to recover his composure, urged on by Robert, but his efforts met with limited success. He had hoped to replace life's unwelcome ambiguity with a rigid framework in which virtue brought its own reward and evil rarely went unpunished.

They attempted to discuss the future, to determine what was likely to become of them but soon abandoned speculation in favour of attempts to improve their circumstances. The authorities encouraged their irresponsibility. Delighted at the prospect of seeing the back of them, they grew more benign with each day that passed.

Robert was delighted to learn that penal servitude meant their return to London. The mitigation of their sentence confirmed him in his view that

England was a sanctuary, distant from the war, where civil liberties were enshrined in statute and life was governed by rules, written and implicit, that he knew and respected. Such thoughts stifled any misgivings about the future. He felt a sense of triumph that a scholar and a pacifist like him, lacking any experience of hardship, had survived the army's enmity. He wondered what had saved them. Had the army in a rare display of common sense pulled back from the brink or had his father and his allies forced them to climb down? He later learnt that Herbert Asquith, the Prime Minister, prompted by certain members of the Cabinet and the leaders of the No-Conscription Fellowship, had intervened successfully on their behalf.

They made their way back to London under guard. Waiting on the quayside for transport to England, they were confronted by a hostile crowd of townsfolk and soldiers going home on leave, enraged that a group of conscientious objectors were leaving the front unscathed. Robert thought it a foretaste of things to come. Once aboard the waiting ship, the incident was forgotten. They hugged each other as the ship weighed anchor and rejoiced that they were going home, breaking off from their celebrations to hold a service in which Robert read aloud from his father's bible and they bowed their heads in prayer for the safety of those engaged in the hostilities. Later, back in England, they discovered the extent to which their prayers had been in vain and that the Somme offensive, epic in its scale and consequences, had devoured many of the troops that they had left behind.

PART III

September 1916

CHAPTER 13

Michael tried not to look at his watch but his eyes seemed drawn to it by forces beyond his control. Its fingers were stationary, frozen in place; every minute recorded felt like an hour and the whistles seemed further away. He wished he was not standing so close to the ladder. He hadn't intended to be one of the first to go over. It was likely to reduce his prospects markedly but there was nothing that he could do. To hesitate would be seen as an act of cowardice, a willingness to turn his back on his comrades and would be met by a fierce reprimand by those urging him forward.

When the order came to 'fix bayonets', Michael drew and fixed his bayonet with practised ease. Holcombe, his close friend and constant companion, was barely able to hold his rifle upright. Michael handed him his rifle, his bayonet fixed, and took Holcombe's from his trembling hands, along with the bayonet that he was waving uselessly in the air.

He whispered, "When I tell you to fix bayonets?"

Holcombe was quick to reply, "You don't fix."

"When I say 'bayonets'?"

"You fix bayonets."

The parade ground ritual complete, they exchanged rifles again. Two rifles, two bayonets fixed. The transaction seemed to calm Holcombe. His hands had stopped shaking. He held his rifle firmly. He stared at the ladder with fierce concentration as if noticing it for the first time.

He said, "It's no good - I can't do it."

Michael moved closer, crowding him against the trench wall, pinning him to the damp clay. He placed his hand on his shoulder. His tunic felt soft to the touch as though the person inside it had shrunk. "Of course, you can do it. You can go over, like the rest of us." He stared into his friend's eyes, up close, so that he felt his hot breath on his face. "Say it, go on, say it: I can go over."

He waited expectantly, his lips framing the words that he wanted to hear. His gaze was uncompromising, his eyes shadowing Holcombe's. He made him repeat what he had said several times.

"I can do it," Holcombe whispered, "I can go over like everyone else."

Michael said, "It's what we came for, what we've been trained to do."

"That's right," Holcombe said, masking his fear in a show of bravado.

"Well done," Michael said, summoning a smile. "It won't be long now."

~

Ten minutes before they were due to go over, Lieutenant-Colonel Beaumont-Dart, the battalion commander, inched past the waiting soldiers, a confident expression on his face. He held a watch in one hand, a service revolver in the other and a whistle hung from a lanyard around his neck. Behind him, the British guns were in full cry. No tell-tale pause this time, no abrupt cessation ten minutes before the troops went over, allowing the German machine gunners time to take up their positions, identify the gaps in the wire and greet the approaching soldiers with a fusillade few would survive. This time the guns would fire up to the whistles, lifting as the troops advanced, targeting the enemy's second line and support trenches. He hoped everything would go according to plan. The staffs, distrustful of their conscript army, planned the attacks in enormous detail but when the wires had been ploughed up by enemy fire, many of the signallers were dead or wounded, and there was only noise and confusion, it was all too easy for the artillery to neglect the troops.

As he made his way back to 'A' Company dugout, he peered at every officer and soldier. He wanted them to know that he was watching them, that he had high expectations of them. He didn't anticipate any problems. They were a decent lot and had been well-trained, although some of them were drafts rushed into the line to make the battalion up to strength. They were keen as mustard though they had seen things a soldier shouldn't see before going into battle. That was why he had been so generous with the rum ration. He had felt that it was the least that he could do.

Several days before, the battalion had stood on a ridge in the rain watching broken lines of figures advancing ponderously across the plain below. Puffs of red, green, black and yellow smoke had risen up to greet them. They had seen the fountains of clay and chalk thrown up by the shells and heard the clamour of machine guns, field guns, mortars and heavy guns, each with their distinctive voice and rhythm. The troops had longed to play their part. None of them had foreseen that the battalion's first task on arriving in the line would be to bury the dead. A week earlier, from the trench in which they now stood, another battalion had gone over. When they had relieved them, most of the casualties had still lain where they had fallen, blackened by the sun and the rain. The battalion had been given the task of collecting and burying the bodies. It had been a cruel irony, given their resentment at being in reserve. Many of the casualties had died before having an opportunity to release the bolts on their rifles. They had been strewn across the open ground, shapeless mounds on the still, brown earth. Some hung from the wire that had impeded them. Some had been buried by the earth thrown up by exploding shells only to be exhumed by later bombardments. They had grown used to the distorted faces, torn limbs and shattered bodies as they collected the identity discs and pay books, loaded the remains on to stretchers and dumped them into the vast shell crater that was to serve as their tomb. The burial party hadn't flinched or ceased its efforts when shells fell amongst them. What none of them had anticipated was the stench of the dead. It had polluted the air, clinging to their clothes, hair and skin long after the corpses were gone, a persistent reminder of the odds against their survival.

He noted one of the soldiers was on the point of collapse. There was a wild look in his eyes, like a bullock in the chute before the bolt is fired into its temple. He was about to urge one of the subalterns to deal with him when he saw his companion put his arm around him. That was why they were persuaded to scale the ladders and rush forward. They didn't do it for King and Country, whatever their families might think. No one fell to the ground with the national anthem on their lips. They didn't respond eagerly because they were told to or feared reprisals for failing to obey orders. They did it so as not to appear cowardly or foolish in the eyes of their comrades. When the whistles sounded, and they had abandoned the trench, mutual support was the key to survival. Only once had he forced a soldier up the ladder at the point of a gun. Ten minutes later, the poor lad was dead, torn to pieces by shrapnel. He had promised himself that he would never do anything like that again, though he knew that if anyone refused to go forward he would have little choice but to compel him, for the sake of the others.

~

Captain Reynolds kept thinking about the letter he had received from home before they went up. It had contained the kind of news no man wanted to hear. His fiancé had written to him breaking off their engagement. She had said that she fallen in love with somebody else. He would have forgiven her had she fallen for a fellow officer; he had been away for a year and had been a poor correspondent, but the object of her affections had been some worthy citizen whose work in a Government ministry meant he couldn't be spared for the war.

He could no longer imagine life back in England. It seemed a distant memory, vague and uncertain. He was purportedly fighting to protect a way of life, the things that he cherished and yet found it difficult to conceive of anything but the war. Even out of the line, it still dominated his thoughts. Playing football for the battalion, immersed in a book, drinking with friends in an estaminet, the conflict was always with him, like a dull toothache, ready to flare up at the least provocation. The dangers, the hardships and the responsibilities lived on in his mind, as did the men of his company, living and fallen. So many had come and gone, with him one minute, gone the next, arbitrarily removed from the scene. That was why the loss of his fiancé troubled him so little, though he had been immensely fond of her. She was merely someone else removed from his life without warning, whom he would learn to forget.

He watched the line of men in the trench, huddled together for safety. He had checked their rifles and kit, patting them on the shoulder, giving them a word of encouragement, a ready smile. He had wanted to convey to them how much he admired their courage and fortitude, how much strength he derived from their stoicism, their generosity, their anxiety to do well. Without their example, he would have crumbled a long time ago. He wished he could reassure them, tell them with conviction that they would prevail but he knew most of them were doomed and that their efforts would have few consequences for the course of the conflict. They were all trapped, even the Generals who ordered them into the line. They had been trapped since three mighty armies had closed on each other. His responsibility was to discharge his orders, conveying them to the men, ensuring their commitment, their willingness to fight. Then, like a malevolent god looking down on the world with a jaundiced eye, the conflict would determine who would live and die. That was why no letter from London, however painful and unexpected its contents, would ever disconcert him.

"Follow me," Michael said to Holcombe, "go where I go, do what I do."

He spoke with authority though he had no idea where they were going or what they would find there. There had been a briefing of sorts before they went up but it had been long on rhetoric and short on specifics. The CO's oration had reminded him of his headmaster on Speech Day. Each year, that most unassuming of men, strode to the pulpit and unleashed on his audience a declamation of such length and complexity that those hearing it for the first time were wholly nonplussed. Yesterday, what little that had been comprehensible had been drowned by the guns. They had seemed to intensify their efforts at the sound of the CO's voice.

"Let me go first," Holcombe said. He wanted Michael to see him up safely, to push him if he hesitated, to curse him if he tried to turn back.

"I'll follow you. No waiting though, when you're over. Go forward with the others. Stay in line. I'll catch you up. We'll advance together, the two of us, side by side."

~

Second-Lieutenant Brigham had mounted the ladder. He had ascended as far as he could without exposing his helmet above the parapet. He could hear bullets embedding themselves in the bags and a trickle of sand ran down his back as he waited, suggesting their appearance would come as no great surprise to the enemy. He preferred not to think about what would happen when he led the platoon out. Few of his classmates had survived the first two years of the war. It seemed at times that his was the only name missing from the school's roll of honour. Many of them had lasted only a matter of weeks before succumbing to shrapnel and machine gun fire or the other hazards of trench warfare. Strangely, he had never regretted enlisting nor sought to exchange the infantry for some less hazardous activity. He still felt, in spite of it all, that he was where he was meant to be and would go on doing his duty as long as he could, leading the men who followed him blindly, trusting him to do what he could do to ensure their survival, though he was the youngest among them.

He wondered what it is was like to command a division or an army, to be one of those exalted personages he had seen being driven to conferences in gleaming staff cars as his battalion toiled up the road to the front weighed down by packs, attempting to march in good order, to muster a song, shoulders buckling under the weight of their kit, their boots biting into their ankles. He imagined them standing over a table draped with maps, planning an advance here, a bombardment there, confident that their plans would be implemented by a hierarchy of officers. He assumed when he scrambled down the communications trench and into the forward positions that there was plan, a strategy capable of winning the war, but when the men were crowded together, apprehensive but eager, waiting on the whistles, he couldn't help but wonder why there were so few signs of success.

He straightened his shoulders, reminding himself he had a job to do. The voices below him had fallen silent, each man alone with his thoughts and misgivings, wondering what might have been, now that it was too late to change anything and all that mattered was surviving and giving a good account of oneself. Their faces were masked by their helmets, their movements restricted by the burdens they carried and the walls of the trench. He knew only that he had to get them over the top and into position and lead the advance, going forward in broad daylight, proceeding slowly in lines, as best they could. He hoped that the artillery had done its work but feared that the machine guns would be waiting. There would be gaps in the wire. The shrapnel would have seen to that but there wouldn't be enough of them. He wished he could do more to protect the men. He and Sergeant Fox, the NCO who never left his side, translating his orders into a vernacular that the men could understand and obey, had done all they could to prepare the men for the ordeal to come. Their letters home still rang in his ears. Some of their writing was barely literate; he had to finish their work; others wrote poetry or revealed insights that were unfamiliar to him with his private education and ignorance of life. He knew the generals regarded them as an undifferentiated mass. How else could they sacrifice so many lives with the flourish of a pen or a word of command? But the men in his platoon were all 'God's children' as the padre might say; each with a family who worried about them and yearned for their return. To all of them, and the hinterland they represented, he had a duty of care. This was not the first time he had gone over. He was nineteen years old and an experienced officer. He only hoped that he would prove capable of doing his duty again.

~

"I want you to have this," Holcombe's voice had become a curious whine as he struggled to control his distress. He fished a letter out of his pocket. Its edges were curling and the address was smudged where the rain had soaked through his tunic.

"What is it?" Michael asked. This was not the time for anything complicated. He was too much on edge. He wanted no part of any last, heartfelt request.

"It's a letter to my mother... just in case."

"Why are you giving it to me?"

"I've got another one," Holcombe patted his tunic, impressed by his own ingenuity. "I wrote two. They're identical. I thought if anything happened to me, you could post on the one I've given you. It increases the odds that she'll get something from me."

Michael took the letter and placed it carefully into the pocket of his tunic, smiling reassuringly. "It would be easier if you survived and sent it yourself."

"I'll do my best."

Michael gave him a gentle punch on the arm. "You're like my brother Robert. You think too much. It's not good for you. Sometimes, you just have to get on with things and hope for the best."

He was aware that Brigham was looking down on them, a worried frown on his face. He touched the pocket that contained Holcombe's letter. It hadn't occurred to him to do anything like that. He had written home several days ago, a long, discursive letter anticipating that they were about to go into the line but had stayed clear of their immediate future, not wanting his words to give rise to concern. He had confined himself to housekeeping matters, the things that he needed and missed, and wry observations about the ways of the army. He had revealed his hopes and fears in his letter to Alice. She was his confidant. With her he could be frank..

He looked down again at his watch and the whistles blew, one after another, in quick succession. The guns lifted, the explosions creeping forward in anticipation of their advance. The drills, the marches, the bayonet charges, the firing practice had all been for this. Brigham reached the top of the ladder. He tumbled over the sandbags and picking himself up, reached down for the others, urging them upwards with swift waves of his hand. Everyone scrambled up the ladders as fast as they were able. Holcombe hesitated halfway. His fears had returned. Michael gave him a shove, as hard as he could, from below. Holcombe kicked out impatiently and his foot struck Michael's shoulder, almost dislodging him. He resumed his ascent, methodically, like an old man climbing the stairs but Michael was satisfied that he would go over now that he had little choice. Behind them, others pressed forward, done with nursing their fears, anxious to get on.

The Germans knew they were coming. They were ready and waiting. How far had they advanced before they struck? It was hard to tell. Their trench was behind them, the enemy's seemingly no nearer, when they were cut down. The firing was remorseless, the bullets biting into their victims, not once but many times before they went down. They were urged to remain upright, to advance with their bayonets extended, to walk towards the fountains of death without flinching. Michael's pack grew heavier with each step that he took. His entrenching tool had come loose. It bit into his thigh. His water bottle had been struck by a bullet. Its contents soaked into his tunic. He wanted to throw himself to the ground, to cast off his pack, to remain there motionless in an attempt to survive but the ground lacked cover or obstacles and they were being urged to walk on. Soon their numbers thinned. Large gaps opened up in the line. The sound of the guns grew louder, those of both sides coming together in a climax that tore at the ground, filling the sky with earth and stones, throwing men high into the air as Brigham strode on, urging them to keep up.

Some writhed and screamed when they fell to the ground, their agony audible above the noise and confusion, the whistle of incoming shells. Others collapsed and crawled blindly, like moles in the sunlight, nursing their shattered limbs as best they could. Holcombe was strangely silent when a shell tossed him aside. He rose and fell like the others but didn't cry out in pain or surprise. He didn't call for his mother or turn to his comrades or demand that somebody put an end to his anguish. Michael saw him take the force of the explosion, witnessed him go down, legs folding neatly beneath him as he fell, knowing there was nothing that he could do to save him. The bearers would collect the wounded, conveying them back to the dressing stations as best they could, whilst the dead would be left until the hostilities ceased. Meanwhile, he was condemned to go forward, to advance in good order until they were pulled back. It was his reward for having been spared. His turn would come soon enough. He hoped it would be swift and clean.

CHAPTER 14

Robert was familiar with the detention barracks at Wandsworth. A wing of the civilian prison controlled by the military authorities, its treatment of prisoners had prompted questions in the House of Commons. Though the Central Tribunal had elected to meet there for reasons of convenience, it was a timely reminder to Robert and to other conscientious objectors of what lay in store for them.

He had been given little guidance as to the nature and timing of his hearing. He found himself reading the letter addressed to him by the tribunal as he waited in a crowded room for admittance. He had no lack of arguments to put to it. He'd had little else to think about since his return from France but he knew little of its views and had no knowledge of the stance it had adopted. He saw its activities as a further example of the continuing tensions between the civilian and military authorities.

The room was no more noteworthy than any of the others in which his beliefs had been scrutinised. It was a makeshift conference room, its walls a uniform grey, dominated by a boardroom table that bore the scars and stains of use, surrounded by a medley of chairs that looked as if they had been purchased from the second-hand furniture shops of the district and a faded carpet, frayed at the edges. The table contained an array of blotters, notepads and pens lined up precisely in front of the chairs. The chairs on one side of the table were occupied by a chairman, a committee member and a secretary, in front of whom sat three piles of paper and a list, several pages long, of the objectors due to appear before them.

The rest of the chairs were empty and Robert was given no indication as to which of them he was expected to occupy. He assumed from the world-weary look on the chairman's face that much of his day had already been spent wrestling with the claims for exemption. He supposed that the central tribunal's cases were the most intractable, the ones most likely to cause controversy and those most suitable for conveying policy to the legion of tribunals throughout the country. He, by contrast, was energised by thoughts of a compromise, feeling that his beliefs had been given a new legitimacy by his involuntary visit to the front.

He pulled up a chair directly opposite the chairman. They regarded each other across the table, one thoughtful and wary, the other animate and eager to start. The chairman's face betrayed nothing of his thoughts. His greeting was cursory, unenthusiastic. He extracted his watch from his waistcoat pocket as Robert sat down, although there was a clock on the wall opposite him, and stared at it as if he could not quite believe the time. He looked expectantly at the secretary. He announced Robert and his history with a formality unsuitable for an audience of three.

The chairman, a plump, choleric man with unwavering blue eyes and a bristling moustache, whose waistcoat threatened to burst through its buttons, introduced himself. He indicated that he was a senior official in the Home Office. His companion was a mayor from one of the London boroughs. Robert recalled seeing his photograph in the local paper but could not recall the reason for his prominence. That was the way of the war. It had created a new world, elevating certain civilians unexpectedly, consigning others to obscurity, changing everything and everyone that crossed its path. The secretary, a nervous, bumbling man, seemed in awe of the chairman and sought to anticipate his needs with anxious glances. He checked his piles of paper constantly. The tallest contained the cases still to come. The other two were cases they had considered. He passed a paper to the chairman, before falling back in to his chair, fountain pen in hand, poised to take notes of the proceedings.

Seeing the mimeographed letter in Robert's hand, the chairman dispensed with any introduction, assuming that it told Robert everything he needed to know. He cleared his throat ceremoniously, leaned forward, hands clasped firmly before him and said, "You are, of course, acquainted with this committee and understand its purpose?"

Robert looked at him guardedly and said, "I've read the paper that was handed to me at the door."

"You know what we're about?"

"I understand that my future's in your hands."

"I would have thought it was in yours," the chairman said without enthusiasm.

He nodded slowly as he spoke. The law was clear and it was up to the objectors how they dealt with it but so few of them agreed with him. They insisted on arguing and nit-picking and testing the committee's resolve. He supposed if things were simple, his intervention wouldn't be needed and everything would be dealt with at the local level, as had been the Government's intention. The mistake had been to build into the legislation an appeal process. It was inevitable that certain people would see it as a further opportunity to air their beliefs.

"Well, what have you decided?" he asked mildly. "Are you willing to accept alternative service? Will you sign the form agreeing to the work prescribed and conform to all the regulations regarding your future conduct?"

He considered the question entirely reasonable. He had asked it many times that day and would ask it many more. Robert thought it a provocation. It was as if time had stood still, as though the agony of having been sent to France had passed him by and the fear and despair of those dark days had never been. He was required to prove himself again, to establish his credentials. How could he reconcile himself to civilian work granted so begrudgingly when he had already offered up his life for the cause that he espoused?

"No, I won't," he said, with all the conviction that he could muster. "I'm as unwilling to accept conscription now as I was six months ago."

The chairman gazed thoughtfully at Robert, disappointed but unsurprised. He knew Robert's family, remembering his father as a stubborn, unworldly man with a fierce intensity in respect of matters he believed in. He might have done something with his life, had it not been for his monumental principles. They were like sandbanks concealed below the water. Every time he put to sea, his ship ran aground on them. It was not in the least surprising that Robert had chosen to follow in his footsteps.

The secretary, poised to reach for another paper, stopped abruptly, knowing that Robert was going to be more difficult than he had anticipated.

"We propose to offer you an alternative to conscription," the chairman said, "civilian work without the intervention of the army. It's been devised with the likes of you in mind."

"I'm aware of that," said Robert, "and am grateful for all your efforts but, unfortunately, it doesn't make any difference."

"I know you've been in France. I'm familiar with what happened there. All most unfortunate." The chairman turned to his companion and shrugged dismissively. "Then, that's the army for you. What can you do? At least, you didn't come to any harm."

"It was a close-run thing."

The chairman waved Robert's papers in the air before saying, "Nobody doubts your sincerity or dismisses your views. That's not the issue here. We're satisfied that you have an objection to military service on grounds of conscience. We're merely saying that you have to meet your obligations in some form or other. You will be transferred to Section W of the Army Reserve where you won't be subject to military supervision or discipline, providing that you undertake civilian work under the conditions determined by this tribunal."

"That misses the point of my objection," Robert replied.

"I fail to see what else we can do for you," the mayor said, struggling to mask his impatience.

Robert recognised the chasm that lay between their neat, administrative solution and his burning passion, heightened by his experience in France. He wondered if his tormentors had the least inkling of conditions at the front. They saw the papers and read the despatches but did they really understand what it was like? They must have seen the casualty lists, newly augmented by the debacle on the Somme? Yet, here they were weaving their neat compromises whilst thousands died and suffered. They were reasonable men with commendable motives blinkered by their ignorance.

He turned back to the chairman and said, "There's nothing you can do. I'm delighted that you recognise my sincerity, though I wish it hadn't been necessary to receive the death sentence before anyone believed that I meant what I said. Unfortunately, the legislation has offered an administrative solution to a moral problem. Conscription remains conscription for military purposes whatever duties it gives rise to. Six months ago, I was more willing to compromise. I intended to serve my country providing that I wasn't required to enlist. Now, I've been to France and observed the ways of the army at first-hand, my views have hardened. I doubt that anyone could have seen what I witnessed and not been affected by it. I am not about to undergo forced labour, build roads or till the land, whilst others sacrifice their lives. My brother's at the front, in the infantry, in harm's way. What am I supposed to say to him when he comes home on leave, that I've taken up some comfortable role, rather than do what he's doing? No, if I'm to be conscripted - and what you're suggesting is still conscription whatever gloss you put on it – there's only one honourable place for me and that's in the line."

"Then go to the front," the mayor said. "If that's how you feel about it, enlist - do what your brother's done."

Robert said, "I won't be conscripted. It's contrary to everything that my family have believed for more than two centuries."

"That's not what your brother thinks," the Mayor said with no small satisfaction, "he's seen his way to doing his duty."

"He has my support," Robert said. "I wouldn't condemn him for a moment. We have to make choices - as individuals that's what we do. We identify actions that accord with our religious and other beliefs, pursue them vigorously and live with the consequences."

The chairman sighed heavily. He rubbed his brow with his forefinger, scratched his head, nodding thoughtfully. He could see Robert's point. If he was opposed to conscription for genuine if misguided reasons and had shown himself willing to sacrifice his life for his beliefs, supervised, civilian work was unlikely to satisfy him. For him, it was different. He was a fixer, by nature, a seeker of compromise. His whole life had been spent in Byzantine committees, seeking solutions the way other man sought favour, finding words sufficiently ambiguous to reconcile opposing parties, allowing opponents to claim victory or cloak defeat in vain and boastful phrases. He was not ignorant about the war. Its consequences were plain to see. But they were unavoidable: that was the point, and Robert's opposition was a direct challenge to the whole, painstakingly constructed scheme of exemptions he and the tribunal had put in place.

He decided to make one last attempt to convince him of the merits of supervised, civilian work.

He said, "Many men have come before me with their excuses whom, frankly, I regard as no more than shirkers. They want to put their self-interest before the successful prosecution of the war. You should hear the stories, the lame excuses that are aired in this room. They make me cringe when I think of the sacrifices that others are making. Then you have the employers: how many of them really need the workers they are seeking to keep? Profit makes the wheels of industry turn - I understand that - but at a time like this it should be secondary to the successful prosecution of the war. Your sincerity is self-evident. You've shown that you are prepared to die for your beliefs. I don't share them in the least degree but I respect them and the stand you have taken on them. But I ask you – as a man of the world – why go on with this? What good does it do? Why suffer further punishment when you are being offered an honourable compromise - a way to satisfy both your conscience and your country?"

He settled back into his chair to wait for Robert's answer, pleased with his turn of phrase and, for a few moments he was confident that he had sown the seeds of doubt in his mind. He sensed that Robert had no appetite for strident opposition. He wasn't one of the awkward brigade that he was used to seeing. He wasn't a socialist or closet revolutionary or one of those declaratory Christians, always looking for a cross. He was a devout but reasonable man who had boxed himself into a corner and needed to find a way out. That was what the Act in its latest form was meant to offer. He peered at Robert expectantly, arms folded across his chest, an encouraging, almost beseeching look on his face.

Robert took a deep breath as he thought about his reply. He was in no hurry to speak and recognised that his future hung on his response. Silence was his constant companion. He was used to being alone. He no longer felt the need to communicate his thoughts, to fill an awkward pause with empty words.

Eventually, he said, "I realised in France that there was no way to satisfy conscience and country. The Government deserves my loyalty - of course, it does, I'm a citizen with rights and obligations like everyone else – but only whilst I share its goals. Ultimately, my loyalty's to my conscience, to those truths that I regard as fundamental to my humanity. I don't doubt you can find some obscure niche for me for the duration of the war but you'll never persuade me to take advantage of it – not whilst the war persists."

The sympathy with which the chairman had cloaked his plea vanished in the face of Robert's words. His features hardened; animosity, barely concealed, replaced his understanding. He was officialdom again: a bureaucrat with rules to implement, a process to progress.

He said, "Well, in that case, I can't help you. If you persist in refusing to recognise your obligations, you're nothing more than an anarchist."

"The fact that I don't recognise your right to sit in judgement on my conscience doesn't make me an anarchist."

"Let's move on, shall we?" said the mayor. "The matter's out of our hands."

The chairman's affirmation made it clear his patience was exhausted. He had done his best for Robert. Now the law would prevail. What a stubborn man. What did he hope to achieve by his recalcitrance? He turned to the secretary and with a brief wave of his hand indicated that he was ready for another file. The secretary added Robert's papers to the smallest pile before him. Only three so far, he noted, fewer than he'd feared.

The chairman watched Robert leave the room and listened to his steps echo down the corridor. He could not avoid some misgivings, a niggling sense of failure. But what was he supposed to do in the face of such intransigence? In every walk of life, there was always a minority that eschewed compromise. He had learnt that he had to ride roughshod over such people if he was to get things done. Yet, men like Robert always left him with a feeling of unease, a conviction that he should also be capable of passion, of an ardour free of pragmatism.

When the door had closed on Robert, he said to his companions, "With his religious beliefs, he was bound to finish up in prison, or worse."

"He's a martyr," the mayor said dismissively, "all his lot are."

"Well, he'll suffer for it. After a few months' hard labour, he'll rue the day he turned down our proposals."

CHAPTER 15

There was something intimidating about leaving the trench at dead of night, groping one's way across no-man's land on a mission of uncertain value. Some men welcomed the darkness, seeing in its presence a respite from the dangers that daylight brought, but Michael never quite believed in its false security. It was all too easy for flares to go up, for shelling to ensue, for men to be exposed by unexpected hostilities or sentries alert to their activities. So when 'A' company was nominated to go out on a raid he was dismayed to find that Captain Reynolds had him in his sights. The plan was that they would cross over to the enemy line under cover of darkness. Splitting into two groups, one would infiltrate the enemy trench in search of prisoners whilst the other would provide covering fire if its presence became known.

They went across at two o'clock. Further up the line the night sky was alive. Guns flashed and spat as the artillery of both sides raged at each other but the ground in front of 'A' company was eerily silent. It seemed that the war had deserted it, leaving only a denuded landscape filled with strange shapes, the detritus of the recent conflict and air, freed of cordite and the damp earth of the trenches, that was heady to breathe.

Michael felt conspicuous as they edged forward. Every tree stump seemed like an enemy sentry, alert for his presence, any unexplained sound or movement the prelude to hostilities. The sky was cloudless and the stars formed intricate patterns on a palate of indigo so that the blackened faces of the men were visible to each other. The line that was their objective was silent. Nothing moved or stirred there as if it were unoccupied yet it needed only a chance accident and there would be no hostage taking, no intelligence to take back to brigade, only a fight for survival, a retreat pursued by an enemy bent on revenge.

Captain Reynolds was dismayed to find himself leading another raid. He knew it was useful to ascertain the nature and strength of the enemy's dispositions. He also understood that it was incumbent on soldiers to inflict casualties on their foe. He had heard these arguments many times, and others besides, but no longer believed them. Raids were little more than a means to keep the troops 'on their toes', another way for commanders to demonstrate their zeal. In his experience, German soldiers were no less ignorant about their leaders' intentions.

They didn't cross over directly but took a circuitous path, skirting the edge of a wood, hoping to exploit what little cover there was. The wood itself was long gone - the artillery had seen to that - but tree stumps, denuded branches, craters, large and small, punctured the earth that had been its habitat. Everyone dutifully followed the captain. His presence was reassuring, his self-confidence inspiring. Brigham was like a small dog, snapping at his master's heels, his diligence vaguely unseemly, his excitement unwelcome. Sergeant Fox, a silent, brooding presence, looked right and left, urging on the others when they failed to keep up, watching all the while for signs of enemy activity.

Michael brought up the rear. Last out of the trench, he found himself struggling to cross the rough terrain, weighed down by the bombs he was carrying. His closest companion kept stumbling in the darkness. Michael watched him anxiously, afraid that his clumsiness might betray their position or that they might lose contact with the others.

When they reached the gap in the wire that had been identified earlier, the group split into two halves; those going right acting as cover, whilst those going left tried to snatch the German infantrymen whose presence was eagerly awaited at Divisional HQ. For a while, both teams made good progress, approaching the German line without incident. Then, as they convinced themselves that their arrival had gone unnoticed, they encountered a German raiding party returning to their trenches.

Within moments, the two sides were firing indiscriminately into the darkness as they attempted to circumnavigate each other. It was clear to the captain that all opportunity for surprise was gone. He passed the word along that they were to turn and go back. The plan had gone awry. The taking of prisoners would have to wait until the sector had quietened and patrols could go out undisturbed.

When Michael's group turned to go back, a machine gun opened up on the gap in the wire. Someone had been seen stealing through it and now everyone was trapped by a fusillade that threatened to ignite the whole line. Shadowy figures stole along the wire, fanning out in both directions in search of gaps. They were soon pinned down, seeking cover wherever they could: behind tree stumps, in shell craters or wherever a hollow promised respite from the machine gun's raking fire.

Brigham's group gathered in a shell-hole, all eyes on their leader. Michael felt the machine gun bullets tear at his pack as he pitched himself over the lip, falling into the mass of limbs and bodies already there. Some like him were unharmed. Others, less fortunate, lay wounded beside him. They lay still and unmoving or writhed in agony, lost to their anguish. He snuffled at the soft earth like a pig foraging, willing his body to shrink, to disappear from sight, wishing that he could slough it off like an overcoat. When, in a moment of foolishness, he looked up, his helmet was struck by a bullet. The strap cut into his chin as it rocked back on his head. When he recovered his composure, he saw that his companion was crawling up the side of the crater, a patch of blood on his tunic, but otherwise unscathed.

"Where are you going?" he called out, struggling to make himself heard above the sound of the guns.

The soldier turned to address him, his eyes betraying no sign of recognition. He attempted to rise to his feet but Michael pulled him back, throwing himself upon him, the weight of his body pinning him down. A hail of bullets kicked up the soil behind them.

"Keep still," he hissed, "or you'll get us killed. We can only wait here until they forget about us. Anyone who stands up is done for."

The soldier lay unmoving, his face unrecognisable. Blackened and muddied, with traces of blood, it was the face of a stranger. Michael felt like a father with an unwary child. He didn't resent the responsibility. It was a source of strength, a constant reminder to remain calm and vigilant. They lay spreadeagled on the ground as the conflict ignited the length of no-man's land, its destructive flame vaulting from one position to the next, the sound of machine gun and rifle fire dwarfed by the intermittent scream of shells and the thunder of explosions as the guns vied for dominance. The night air filled with smoke and dust so that they could scarcely breathe. Who was attacking where? There was no way of knowing. Still less did they care. Their concern was to avoid the machine guns that threatened to exact a fearsome toll on their numbers. Eventually, the firing died down. There was more activity further down the line. Fresh troops had issued from the trenches. They were visible when the flares went up. Michael could see huddled figures moving forward in groups, their advance broken up by the dead and the wounded, their leaders attempting to locate gaps in the wire.

Brigham crawled towards Michael. Michael viewed his arrival with misgivings, fearing he was about to ask more of him, unwilling as they were to lie in the crater until the conflict subsided as others less bold might have done.

The lieutenant was wounded; one arm hung at his side. If his wound was painful, he chose to ignore it, the only sign of its presence being the makeshift tourniquet binding it tightly. He knew that they needed to break out. The brief lull in the fighting was their last opportunity to escape, though it might cost them their lives.

He said, "We have to deal with that machine gun. It's the key to everything. If we make a run for it, it'll finish us off."

He spoke with a certainty that Michael had not witnessed before. The emergency had given him courage he was keen to display. He was aware that their lives were in his hands.

The sergeant agreed, "We have to go after it; there's no other way." His blackened face loomed large and his eyes shone like lamps in the gloom.

It would be dawn soon and they would be trapped, able to be picked off at will or forced to surrender, observing the wounded as they suffered and died.

"I need six of you." Brigham looked at them expectantly. "The rest stay here. Once the machine gun's silenced, rush for the line. We'll have to bring the wounded out as best we can."

Michael was reluctant to leave the crater, even when daylight threatened to expose their position. Without it, they would surely have died.

Brigham crawled round the crater, wincing when his arm touched the ground. His instructions were received in silence. He and the sergeant were to lead the attack, Michael and others going with them. The walking wounded would be led back to the line when the time was right. The rest would have to wait until the bearers came.

"We'll be on our way then," Sergeant Fox said, unconcernedly.

Michael wondered if he ever showed fear. There was certainly no sign of it. His matter-of-factness was a source of comfort but also a cause for consternation for those unable to replicate it.

He inclined his head towards the enemy line. None of them dared to stand up, to test the proposition that the enemy was distracted and would leave them alone, though the battle had taken on a new direction. They lined up against the side of the crater, waiting on the order to go forward. Sergeant Fox rose abruptly. The others waited with bated breath. He remained unmoving for several minutes before urging them on.

Brigham was the first out of the crater. He crawled over the rim, lay still for a moment in the darkness, like some vast insect, and rose to his knees. The others joined him, all of them crouching, insufficiently confident to stand, as the sergeant had done.

"We go now," Brigham whispered fiercely, "keep to the left."

The lie of the land offered a degree of cover if the guns opened up again but Michael felt certain that it would fail to save them if they were spotted.

"Keep your bloody heads down," the sergeant hissed as they stumbled forward, starting at every shadow, praying that no lights would go up. Freed of their kit, they moved faster, Brigham struggling to keep up. His face was pale, his tread heavy. He should have remained with the wounded but no one had cared to suggest it.

When he started to fall back, he waved the sergeant forward, making a clumsy gesture with his good arm. He continued to follow them as they began to run.

The sergeant took over, Michael by his side. Michael had lost his fear, focused as he was on reaching the enemy sap. His boots scuffed the ground as he tumbled forward. He skirted the body of a dead soldier, a pair of wide, staring eyes, two arms flung out in supplication, noting that the face beneath the helmet belonged to someone he recognised. He tried and failed to remember his name.

Sergeant Fox intended to be the first to the sap where the machine gunners lay hidden. He wanted the opportunity to avenge the casualties of the platoon he had led for so long. He had lost so many soldiers in the two years of the war. He had watched them arrive in the line, officers and men, many of them little more than schoolboys, full of bravado and enthusiasm, their notions of warfare derived from *Boys' Own Paper* and the popular press. He had served several young officers like Brigham, fresh-faced subalterns straight out of public school, ignorant of life, their ways foreign to the men they commanded, with everything to live for. If he reached the enemy sap, had the opportunity to kill its occupants, the gunners who had wreaked havoc on his platoon, he wouldn't do it out of any misplaced sense of malice or a lust to kill, he would strike them down because he felt it wasn't right that so many young lives should have been ended by their malevolence.

They were short of the enemy sap when they were spotted: fleeting figures in the darkness, rifles in hand, scrambling across the landscape. The machine gun swung round, preparing to direct its fire in their direction. The manoeuvre provoked Michael to increase his pace. Stripped of the encumbrances he had ditched in the crater, his progress was rapid. There was no need for stealth, no point in hesitating when they lacked cover. He had made many yards on the others when he reached the sap. It was forward of the line, where a fold in the ground gave the gunners the vantage they needed. They were the first Germans he had ever seen at close-quarters, dealers in death in their coal scuttle helmets, leather respirators hanging from their belts. They pivoted towards him but the move was too late to save them.

He threw himself over the wall of sandbags, landing in a heap in their midst before scrambling to his feet, unhurt. They hesitated, disconcerted by his unexpected arrival, wondering how best to protect themselves. One of them raised his hands in a gesture of helplessness but if it signalled a desire to surrender, it was of no avail. Michael thrust his bayonet at his unprotected chest. The German seemed to fall forward on to his rifle, conspiring with the gleaming blade to effect his destruction. He sank to the ground, almost silently, as Michael drew back. His companion watched in horror, unable to believe that his omnipotence was over, that the machine gun that had made him lord and master of the open ground irrespective of the numbers thrown against them, was unable to save him. He tried to scramble out of the sap before falling back against the parapet, mouth agape, shoulders hunched, hands fluttering uselessly. He reached for the knife that hung on his belt only to receive a sharp blow to the head from the butt of Michael's rifle. Slumped against the side of the sap wall, blood trickling down his face, he raised his hands in protest, fearing the worst.

Sergeant Fox was the only witness to what happened next. If Michael contemplated mercy, there was no sign of it. He towered above the German soldier, feet apart and bayoneted the cowering figure with all his strength. He levered the bayonet free and stabbed him again, not once but many times, chanting the ritual of the training ground: long points, short points, parries, jabs, as though the defenceless soldier was one of the straw figures on which he had practiced enthusiastically on the training ground. He was still stabbing, still shouting when the sergeant reached him. The two struggled before Michael fell back exhausted against the sap wall, his tunic streaked with blood, a look of awe and triumph on his face.

The others gathered round him before pressing on, all thought of retreat forgotten as more troops crossed over. Michael averted his face from the havoc he had caused. He didn't regret the blood he had spilled but he wondered at the enthusiasm with which he had struck and what would have happened without the sergeant's restraining hand.

Spared the murderous fire, others soon joined them. They began to bomb their way along the German trench. The trench, so long a refuge, was now a trap. A breakthrough further up had cut off its occupants; they were harassed on all sides. The fighting was fierce, hand-to-hand, spilling out on to the open ground, shadows fighting in the darkness. The defenders fought tenaciously until, as the night gave way to the dawn, they were overcome, their line occupied by the enemy.

Their progress was arrested by a runner from the British line. He arrived amongst them, wild-eyed and breathless, saying that they had been told to retreat, that no reserves were available to consolidate their gains. Michael didn't want to retreat. He wanted to go on. He felt indomitable, capable of anything. Nobody could harm him or restrain him. Then, when the order to withdraw was given, he became aware of his fatigue, thirst and hunger, the hazards awaiting them.

He scanned the faces of his companions, wanting to know who had been cut down, who had survived, which of the wounded he could help to the line. Sergeant Fox was by his shoulder but there was no sign of Brigham. When he asked after his whereabouts, Fox said without ceremony, "He didn't get this far. We'll look for him on the way back." He glanced up at the sky, the faint light on the horizon, saying, "We'd better get going. There's little time left."

With heavy heart, they started back, knowing that by dawn the German line would be repopulated, its positions strengthened, its machine guns ready and eager to repulse the next assault.

The British guns fired vigorously, intent on providing cover for the retreating forces. Shells arced over the soldiers as they struggled back, bringing in the wounded as best they could, leaving others to the bearers who rushed past them in search of casualties or carried the wounded to the dressing stations. The guns illuminated their path, sudden flashes, red streaks lighting the sky, uncertain street lamps, parting the blackness. Michael looked for Brigham, scanning the faces of the dead and the wounded, but there was no sign of him. He overtook a soldier crawling on his hand and knees towards the line and hauled him to his feet, urging him on with words of encouragement, dragging him when he could no longer support him.

A shell fell in their midst: a rush of air, a deafening noise, earth thrown skywards, the smell of cordite, the cries of the victims, an ominous hush. Michael was blown off his feet by the blast. He fell awkwardly, the wounded soldier landing on top of him. The two of them lay there, too stunned to move until a figure appeared by their shoulder, urging them on.

Captain Reynolds's head was bare. His uniform was torn and bloody. His expression was thunderous, an angry mask. He clutched a rifle, shaking it furiously in the direction of the British guns.

"They're shelling us," he shouted at the top of his voice. "Our own bloody side." He looked with dismay at the remnants of the force he had led out; so few of them were left standing and many of the survivors were wounded and unable to make their way back unaided.

He began to gather those able to move, organising help for the others as best he could. Inspired by his example, Michael staggered to his feet, his head spinning, his vision blurred. He reached for his companion but he was lifeless, having taken the full force of the blast. He looked for someone else to assist. There, edging his way towards the line was Brigham. His arm, free of its makeshift tourniquet, hung loosely by his side. He lurched over the uneven ground. His blackened face was streaked with blood but there was a look of determination in his eyes. He looked at Michael expectantly. Michael put his arm around him and, leaning heavily on each other, they headed for the trench they had left so reluctantly.

CHAPTER 16

Alice entered a room divided into stalls barely larger than a telephone box, separated by two thick screens of wire, a foot apart. A warder directed her into one and stood immediately behind her, feet astride, hands clasped behind his back, dashing any hope of privacy.

Her irritation had been growing from the moment she entered the prison. There was something about the forbidding, grey stones of the keep, the bars on every window, the solid doors with their multiple locks that made her want to hurl herself against them.

It was her first opportunity to meet Robert since his return from France.

She wondered how he felt about her visit, as the other cubicles filled up and the warders lined up behind the visitors. Some were impatient to get on whilst others looked about them anxiously. She was nervous at the prospect of meeting Robert again. It had been so long and so much had happened to them both. A door opened at the end of the room and the prisoners filed in. She thought them a sorry sight in their drab garments, shuffling forward as if they had forgotten how to walk, blinking in the light. They milled about uncertainly, wasting precious moments whilst they waited for the warders to direct them to the visitors, seemingly incapable of deciding for themselves which one was theirs.

Robert stood there before her. He started towards her, unmindful of the barrier that divided them. His appearance shocked her. He looked worn and diminished, his reduced stature exaggerated by the prison clothes that hung about him loosely. His hair was short, shorn roughly, his pallid face unshaven. He waved to her cheerfully and then, confronting the wire that separated them, fell back defeated.

She said, "Robert, are you all right?"

She reached out to the wire, wanting to touch him, to feel his hand in hers but the wire was impenetrable and the desks impeded her so that even his finger tips were beyond her reach.

"When I heard they'd taken you to France, understood what that meant and why they'd done it, I thought I'd never see you again. Yet here you are, alive and well. I can't believe I'm able to talk to you; it's something I've wanted to do for such a long time. If anything had happened to you, I would never have forgiven myself."

"What makes you say that?"

"I was the one who encouraged you to resist conscription. I knew where it might lead but I'd no idea that it would place you in danger."

"How could you have known that? Nobody was more surprised than me. There again," he said in an effort to comfort her, "it turned out all right in the end, thanks to your efforts. Here I am, back in England, in Wandsworth Prison, at His Majesty's pleasure."

His face broke into a smile and he was the old Robert, the brother to whom she had always looked up, who had guided her when she was uncertain, amused her with his wry observances, involved her in his earnest discussions. Noting her discomfort, he said anxiously, "Do I look terrible? I suppose I must, after so long in solitary confinement."

"Oh, not at all. You look fine. I'm surprised to see you looking so well." Then, she spoilt the effect by looking around and saying with a shudder, "But what an awful place you've ended up in."

"The worst is not being able to sleep. If I could rely on having a few hours every night in which to escape from the squalor and the tedium, I'd be fine. But it's difficult to sleep without fresh air or exercise."

Alice said, "It must be very hard," and shivered slightly as if a door had opened and a draught had been directed on to her.

He wanted to pour his heart out to his sister after so long apart but forced himself to suppress his feelings for her sake. There was too much pain, frustration and disappointment bottled up inside him to permit its release. It was better to suffer the indignities in silence when there was nothing she could do to help him. With a conscious effort, he asked after their parents, about Michael and how he was faring, wanting to deflect her from enquiring further into his circumstances.

Alice observed his difficulty in forming words. His hesitancy made her impatient. She wanted to learn everything about him before they took him away.

He said, "I'm at the second stage of hard labour. I'm allowed to go to the workshops. We spend the day making rope mats. We're like cattle, lined up in pens. We thread rope through strips of canvas with a knife and needle and sixty of us drink from the same rusting can to slake our thirst."

"Have you spoken to any of the others?"

He looked across at the warder who stood by Alice's shoulder, his face segmented by the two grilles that separated them. The warder looked away, affecting nonchalance.

"We mutter to each other in the exercise yard and exchange a word or two in the workshop. That's about the extent of it, really. I'm trying to abide by the rules. I feel our cause is best established by ensuring our behaviour's beyond reproach."

"Oh, no," Alice said, "that's unnecessary. The fact that you're here speaks oceans about your determination to do what you believe to be right. There's no need to do more. Don't worry about what anyone thinks of you."

She gestured towards the line of warders. "Their views are of no consequence. Your task is to endure imprisonment. Everything else can wait until you're released."

"I suppose you're right. All I can do is try to make the best of my circumstances."

Alice decided the time had come to put to him the question that had been on her lips from the moment that she had entered the prison and had seen the consequences of the actions that she had urged upon him with such enthusiasm.

"Have you thought about alternative service? Many objectors - even those who were shipped to France - have agreed to join the Home Office scheme. It's far from ideal and there will be difficulties when its futility becomes clear but you would have a life of sorts - and it wouldn't be conscription, not in any formal sense."

"The experience in France has hardened my views. It wasn't something I bargained for. When I think back to the tribunal, to my hopes and expectations, I writhe with embarrassment. I was naive and arrogant to believe that I could defy a government so committed to the war."

"We didn't think it through. We believed our good intentions would protect us."

Alice thought back to how proud she had been of Robert's obduracy. Why had she burdened him with her idealism? She had acted like one of those shrill, unthinking women who despatched their unsuspecting sons and husbands to the front. She deserved to watch him suffer, to acquire painful memories each time they met.

He said, "Well, I'm committed now. There's no going back. I'll get used to it in time. They say the first few weeks of prison are when the shock of deprivation is at its greatest. Now, at least, I'm allowed out for exercise every day. I go to chapel, write letters and receive visitors. It's a life of sorts."

"Not much of one."

"It's what I chose to do."

He smiled encouragingly at his sister but she failed to respond. She was too shocked at the conditions to make light of them. Her father had attempted to prepare her for her visit but his words had meant little when they were so alien to her experience of life.

Robert asked how the family had fared in his absence. He was conscious that their time together was almost over, that Alice would depart and he would be alone once more. He found it hard to imagine family life. Though it was only a matter of months since they had been together, the isolation of prison had made it seem like a lifetime. His memory had become like an old man's: his recollections of childhood were vivid whilst the events of recent months were a blur, a jumble of conversations and occurrences that made little sense, appearing in fragments, unanchored by anything safe or familiar.

"How's Michael, is he safe and well? I received a letter from him. It was my first letter after I came here. He appeared to be thriving but you can't tell."

Alice had encouraged Michael to write and the others had held their letters back so that his would be first. She had wanted her brothers to communicate in spite of their circumstances. With Michael, there was no knowing when the letters might dry up. As it was, with every delay, their hearts stopped, fearing the worst, only to discover that he had been distracted or diverted from writing, forgetting how much they hung on to his every word.

She said, "Michael's a hero. He was spared the early weeks of the Somme offensive but got caught up in things later. There was a raid that went badly wrong. He stormed the machine gun position that was doing all the damage." She added matter-of-factly, "He's going to be decorated for his bravery."

"I always thought he would make a good soldier."

"He asks about you a lot. When I tell him what you've survived, he demands to know what we're doing to help you. I've told him that I'm working for the No Conscription Fellowship and have been for months. He doesn't seem impressed. His letters imply we should be doing more on your behalf."

"He doesn't understand how difficult it is for you. When I next write to him, I'll tell him that you're doing all you can."

She said she had joined the NCF for his sake, that she had begun as a clerk, filing letters and messages from prisoners, trying to keep track of them. The Defence of the Realm Act which had led to the arrest of so many of her colleagues had made her prominent. Now she was editing *The Tribune* and doing more besides.

He said, "Knowing there's an organisation, dedicated to supporting objectors in the prisons and the camps, gives us hope. It's all too easy to believe that you're entirely alone, neglected by a world that has more important things on its mind than the fate of those foolish enough to oppose conscription."

"We know more about you than we do about Michael. The censor keeps us in ignorance of his whereabouts. Every letter home is read by a superior officer and some of its contents redacted. A few journalists are permitted access to the fighting but they have to be approved by the army and accredited as captains. The result is that civilians know very little. Every action is trumpeted as a victory. The newspapers speak of advances, of battles fought and won and yet the casualties keep mounting and the front hardly shifts."

She longed to reach out and touch him, to hold his hand or stroke his cheek. He spoke of a sort of life, of making do but his appearance belied his words. Had he seen himself lately? Did prisons have mirrors?

His eyes were bloodshot. His face was pale, almost grey. The little hair that they hadn't cut off was dirty and matted. His clothes hung about him as if he were a scarecrow. He had been the picture of health six months ago. How could he talk of prevailing when his appearance spoke only of anguish and hardship? She wondered if their menfolk recognised the consequences of their platitudes. Were they aware that every sentence they wrote or uttered was scrutinised for brittle optimism, for clues as to their well-being, that whole families waited for news, their hopes suspended by a thread that might break at any minute, dreading the prospect of silence, fearing still more the news another day might bring?

Robert asked, "What's father up to? I can't imagine he's resting on his laurels, after his visit to France."

Alice said her father's attitude gave her grounds for concern. It wasn't that he was idle or had stopped caring but the optimism that had buoyed him up for so long had evaporated leaving only dour application and a feeling of futility.

"You know how optimistic he used to be, how convinced he was that something could be done to truncate the war? Since he's been to France and seen the scale of the conflict, he talks of it being a climacteric, a crisis of such magnitude as to be beyond the scope of individuals or governments to halt."

"So what's he doing?" Robert asked, convinced that his father would be doing something, that inactivity was something that only a serious illness would prompt.

"He's become a Quaker chaplain. He visits camps and prison indefatigably. He attends a regular service in Wormwood Scrubs. He hardly talks about the war any more. I think he wants to talk about it, that it's still uppermost in his mind but he restrains himself as best he can.

Odd isn't it? After all he's done. He's trying to help us by avoiding the subject, by focusing on the things he can do."

Robert declined to comment on his father's behaviour but his expression spoke volumes. There had been a time when his father was full of declarations, when he wrote copiously, made speeches, went to protest meetings and campaigned strenuously against the war. Where had it got him? Conscription's false equality had undone all his efforts. Perhaps, he was right? There was little point in railing against the war. Helping others, working to mitigate its consequences was preferable to calling for its cessation with empty words.

Alice said, "There are lots of letters waiting for you at home."

"I look forward to reading them."

"Many of them are from America."

"My friends must be wondering why I haven't been in touch."

"Most of them are from the same person - a young woman to judge by the handwriting. Were you expecting to hear from her?"

The handwriting was striking; neat and regular with sudden flourishes. Each letter carried the same Pennsylvania address on the back of the envelope. She had been tempted to reply to one of them, explaining Robert's silence but had thought better of it, deciding that she should speak to him first.

Robert was silent for a moment, avoiding Alice's gaze. She watched him through the mesh. She saw a look of sadness in his eyes, a fleeting expression, there for an instance, before making way for the mask he donned to hide his feelings.

He said guardedly, "I'm not surprised she's written."

"What's her name?"

"Mary."

"You've never spoken of her. Is she the reason you came back?"

"I told you why I came back."

She stared at him intently, a frown on her face. "I've never understood why you put yourself in this position, when you could have so easily avoided it. Why didn't you stay in your teaching post? You told me it was the culmination of everything you'd worked for and that you were fortunate to become a professor at an early age. No one would have thought any the worse of you if you hadn't come back. We urged you to stay away, knowing what was likely to happen if you returned. Now it seems you had a friend in Pennsylvania..."

"Whom I cared for greatly but lost."

"Was that sufficient reason to leave?"

"It went badly wrong."

"It must have, to have led to this."

The warders were stirring. Their time together was almost up. The prisoners and the visitors were beginning to part, some reluctantly, often tearfully, others relieved that their unsatisfactory encounter was over.

When Robert rose from his seat with a show of dismay, Alice leaned forward and said, "Would you like me to write to her?"

"You don't know her address?"

"She writes it on the back of the envelope. She's American – that's what they do. Shall I write to her or not? What do you think?"

"You'll tell her I'm in prison and nothing more?"

"Nothing else."

"You won't open her letters?"

"They'll be there waiting for you when you come home."

"What if she writes back?"

"I won't reply."

He felt a hand on his shoulder and a voice urged him to step back. He said, "Tell her I'm in prison and can't be reached –nothing more."

"Shall I tell her that you're thinking of her?"

"I don't think she'd welcome that."

He gave Alice one last, lingering look as the warder on her side of the barrier, motioned her to leave. He sought to remember every aspect of her appearance. She was wearing new clothes and looked conspicuous, affluent and slightly grand, as if wanting to be distinctive for his sake, to plant an image in his mind that would endure until her next visit. Yet, she was really no different from the other visitors in their worn clothes, tight bonnets and dull boots. They were all fragments of families seeking to link up with the missing pieces beyond the wire.

He called out, "I won't give up - not yet."

She said that she had never doubted it and the old pride in his stance rose up in her breast though she fought hard to conceal it.

"Do whatever's necessary to make life bearable. Your presence here's proof enough of your devotion to peace."

"You have to leave," the warder said, inserting himself between her and the gauze so that her view of Robert was impeded.

She backed towards the door. Her eyes fixed on Robert, she collided with a woman in a long, black coat who dragged a whimpering child behind her. She consoled herself with the thought that Robert would be released soon, that they would commute his sentence, offer him a reprieve in the manner of the suffragettes. But what difference would it make? They would only conscript him again, he would refuse to fight or work and the whole cycle of reprisals would begin anew. Many men had survived, even prospered in prison, sustained by their convictions but Robert wasn't made of the stuff of martyrs. Prison would destroy him if he remained within its confines for too long.

Led back to his cell, Robert followed dutifully, overjoyed at seeing Alice. His elation remained with him until nightfall. Then, as the light faded, he slipped back into his old despondency, welcoming it like an old and trusted friend. The long awaited visit was over. Nothing for another month but two letters in and out. He understood why few prisoners wrote to their families or welcomed their visits. Their absence was too great to bear. He vowed he would welcome all contact with family and friends though he knew how hard it would be when he missed them so much.

His thoughts turned to Pennsylvania and all that had happened there and he began to relive the events that had brought him back to England.

CHAPTER 17

Michael returned to the line bearing the ribbons of the Distinguished Conduct Medal. It had been presented to him by the corps commander at a brief parade. The medal was an unwelcome reminder that Holcombe had gone. Michael had seen him being carried to the casualty clearing station. There had seemed little prospect of him surviving. He wrote to his parents, speaking of his valour, but his words seemed contrived. He wrote to Holcombe several times but there was no reply. The consolation was that there was no news of his death. He vowed to stay in touch with him and to visit him when he was on leave.

His gallantry brought him to the attention of the battalion commander. Lieutenant-Colonel Beaumont-Dart seemed affronted by Michael's lowly rank, as if no one of his background and education had any right to be a private. He spoke of the officers that he had lost and the need to replace them and looked at Michael meaningfully, hinting that any attempt on his part to gain a commission would be looked on favourably.

Michael said nothing. He had no objection to becoming a junior officer, though the casualty rate was hardly an inducement, but felt that promotion would be inappropriate for someone of his background.

Beaumont-Dart was a tall thin man, with a pronounced stoop, a long, thin face, a small moustache he fingered constantly and a high-pitched voice. He lacked the presence and the carefully-contrived airs of his peers, most of whom found him too earnest. Though a stickler for discipline, he cared little for his own appearance, frequently appearing with loose buttons hanging from his tunic, his boots scuffed or dull and apparently in need of a shave. His career had been pedestrian in spite of the opportunities for advancement afforded by the war. What made him remarkable in the eyes of his fellow-officers and subordinates were his indefatigable efforts on behalf of the battalion and his growing conviction that the army's tactics were a tragic waste.

He had been horrified by the carnage on the Somme. He had attended the roll calls of his denuded companies and had marvelled at the blind optimism that had sent them forward, concluding long before the Field Regulations adapted to the new realities that was what was needed was tactical mobility: short rushes forward by unencumbered troops in pursuit of limited objectives, supported by others able to leapfrog the positions gained.

~

It was winter when they went back into the line, bolstered by a draft of new recruits, but still below battalion strength. The sweltering heat of the summer was forgotten and the rain that had reduced the ground to a morass of mud that bogged down all the guns and transport had given way to crisp, clear days and bitterly cold nights. Ground once treacherous underfoot had frozen solid so that the dug-out timbers set fast and the wheels of stationary limbers became unyielding. When supplies moved up at night, it was possible to hear the ring of the horses' hooves on the stubborn ground and the curses of the drivers as the carts lurched forward. In the trenches, men in greatcoats huddled together for warmth, attempting to evade the wind that pierced their clothes, glazed their ears and lips and turned their breath into curling plumes of smoke.

It had been a day of heavy casualties, no ground gained or lost. There had been a brief assault on the German line and a swift counter attack by its defenders. No fighting of great substance but sufficient to cover the ground between the lines with a carpet of casualties. Dusk brought with it squalls of snow, the first of the winter, which covered the trenches, draping the earthworks, the wire, the saps and the look-out posts in a white shroud, slowing the passage of the casualties down the communication trenches, hampering the limbers as they brought up fresh supplies. It had imposed a sudden awkward silence on the bustle of the line and halted the spasmodic firing that issued from both sides.

Michael was on sentry duty. In the trench opposite were Prussian Guards whose zealous ways were irksome. Snipers waited patiently for any moment of carelessness likely to expose men to their fire, Michael stepped down to brush the snow flakes from his greatcoat, clap his hands and stamp his feet in an effort to keep warm and rid his rifle of the snow that lined its barrel before peering carefully across the strip of land that separated him from other freezing figures. Between the two sides, on the rough, unyielding ground, lay the wounded. Some had been brought in by the bearers between lulls in the fighting but most lay where they had fallen, huddled in the craters, strewn across the open ground in rude disorder. Every effort to retrieve them had been met by fire from the German side and every head above the parapet risked a sniper's bullet. Though the German wounded lay abandoned in the snow, there was no way either side could effect a truce, so that the casualties were condemned to lie unaided. They stirred as the wet snow caressed their faces. Michael heard them shift and groan; waves of pain that came and went, followed by short silences. A voice called out to God repeatedly; someone hailed his mother, hoping she might ease his anguish; another coughed harshly, a guttural sound, plaintive and unceasing.

Five men, Captain Reynolds, Lieutenant Brigham, Sergeant Fox and two soldiers from the recent draft, approached Michael's vantage point as the sounds from no-man's land grew louder. They looked at each other anxiously, unsure what to do.

Michael stepped down from the fire step and said loudly, "Sir, permission to form a party to bring our wounded in?"

Captain Reynolds, who knew Michael well, looked at him carefully, a worried frown on his face. He remained silent for several minutes, shifting uneasily from one foot to the other before saying in a flat, dull voice that made his anguish clear. "There's nothing we can do, without the cooperation of the other side. "

"Perhaps if we made a start, they would do the same?"

Sergeant Fox's countenance was stern and unforgiving. "We've sent men out already; they're out there with the rest."

"They'll die if we don't help them," Michael said, his voice verging on panic.

"Easy lad," the sergeant said, placing a reassuring arm on Michael's shoulder, "we'd help them if we could but if you put your head above the parapet, it'll be the last thing that you do."

Michael thought back to when he had lain in a shell crater amidst a heap of dead and dying soldiers. He had seen the anguish and helplessness of the wounded, their desperation to regain the shelter of the line, their desire to be on the conveyor that went from field dressing station to casualty clearing station to base hospital on which their prospects depended. For many casualties the journey was short. The important thing was to embark on it, to be conveyed back to the line. Abandonment in no-man's land was almost certain death.

"What's that noise?" the captain asked his gloved hand across his mouth.

The six of them stood silently. As the snow began to fall in earnest, the figures above them began to voice their unease. A gurgling, a wailing, began to sweep the open ground. Fitful at first, it grew more persistent until it formed a chorus, a succession of screams that sprang from man to man. Their wild, piercing cries soon combined to form a single scream, a communal anguish in hundreds of despairing throats as if every casualty had overheard the company commander's observations and had decided to rise up in protest against them.

Captain Reynolds hastened back to the battalion dugout, the others following behind. He was at a loss as to what to do about the men still out on the open ground and wanted to talk to the CO. The dug-out comprised a sheet of corrugated iron for a roof, weighed down by sandbags, a narrow entrance shored up by timber and other trench miscellany, a spluttering stove above which a kettle hung from a makeshift gantry and a collection of empty ammunition boxes that served as seats and tables. In the corner was a bed made up of further boxes and a door; two cushions and a pile of blankets provided its only comforts.

The colonel was sitting in front of the stove, breathing in the obnoxious fumes, cradling a tin cup filled with steaming tea, his helmet at his feet. He looked up as the others entered, without enthusiasm. The expression on their faces told him that they brought unpalatable news.

"Sir, can you hear that noise?" the captain asked.

"Indeed, I can."

"It's getting louder," said the captain, though it was obvious.

Beaumont-Dart inclined his head to one side and listened carefully. Not liking what he heard, he reached down for his helmet, saying, "We'd better see what's going on." He brushed the curtain aside and stepped out into the twilight. Pausing for a moment to allow his eyes to adjust to the gloom, he made his way down the trench to where the noise seemed loudest, noting in passing the effect that it was having on the soldiers, disconcerted by the unseemly chorus issuing from no-man's land. Many of them had covered their ears with their hands or had bundled mufflers around their heads. Others were talking loudly or shouting to each other in an effort to drown out the noise. One man had fallen to his knees, hands raised in supplication. Several muttered songs to themselves. Some stood at the ready, waiting on the order to retrieve the wounded whilst others gathered ominously at the head of the communications trench, as if preparing to desert their posts until the noise subsided.

"We have to bring them in, sir," Lieutenant Brigham interceded.

His face was pale, his hands were shaking; he seemed at the end of his tether. The others resumed the arguments, aired earlier, in favour of some form of intervention.

The colonel listened to them carefully before he shook his head. He peered at Captain Reynolds and a look of understanding passed between them. He said, "No one leaves the trench until we can be certain that the Boche won't fire on us."

"How'll we know what their intentions are, sir?" asked Brigham.

The colonel said, "You'd have to ask some men to risk their lives."

"Why don't we call for volunteers and take a party out, sir? We might get away with it, if we move quickly,"

"Who would lead them, you, I suppose?"

"I would, sir, most certainly," Brigham said, determined to convince the CO that he was not proposing something that he was not prepared to do himself.

"Well, you'll stay here and sit it out with the rest of us. You might be prepared to die for your wounded comrades but the men whom you command deserve a better fate."

"Even if they volunteer, sir?"

"Especially, if they volunteer. There's nothing we can do without the help of the Boche."

"A white flag…"

"It would be invisible in these conditions." The CO stretched out his hand and watched the snow flakes gather in the palm of his glove

Shots sounded further down the line. They thought it was a raid at first, one of those vicious and unpredictable forays that punctuated every day as each side sought advantage. It was why the enemy could not be trusted to withhold their fire. But it wasn't a raid; it was nervous soldiers firing on their wounded comrades in an effort to truncate the chorus of distress from no-man's land. Others had thrown down their weapons and were rushing down the trench. It was clear morale was crumbling and that something would have to be done to maintain discipline.

The CO recalled the soldiers singing softly to each other in an attempt to distract themselves from the noise. Perhaps it could be employed to good effect on a grander scale? He turned to Sergeant Fox. "Get me Morgan. On the double. "

The sergeant looked at the CO in amazement. What did he want Morgan for? Where was he? He had no idea but he would find him if it helped to keep the men under control. As if to emphasise the urgency of the matter, a soldier nearby slipped his rifle off his shoulder, loosed the firing bolt and went to mount the fire step.

Captain Reynolds was quick to bar his way.

"Where do you think you're going with that?"

He thought the soldier was about to defy him but he changed his mind. He slumped down dejectedly on the step, his rifle across his knee and said, "It's the noise, sir. I can't stand it. It'll go on all night unless we do something."

"We are going to do something," said Captain Reynolds, assuming a look of quiet confidence. He thought he knew what the CO had in mind. It was a long shot but it might prevent a dangerous collapse of morale.

He ordered the subalterns and NCOs to move along the line, calming the men as best they could and directed them to ensure that nobody did anything foolish. One man had been shot already, picked off by a sniper when he poked his head above the trench to see what was going on. The bearers were loading him on to a stretcher though the captain suspected that by the time they reached the dressing station, there would be little they could do for him. Above his head, a Very light took flight, prompting a burst of machine gun fire and further protestations from the men abandoned in the snow.

Sergeant Fox threaded his way along the trench. His short, wiry figure was made for trench warfare. There was no danger of his helmet appearing above the parapet and he was capable of squeezing through the smallest of gaps. Men were scattering in all directions, throwing down their weapons, tearing at their uniforms, to rid themselves of the excruciating cries. They thrust aside the officers attempting to restrain them, mindful only of the anguished bodies in the snow, the rising chorus of distress.

Finding Lance-Corporal Morgan wasn't easy. He was further down the line than he'd anticipated, busy helping to calm his platoon. His officer was slumped against the trench wall, his head in his hands, in a vain effort to stifle the sounds from above.

"The CO wants you in the dug-out," he said to Morgan without ceremony.

"What about him?" Morgan pointed at the officer.

"He can wait, you've got other things to do."

They squeezed past the soldiers, the officers vainly trying to calm them. The snow was falling heavily. The duckboards were treacherous, the sandbags above their heads, a whitened mass. Morgan was a big man, ponderous, slow-moving but also imperturbable. Nothing disconcerted him. He had greeted all the hardships and hazards of their months in the line with the same ready stoicism. Now his coat was open, revealing the scarf and knitted waistcoat beneath his tunic that added to his bulk. He wore his helmet at a jaunty angle as if it were too small for him. He was breathing heavily by the time he and the sergeant reached the dug-out.

Morgan presented himself to the CO with his usual matter-of-factness. He might have been in the depot counting off the draft. He said, "You wanted me, sir?"

"Not you, Morgan," the CO said. "I want your voice, the one you sang with in the concert."

"They parade together, sir."

The CO looked at him suspiciously. The previous week, the battalion had put on a concert at divisional HQ. They had distributed sheets of the words of the popular music hall songs and had urged the whole assembly to sing. The men had loved it, demanding encores, until it seemed that they would never tire of the sound of their voices or go back to their billets. Even the General had sung along with the rest. The orchestra had been made up of whatever instruments and musicians could be found. It was amazing what men brought with them to the front. During the choruses, Morgan's voice had towered above the others. The colonel, conducting the orchestra, had relied on his insistent baritone, motioning him when to start and stop, but otherwise following his lead. His example had converted a motley crew of songsters into something resembling a Welsh Male Voice choir.

"Good, because you're going to sing."

"What now, sir?"

"It'll help to calm the men, distract them from what's going on out there."

"On my own, sir?"

Morgan shivered, flapping his coat to shake the snow off it. To Michael, he seemed like a bear emerging from hibernation in search of food, irascible, baffled, with a hint of desperation.

"Of course not, everyone will join in, just as we did last week. But you will lead, that's the point. Everyone will follow you."

"What am I going to sing?" Morgan demanded, desperate to avoid the responsibility that had been thrust upon him.

"Anything you like, music hall, marching songs, hymns, I don't care, though it would be helpful if others knew the words. You get the point, don't you? We need something to calm and occupy the men until things settle down again."

"Do we have any musical instruments?"

The colonel looked at the others in desperation. The sergeant stepped into the breech as always. He said, "We have a bugler. Stephens will have his mouth organ with him. He can play anything on that. And there's Brown..."

"What does Brown do?"

"He's a violinist, sir."

"He'll have his violin with him? Here?"

"Oh, yes, sir, he takes it everywhere."

"Well, we need all these people. Take them and Morgan and anyone else who looks like they can sing to the top of the 'comms' trench and get them started. The others'll join in soon enough."

Sergeant Fox prepared to get on his way but everyone could tell he wasn't keen on the idea. His thoughts were with the wounded. As the senior NCO, he felt they should be doing more to get them in, even as he recognised the practical difficulties in going to their aid. For him, it was a matter of honour not to let them down.

The men turned up a bewildering variety of musical instruments. Captain Reynolds wasn't in the least surprised. Soldiers carried all sorts of strange things round with them: charms, mementoes, mascots, books. Nothing surprised him any more. Nor did he mind if it helped them get through a strafe. He knew of one subaltern whose mother had insisted that he wore a large medallion. He wore it every time he came into the line. When he was shot, the bullet had embedded itself in the metal but had failed to penetrate it. It had hung above his heart.

The makeshift choir and orchestra assembled at the top of the communications trench and began their concert. They were hesitant at first but they soon got into the swing of it, improvising or humming when they didn't know the words. When their limited repertoire of music hall songs was exhausted, they switched to marching songs and soon everyone joined in, in a fevered, manic effort to muffle the sounds from no-man's land. Their singing was not a thing of beauty. It was not even very loud in spite of Morgan's labours but it served to stop the haemorrhage of discipline that threatened the integrity of the line. The colonel scrambled up and down the trench, ignoring the snow, the biting wind, speaking to every soldier. Some he treated brusquely, ordering them to take up their positions or to pick up their fallen weapons. Others he comforted as best he could, remarking with approval on their steadfastness but most of all, he urged them to sing, insisting that they join their voices with the others led by Morgan, until a discordant chorus of voices and instruments filled the night, drowning out the cries of distress from no man's land.

It wasn't enough to satisfy the men. There was something unmanly about doing nothing to bring the casualties in. If loyalty meant anything, it meant attempting to save the wounded and the dying, meant transporting them to the dressing stations wherein lay their only hope of life and when that failed, affording their remains a decent Christian burial. When Captain Reynolds looked at the resigned, bewildered faces of the men, their stoicism reinforced his belief in honour and discipline, the values that had brought him to that place. He knew that the CO's actions were the right ones. The men had to be restrained. Theirs was an active front.

They had suffered many casualties. They dared not let the company loose in no-man's land without cooperation from the other side.

Eventually, a few men did go out but it did no good. No sooner had they left than the flares went up, their cascading light throwing into stark relief the falling snow, the wounded crawling to the line, the stretcher bearers loading up the casualties or stooping to put water to their fevered lips. The rescuers scrambled back into the trench, tumbling over the side in their eagerness to escape the fusillade of fire from the other side. If the Germans were inclined to bring in their wounded, there was no sign of it. No one thanked the CO for the singing. No one had any sympathy for Morgan who by dawn had lost his voice but there was no doubt the unseemly chorus had done the trick. Thanks to its distractive power, the line remained intact.

The sound of the casualties grew fainter as the night wore on. There was no attack at dawn as many had feared. The ground was blanketed in snow, the guns were silent and in no-man's land nothing stirred or moved. The wounded had perished in the night.

They lay where they had fallen, covered in snow: groups, lines, individuals, scattered carelessly across the landscape, their features only visible in silhouette, their bodies, forsaken and grotesque. One man sat bolt upright, his frozen entrails in front of him. Others had died whilst crawling to the parapet. Several had reached it, their arms dangling over the edge, unnoticed in the darkness. In the distance, a kneeling sentry, supported by his rifle, looked out purposively, with dead, unseeing eyes, as if to warn the others of the enemy's approach.

The colonel wondered afterwards if he should have acted differently, whether something more in keeping with the heroic folly of the war would have been better suited to their circumstances but having led so many men to their destruction he had tired of mindless sacrifice, wanting only to keep the troops safe so that when the war was over, they could celebrate its passing and remember those left to death's embrace whom they had known so well.

PART IV

April, 1917

CHAPTER 18

They met in the doorway of the No-Conscription Fellowship, at the foot of the winding staircase that led up from the street. Alice had unlocked the outer door which was heavy and difficult to shift, wedging it ajar with her foot whilst she sought to clear away the pile of letters that had collected behind it.

"Here, let me get those," said a friendly but unfamiliar voice. She stepped aside whilst the man who had spoken bent before her and swept up the letters, stacking them neatly before placing them in her arms.

"Thank you, you're very kind," she said as she turned to go up the stairs, scarcely glancing at him in her eagerness to begin work, save to note that he wore the boots, puttees, tunic and cap of a captain. To her consternation, he followed along behind her, his tread heavy on the stair.

Before she could ask him who he was and what he thought he was doing, he said, "I hope you don't mind me coming in uninvited. I was hoping to speak to Alice Bennett. If now's not a good time, I can always come back."

He seemed to have difficulty mounting the stairs. His breathing was laboured and his step uneven. When he reached the top, he paused to collect himself whilst Alice unlocked the inner door. He watched her intently, keen to learn more about her, before delivering his message.

"You're Robert's sister, aren't you?" he said as he entered the room. "I was told that I might find you here."

"Robert…?"

"Robert Bennett – one of the conscientious objectors who was shipped to France and sentenced to death."

"You know him?" Alice asked, her interest quickening as it always did when Robert's name was mentioned. She knew most of Robert's friends. The Captain was not amongst them.

"Well, I don't know him exactly, but I've met him and had an opportunity to study him. The likeness is unmistakeable."

He added in a poor attempt at gallantry, "Of course, you're much prettier."

"I'm pleased to hear it," Alice said, acknowledging the unexpected compliment with a faint smile. "Where do you know him from?"

"The court martial," the Captain said, after some hesitation.

He had intended to conceal the connection until later but now he had met the woman he supposed to be Robert's sister, and was taken with her appearance, he was eager to tell his story.

Alice stopped what she was doing. She was sorting the mail into piles ready to distribute it to the others. There was so much of it. Keeping track of all the objectors was a full-time occupation. The army made no effort to be helpful. Even the Government was kept in ignorance. One of the Fellowship's tasks was to keep the Government informed of the facts that, wilfully or otherwise, the army concealed.

"You were present at the field court martial?"

"I was one of the four officers."

"Then we'd better talk."

To conceal her mounting confusion, Alice added, "I was about to make a cup of tea, would you like one?"

"I certainly would," said the Captain.

He had been awake much of the night, wrestling with his thoughts, trying to decide whether he should seek out Alice and tell her what had happened in France. It was part of a larger question he was trying to answer: where did he stand in relation to the war? Was he going back and, if so, in what capacity? It was all very straightforward in the line. There was little time for doubts or misgivings. Wounded, with the prospect of months of convalescence ahead of him, it was a different matter. Doubts long concealed had surfaced, brought to a head by recollections of Robert's treatment. He needed to discuss them with somebody sympathetic if they were not to impede his return to the line.

He looked round the cluttered office whilst Alice boiled a kettle of water in the tiny kitchen at the back of the room and took two cups and saucers from the cupboard above the sink. The scene was chaotic: cards and papers were heaped upon the desks and furniture; half-open drawers were filled to overflowing; the walls were papered with lists and photographs. There were letters from guardrooms, detention barracks and prisons, some long and discursive, others scrawled in pencil or scratched with needles. There were reports from chaplains and other prison visitors, court martial and tribunal statements, announcements and judgements. Every letter had been recorded, its origins entered painstakingly on to index cards so as to show at a glance the state and whereabouts of every prisoner. Some of those listed had been prosecuted several times. One corner of the room was the editorial office of *The Tribunal*, its desks strewn with galleys, cuttings and readers' letters. He looked in awe at the confusion. He had imagined resistance to conscription to be confined to a handful of cranks and troublemakers. He had not imagined that the objectors in France were the tip of the iceberg and that beneath it lay a community of protesters.

When Alice returned with two mugs of tea and a packet of biscuits, he was feeling more at home. He was perched on the corner of the desk, one leg swinging idly, the other planted firmly on the ground. Feeling at home was a trait he had perfected in the army. There you never knew where your next square meal was coming from or when you would get a good night's sleep.

"So," said Alice, falling into a chair opposite him and looking at him with a directness that disconcerted him, "How did you come to be involved with Robert? Did you volunteer to sit in judgement over him?"

"I didn't volunteer; no one in the army does, if they've got any sense. I was preparing to go up when I was summoned, out of the blue. They had a colonel lined up and needed a major or captain. Our sector was quiet at the time so they thought I could be spared. Not that I was gone for long. The whole thing was almost over before it started."

"Men's lives were at stake – that surely made it a matter deserving careful consideration?"

"They were guilty. They didn't deny it. The witnesses weren't needed. They contested the right of the army to spirit them to France…but that cut no ice with anyone."

"That was the crux of the matter, surely?"

Watching her features transform themselves from something gentle and inviting into something hard and unforgiving, he felt a sense of loss. He wanted her to believe that he had been powerless, lacking all discretion in the matter of her brother's fate.

"I believe they also requested proper legal representation but were denied it."

"The army provided that, though it wasn't really necessary."

"Robert thought it was."

"We weren't there to determine matters of jurisdiction. That wasn't what we were about."

"What were you about?"

"We were there because they'd disobeyed the lawful command of a senior officer. No one disputed that. They wouldn't wear uniforms; they wouldn't drill; they wouldn't do fatigues; the insubordination was endless."

Alice's eyes narrowed dangerously as she struggled to keep her feelings in check. She said in a low voice he could scarcely hear, "You found them guilty knowing that they would be sentenced to death?"

"Four officers were present. The sentence was unanimous. It was the sentence prescribed by the Military Manual."

"You had no discretion in the matter?"

He looked at her with misgivings. "I was angry and frustrated at the time. I didn't want to be there. My battalion was going up the line. I had a bad feeling about it. I felt I should have been with them, not listening to civilians voicing their objection to a war we were trying our best to win."

"So why are you telling me this now?"

"I thought that you might want to know what happened to your brother. I also wanted to apologise and to try to make amends. What I did was wrong."

"Mind you," he added, as she stared at him angrily, "it wouldn't have made any difference in the end. There would almost certainly have been a retrial if we had failed to reach a unanimous verdict. The circumstances of the trial were so unusual that the outcome was always going to be a matter for GHQ."

"You couldn't have known that at the time?"

"I couldn't be sure. There was no precedent on which we could draw. No, I deeply regret my part in your brother's trial. Had the death sentence been carried out, I would never have forgiven myself. Thankfully, it didn't come to that."

Alice shook her head in bewilderment, impressed that he had come to tell her his story but angry at his part in it. It seemed to her that Military

Manual was a device for relieving everyone of the responsibilities for their actions. Its imperatives could lead them anywhere. That was why it was so important to defy its power and influence, why Robert had been right to resist all compromise in the matter of conscription.

She said, "Even if they were deemed to have enlisted under the terms of the Act, the authorities had no right to ship them to the front. That was just a clumsy attempt to intimidate anyone thinking of going down the same road."

"I hadn't really thought about it like that."

She said eagerly. "So have you changed your views? Are you sympathetic to our cause?"

The least remarkable thing was a man in uniform. The world was awash with khaki. It swirled around the railway stations, parks and squares; it filled the cafes, clubs and restaurants to overflowing, until it seemed that every man in London was destined for the front. Yet, it was the first time that a man in uniform had ever ventured into her office. The NCF was dedicated to keeping men out of uniform, to opposing conscription in all its forms.

He said, "I'm here because of Robert, because I was impressed by his courage and his demeanour, because he was prepared to die for what he believed in. I didn't care for the others greatly. I found them blinkered and selfish but I felt he was doing what he did with his eyes open, because he felt it was the right thing to do. Don't understand me," he added hastily, when he saw her look of appreciation. "I don't share Robert's views. I chose to be a soldier and will always do my duty, whatever my misgivings about the war. But it's no small matter to risk your life for your beliefs, whatever they are. It would have been easy to recant, to agree to some compromise. I suppose I'm paying my respects by coming here, not just to Robert, but to everyone who was with him in France. Those conscientious objectors were a rum lot - no doubt about that - but they were brave and didn't deserve to die. It seems a long time ago now...but it's been on my mind. I tried not to think about it too much," he glanced down at his leg and gave it an exploratory rub, "but when I was wounded and had time on my hands, I thought I might try to make amends. When I heard about you, I decided I would tell you what happened. I thought it might do some good."

"That's remarkably generous of you. We don't see many soldiers here. Supporting conscientious objectors is not a popular pastime."

"No, I don't suppose it is. Mind you, I don't get it, if I'm honest, - conscientious objection. I can't understand why anyone who wasn't a shirker wouldn't want to fight for King and Country. But that's not the issue. Robert felt very strongly about conscription – to the point of being prepared to die for his beliefs. People like that shouldn't be required to enlist. They're not going to fight. It would be far better to find something useful for them to do, something far from the front."

"I couldn't agree more."

"The death sentence was commuted to ten year's hard labour, wasn't it? That's what they said at the parade."

"It was reduced to one hundred and twelve days."

"So he's a free man?"

"He was released - it's happened twice now - each time he refuses to do anything and ends up in prison again. When he returns to prison, he's placed in solitary confinement, on bread and water for thirty days, before he receives any privileges. It's two months before he's allowed any visitors, any correspondence in or out, anything to read or even the right to work in association.

"So why doesn't he cooperate in some degree? There's lots of useful civilian work that he can do. What's wrong with that?"

"He won't do anything that involves conscription. He feels very strongly about it after what happened in France. He thinks he should be free to decide for himself how best to serve his country."

"I draw the line there. Everybody has to aid the war effort in some way. Otherwise we couldn't fight. Then, where would we be? The Germans would walk all over us. We'd lose our freedom and our self-respect. That makes no sense at all."

"He wants to help mitigate the effects of the war."

The Captain looked at her suspiciously. She was a forceful and articulate woman, no doubt about it; he doubted he'd get the better of her, not when any arguments he might put up had been refuted by her kind in courts and tribunals the length of the land. He recalled the carnage he had witnessed; the comrades he had lost. He loathed everything about the war. How could he not after everything he'd seen? But he hadn't come to the NCF to voice his distaste for the conflict or to offer his support for the absolutists but rather to tell her that their efforts were in vain. Officers like him and the soldiers they led were committed to the war, regardless of its cost. They felt they had no choice but to go on with it for as long as was necessary.

He sat down in a chair facing her, his legs stretched out in front of him. His black hair was parted neatly; a moustache bisected his face. His eyes were unblinking as they gazed at her face, and his arms, folded over his chest, spoke of his determination to represent his views. But as he began to speak again, there was a tread of feet on the stairs. The door of the office burst open and a young woman with a shopping bag in each hand said brightly, "I've been to the grocers…"

"Oh," she added, observing the captain, "I didn't know we had visitors." She waited uncertainly until Alice said, "Betty, this is Captain…"she turned to him apologetically, "I'm sorry I don't know your name."

"Captain Malcolm Fielding: Thirteenth Battalion, The Rifle Brigade."

The Captain rose from his chair and inclining his head towards Betty, extended his hand in greeting to Alice.

"Captain Fielding attended Robert's court martial," Alice said, "he was just telling me all about it." Her voice, lilting in a manner that he relished, was calm but he couldn't help but notice that she was blushing slightly, uncomfortable to be found alone in his presence.

"Oh, then I'll let you get on," said Betty, feeling that she was intruding, "but I must put these things in the cupboard. I've had a good morning with the groceries but it's becoming quite difficult to find what we need."

"Let me help you with those," Malcolm said, rising from his chair.

"Don't worry about them," Betty said, with a fling of her head. "I've got them this far."

She started forward. The door downstairs slammed. More feet could be heard on the stairs. Several people ascended, chattering amongst themselves.

"I'm keeping you from your work," Malcolm said, "but I've more to say, if you care to hear it?"

"I miss Robert terribly. All I have are the fragments that he's managed to tell me in prison and the short letters he's allowed to write home."

"It was only one short meeting – that, and a parade afterwards."

Drawn to her quiet dignity, the sadness in her eyes, he gazed at her fondly. Hers was an attitude he had encountered often since his return. A robust, cheerfulness, determined optimism, masking feelings of uncertainty together with a barely-concealed anxiety for loved ones exposed to danger. At least Robert was safe; he wasn't in the line. He was in some draughty prison cell, half-starved and bored beyond belief, no doubt, but better that than the dangers others faced in France.

She said, "I'll come down with you and see you out."

They threaded their way between the desks. Betty watched from the door of the kitchen, convinced that she was witnessing more than a discussion of Robert's circumstances. What a handsome man, she thought, so tall and straight. Just what Alice needed to free her from her concerns. She only hoped her seriousness wouldn't scare him off.

They squeezed past other women on the narrow stairs on their way up to the office; they stared openly at Malcolm as he paused to let them past.

"An inquisitive lot, aren't they?" he said when they reached the street.

The road was thronged with traffic and pedestrians on their way to work. The front and the home front. Different, separate worlds, each untouched by the other, until you looked behind the scenes, asked people how they felt, heard their concerns and realised that the two were held fast by ties of flesh and blood and that everyone was carrying on as best they could because nothing else made sense.

"We don't see many soldiers here," Alice said, a smile on her face.

The observation made them conspirators. Though she had known this enigmatic officer only briefly, she was strangely drawn to him, believing there was a link between them that went beyond her brother. She felt sure that he would suggest that they meet again and knew that after a show of reluctance she would agree to his request. Their rendezvous would take place the next day or soon afterwards as was the way when time was short and not to be wasted and no one knew how long they had.

Before they parted, their arrangements made, she said, "How long will it be before you go back?"

"I don't know. I'll go back whenever the War Office Board decides that I'm fit for duty. I've no idea when that will be."

He spoke regretfully, suggesting that the front was his home. He was not the first soldier Alice had encountered who was uncomfortable out of the line. It must be strange, life in all its ordinariness going on around them, trundling along, everyone trying to make the best of things.

She watched him limp down the street, one leg striding out, and the other trailing behind him. Something had also happened to his arm, one arm swung out briskly whilst the other hung loosely by his side. She concluded that it would be some time before he went back to his battalion and the idea pleased her, stranger though he was.

CHAPTER 19

Robert's new sentence began like his last. A lorry deposited him before the prison's iron gate, adjacent to the long, grey porch and narrow, stone-framed windows of the gatehouse, leaving him to make his way across the yard beneath the watchful eye of the receiving officer. It felt strange to be delivered and signed for like a parcel. He sat resignedly on a low, wooden bench whilst a warden recorded his particulars into the body receiving book, peering myopically at the half-filled page, tongue protruding from between his teeth as he copied Robert's details from the invoice.

"Defence of the Realm, eh?" he said, looking at Robert with stern disapproval. "Nice how do you do, that is, when there's a war on."

Robert said nothing, buffeted and fatigued as he was by the journey. It was all he could do to answer the questions put to him.

When the set of entries was complete, the warder stood back from his desk and blotted the open page with elaborate care. "Now when I call your name," he said loudly, as if Robert was hard of hearing, "You stand up, say what your occupation is, what your sentence is, what your religion is and how much money you came in with."

Robert had ceased to resent foolish orders and instructions. Obeying them was easier than argument or blunt defiance. He no longer marvelled at stupidity or pondered on its origins, focusing on those aspects of his life that preserved his thoughts from unwanted intrusion. He supplied his details unthinkingly, waiting patiently while the officer recorded his replies.

"There," the warder said, "that's you sorted. You're here."

He led Robert into a long room with small cells on either side of a narrow passage. Hot water pipes lined the ceiling, their paint flaking. Two men sat behind separate desks at the end of the room, talking quietly. They ignored the visitors until they were standing in front of them. Robert's escort left abruptly, leaving his papers on the desk. They lay untouched for several minutes until one of the warders picked them up and began to scan them with interest. His scrutiny gave way to a token grimace of welcome. The other reached for the ledger that lay upon his desk. Together, they began an inventory of everything that Robert wore and carried, ignoring the information compiled previously. One of them whistled tunelessly, pausing intermittently to glance Robert's way. His companion frowned at these signs of recognition. If Robert had hoped for a brief exchange of pleasantries, some awareness that there was more to him than a few columns of dry facts and a cluster of belongings, he was disappointed. He was weighed and measured. He stripped as ordered and plunged into a bath of tepid water. When he emerged his prison clothes awaited him: a green flannelette vest with matching pants, a white cotton shirt, socks, a grey, cloth suit and a jacket decorated with broad arrows. Directed to a small reception cell, he waited for the prison doctor to confirm his fitness for hard labour. He sank on the unmade bed, arms folded behind his head, feet dangling and lay there undisturbed until the doctor came.

The doctor was short with greying, bushy hair that hung about his ears. The eyes that peered out from behind his thick-rimmed glasses lacked sympathy or humour. Robert stood upright whilst he took his pulse, peered down his throat and tapped his chest. He asked several questions in quick succession, barely waiting on Robert's answers.

"You've got itch but otherwise you'll do," he said after several minutes' scrutiny. He picked up his unopened bag and retreated from the cell, offering no solution for Robert's malady. Later, when they brought him a tin of porridge and piece of thick, dry bread, Robert seized them eagerly. He crossed into the hall of the main prison the next day, testing his impressions against the experience of his previous sentence. He was reminded of his first day at boarding school, when everything had seemed so large, cold and forbidding. Doors were locked and unlocked; the landings echoed with the sound of footsteps. He listened vainly for voices as he passed the prisoners toiling at their mailbags. Some worked with lowered heads, their needles twisting awkwardly; a few looked up with interest but no one uttered a word of greeting or gave him a friendly smile. That night, prompted by the thought of the unopened letters that awaited him at home, he began the first of many fractured dialogues with Mary, his former student, and relived the events that had conspired to bring him home.

~

She always sat in the front row of the lecture theatre, directly in his line of vision, so that he couldn't fail to notice her, alert and attentive, pen in hand, transcribing every word he uttered. She was a striking girl, with a pretty face and good colour, conspicuous amongst the sea of faces that looked down on him from the tiered rows, auburn hair falling across her shoulders or tied up in a bun, exposing her slender neck, high cheek bones and soft, green eyes. When she wasn't writing or shuffling her notes, she gazed at him fiercely, hands folded neatly on the desk, her eyes following his. If he hesitated, seeking a place in his notes or searching for a turn of phrase to illustrate a point, she looked up expectantly, waiting on his words. She never huddled with friends or broke off from animated conversations when he entered the room like so many of his students and rarely smiled, save to acknowledge the modest jokes with which he punctuated his lectures. If anyone around her spoke when he was speaking, she would frown, a small gesture of annoyance that he grew to appreciate. Her attention rarely strayed. She never assumed the vacant look of so many of his students when he spoke for too long. He anticipated her diligence and was comforted to find her in her usual place. He missed her when she was ill and speculated about what she did outside the classroom, believing her alone like him. He came to know her better when she attended his seminars. She rarely spoke without prompting and her words were hesitant, involving frequent glances at her companions, but when she was persuaded to speak, she talked sensibly and showed evidence of thoughtfulness. Her work was a faithful replication of his lecture notes: the same evidence, the same sources, the same arguments, with little of her views. When he asked for her opinion in tutorials, there was little response. He was not surprised by her reticence. Many of his students lacked views of their own but she was arguably the worst offender, the one who replicated his arguments and texts most faithfully, the one most likely to keep her thoughts to herself. Her predictability disappointed him. He wanted her to do well, to flourish as a result of his teaching, but she offered nothing beyond her rapt attention and her ability to record and represent faithfully all that he said. He had dismissed her as a run-of-the-mill student when she surprised him with a piece of work of great quality, an essay that made him believe that she had been biding her time, awaiting her moment to evidence her worth.

"This is all your own work?" he asked, when he discussed her essay with her. "Oh, yes," she replied, her eyes widening in surprise. "I worked very hard on it. The subject interested me greatly." "It certainly did," he replied, believing her readily, because he wanted her to succeed and welcomed any work that was outstanding. He was especially pleased because he had thought that she was struggling to keep up and had been wondering how best to help her. When he asked, "Would you mind if I showed this to the others?" her eyes filled with alarm. She said she didn't want any prominence and he agreed to say nothing. She left his office nursing her paper, pleased with her distinction.

Once her efforts had caught his eye, he paid her more attention and she responded well to his encouragement. She became bolder, more forthcoming in her seminars and tutorials. He delighted in hearing her voice, the cadences it contained, as she presented her work. She spoke up in class when he struggled to engineer a debate amongst students who preferred to remain silent. It seemed that all she required was time to prepare herself, to know in advance what was expected of her, in order to find her way to the truth. It was an approach that he appreciated. It seemed to mirror the care and diligence that he always brought to his work.

One day, she appeared unexpectedly at the door of his office. It was a fine autumn day. The sun was bright, the chill in the air hinted at the winter to come and the wind had prevailed on the leaves on the grass to dance to its tune. He had put the day aside to complete the paper he intended to publish, but had made little progress

"Am I interrupting you?" she asked as she stepped into his office, her books beneath her arm.

"No, not at all," he responded, "I was about to go out for walk."

"I would offer to come with you," she said, surprising him with her boldness, "but I'm not sure it would be proper for us to be seen together."

"No, I don't suppose it would. Is there something that I can help you with? Is that why you came to see me?"

"I'm struggling with the work you gave us and would welcome your advice."

They spoke about her paper but their hearts weren't in it. They began to speak about themselves, their backgrounds and their lives at the college. Both of them were lonely in their different ways. Robert's academic life was full and challenging but there was no one he was close to, no one to whom he could reveal his unease about what was happening in England, his guilt at being away, the extent to which he missed his family and friends. She confessed she was shy and found it difficult to meet others, that there were eager young men in abundance but few whom she found interesting and none who had captured her heart.

Thereafter, they sought out each other at every opportunity, respecting the formality that was appropriate between teacher and student but finding excuses to meet and talk, even if it were only a fleeting exchange in a crowded corridor or adjacent desks in the library that facilitated whispered asides. Her work impressed him with its originality, her subject knowledge and her desire to improve. He told her that she would gain an exemplary degree and encouraged her to think about research and teaching, perhaps with a view to mirroring his progress. He noted that she was not drawn to the idea, meeting it with a sad smile, as if such ambitions were beyond her. The difference in their ages rarely troubled them. He regarded her as his disciple. Where he led, she followed, seemingly content to have him set the agenda, providing always that she had his attention, that his affection for her was clear. As they grew to know each other better, they contrived to meet alone, away from the campus, where no one was likely to recognise them. He was struck by the strength of her moods but thought nothing of it. Sometimes, when they met, she was full of life, exuberant, almost boisterous, inclined to tease and provoke him. Then he basked in her smile, delighting in making her laugh and never tired of studying her demeanour, noting every change in her expression. At other times, she was despondent, insisting her work was poor, complaining about her family, convinced that he would go back to England and that she would be left on her own. If he prompted her to mix with her contemporaries, to join the clubs and societies that would introduce her to others, she claimed that he was trying to get rid of her and insisted that she would not be prised loose. When she was sure they were alone, she would take his arm as they walked down the street and would encourage him to kiss and to hold her. At first, he was reticent, believing that his obligations as her teacher outweighed his affection towards her, but his resistance soon crumbled and, he held her tightly, whenever they were unobserved and she delighted in his embrace. He began to take care over his appearance, casting aside his old suits and sweaters, the ones that the moths had feasted upon and that he had worn for so long, buying whatever she selected and proudly wearing her choices.

Once, in his study, she rushed into his arms, whispering endearments. When he urged her to step back from the window and hurriedly closed the door, she cried, "You're going to leave me, I know you are. You want to go back to England. You've heard from your sister again. It's written all over your face." He informed her that his family had advised him not to go back but at such times she was inconsolable and nothing he said or promised arrested her fears. It was true: he had an increasing urge to return to England but when he held her in his arms, he thought only of her presence.

It became clear to him after several months that the future that he had envisaged, whereby they kept their distance until her studies were over, was proving impossible. Their need for each other was too great, patience and prudence too hard to bear. When his course changed, there was a precipitate decline in her work. She failed to turn up for several of his lectures. She became indiscreet about their relationship, making no effort to conceal their contact or to consider the complications to which it might give rise. It became clear that she dreaded the examinations that would determine her future. In vain he assured her that she had little to worry about but, unconvinced, she began to demand hints as to what the papers might contain and asked for guidance in respect of her revision. "Stop worrying," he told her, as she continued to bother him, "it's going to be alright. You know I can't tell you what the questions are likely to be."

He might never have discovered that she was a plagiarist had a colleague not mentioned a student who had excelled in his history degree before going to Yale to undertake postgraduate work. She gave him an essay to read and as soon as he started to read it, he realised he had read it before. When he compared it with what Mary had written on the same topic, there were few differences. Certain sentences had been changed, often clumsily; some paragraphs had been reordered so that the arguments were less striking but substantially the submissions were the same. There could be little doubt that Mary had copied her essays and that only her early, hesitant submissions had been her own work. He acquired further papers from the same student. His conclusions were similar. Mary had changed each paper marginally but otherwise the work had been copied.

Meanwhile, their relationship had spilled over from a friendship between teacher and student to that of lovers. It had been her suggestion that they go away for the New Year, though he needed little persuading. The campus was deserted, staff and students alike having retreated to their families, leaving only a skeleton staff and a few expatriates in place. He had resolved, without enthusiasm, to spend the holiday in the library, engaged on his research. He had also intended to make up his mind about whether he would stay on in response to the Principal's pleas or whether he would give notice of his intended return to England. As it was, his anticipated isolation gave way to three wind-swept days on the Atlantic coast with Mary: hours of bracing walks along deserted beaches, dinners by the hotel fireside amid flickering candles and nights of passion in a large four-poster bed with curtains around it. His most earnest wish was that it would never end.

When he broached with Mary the subject of her plagiarism and its likely consequences, he quickly realised that he had led himself into a trap. She regarded their time away together and all that it had entailed as her guarantee that he would ensure that she would pass her exams and that her plagiarism would go undisclosed. She expected him to give her the examination questions or to coach her in her responses and to conceal the fact that her previous work had not been her own. Her last essay, all her own work, made it clear to him, that without his connivance, she was unlikely to meet the standard required. He doubted she had set out to compromise him, he didn't see her as wicked or crafty, but it was where the logic of their behaviour had taken them and now she expected him to support her deceit.

He said, "I really have no choice but to report everything you've done to the Dean." When she had pleaded with him and found him unmoved, she asked, "Will you tell him about our relationship, our time together, the encounters in your study, the long walks, our New Year by the shore, because I'll tell him everything if my survival requires it."

It never occurred to him, after her clumsy attempt at blackmail, that he might accede to her wishes. He knew he had behaved unwisely and felt he had no choice but to own up to it. He decided to speak to the Dean immediately, to lay the facts before him and to tender the resignation he would surely require of him. It never occurred to him that there could be any other outcome when the facts were known. He avoided Mary, hoping his resignation would spare her the humiliation of an enquiry into their conduct. She made little effort to seek him out. Her seat in the lecture theatre was unoccupied; she submitted no further work and her name was absent from the pass list that went up on the notice board at the end of term, several days after he had left for England.

CHAPTER 20

Alice felt uneasy about losing all restraint over someone whom she hardly knew. It was a far cry from the Quaker circles in which everyone knew everybody else, moved seamlessly between each others' homes, worked in the same businesses and attended the same Meeting Houses. "I know his mother," Louise would say on being introduced to someone or, "Robert was at school with his brother." Bennett also drew on his network of Quaker acquaintances to offer advice. Though they were rarely critical, her parents' observations made her feel that everyone she introduced to them was lacking in some way. Malcolm was an unknown quantity, which was welcome, but it also made him dangerous. It wasn't like her to lose her head easily, she told herself, as she picked over his every word, searching for signs of affection. Now, as she hurried along the street, tugging at her skirt, adjusting her hat, she hoped her lateness would not deprive her of his company, knowing that if his patience failed him, she had no means of finding him again.

She found him on the steps of the Albert Memorial, their rendezvous, a restless, troubled figure, peering anxiously about him. His impatience pleased her, giving her confidence. He extended his arms in greeting, a broad smile on his face. He seemed shorter and fairer in the crowd than he had in the cramped room of the NCF but he was still several inches taller than her and his solidity contrasted with her slightness. His face, no longer youthful, had a maturity than suggested he was older than her brother. One of his cheeks was scarred. She had barely noticed it at first, a thin, faint crimson line that started below the eye and ended above his moustache. When he stroked it with his index finger as if it was newly acquired, she supposed it to be a legacy of the war. One hand hung by his side; the other shielded his eyes. He rushed towards her when he saw her and said, "I thought you weren't coming."

Finding no hint of reprimand in his greeting, Alice stifled her explanations, kissed him lightly and linked her arm with his. They set off down the path that crossed the park, eager to put the crowds behind them in favour of a quieter place. They walked through the park, paying no attention to those around them or caring where they went. Malcolm strode out briskly, Alice skipping periodically to keep up, until his pace slowed and he began to limp.

"Are you all right? Would you like to rest?"

She steered him towards a bench, intending to sit with him until he recovered, but he resisted her efforts saying, "No, I have to do it. The doctors insist on it. I have to exercise every day if I'm to have any hope of going back."

"Well, rest for a while," Alice insisted, tugging on his arm, "and then we'll carry on."

They had made no plans and had no destination in mind. The sun had brought them out, as it had the whole city. Malcolm said walking in the park had become his passion. He told her how much he enjoyed the freedom to stand upright after the cramped conditions of the trenches, and the ability to stride out, free of the mud that, during the worst of the rains, had made every step a labour.

They walked from Kensington to Marble Arch. It was the weekend and the crowds were out. Young women clung to soldiers' hands or paraded arm in arm. Children shepherded by nannies, parents or siblings raced between the trees. By the Serpentine a band was playing vigorously, not the military airs typical of the early months of the war but sprightly music hall tunes, one after the other in quick succession. Women moved among the onlookers, shaking tins beneath their noses, competing without shame for contributions to their causes. On the placid waters of the lake, boats jostled each other, filled to overflowing, spilling arms and legs over the side as oars rose and fell, whilst onlookers queued patiently to occupy the vacant craft. Faces tilted at the sunshine, tall, pale flowers seeking the light. The scene reminded Alice of another weekend when the sun had shone brightly and the parks had been filled to overflowing. Then, there hadn't been a uniform in sight or any talk of war and the man whose arm she had taken on that day had not been a soldier but one of the solid professionals of whom her parents approved.

"What did the doctor say?" she asked when they stopped to rest again, knowing that earlier he'd had an appointment in Harley Street. He claimed that he had been looking forward to it, hoping for good news. His silence on the subject suggested that the tidings had not been entirely to his liking.

"He was non-committal about when I'd become General Service again. I'm not much further on."

"Do you mind not knowing when you're going to go back?"

"I hate the uncertainty. I just want a date, something I can work towards. If I knew when it was going to be, I could relax, enjoy the respite. As it is, I feel on edge, like I used to do in the line when word came down that there might be a strafe."

"Why are you in such a hurry to go back?"

"I don't want to go back – not since I've met you – but nor do I feel I belong here."

"I can understand that," Alice said, waving vaguely at the happy, boisterous crowds. "This must seem very strange when you've just come out of the line."

He looked at her suspiciously, hoping that she was not going to destroy the happiness afforded by her presence with some ill-timed broadside against the war.

He said, "Well, good luck to them. Let them enjoy themselves. Why not? The war's made every minute precious."

He pointed to a soldier, laughing loudly, swaying, his arm around two girls who were giggling, attempting to break free.

"He's probably going out tomorrow. Maybe, this is his last day with his friends? They might never see each other again. Who knows? What's he to do but grasp the moment? Nothing else makes sense."

"That's always my fear," Alice said, "that I'll get to the end of my life and feel that I haven't done enough with it."

"Isn't that what everybody feels when the time comes?"

He thought of the deaths he had witnessed, the soldiers who had expired in his arms. Few of those deaths had been contemplative or timely. He recalled only the the look of horror and surprise on their faces as they fell.

"You don't resent the civilians in their reserved occupations or the civil servants in their government departments, far removed from the conflict?"

"I find it comforting that life goes on in spite of everything."

"What are you going to do after the war?"

She often asked herself the same question. Now, she had a mission but what would she do later? The war had thrown her old life into confusion but had failed to offer any guidance as to what might follow.

"I don't know. Go back to being a barrister, as if nothing's changed? That's not going to work. I'm thirty four in a month's time and feel my life is over, that everything significant has happened already."

"Your old life will be waiting for you."

"It won't be as I left it, though. The war has changed my outlook, as it has for everyone. Look at women of your age. A million of you doing men's jobs, jobs no one thought you capable of doing. Do you think you'll give all that up, go back to the old ways when you've had money of your own to spend and enjoyed the freedom brought on by the war? What'll happen to men who have seen and experienced things that they could scarcely imagine? Will they slip back into their old ways? That'll be impossible for me, and I won't be alone. I'll miss the men for whom I was responsible, who looked to me for leadership, and wonder what became of them."

"You'll get back to them soon enough," Alice said, wincing at his desire to leave her even as they grew to know each other.

"I might be posted to another unit or go back to my old battalion and find it full of strangers."

"People forget each other more easily than you think."

"That's rather cynical, isn't it?"

"I'm usually a hopeless optimist. My mother speaks of my relentless, good cheer as if it were a disease."

She considered her mother's words for a moment and said, "It makes me sound rather naïve and foolish, doesn't it? But I try to see the best in everybody and to make the most of things. That's important, isn't it, especially now, when everything's so awful?"

"It's vital in the line, especially for an officer. He sets the tone. He has little choice but to remain optimistic, to believe that things'll improve. It's a good thing too. The effort to appear strong and decisive helps make us so."

"People will forget what the war was like. I don't mean that they'll be ungrateful or cease to honour the casualties but our lives have a momentum that compels us to get over things. That's what'll happen after the war. People'll adjust to the loss and be grateful for the improvement in their fortunes."

Malcolm gazed at her fondly. He often looked at her in silence, saying little or nothing, taking her hand or touching her arm, his eyes searching her face, as if in pursuit of her feelings. Now she returned his gaze without embarrassment, flattered to be the target of his admiration.

"I won't be going back to what I did before. That much is certain. For better or worse, the war has changed me. I'm a different person from when I enlisted. I've lived in the war's shadow for a long time and won't easily be free of it."

"What'll you do? Relive your battles like some retired general? Lament your fallen comrades and seek to conjure up their presence? There are many possibilities but few I'd recommend."

"I'll travel to some far-flung corner of the world: South Africa, Australia, New Zealand – it doesn't matter where. Somewhere far from Europe, that has a future, untainted by war.

"You're forgetting it's a world war. Few places haven't been touched by it."

He laughed at his conjectures, shaking his head.

"You do this to me. You ask questions which I can't answer. The war might go on indefinitely or I won't survive it. The future isn't under our control."

"The war'll end when the opposing armies sink exhausted to the ground. Then, the Government will declare a momentous victory. Every general will receive a stipend and write his memoirs and every town and village will build a monument to its 'glorious dead'."

Malcolm watched three girls stroll by. Young and pretty, they were full of themselves, parading in their new clothes. They wore skirts revealing ankle and calf, gaudy Paris hats. One of them acknowledged his admiration with an imperceptible nod of the head. Alice watched without resentment, neither moved nor jealous. She was surprised to find herself the object of attention. She only wished she had a taste for striking clothes, for brassieres and lipstick. Other, worldlier girls, made her feel dull and staid. The poor were growing richer whilst the prosperous grew shabby.

"Look around you," she said, as they neared the edge of the park, within sight of Oxford Street and Edgware Road. "What do you see?"

"People enjoying themselves; soldiers, on leave, spending a day with their families. Tomorrow, it'll be business as usual. The men will go back, the women will return to the factories and the bus stations and those in reserved occupations will go back to doing whatever it is they do whilst we fight their war."

He stopped and looked about him as though he had lost his way. He was back at the front, poised on the fire step, a whistle to his lips. Dawn was stealing across the untenanted land. The guns had lifted, shrapnel, high explosive, mortars having rained down on the enemy, delivered by a line of guns, axle to axle, of every shape and size. They had been promised that nothing would withstand the barrage, that the wire would be cut, the trenches destroyed, the machine guns silenced and had believed the persistent voices that had urged them on. A line of soldiers waited nervously; beneath the shadow of their helmets, their faces anxious, they watched each other closely. He wondered why anyone obeyed his orders, why they braved the shells, the machine gun fire and the wire. Platoon, company, battalion, division, they always responded, not because of the fate that awaited the reluctant or an implacable hatred of the enemy but because they relied on each other. He would miss the loyalty, the spirit of sacrifice, the mutual respect. It was incomprehensible to those who hadn't experienced it. When the war was long forgotten, the spirit of the trenches would dominate his consciousness.

Alice said, "I want to help you forget, not for ever, but for now, whilst you're with me. I want to dominate your thoughts. When you go back, I want to be your fondest memory and, when you return, I'll be your bridge to civilian life."

She blushed, taken aback by her own boldness.

He slipped his arm around her waist, pulled her to him tightly and said, "I'd like that very much," and kissed her on the lips.

She was conscious of the fabric of her dress against the belt and buckles of his uniform, the hide of his brightly polished boot against her calf. She had never kissed anyone in public before. She gave no thought to fighting the wave of affection that overcame her or to resisting its persistent tug. She was happy to be borne aloft, free of all restraint. It had been a long time since she had loved anyone and now she had found someone to care about, she gave no thought to restraint.

Their intimacy subsided when they left the park. Malcolm, limping badly, clutched at Alice's arm. She wondered where to take him for tea. She wanted to demonstrate that she was an independent woman, with means of her own. She decided on the Maison Lyon, a five story restaurant at Marble Arch, one of her mother's favourites. They passed through the ground floor food hall with its hams, cakes, fruits, hand-made chocolates, wines and cheeses. No sign of war-time shortages there. There was food from every corner of the Empire, even ample bread, though the Government was attempting to ration it. The restaurant on the third floor, its tables stretching in every direction was crowded, full of parties eating and drinking heartily. With the help of an elderly waiter, they found a table. His hand shook as he took their order. The war had given his career a new lease of life.

Seated at their table, waiting on their order, Alice said, "Do you always wear your uniform?" and ran her finger lightly down his tunic, tracing the insignia, the folds and creases of the cloth as the waiter bustled round them, unfolding napkins with a flourish, aligning knives, forks and spoons on the table cloth.

"You're not embarrassed at being seen with me, are you?"

Malcolm's tone betrayed a quiet anxiety, a degree of doubt she found surprising. He didn't know what to make of her stance against the war or what it meant for them.

"Go on; admit it. You're afraid you'll meet someone you know."

"That's more than likely."

Alice had already seen somebody she knew. There were no doubt others present whom she would recognise. Her family had the relationship with tea that the nation had with alcohol. Every day was punctuated by the same ritual of tea, sandwiches and cakes wherever they happened to be.

"No, I'm not embarrassed by your uniform," she said, knowing other women welcomed their liberating presence. They enabled them to thrust aside the manners and conventions of the times. For her, it was a signal that she and others of like mind swam against the tide.

"What matters is the person – not the clothes he's wearing. We're not bigots because we oppose the war. Nor are we unappreciative of the sacrifices that others are making."

"I never thought it would last so long."

"Nor did Robert. His path isn't an easy one. I know his life isn't in danger but his road's hard to travel. Hard labour is well-named: solitary confinement, punishment diet, lack of exercise, the rule of silence, all exact a heavy toll. For those in and out of prison, like Robert, it's especially hard."

"I'd like to meet him again,"

"To make amends?"

"We wouldn't agree about the war but we'd have other things in common."

Alice began to talk about Robert. Malcolm listened carefully, noting the admiration with which Alice spoke of him. The light in her eyes, the proud smile when she said his name and her obvious affection for him made him jealous of the life that they had shared.

He said, "I knew a chap like him at school. A splendid chap in many ways; an athlete, very bright. He won a scholarship to Oxford but didn't get anywhere. The problem was he didn't fit in. He was against everything. Some chaps are like that, aren't they? There's nothing wrong with it. It takes all sorts to make a world. But they pay a price for their stubbornness."

"Everybody's very fond of Robert. He's only different from everyone else in so far as he refuses to be conscripted."

The table next to them was boisterous: an extended family, jousting noisily. They erupted periodically at a joke well-told. A plump, florid man, at the head of the table watched everyone around him with benign satisfaction. Not a young man, by any means, thought Malcolm, but still young enough to enlist. His demeanour suggested he had done well from the war. What compelled some men to fight whilst others stood aside? He had always felt that he had no choice and, even now, knowing of the war's excesses, he would do the same again.

He said, "I don't understand why the army persists in persecuting men like Robert. If a man doesn't want to fight for his country, he'll be no good in the line. Mind you, there are other things that he could do, short of fighting, if he cared to," he added, without enthusiasm.

"Why can't people respect Robert for his viewpoint, for his genuinely held conviction? I don't understand why the authorities can't treat him fairly."

"Fairly?"

Malcolm repeated the word with an air of incredulity. He spoke more loudly than he meant to, attracting the attention of the couple opposite.

"Whatever he believes in, he won't find fairness anywhere. There isn't any fairness now. What's fair about shells that blow men to smithereens and leave their companions unscathed? What's fair about machine gun rounds that mow down whole platoons without discrimination? Robert's entitled to act according to his beliefs. Of course he is. I support that absolutely. But he must expect to suffer for it. Suffering is the war's gift to those who care."

His eyes were drawn again to the adjacent table, to the man presiding over the unruly party there. There was no sign that the war had torn his life apart. He seemed immune to everything going on elsewhere. Didn't that make his point? Life's rewards were distributed randomly. He hadn't thought like that before the war, assuming there was a sort of rough justice whereby the cleverest and most industrious were successful and the impoverished were the victims of their fecklessness. Now, after two years in the line he appreciated the randomness of good fortune. He wondered if he was becoming a socialist, and whether, in the absence of divine intervention, mankind's only hope was to help one another.

Alice wanted to meet his gaze, to ask him to forgive her thoughtlessness, but couldn't find the words. Her fears for Robert's safety blinded her at times. How many of those who had rushed forward unthinkingly at the start of the war were now trapped by its demands? It was the familiar dilemma: the argument against Robert's stance that she could never refute. What right had objectors to complain about their woes when others suffered more? Fearing that they were on a collision course, she rushed to make amends.

"Would you like to visit our home in Barnes? Robert won't be there, of course, nor Michael. But my parents would be pleased to see you. They are always keen to meet my friends."

He offered her a cigarette before replying, producing a silver lighter from his pocket that produced a flame after several flicks of his thumb. When their cigarettes were lit, he sat back in his chair, inhaling deeply.

He never smoked in the trenches, believing in the cautionary tales about smoking, but out of the line he delighted in the Turkish cigarettes it was possible to obtain if you knew where to look. Alice puffed nervously on hers, stifling a desire to cough. She disliked cigarettes. They made her head spin but she hadn't wanted to refuse.

He said, "Are you sure that's a good idea? I wouldn't want to disconcert them by my presence."

Alice smiled mischievously. Did he think that they were precious? They might be ignorant of the war's true nature but no more so than other families. No, if she had any reservations, they were of a different kind. Her parents would see in Malcolm's presence a change of sides, a new commitment on her part.

She said, "They're nothing if not open-minded. But, if you think that it's too soon for that, I'd understand…we haven't known each other for long."

"No, I'd be delighted to meet them," Malcolm said, his ready answer belying his misgivings.

Concealing her elation, she said, "I'll organise it right away."

CHAPTER 21

Malcolm's visit coincided with the first daylight bombing raid on London by German aircraft. Sweeping in from the east, conspicuous amidst a clear blue sky, they targeted the unprotected streets. The East End bore the brunt of the attack and though the big guns in Hyde Park coughed defiantly, they failed to protect a civilian population taken unawares. The explosions were audible in Barnes. People gathered in the streets to find out what was going on, their curiosity overcoming any concerns they might have for their safety. "Come back inside," Bennett urged, even as he leaned precariously from a bedroom window, clutching a telescope and pointing at the sky, but the planes were barely visible and the onlookers ignored him in favour of animated conversations about what was going on. Later, when they saw photographs of the damage and learnt of the direct hit on a primary school in Poplar, they grasped the true nature of the threat they faced.

The time for Malcolm's arrival came and went. Alice walked to the station hoping to meet him but returned saying that there were few trains. The cook, their one remaining servant, stomped around the kitchen, making clear her displeasure. They decided to start without him rather than waste food at a time of growing shortages. Alice grew more anxious with every minute of his absence. Where was he? Had he changed his mind? In spite of many hours of conversation he was still a stranger. He was willing to talk about the hostilities; his frankness on the subject was a revelation, but he spoke rarely of his personal circumstances and she hadn't pressed him. It wasn't that she wasn't curious. She preferred him to volunteer the information that would enlighten her.

His belated arrival was the signal for an outburst of activity. He appeared suddenly at the front door, flushed and excited.

"I'm sorry I'm late," he declared breathlessly, as he shook the outstretched hands. "The bombing stopped the trains."

Bennett leapt to his feet, as though he had forgotten that he was coming. He looked him up and down, making no effort to conceal his scrutiny. Malcolm was older than he had anticipated, with a gravitas that impressed him. His grey eyes contained a wariness that suggested that the world was not to be trusted, even when it seemed at its most innocent. Alice noted that he appeared unperturbed by her father's inspection He was deferential to him, charming to her mother and displayed a warmth and enthusiasm towards her she felt that she could reach out and touch. She rewarded him with her most dazzling smile and touched his arm frequently. She wanted her parents to know that this was no war-time dalliance, but that the man, whom they were meeting, would feature in their lives.

Malcolm had abandoned his uniform in deference to his hosts' views. He sported a dark flannel suit with a waistcoat. His boots and puttees had given way to a pair of highly polished brogues. The effect in Alice's eyes was to make him taller, leaner and more handsome. He sat benignly in his chair, happy to be the centre of attention, whilst the preparations went on around him, before taking his place at the table, a course behind the others, addressing with relish the heaped plate of food before him.

"I hope it's all right," Louise said, as she urged him to tuck in, "eating well is such a struggle in the face of shortages."

Malcolm proceeded to clear his plate. Alice was unsurprised. She had never known him to leave a morsel. He was always hungry, no doubt a legacy of life in the trenches, though she had heard that, out of the line, the officers ate well. He was also trying to put on weight in order to please his doctors. Unconvinced, Louise continued her litany of apologies. Their last maid having recently departed for better paid work in a munitions factory, she found it difficult to cope.

Alice said, "Oh, Mother, do stop fussing."

Louise sank back into her chair, smiling ruefully. Minutes later, she was clearing away the plates. Alice joined her in the kitchen and Malcolm and Bennett were left alone.

Bennett sat at the head of the table, oblivious to the fuss going on around him, asking questions with a show of interest, determined to win Malcolm over. Alice hoped that his attentiveness was not a prelude to mischief. Her father could be so disarming. Then, when the trap was baited, the prey lured in, he would spring it, asking an unwelcome question or generating controversy. She hoped that Malcolm would decline to fall under his spell. She had no wish to share his loyalties with any other member of her family, least of all her father.

"What do you think of the bombing?" he asked when Malcolm had laid down his knife and fork. "Not what you expect, when you are travelling across London, minding your own business?"

He made no effort to conceal his outrage that civilians should be placed in such jeopardy. Moreover, he didn't see the point of it. What purpose did it serve other than to worsen the enmity that existed between two great nations?

Malcolm shared his indignation. His train had halted at Vauxhall, in sight of the station but short of its platforms. He had glimpsed the aircraft through the grimy window and heard the explosions and the faltering guns. There had been an eerie silence afterwards, as though everyone was holding their breath. A well-dressed woman in the compartment, whom he had scarcely noticed before, had thanked the soldier next to her for keeping her safe. She said nothing to Malcolm in his civilian clothes, pausing only to give him a withering glance as she left the train at Clapham Junction.

He said, "They've no right to assault our cities in this way. War's a matter for soldiers and armies. It has no business here, amongst our homes."

Bennett agreed without conviction, a vexed look upon his face. He felt Malcolm had no inkling of the profound changes that the war had prompted. The malevolent machines, high in the sky, heralded an age of total war.

"Soon no one will be safe. Then what'll become of the pacifists? Who'll make the arguments against conscription when there's no refuge for the innocent? The air raids cut the ground from beneath our feet."

Louise said, overhearing them, "What must Robert think, languishing in prison?"

She had been unusually silent over lunch, focused on providing for their guest, but she had listened to Malcolm with great care, watching him and Alice, the looks that passed between them.

Malcolm offered no opinion. The arguments for pacifism quite eluded him though he had little time for strident nationalism. He thought it best that everyone reach their own conclusions about the war.

Alice proposed that they move to the sitting room, to the armchairs and sofa clustered round the fireside, even though the roaring fire of the winter months had been reduced to a silent heap of wood and coals. She was not about to allow Bennett, brooding on the bombing, to plunge them into dark despair.

When they were seated round the fireplace, she said, "I wonder if Robert heard the bombs. Hidden away as he is, he probably heard nothing. He's only five miles away, but he could be in America for all we see of him."

"How's he getting on in prison?" Malcolm asked. He thought the question rather foolish but felt obliged to ask it. How did anyone get on in prison?

"Not well," Bennett said. "He doesn't have the temperament for prison. His mind's too lively for his own good, always has been. It makes him a formidable scholar but means he's ill-equipped to cope with the futility of prison."

"Did he know what he was getting into?"

"We told him before he left America that he might be imprisoned if he declined to enlist. But he wasn't deterred," said Bennett, his voice lifting proudly. "He felt it his duty to be back amongst us, speaking out against the war, doing what he could to help those most affected by it. Sadly, he never had the opportunity to do anything useful. He was arrested almost immediately and has been in and out of prison ever since. Such a shame," he added sadly, "to be shut away when he could have done so much."

"You must be very proud of him," Malcolm said, touched by Bennett's admiration for his son. "To come back to England when he did was no small thing."

"I was very moved by his courage. I hope he isn't in prison too long, though I'm prepared for the worst."

Alice watched her father carefully. His long face, framed by his thinning black hair, the thick-set beard, normally so solemn, often wary, was wreathed in smiles. His eyes, dark coals set deeply in their sockets, shone with pride. He had no inkling that Robert had possessed other reasons, undisclosed to anyone but her, for coming back to England - how could he when she had snatched up the letters from Pennsylvania and hidden them from view - reasons so potent that Robert had come back in spite of knowing he might have to go to prison. She thought of the letters, the bundle in her bedroom, tied neatly in a ribbon, hidden from her parents' gaze, waiting for Robert to open them. She had replied to them as promised: a brief statement of Robert's circumstances, an explanation for his silence, hoping that her note would end the correspondence. There would come a point when Robert would have to speak to his parents, revealing the reasons for his return, but for now, uneasy though it made her, she was willing to allow her father to bask in the reflected glory of his son's homecoming.

Bennett said, "Do you think the war'll go on to the bitter end?" He looked at Malcolm expectantly, as though his service gave him insights denied to others. "If we could have found our way to a truce, the country might have been spared conscription."

"I never thought it likely, did you? President Wilson's overtures have been ignored. France will never negotiate whilst Germany occupies her country and her army's undefeated and now that victory looks imminent in the east, Germany will fight in the west with a new resolve."

"If only there were some appetite in London for a negotiated solution?"

Malcolm said quite robustly, "You can't prosecute a war and negotiate with the enemy at the same time. The war will only end when one side prevails over the other."

"The conflict is stalemated and the casualties increase."

"If the Germans were inclined to negotiate," Malcolm said, recalling that he had been stranded on a train at Vauxhall whilst German bombers wheeled above the city, "they wouldn't be bombing our homes."

"The end will come quickly and in a way that no one can foresee."

Bennett spoke without optimism, resigned like the rest of the country to seeing it through. The conflict had drawn everyone into it until soldier and pacifist were all part of the same jumbled heap, struggling to survive in a world that had lost its way. It was rumoured that a big push was about to begin in the corner of Belgium where the fighting had already cost many lives.

"That's enough of that," Louise said determinedly when she returned from a further visit to the kitchen, "I'm sure Malcolm doesn't want to talk about the war."

Malcolm seemed unconcerned at the direction that the conversation had taken. He was slumped in an armchair, head resting against the cushion, looking entirely at ease.

Louise noted that he and Bennett appeared to have hit it off, no matter that they held such different views. But now she wanted to know more about the man who had captured her daughter's affections. She placed a cautionary hand on Bennett's arm and said to Malcolm, an innocent smile upon her face, "Tell us something about your family. What do they do? Where do they live? How has the war affected them?"

"Well," Malcolm said, a little nervously Louise thought, observing him closely, "I've been at the front for three years, I'm a bit out of touch with everyone."

"Even with your own family?"

Louise made no effort to conceal her surprise. Her son wrote to her each week without fail but then she was not interested in Malcolm's relationship with his parents. What she wanted to know was what other relatives he had and how Alice's prospects might be affected by them.

Malcolm answered few of her questions, preferring to ask questions of his own, suggesting a knowledge of her family she found surprising. She hadn't realised Alice had told him so much about their lives and activities. He seemed particularly interested in Michael.

Much to Louise's annoyance, Bennett did little to help her enquiries. He wanted to return to the war. How often did he have the opportunity to talk to a serving officer, to exchange ideas with someone with first-hand experience of life at the front? He was flattered by Malcolm's willingness to engage with him and thought it more than good manners. He felt he respected his views. He had grown discouraged by his political impotence. He kept himself informed; the maps and newspaper cuttings in his study were evidence of that. He prepared his speeches and articles painstakingly, seeking to persuade the dwindling audiences to his viewpoint. But what good did it do? The objector's numbers remained meagre. Conscription held sway. Were it not for Robert, he would have attended to his ministry and left politics alone.

Alice followed her mother's conversation with Malcolm with interest. She and Malcolm exchanged looks, a meeting of eyes, a faint, complicit smile. She shivered slightly after each glance, feeling that another aspect of her emotions had been laid bare. Though her feelings had led her into uncharted waters, she gave no thought to turning back. She wanted to lie in Malcolm's arms, safe in a world that she found so uncertain, her future and his linked irretrievably, all else put aside.

When her mother's questions became tiresome, she intervened, intent on rescuing him, even though she also wanted to know more about the man who had captured her heart. Her questions were not for her mother's ears. They concerned his affection for her and whether her burgeoning love for him was reciprocated.

Malcolm said that it was time for him to go. Alice offered to walk with him to the station, saying that if they left now she would get back before dark. Louise felt that aspects of his life, important to Alice, remained undisclosed. She wondered if suitors no longer bothered to win parental approval? Why should they respect their elders' wishes when they were dying in an old man's war? Alice wondered if her plan to make Malcolm a member of the family had failed. Perhaps she had misjudged his feelings? Perhaps he had too many sharp edges to fit comfortably into their ordered existence? It was a sign of her commitment to him, a public declaration of loyalty, that when he rose to leave, she hastened to his side.

Together, they mouthed the platitudes of leave-taking.

"Come and see us before you go back," Bennett said. It was the first time that any of them had mentioned his return to the front. It had been the ghost at the banquet, present but unacknowledged.

"Oh, I will," he said, speaking with an enthusiasm Alice doubted that he felt.

"We'd love you to come back," Louise insisted, "It's been such a short visit."

"I'll try my best," he said, as he backed out of the door, helping Alice on with her coat, before waving goodbye.

Louise watched them walk to the front gate. Their behaviour was circumspect: they remained apart but their hands entwined as they turned the corner, their shoulders touching. She heard their footsteps falter behind the hedge as they stopped to kiss.

"How did it go?" Malcolm asked as they walked down the road.

"Well, I thought," Alice said, with an encouraging smile. "You might have talked more about Robert though; his predicament is very much on their minds."

"His life's not in danger like Michael's."

He was tempted tell her what it was like, because these civilians with their strange notions about the war knew nothing. How could they? Their worst imaginings couldn't do justice to its enormity or conceive of its malice. He decided against it, lapsing into a thoughtful silence, knowing it wasn't fair to alarm her.

"Why were you reluctant to talk about yourself?" Alice asked as they neared the end of the road.

She had taken his arm, proud to be seen with him, hoping that they might meet a neighbour, a witness to their intimacy. She had a reputation for rarely being seen with young men. She was thought too serious to retain their interest. The way she spoke and dressed also suggested a degree of indifference. She felt that the earnest young men drawn to her looks and intelligence were too young and knew too little about the world. Malcolm was older. The war had matured him. She respected him and was disinclined to hold back.

"I've lost the art of small talk. There's little time for it in the line. You're too busy attending to the endless directives and seeing to the needs of the men."

"There's always the officers' mess."

"I'm not a regular officer. Though most of them are long gone, the traditions live on. The forced jollity makes me uncomfortable. The hierarchy intrudes. Even close friendships have to respect its demands. I'm more at home with the men. You know where you are with them. They want to have a bit of fun, a drink and a laugh and to get the job done so that they can go home to their wives."

"You need some women to fuss over you, to loosen you up a bit, make you behave properly. Women of the right kind," she added hastily, "not the ones you're likely to meet behind the lines."

He thought of the efforts to keep the men out of trouble. He never understood why they queued for sex, even when they were out of the line for only a few days and it might be their last opportunity. He found the idea uninviting. Even the private arrangements available to the officers were unattractive He wanted to rest when he was free to do so. The high jinks others preferred were not for him.

He stopped suddenly, took Alice's shoulders and held her at arms' length, his head on one side, staring into the twilight.

"What is it?"

"Can't you hear the guns?"

She thought he meant the guns in Hyde Park. Then she heard a distant boom, not one, but a whole series of them. They carried on the evening breeze, faint but unmistakeable, audible only briefly before the sounds of the village, the wind in the trees, the noise of a barking dog drove them away. She thought she might have imagined them, like the sound of the waves in a sea shell, but the severity of Malcolm's reaction confirmed that it was the sound of artillery, reminding them how little time they had before he went back.

He said, "It's getting dark, you'd better go."

"I want to see you on to the train."

Something had changed as a result of the visit. She didn't want it to end; it had given rise to an intimacy that hadn't existed before.

"You can't walk back on your own in the dark."

"Then you'll have to come with me."

"We'll sleep on the grass."

"What a lovely idea."

They walked arm in arm, as the darkness descended, cloaking them in shadow, neither of them wanting their journey to end.

They would soon spend the night together. He was sure of it. He had taken a flat in Chelsea for the duration of the war. He had wanted to invite her there ever since they had met but had held back, even though his return to the front gave him licence to throw aside the conventions, knowing she would indicate when the time was right. That was one of the things he loved about her. She was frank and honest, and could be relied upon to say what she thought. He had advised so many men returning home to their wives and fiancés against adding to the population of loved ones bringing up children alone when the odds were against them becoming dutiful parents. What did you tell a member of your battalion when he asked you his chances of surviving? Few of them heeded his words. They felt an urge to leave children behind, believing it to be an immortality of sorts.

They parted at the station, leaving Malcolm to wait for the train. They agreed they would meet again soon, that he would collect her from work.

She watched him make his way along the platform. He was moving more easily now, the limp that he had possessed when she met him and that she regarded as a part of him, no less than his dark hair, his moustache or the long fingers that had played a tattoo on the table when he was restless, had almost gone. He would appear before the War Board again soon. She didn't doubt that they would instruct him to go back. Then, when would she see him again? There was no way of knowing. The war had made the future uncertain, raising questions that no one could answer. She decided she didn't care anymore. She was determined to live for the moment. She owed it to them both. The future, the challenges it posed, could take care of itself.

It was dark when she returned to the house. The roads were deserted and the common silent but though the streets were dark, the lamps unlit, a bold moon and a sky embroidered with stars illuminated the paths. On the corner where the trees gave way to houses, a fox sat scratching itself, its hind leg in the air. It scrutinised her until, satisfied that her intentions were benign, it returned to its labours, unperturbed by her presence. She opened the gate to the front garden. It hung loosely, scraping the stones as it swung back. Closing the front door, she wondered what to do next. She was keen to know what her parents had made of Malcolm but didn't want to solicit their views. Bennett was in his study, writing a piece for the newspapers. Louise didn't appear to have left her place in the sitting room. She was upright in her customary armchair, holding aloft one of the large Victorian novels that she read habitually, but paying it scant attention. There was a vexed look on her face. When Alice sat down in the chair opposite her, she said. "You do know he's married, don't you?"

She waited a moment or two for her words to sink in before adding, "I think you might have warned me. I know it's none of my business. It would have been helpful to know, that's all."

Alice concealed her consternation, but there was a tremor in her voice and her hands were clasped tightly. She wanted to shout her denials at the top of her voice, to insist that Malcolm would never deceive her, but, respecting her mother, elected to understand better how she had come to such a view.

"Oh, I've done it now, haven't I?" Louise said, placing her book on the table beside her. "I didn't mean to alarm you. I don't have much to go on. Perhaps, I should have kept my views to myself?"

"What makes you think he's married? I didn't hear him say anything that meant he was spoken for and I was with both of you the whole time."

"Yes, I couldn't help but notice that."

Louise leaned forward, pulling her shawl around her. She wore it all the time now they were saving on coal. It frequently slipped from her shoulders. Alice had bought her a clasp to keep it in place but it hadn't helped.

"It wasn't what he said but rather what he didn't say that caught my attention."

"You certainly asked a lot of questions about his family. I thought some of them a bit pointed, if I'm honest."

"Well, exactly, and he didn't answer any of them, did he? You surely noticed that?"

"That's not true."

"He pretended to answer but divulged very little."

"That's it?" asked Alice, surprise and relief in her voice.

Her mother's assertions had struck a raw nerve. She knew little about Malcolm, in spite of their hours together, and it had been troubling her, causing her to manage her feelings carefully, as she struggled to put her doubts from her mind.

She said, "He might be intimidated by the fact that we're a Quaker household, known for campaigning against the war, whilst he's the opposite - an army captain, wounded in action, soon to return to the front."

"He's a barrister, isn't he? Not a profession I would associate with the shy and retiring! Quite the opposite, I would have thought."

"He's been in the line – it changes people."

"He's certainly acquired the habit of command. But, I don't want to alarm you; you're free to take up with whoever you choose. I just don't want you to get hurt. You seem very fond of him and it's not hard to see why. He's an attractive and articulate man. He's not young though, is he? That makes it all the more surprising that he isn't attached."

"Everyone has a past," Alice said, mindful of her own false steps. "He's hardly likely to talk about it on a visit to my parents, is he? I think you don't really have cause to worry".

She concluded with a bright smile but, if it was meant to reassure her mother, it failed to work.

"There's something else," Louise said, after some hesitation, "another reason I thought he was married."

"What's that?" Alice asked with trepidation, drawn to her mother's assertions like a moth to the light.

"I've been married a long time. Everybody I know is married, as are many of their children. I watch them with interest, especially the young. Married men of our class have a way of doing things. They're used to being looked after, to being made comfortable. They expect to be listened to by their wives and their families and to have the last word. We wives flatter and obey them. Every wife does it, whether out of devotion or habit. It oils the wheels, allows us to get on with our lives and to assert ourselves in respect of the matters that count. I couldn't help but notice how he made himself at home. He expected his food to be on the table, to have everything brought to him. He took up his position in the armchair by the fireside as if the indentations in the cushions were his. He spoke, he held court…we listened…he expected it…didn't you notice?

"He was our guest, in our home for the first time. We chose to place him centre stage. Why wouldn't we in such circumstances?

"I expect you're right," Louise said, fearing that her words might become a barrier between them. She was unsurprised that her warning had fallen upon deaf ears. She had been like her daughter once, committed irretrievably, deaf to advice, determined to marry, whatever the consequences, Perhaps it was the only sure route to matrimony? There were never any guarantees that it would end well.

"I have no real evidence to go on. You'll establish his status soon enough…and whatever it is, you'll go your own way. You always do in the end and why not? That's how it should be at your age. I'm delighted you've found someone you care for. It's only what you deserve. You've been on your own too long."

"I have, haven't I?"

Alice had often told herself that it didn't matter, better that than being married to the wrong man. She had her family and her work and that was enough. Except that it wasn't and never had been. There had always been emptiness there. She wanted someone whom she could love and respect without reservation, who would reciprocate her feelings and weave his life with hers. There had been times when she had come close to success but for the most part, she had been burdened by doubts. She hadn't made enough effort to crystallise things, to organise her life to suit somebody else. With Malcolm, it felt different. Loving him seemed part of the natural order. Her whole being changed in his presence. The thought that he had sought to conceal his true circumstances was painful to contemplate. Now her mother had sown the seeds of doubt in her mind, she would have to discuss it with him, even if it caused her to discover that he was not whom he purported to be.

"Let's talk about something else," she said brightly and convinced that she would consider her words and act on them, Louise was quick to agree.

They had much to talk about. They saw little of each other in spite of living in the same house. Alice's work at the NCF was time-consuming and Malcolm took up her free time. Louise undertook ever more visits to soldiers' families, helping mothers to make ends meet or to grieve over their sons. They had hoped to see Robert when his latest sentence concluded but their hopes had been dashed. There were letters to write to him and to Michael, who had become a prolific correspondent. They spoke of these things and others long into the night and it was like the old days before Malcolm had brought new joys and uncertainties into her life.

That night, as she lay in bed, Bennett snoring gently beside her, Louise added her fears for Alice to her anxieties about the war. Michael was somewhere in France - perhaps participating in some foolhardy advance. She could only hope that he would remain safe as the hostilities dragged on and the casualties mounted. She thought also of Robert. His health was declining and if the harsh prison regime continued who knew what the effects of solitary confinement and the rule of silence on a mind given to introspection might be? Even when he secured his release, his difficulties would endure. Few of those who had lost sons and brothers would rush to employ someone who had stood aloof from the conflict. Now she was convinced that Malcolm would hurt her beloved daughter though Alice couldn't see it and wouldn't until it was too late. She began to pray, calling upon God to protect her family, hoping that her devotion would keep them out of harm's way.

CHAPTER 22

He rested on his elbow, gazing down at her fondly. She pulled the sheet over her to conceal her nakedness but her foot caught in it so that her breasts remained bare, white against a white sheet. She lay back on the pillow, one arm draped across her face as though shielding her eyes from the sun whilst the other ruffled his hair without thought or purpose. When he leaned across and kissed her lightly on the lips and she felt his warm breath on her face, she pulled away from him, looked at him expectantly and said, "Mother thinks you're married."

He had realised there was an issue when they had met for lunch. Every word he had uttered had been weighed and appraised. She had ordered her food without interest and had picked at it desultorily when the plates came. They had returned to his flat and had done all the things they usually did: throwing off their clothes, falling back on the bed in a tangle of limbs, giving themselves to each other with all the abandon of which they were capable. The sighs and cries, the modest chorus that excited them, had been the same as always but there had also been a new detachment that had suggested Alice was going through the motions and that her thoughts were elsewhere.

He gazed at the ceiling with rapt concentration, as if the answer to her question was to be found there, before shaking his head vigorously and saying, "What made her think that? I answered her questions as best I could. What more could I have done?"

"It was what you didn't say that gave her cause for concern. She thought you looked and behaved like a married man."

"How does a married man behave?" Malcolm asked, a touch of scorn in his voice.

"I can only repeat what she told me. I'm no expert in these matters. She observed the way you made yourself at home, the way that you sat back and prepared to be waited on. She said you were someone used to being comfortable, who had an expectation that his needs would be met."

"Oh," he replied, his geniality returning, though it had a slightly forced edge to it. "She's referring to the officer in me. You give orders and they're obeyed. That's how it is in the army. I have a servant who meets all my needs. When you're back in London, you expect more of the same. I didn't realise it was so noticeable. I obviously need to make more of an effort to get back to civilian ways."

Alice's expression made it plain that she was unconvinced. She searched his face, lips pursed tightly and when she spoke her words had a note of urgency.

"Whenever she asked about your family, you evaded her questions. You kept changing the subject, bringing my father into the conversation. You gave us both the impression that you had something to hide."

That wasn't quite how she remembered it. She was exaggerating her mother's suspicions in an effort to get at the truth. Her mother's viewpoint had captured her thinking, intruding when she least expected it, making her intent on learning the facts for herself.

She said, "Of course, what mother thinks doesn't matter greatly."

"Well, it does if you believe what she says."

"Answer the question, then: are you married or not? That's all I want to know. How the army's affected your personal habits can wait for some other time."

He said, "If you're so suspicious, what are you doing here? I didn't force you come to my flat."

"No, you didn't. I came to you of my own free will, as I always do."

She was inclined to say that she regretted it, that it would have been better to wait until she was certain that he wasn't misleading her, but her passion had got the better of her and it had been easier to give in than to resist.

"Yes, I'm married - in a manner of speaking."

"What does that mean: in a manner of speaking? You're either married or you're not. Which is it?"

He took a deep breath. His heavy sigh increased her misgivings. She wanted to bury her head under the pillows, shut out his reply even as she urged him to go on.

He said reluctantly, "Your mother's right – I'm afraid. I've been married for eight years. I have two children; they're six and four. My wife and I are estranged. We don't live together any more."

His face softened at the thought of his children before becoming hard and business-like again. He said, "This is my home now. It's not much, I know, but it'll do until the end of the war."

"No, it isn't much," Alice said, looking it over as if seeing it for the first time. "It feels temporary, as if you've just moved in, and have no intention of staying."

It had occurred to her on their first night together, when her clothes lay in a crumpled heap on the floor and they had stumbled towards the bed, locked together. The flat contained no traces of his presence: the pictures on the walls, the ornaments lined up on the mantelpiece were commonplace artefacts, part of the token, half-hearted embellishments found in rented property. It had been a place meant for strangers, for visitors having no stake in the premises. It could have been a home if somebody had elected to decorate and furnish it to accord with their tastes but in the absence of any effort to improve its appearance, it had looked what it was: a rendezvous, convenient and bland, where lovers could meet undisturbed.

"I took it to be near your work. My furniture and most of my clothes are elsewhere."

"In the family home, the home of your estranged wife?"

"No somewhere else, in rooms that I rented at the start of the war."

"So this is a love-nest? I'm supposed to be flattered that you took somewhere nearby so you could meet me - or anyone else for that matter?"

"There's no one else, you know that."

Alice was unimpressed. "Does your wife know about this place? Does she send your post here? I haven't seen any letters lying around. What about me? Your mistress?" She said the word with ill-concealed contempt. "Have you told her of my existence, that you've found somebody else?"

"I don't think she cares what I do any more."

"The mother of your children doesn't care what their father does? Are you sure? What have you actually said to her? Have you spelt it out?"

"Quite sure. She wants nothing to do with me. She's made that very clear. But no, I haven't told her about you. It's still early days and I saw no reason to provoke her, to make her think even less of me than she already does."

"Early days?" The words rang in Alice's ears. They might be early days for Malcolm but for her there was already a history, a brief but eventful past, and a raft of expectations with regard to the future that had been suddenly and cruelly dashed.

He wondered why it was so hard to speak the truth. His wife had a hold over him he found hard to describe. She had left him for somebody else but he knew that as soon as she discovered he had a lover, she would demand that he came back to her and he would struggle to resist. There was no point in returning to her side. She was unable to confine herself to one man, even the father of her children. She pursued men she didn't care for, men whose devotion soon bored her, men whom she dispensed with easily, without regard for their feelings. There was something about their marriage that failed to satisfy her. What was it? Did her need for attention, flattery and devotion, desires that lay beyond his capacity to provide to a sufficient extent, force her to seek them elsewhere? His inadequacy had devastated him until he had realised his rivals suffered the same failings and that her needs could never be satisfied. Then, there had been an overwhelming sadness and the recognition that he was harnessed to a marriage that was bound to fail.

They lay motionless. The arm that lay across his chest was lifeless. Its owner neither moved nor spoke, except that her breast rose and fell against his shoulder and her eyes struggled to fight back her tears. The noises from the street below: the clanking of trams, the raucous call of the car horns, the tattoo of the horses' hooves on the cobblestones, the cry of the newspaper vendor passed her by. He had a wife and two children whose existence he had concealed. She was his mistress, the woman he turned to when his wife was unavailable. How many women did she know who had fulfilled that unsatisfactory role?

She said, "Why didn't you tell me you were married? Why did you allow me to think you were available, that we might have a future together, when all the time you were spoken for?"

He looked down at her earnestly, with an intensity that was new to her, a determination to prevail. His face was red, as if from great exertion, but his eyes avoided hers, sliding way like a creature at dusk, unwilling to confront an intruder.

He said with great care, "The time never seemed right. If I'd told you I was married when we first met, you wouldn't have had anything more to do with me. None of the wonderful times we have had together would have happened. Later, I was afraid to put our relationship at risk by telling you the truth. I had backed myself into a corner and couldn't see any way out."

Alice was unmoved. "Anything would have been better than waiting until I wrung a confession out of you. And allowing me to introduce you to my parents? What were you thinking of, allowing me to invite a married man to their home?"

He said with dismay, "You were so insistent, what else could I do?"

"You could have told me the truth. Why were you so certain that that would have been the end of us?"

"Because of your background, your family, the kind of person you are."

"You'd be surprised what a woman is capable of doing when she is truly in love."

"Are you truly in love?" He turned to her eagerly, his face alive. He placed his arm on hers, pulling her towards him and said, "Will you forgive me for what I've done?"

Alice shook her arm free, moved away from him and said, "You don't understand me at all, do you? You haven't the least idea what I'm like or what I want. Of course, I regret the fact that you're married, but it doesn't matter to me that much, provided you're sincere when you say that you love me and have no intention of going back to your wife. Couples come together, fall apart. It's in the nature of things. The point that you haven't grasped, is that you lied to me. You allowed me to think that you were free, that I had you to myself, when all the time I was sharing you with someone else."

"I've told you. My wife and I meet rarely and never in circumstances such as these."

"She's still your wife."

"I didn't lie to you outright. You didn't ask me if I was married and I didn't speak about it. The subject never came up."

She sat upright on the bed and the bedclothes fell away from her, revealing her nakedness but she no longer cared. The time for becoming modesty was past. That was something appropriate for the man she cared for. This other man, this stranger, could feast his eyes upon her for all she cared. She pivoted to the side of the bed, turning her back on him, her legs dangling over the edge. There was a look of fury and deep disappointment on her face. When he attempted to reach out for her, she twisted away. Rising to her feet, she said, in a voice she scarcely recognised as her own. "Was I supposed to ask if you were married? "

Pointing, an accusatory finger at him, she continued. "You're suggesting that the onus was on me to establish the truth? How dare you? You should have been honest with me at the start. You ought to have allowed me to make a choice about our future in the full knowledge of the facts. But no, you lied and obfuscated instead...and you're still squirming...even now, you're reluctant to speak the truth... You say I might have turned my back on you had you been frank with me. Well, I might have... but that was a risk you should have taken - anything would have been better than this horrible deceit."

She strode across the room, stooping to collect the clothes scattered on the floor and went into the bathroom, slamming the door. He heard the water run into the washbowl, the flush of the lavatory but lay unmoving on the bed, making no effort to pursue her or prevent her from leaving. He knew how stupid he had been, that his deception was unforgivable, his excuses lame. What he had said was true: he had resolved to tell her the unvarnished truth but each time his nerve had failed him. Her mother had been right to be suspicious of him. Now she wanted nothing more to do with him. All he could do was to keep silent, for fear of making matters worse. Soon, the war would claim him again and afterwards, if he saw it through, he would attempt to make it right with her in the hope that she had forgiven his deception.

He was dressed by the time she returned to the bedroom, ready to leave. Her dress was arranged neatly; her hair was tied back, exposing the neck that he so loved to caress. Her coat was thrown over her arm and in her hand she held the hat that they had chosen together. He had seen it in a shop window near where she worked and had insisted that she try it on. It had so suited her face and colouring that he had purchased it for her. Now seeing her standing before him, poised to depart, he abandoned his vow of silence and called out to her, his voice full of pleading, "Don't go; not yet. Don't leave without hearing me out."

His plea stopped her in her tracks. Seeing him in his uniform, his tunic unbuttoned, it scarcely seemed possible that a matter of minutes before, she had been lying in his arms, exalting in the touch of his fingers and the taste of his lips. Now the bed was cold, the impression of their bodies on the sheets gone and all that remained were bitter memories and the presence of the man who had misled her.

"There's nothing more to be said. Your behaviour speaks for itself."

"Wait a few minutes, allow me to explain, things aren't what they seem."

He edged towards the door, intent on detaining her until she heard him out. If she walked out of the door in her present frame of mind she would be gone for ever. There would be no reunion after the war. That was fanciful thinking. She was an attractive, young woman. There would be no lack of suitors. They weren't husband and wife. They had no children to care for. They were bound only by their affection. She had her parents and siblings and the hinterland of relatives and friends that she had told him about whilst he had only a wife who had rejected him for somebody else and two children whom he hardly knew. When he was in the line, he had often asked himself who would mourn him when he was gone. If Alice left him, he would be alone in the world and when a shell or bullet came his way unbidden, he would be erased from the earth as surely as if he had never inhabited it.

He said again, "My wife and I aren't together any more." He struggled to keep his voice low key, to conceal his distress. "We haven't been together since I enlisted. That was why I was eager to go. I didn't join up out of misplaced optimism or unreasoning zeal. I had no great urge to serve King and Country. I had an opportunity to take a job at the War Office. I insisted on going into the infantry. I wanted to be in the thick of it. It seemed the only thing to do after my wife had betrayed me and I didn't care whether I lived or died."

"Betrayed you?"

"She ran off with someone else, leaving me to look after two small children whilst she gallivanted round Europe with someone she hardly knew. It was a spur of the moment thing, but it wasn't the first time nor, if we had stayed together, would it have been the last. I would have forgiven her had she shown the least sign of remorse, but she shrugged it off and said there was no guarantee that she wouldn't do it again. It was then that I resolved to enlist and have been at the front ever since. The battalion's my home. The men are my family. Before I met you, there was no one else."

"What's your wife's name?"

"Geraldine."

"What a lovely name. Don't you ever see your children? You must write to them, must long for their presence, even if you have no urge to meet their mother again?"

"Oh, I do... how could it be otherwise...they're my children? But Geraldine's gone back to her family, taking them with her. I'm a stranger to them. She's made sure of that. I've seen them once since I went out. She's turned them against me. It's her revenge because I won't take her back on her terms."

"Why don't you go back to her? Isn't that a price worth paying to be with your children? She's their mother, after all. Why don't you forgive her and become a family again?"

"It's too late for that. She's humiliated me enough. I'm done with her. There's no turning back. And anyway, I've met you..." his voice trailed off.

He began to button his tunic and reached down for his boots, watching her prepare to leave the room. It was painful to look down on the bed they had shared, addressing each other in terms of endearment that they would never repeat. He couldn't get over his foolishness. What had possessed him to act as he had? There had been a story to tell. Why had he not related to her everything that had happened? She might have been sympathetic had he spoken out at the start.

He asked, "What can I say or do to convince you that I meant you no harm?"

He stood before her, his hands on her shoulders, staring into her eyes with a fierce intensity. Had he sought to deceive her? Could she trust him? She didn't want to lose him, God knows, but she couldn't love someone who couldn't be relied upon to be honest. She shivered as he pulled her to him but put up no resistance when their lips touched.

When he released her, she said, "You can do nothing more. It's up to me now. I have to consider how I feel about you in the light of everything you've told me and decide what I want to do."

"That's right, you must."

He was eager now, full of encouragement, sensing that the tide was turning in his favour. "Of course, it's up to you but don't doubt my sincerity when I tell you I love you and that I want to return to you after the war."

"What about Geraldine? She stumbled over the name. "Will you divorce her? Will you ever be free to marry somebody else?"

"Most certainly, after the war."

"Oh, the war..." she said plaintively "...always the war, speeding things up so there's no time to think, a dark cloud of uncertainty over the future.

I know this," she said, attempting to marshal her thoughts into some sort of order, "I want your assurance that you've told me everything that has a bearing on our relationship, that there's nothing hidden, no dark secrets about which you've kept silent which I have to find out for myself."

After a long pause that filled her with dread, he said, "No, you have my assurance that there's nothing else."

"You're quite sure?"

"Quite sure," he repeated, even as he became aware of an issue that would surely trouble them at some point in the future.

His wife had been adamant at their last meeting that she would never divorce him, for reasons that had been unclear. For all that she had abused his affection, she would never allow him to leave her for somebody else. But that was a matter, he told himself, relying on the logic that had prevailed before and had been his undoing, he would address after the war. Why raise the matter now? Alice was weighing up their future together. Why put another obstacle in their path? It had been that way since the first time they met. He had been lost to everything but his passion, prepared to say anything, providing it ensured she remained in his arms.

They regarded each other warily, unsure if their quarrel was over or about to return with all its old force. But Alice's anger had evaporated. She knew that he should have revealed his true status at the outset, as she had insisted, but would it have made any difference? She was no longer sure. She suspected that she had been committed to him from the moment they met. She was no longer in control of her feelings and nor, she suspected, was he. She had seen for herself how distraught he had become at the prospect of her leaving and had been reassured by it. His deceit had been foolish in the extreme, even cowardly, but she doubted it was the action of a man unworthy of her love. He had sought her out, had declared his intentions without hesitation and showed every sign of wanting to return to her at the end of the war. If that was truly the case, the niceties, the details could wait until then. Her mother would have to make up their own mind, but she had little doubt that when she observed the strength of her affections for Malcolm, she would support her.

"I'm sorry I misled you," he said when he judged the time for a final apology was right. "I only hope that you can see your way to forgiving me, knowing that I won't let you down again."

"I'm sure you won't," Alice said, warming to his appeal. When he stepped forward hopefully, she allowed him to kiss her again.

But though she clung to him as if their recent dispute had never occurred, she wanted to leave the room that accommodated them and never see it again. He was still somebody else's husband, whatever he might claim, and she had no business sharing his bed. If anything of that nature was to occur, and that was certainly not her intention, they would have to meet elsewhere. Only then would it be possible to put their quarrel behind them and learn to trust each other again.

She said, "I have to go now."

The look on her face suggested that she would brook no delay. She donned her hat and coat though she had no destination in mind and he hastened to assist her, a slight smile on his face, believing that he had convinced her of his sincerity and that he would see her again.

He knew that he was up before the War Board in a few days' time and that they would declare him fit to return to his battalion. He greeted the prospect without enthusiasm. His reticence was partly a reluctance to leave Alice but was also a fear, long suppressed, of what he was likely to confront in the line. His dark thoughts weighed down on him as he watched Alice make her way down the street, holding on to her new hat as a brisk wind threatened to dislodge it. He noted the swing of her hips, her upright deportment and her bustling, purposeful stride. He was fortunate to have such a lover. He had revealed her for the attractive and articulate woman she was. He regretted his behaviour but felt little remorse, though he knew he would have to tread carefully, if he wanted to find her waiting for him on his return.

CHAPTER 23

Louise woke abruptly, starting from a deep, untroubled sleep. The room was dark, the curtains framed by moonlight, the place beside her cold. She sat up against the pillows and her weary eyes discerned the shape of Bennett in the chair by the window. He was leaning forward, his elbows resting on his knees. His chest heaved, rising and falling abruptly, as he struggled for breath. She threw aside the bedclothes and hurried to his side. He gazed at her forlornly as she stood before him. His face had taken on a greyish hue. The hand that clung to her nightdress shook noticeably and he rocked backwards and forwards as he tried to acquire the momentum to rise from the chair. His swaying figure reminded her that they were becoming old and vulnerable. She shivered at the prospect that she might survive him, might have to spend her final years alone. She pressed her face against his beard; her closeness calmed him. He clung to her, grateful for her presence.

She remembered when he had been a tall, broad shouldered man with a blacksmith's forearms who lifted her effortlessly or ran the length of the garden, an excited child beneath each arm. He had seemed so upright then, so powerful, so far removed from the ailing man before her. His father had owned a brass foundry, a sprawling factory whose ball valves, stopcocks and gate valves followed British engineers to the farthest reaches of the Empire. The ponderous presses and the whirring lathes had been the cornerstone of a solid, pious life and the pungent odour of the foundries had clung to their possessions until it seemed that home, factory and offices were one vast machine working unceasingly to shape the mountains of brass rod. Every morning they had clustered at the door to watch his father climb into his carriage, finding in his brisk departure, a pride, a continuity, a belief in thrift and diligence that had spanned the generations. Unfortunately, the business that Bennett's father had inherited from his father, which he managed with such a show of confidence, was on the brink of ruin. Mindful only of appearances, of preserving his position amongst his peers, his sudden death revealed an enterprise devoid of customers, burdened by debt.

Bennett joined his two older brothers in an effort to save the business but was unable to replicate their zeal. Sitting in his office, the taste of the foundry on his lips, he looked ahead and saw years devoid of change and inspiration. Soon, the factory, workshops and assembly lines repelled him. He pitied the tired, grey faces that filed past the window at the end of each shift and hated the lines of presses that shook the building with their stamping. His brothers delighted in the factory floor. Standing at the end of the line counting the valves that passed overhead, they felt that they were masters of the machines that melted, poured, hammered and turned the reluctant metal. For him it was a denial of everything he cherished. He was on the point of leaving when the bookkeeper fell ill. His brothers urged him to stay, convinced that he had a financial acumen denied to them and, trapped by the need to nurture the company's fragile finances, he agreed reluctantly.

He had always had a passion for numbers, regarding them as part of a magical, personal world. Where others saw rows and columns, he saw stories and patterns. The factory's books revealed the true nature of the enterprise that was the focus of his family's labours. No matter how hard they worked, how skilfully that work was organised, their profits were determined not by their labours but by the metal price, by the quixotic behaviour of copper, brass and gunmetal on the metal exchanges. Recognising that the profits from successful speculation far outweighed the benefits of proficient manufacturing, Bennett began to play the markets. He spent hours in the clubs that were the refuges of the proprietors, listening to the gossip, watching for the shifts of sentiment that signalled a decisive movement in the prices. He visited the scrap metal yards with their dingy offices, their mountains of scrap and swarf, their lists of prices crudely chalked on blackboards. He opened positions for quantities that weren't required, small commitments at first and then, as his understanding increased, long and short positions far exceeding their needs. He borrowed heavily at times, until the factory's modest requirements were merely a cloak for the huge speculative positions that he had opened on its behalf. He told his brothers little of the risks he took. For him it was an intellectual pursuit. He cared nothing for the money. They never realised that the factory was mortgaged, their homes in jeopardy, their livelihoods at stake and that he, not caring for their orderly life, was gambling with their heritage.

Following the slump of the eighteen nineties, business boomed. With ample funds at his disposal, Bennett combined consistent foresight with a willingness to back his judgement with everything they owned. He no longer confined himself to non-ferrous metals. No commodity market was too fraught, no deal too intricate for his consideration. He was only interested in the outcome, in the complex scorecard that was his taskmaster and prize. He relished the risks, the offers and pledges, the nods of agreement, the handshakes and the pyramid of deals to which they gave rise. Without them, there was only the dull routine of the office, the dusty ledgers and the empty, idle talk. When he rested from his self-appointed task he acknowledged the transformation that he had wrought. He had converted an ailing manufacturer into a prosperous and growing company with interests that ranged the world.

His relationship with his brothers displayed signs of strain as the business prospered. Though he rarely let them down, unwinding his mistakes with truly brutal speed, increasing affluence spawned a new conservatism, a determination to preserve the gains. Bennett was rarely in the office, preferring to work from home or the City of London or to travel overseas. He would brook no interference in his activities, believing speed and detachment to be the keys to his success. When his brothers understood the extent of his speculation, they became indignant. Their attacks grew more persistent when he ignored their protests. They suggested that success in industry and commerce should be founded on the non-conformist virtues of diligence and thrift. They claimed that his success was wealth accumulation for its own sake, even as they banked with indecent haste the profits he had made.

Bennett shrugged aside their disaffection. He understood their jealousy, their reasons for concern. They were dour men, lacking his generosity, always suspicious, always afraid that someone might better them. Bennett had no great liking for either of them and only asked that they leave him alone whilst he worked unceasingly on their behalf. But there was another side to him, a private, deeply spiritual vein that was troubled by their barbs. He had always been a tireless worker on behalf of Quaker causes. He was frugal, devout, an ardent pacifist. His refusal to pay rates in favour of voluntary schools had resulted in the distrainment of his goods. His brothers' criticism alerted him to the dangers of excessive wealth. He might have carried on, had his mother not been haunted by her husband's misdemeanours. His death had revealed that he had been a spendthrift and a philanderer and she feared her favourite son was about to follow in his footsteps. Her misgivings troubled Bennett greatly and the speculations that had once delighted him became a burden. He began to hesitate when he should have been decisive or to be reckless when caution was required.

No matter what he did or where he went, there were accusing faces, voices of dissent. Suddenly, in one of those abrupt breaks with the past that were to characterise his life, he announced he was leaving the business. His brothers mouthed their regrets, urging him to stay, whilst signalling their relief at his departure. By now, their fortune was considerable. It made for financial independence even when Bennett had been paid for his equity. He ended his financial dealings and all mention of his fortune was forbidden. It became his family's provider, welcome but ignored.

He worked ferociously at politics, his new profession, determined to put the past behind him. He developed views on the political and social issues of the day, views that represented the tradition that he had neglected during his years in business. He became a formidable lobbyist on behalf of Quaker causes but influential though he was by virtue of his intellect and energy, it was not enough. He recognised that he had to be in the House of Commons, even a member of the Government, if he were to make his mark. Progressing from lobbyist to Liberal Parliamentary candidate, he was twice defeated in the polls. Rejection in the elections of 1906 and 1909 proved devastating to his self-esteem. It mattered little that his constituency was one of the few that could be relied upon to withstand the Liberal landslide or that he was ill-served by his constituency party. Reform was in the air and, desperate to be one of its drivers, he had been rejected by the voters. He threw himself into his work with renewed zeal but his efforts failed to mitigate his disappointment. Within a year, he had become seriously ill.

He had never been a healthy man in spite of his vigorous appearance. His marriage to Louise had been plagued by a succession of minor illnesses. After his defeat, bad health struck in earnest; an attack of pleurisy, a racking cough that threatened to devour him. Fearing for his health, Louise rushed him to Switzerland, where the favourable climate and her devoted nursing restored his health. His health improved but his nature remained troubled. He failed to settle at anything; he could not bear to be alone. He talked of dispersing their wealth, echoing his mother's view that it was unearned and undeserved, but his convalescence was expensive and he had no income other than his dividends. When Louise gave up the struggle to distract him, he returned to England, a tall emaciated figure with suffering in his eyes and began to work again in spite of his fragile health, the death of all his prospects.

Louise recalled their return with a shudder. His fervour had frightened her. Business, even politics, had wrought a sort of balance; without their demands, issues tore at him. He could be outraged or dismayed by the least matter, lapsing into hurt indifference when his emotion was exhausted. He remained a wheel without an axle, spinning aimlessly, until the outbreak of the war. The war was the defeat of everything he valued. He watched its early progress with astonishment and horror. Yet it was also the making of him. It restored his sense of purpose. He was provoked by the speed with which the war brushed aside the work of peacemakers, internationalists and socialists. Speeches and pamphlets in opposition to it issued from him and though his fevered brain drove his tired body without respite, there was a sense of mission, and a belief in his own usefulness that had made him whole again.

She reached hastily for the bowl that sat beside the bed. Bennett stretched forth a shaking hand and took it from her grasp. When he bent forward and began to retch, she turned away, knowing he would be ashamed of his weakness. She lay back in the bed and feigned a troubled sleep, his racking cough pursuing her until the crisis passed and he fell back exhausted, a limp and forlorn figure.

When, later, he sat upright and asked for Robert's letter, she said, "Not now. Leave it till the morning. You'll catch your death of cold."

"I must read it again whilst it's on my mind."

He sat on the edge of the bed, knowing that if he waited long enough, she would take pity on him and retrieve it from his study.

Wearily, she set off in search of it. She found it in his desk: the rough prison notepaper, Robert's stylish but irregular hand, the eight hundred words permitted by the regulations. Why had he not allowed her to read it? Why had it upset him so much? She eyed the page with grave misgivings and began to read about the events that had brought Robert back from America.

CHAPTER 24

She heard the tidings from the Medical Board at Caxton Hall in tight-lipped silence. It was a building she knew well, having gone there with her mother in 1907 when the Women's Social and Political Union held its first Women's Parliament. Each year thereafter, she had taken part in the annual procession to the Houses of Parliament to deliver a petition to the Prime Minister for the right to vote. Malcolm's visit was a cruel parody of everything she had hoped for. The smiling doctors assured him he had recovered and he purported to be delighted at the news though Alice observed trepidation behind his enthusiasm. It was all very well to enthuse about a return to the line when it was impossible. It was different when the papers were issued and a seat had been booked on the leave train. When she asked him how he felt about going back, he said that he had not expected it to happen so soon.

He was determined to make their last night together memorable even as he attempted to make light of his return. He said he wanted to leave her arms for the troop train, the scent of her perfume on his clothes. He insisted that his fatalism was gone, banished by the promise of her presence and the knowledge of her support. He said he would know, whatever the trials and hardships, that she would be waiting for him and that, he declared grandly, would make all the difference.

"Where are we going for our last night?" she asked with misgivings.

He named a hotel a short walk from Victoria station, saying, "We'll be able to leave for the train at the last minute."

She was inclined to say that she was not prepared to go to a hotel with him as man and wife, even on their last night, but when she thought about how long it might be before they met again, it seemed churlish to turn him down. He said little about the restaurant he had chosen, revealing only that it was in Soho.

They had agreed to meet at the Cafe Royal. He arrived early to claim a table and waited fretfully for her to appear amid an atmosphere of cigar smoke, perfume and alcohol. She was late as always; whether by habit or inclination he never knew, and he was irritated by the delay, feeling that every moment was precious. In a matter of hours, he would on the train for France. It never ceased to amaze him how near London was to the conflict. Two different, separate worlds with little in common. One brash and lively, full of gaiety and laughter, populated by men and women intent on forgetting the war; the other dour and unforgiving, moments of extreme danger separating periods of excruciating boredom. When Alice appeared, she had difficulty finding him. He stood up and waved his napkin to attract her attention. When that failed, he left his prized table and squeezed through the crowd to her side. "This way," he said, taking her hand. They threaded their way back to the table as another couple attempted to occupy the spaces he had saved. When they were seated, he ordered champagne. Alice drank it quickly, which made her head spin, hoping to find in its magic a gaiety that she had yet to feel.

The reason for her late arrival was that her mother had been to see Robert in Wandsworth and had been appalled by what she found there. It was no surprise to witness Robert's pale, haggard face and the weight he had lost. The diet, lack of exercise and isolation meant it could hardly be otherwise. Her greater concern was his lack of spirit. Robert had been one of life's optimists, leavening his resolve with a sharp sense of humour, seeing irony in the least promising situations. Imprisoned, he had become depressed, feeling that he was obliged to go on with his protest for the lack of a better alternative whilst having lost confidence in its power to change anything. He remained opposed to alternative service, believing it a recipe for unseemly disputes, whilst abandoning his opposition to conscription was impossible.

"I have to go on," he had concluded with no great enthusiasm, leaving Louise to wonder how much more he could stomach. Alice didn't care to discuss these issues with Malcolm on their last evening together but they troubled her as she attempted to match his high spirits.

He exclaimed, "Isn't this place amazing?" as they tumbled out into the street. "It's more like a street party than a city in the midst of war."

Cafes, restaurants and clubs crowded the narrow thoroughfares of Soho. Catering for armies of office workers during the day, they indulged soldiers hungry for excitement at night. The theatres were full of new shows, every seat taken, musicals full of colour, fun and uplifting melodies, something to sing or hum on long route marches or to replicate in the entertainments that the troops put on for themselves. Malcolm had taken Alice to several shows - she didn't know how he had acquired the tickets at such short notice – including Chu Chin Chou, for which there were long queues every night and which they had seen twice. She hadn't known what to make of them at first. She wasn't sure that she didn't prefer a night at home but then their exuberance had grown on her. It wasn't so much the events on the stage that delighted her but rather the sight and sound of an audience having fun. There hadn't been enough fun in her life. She began to join in with gusto, surprising Malcolm, who was still adjusting to her quiet solemnity.

"Do you think I'm changing?" she had asked him after one riotous evening, a serious look on her face.

He had answered, "Most certainly - and not before time," receiving a painful dig in the ribs for his pains. "You Quakers are a serious lot. You deserve a night or two on the town."

She did enjoy herself, though not without feelings of guilt. She couldn't quite overlook, even for an hour or two, what was happening to the rest of the family.

The restaurant didn't live up to Malcolm's expectations. It purported to be French, but the French waiters were long gone and the manager had an accent from London's East End. Each candle-lit table was closeted from its neighbour and several were laid up for large parties. The walls, lined with striped wallpaper, faded and peeling, were studded with signed portraits of actors and politicians who stared down with frozen geniality. The menu's choices appeared untouched by the war. Malcolm studied them appreciatively, wondering when he would have the opportunity to eat so well again. He thought Alice looked wonderful and said so repeatedly. Her hair was swept back from her brow in the style he favoured, emphasising her delicate nose, the lips he longed to kiss. Her neck arched prettily as she inclined her head and her eyes, in the half light of the room, seem greener than ever.

"You know how much I love you?" he asked over the top of his menu, a smile on his face.

"Oh, but I do. It's what I live for. You've woken me from a long sleep."

He handed over his money. Officers' expenditure was capped and money changed hands before every meal. He gave little thought to money, curbing his expenses whenever he could, but not bothering greatly how much was available. He was not one of those soldiers who fussed over everything before going into the line. His finances were on a long list of things that could wait until the end of the war.

Alice marvelled at the choices on offer in the midst of meatless days, posters urging them to plant potatoes, the shortages of bread and sugar and resolved to make the most of them.

The food was a long time coming. The waiters, few in number, seemed distracted; the large parties demanded frequent attention and the kitchen gave every sign of being in unpractised hands. The manager with the strange accent hovered around them, giving orders, many of which went unheeded.

Malcolm began to show signs of restlessness at the absence of food, saying, "I think I'd better say something to them, don't you?"

Alice shook her head. The restaurant was crowded and she was happy to wait.

Malcolm summoned the manager and sent him to the kitchen in search of their order. When the food arrived he complained it was cold and only Alice's protests prevented him from sending it back.

She said, "You seem on edge tonight. Are you all right?" When he said nothing, she watched him pick at his food and wondered what had prompted his mood.

His mind had become a diffuse canvas, a confusion of colour, shapes and form. Scenes of strafes reared up unexpectedly, an innocent phrase, a careless gesture invoking a discordant symphony of artillery and machine guns. He recalled soldiers struggling forward over the bodies of their comrades. He revisited landscapes, torn apart by shell fire, affording neither vantage nor shelter. When his visions diminished, shouldered aside by Alice's vivacity, he became a boisterous and carefree companion but his memories had only retreated and would intrude again.

He said, "Don't worry about me. I'll be fine. Now I'm on the point of leaving, the past has become more immediate. Stuff I thought I'd put behind me has reared its head unexpectedly."

"Talk to me about it, if you want to; I'm happy to listen," Alice said, anxious to know what was troubling him. "It's your last night in London; feel free to make of it what you will."

"Oh, I couldn't do that," Malcolm said, recoiling at the thought that he might be a burden on their last night together.

"I can't get over all the food," Alice said, thinking of her mother's daily struggle to find fresh fruit and vegetables, the absence of the meat.

"Look at the prices;" Malcolm said with a laugh, "it's plentiful enough for those with the means to pay."

He spoke of food at the front, the importance of parcels sent from home. He claimed the post kept them afloat, letters and parcels finding them in the most unlikely places. Alice was surprised to hear how well they ate. There seemed to be no shortages there.

Malcolm said, "Beef tea squares kept me going in the line. I'll be on them again before long," he added, without enthusiasm.

His wife had sent them when they were communicating in a dilatory fashion in the early days of the war. He had asked her for some and they had come ever since, long after her letters had dried up. He had thought it a sign of guilt on her part and had distributed them to the men. They greatly appreciated a change from the tea tasting of petrol transported up to the line in Dixies at odd hours of day and night.

He wished he'd had the opportunity to say goodbye to his children. He pretended not to miss them but it was far from the truth. He had their photographs in his wallet and carried them with him everywhere. He had shown them to Alice, making no effort to stifle his pride as he told her their names and ages. They had adored him at the start of the war. He walked into their lives unexpectedly, laden with presents. Now, they looked at him in bewilderment. They understood his comings and goings to be a consequence of the war and spoke proudly of him during his absence but were puzzled by their mother's antipathy towards him and assumed that he had done something terrible to turn her against him. "What are you going to do after I've gone?" he asked during a lull between courses.

"I expect I'll worry - like everyone else. Worrying has become the national pastime for those with friends and relatives in France."

"You can always knit socks and scarves, that sort of thing. The wrong size, of course."

"There's always that."

"Does your mother knit? Mine never stops. Mind you, the odd scarf is welcome when you've been standing in the mud or the rain."

Alice laughed out loud. "Mother knit? Even if the inclination were to strike her, which is unlikely, she wouldn't know where to start. Mother has many virtues but homemaking isn't one of them."

"How do you distract yourself?"

"Oh, I write lots of letters, like the rest of the family, and engage in endless discussions about the course of the war.."

"I'm not much of a letter writer. I write them, of course, but infrequently and they're usually quite short. I've read so many that it's put me off writing them."

He frowned at the thought of separateness that was to come, toying with his glass.

"I'll soon change that," Alice said. "They'll have to put on extra deliveries once I get going."

She noticed that his glass was empty again and that he was drinking heavily and wondered if she should attempt to restrain him.

He said, "Of course, you might find someone else after I've gone. London is awash with dashing young officers looking for someone."

"I'll tell them that I'm spoken for until the end of the war."

"What will you say after that?"

"That's up to you. I won't be your mistress if that's what you're hoping for. I want to marry and have a family with someone who loves me and cares for me greatly. Nothing else would be right."

He wondered how long it would be before she wearied of his circumstances and turned to somebody else. He regarded her as a diamond, one that he had mined, fashioned and set. Others would see her for the prize that she was, whilst he struggled to survive the war and sought to unwind his vexatious marriage.

Raising his glass to his lips, he said, "Well, here's to the end of the war!"

She echoed his words with a smile. Their glasses clinked. The crystal caught the candlelight, casting their faces in a mysterious glow. He said that he had never seen her looking so beautiful and spoke of his good fortune. Though wanting to see the exchange as evidence that they had sealed their future, Alice knew it was another decision postponed until the end of the war.

"What's going to happen to Robert?" he asked as the waiter swept the crumbs from the table and offered them the desert menus.

"I don't know," Alice said frowning, "he doesn't know, either. He feels that he has no choice but to go on with his protest."

"Does he still believe in what he's doing?"

She observed his change of mood, one minute intimate and loving, the next stern and disapproving, and put it down to his misgivings at going back. Now the time had come to leave, his bravado had given way to something more complicated, more difficult to understand.

She said. "It was very simple at first. He had a conscientous objection to conscription and an urge to help those suffering as a result of the war. He was prepared to be flexible about what he did, providing always that he was not required to enlist."

"That was never realistic, was it?"

"Perhaps not? He never had the opportunity to witness for himself the extent of the country's support for the war."

"Would it have made any difference if he had?"

"I doubt it - but who knows - there was little ambiguity in those early months. Everybody supported the war and he might have been swept up by the tide. More likely, free of the army's interference, he would have taken up non-combatant duties, as many Quakers did. He certainly wouldn't have wrung his hands for two years or sought refuge in some occupation, designed to keep him safe. Once the army got its hands on him, he was bound to make a stand of some kind. Robert doesn't go quietly - it's not in his nature. In the event, by the time he came home, and we warned him what was likely to happen, conscription was upon us and he felt as a practicing Quaker that he couldn't join the army. Now he spends most of his time in solitary confinement. It's wearing him down. Soon, the only struggle he'll be engaged in will be the one to survive."

"Unless he gives up, there's always that possibility."

"I think that makes it more difficult. Anyway, he won't join the army in any capacity or undertake alternative service under army or Home Office supervision."

"That's surely unreasonable?"

"He'd probably have agreed with you before they shipped him to France. Now, after what they did to him there, he won't do anything that's forced upon him. Some of the others have agreed to undertake alternative service, though few of them are doing meaningful work. They're being punished for their refusal to enlist and there'll be trouble in due course."

"I find it very strange he won't compromise. It's a position little deserving of sympathy, if I may say so."

"You're just as bad - insisting on going back into the line."

"I'm a serving officer. I don't have any choice."

"Of course you do. You were in the line for two years. You were badly wounded,. It would be quite reasonable to serve in some other capacity.

The army's full of people who have never been near the front or taken part in the conflict and they're not despised for it."

"I couldn't do it, not after what I've been through. It wouldn't be honourable. I would feel that I was letting everyone down. I've served in the infantry for two years. That's where I belong."

"Robert's committed to serving his sentence, whatever the consequences for his reputation and health."

Malcolm was still considering her words when the air raid sirens interrupted his thoughts.

~

The clamour was hidden by the noise of conversation and laughter but it persisted, adopting a note of urgency. It scratched at the window, stole under the door and came through the roof until the ensuing silence made it still louder, urging the diners to take shelter whilst there was time.

Everyone looked at everyone else. Then the men stood upright as one; issuing instructions in knowledgeable voices, they competed to take charge of their guests.

An anxious officer, wearing his napkin, began to usher his party towards the front door. "Quickly, quickly, or we'll be caught in the open," he urged, as some hesitated or lingered.

"It's an air raid," another man said loudly, as if nobody else understood what was happening. "We have to take shelter. It's dangerous to stay where we are."

Somebody shouted "Piccadilly Underground station, that's the place to go," and the diners abandoned their tables and ran for the door.

One officer, a thin, weasel-faced man, still holding his wine glass, attempted to organise an orderly retreat. Everybody ignored him, even those at his table, preferring an anarchic rush for safety.

Women, giggling nervously, gathered their belongings and attempted to put on their coats and stoles. "What a lark!" one of them said, as she adjusted her hat. Others, threaded their way through the narrow doorway, a short step from panic.

The waiters hovered anxiously, unsure what to do or fell over each other as they rushed to the cloakroom, waving tickets and gathering coats. One of them attempted to deliver a tray of steaming food to a table in the centre of the room and a guest, unaware of his presence, cannoned into him and the tray that he was carrying fell to the ground with a loud crash. Another uncorked a bottle of wine as he edged towards the door. When the bottle was free of its cork, a guest snatched it from him. Saying, "Here, I'll take that," in a loud voice, he carried it into the street, determined to make his stay in the shelter a jolly affair.

A handful of guests attempted to make light of the threat, watching those around them with studied nonchalance but as the panic mounted, they ceased their posturing and the trickle of departures became a torrent intent on making the short trip to safety.

"You still have to pay," the manager shouted but nobody took any notice of him save for one man who took out his wallet and placed a handful of notes on the table by the door.

Alice watched as someone else picked them up and stuffed them into his pocket.

They regarded the scene around them with dismay but made no attempt to leave, wanting to cling to the remnants of their last evening together for as long as they could.

When Alice rose to her feet, saying, "We'd better go," Malcolm said, "I'm not going anywhere." He reached for the bottle of wine on the table before him and filled his glass to the brim.

"Malcolm, it isn't safe here. Why don't we take shelter?"

"The Boche are not going to spoil our last show."

"We can come back later or go to the hotel and get something there."

"You won't be any safer on the street."

"I'm not staying here."

"I'm staying," Malcolm said, placing his hand on her arm. He pointed at the seat she had vacated. A harassed waiter held out her coat before turning for the door.

"Malcolm, please, let's go."

"I won't be here when you get back."

"Listen to the sound of the guns."

Though the firing had intensified, the sound of explosions could still be heard, each nearer, more threatening than its predecessor. When a bomb exploded nearby, the whole building shivered. Their table danced: the tall pepper grinder fell over, the cutlery rattled and the plates shook nervously. The rest of the staff headed for the door. Only one other table remained occupied and its diners were preparing to leave.

Malcolm remained in his place. Alice donned her coat, keen to depart but unwilling to leave him. His hands gripping the edge of the table, he ignored her entreaties. He stared past her, absorbed in a duel of his own making, a test of his fortitude in which her feelings had no part to play.

"It's not right…unarmed civilians … it's not right." He repeated the words he had said to her father.

Alice resolved to see it through at his side, even though she was trembling.

The noise of the explosion deafened her. A violent wind tore at her clothes; her hat was snatched from her hand. They were showered with glass and masonry, coating them in a thick cloud of dust. The woman by the window screamed loudly; blood welling from cuts on her face. Her companion slumped over the plates, twisting awkwardly, a sliver of glass in his neck. Tongues of flame licked at the curtain across the door. Alice realised they were trapped, the doorway blocked by timber and masonry. Malcolm remained in his seat, his face expressionless, stunned by the force of the blast. He ignored the flames, the danger they posed, making no effort to protect or comfort her.

"Malcolm, do something," Alice called, her voice conveying the terror she felt at their predicament.

Malcolm jumped to his feet, intent on finding some means to escape from the flames. Alice was comforted by his show of resolve. A serving officer, two years in the line, would know what to do for the best. But he had no thought for her welfare. He ignored the casualties by the window. He rushed for the door, wading through the broken glass and the rubble, clutching at the upturned tables, his progress slow. Attacking the timbers that blocked the exit with manic vigour, he brushed past the flames in the doorway and plunged out into the street.

Alice remained stationary, incapable of movement, conscious only of the noise and confusion, the flames, heat and smoke. She coughed violently, her eyes filling with tears. The room swayed, its contents ebbing and flowing. The movements of the woman on the next table caught her eye. Her neighbour stood up, tumbling forward, no destination in mind, knowing only that she had to leave.

"Help me. I can't see. I can't find the door."

She uttered the cry repeatedly in the hope that she was not as alone.

"I'm here. I'll help you," Alice said, rousing herself from her torpor.

She staggered across the room, the broken glass crunching beneath her feet, fighting her way over to where the helpless woman was standing, gazing around her in a vain effort to locate the door.

The doorway blazed fiercely, the flames fanned by the draught from the street. The smoke in the room grew dense, the injured woman more desperate. She clutched at Alice, her nails digging into her arm, pleading with her to do something whilst there was still time. Alice turned to the kitchen, hoping it might offer an exit to the street but the blaze was intense. The shattered window was their only means of escape. Shaking herself free of her companion, she picked up a chair and struck at the frame, clearing it of the shards of glass that hung there. She pushed the nearest table up to the ledge, placed a chair in front of it to serve as a step, urging the woman on to it so that she could leap from the window and into the street. Once on the table, the woman was reluctant to jump. She clung on to Alice, crying that she couldn't see.

"You can see enough to save your life," Alice said.

Shaking herself free, she gave her a shove. The woman tumbled out of the window with a sharp cry, falling heavily on to the pavement. She lay there motionless as Alice followed, her eyes filled with smoke. She leapt blindly, stumbling over her companion, but staying upright as she fell. She felt a sharp pain in her ankle but gave it no heed. Dragging the woman behind her, she set off down the alley. The woman was bleeding. Rivulets of blood streamed down her face, staining her dress, but she was conscious, protesting loudly, which was all Alice cared about as they struggled to escape the blaze.

Outside the restaurant, there was chaos. A bomb had fallen in the middle of the street. The damage was extensive. The sides of buildings had been torn away, revealing the rooms within, the contents they contained. The street was full of debris. Cars and carriages had been overturned. A panicked horse was struggling to free itself from its traces; another dragged a gutted carriage along the street. A lorry lay upside down, its wheels spinning. She observed shapeless bundles; bystanders caught by the explosion, and wondered if they had been in the restaurant. Firemen and women ran out hoses from a red, open-topped Denis fire engine. There was a line of bodies on stretchers, ready to be loaded into the ambulances that waited at the end of the street. Two policemen were putting up a tape. A crowd of onlookers, bold now that the danger was past, struggled to see what was going on. Vultures, thought Alice, even as her eyes followed theirs, drawn to the distorted bodies, roughly covered, the figures on the stretchers, groaning fearfully. She guided her companion into the embrace of a waiting constable. The woman pleaded for her to stay but Alice had carried out her duty and wanted to be free of her. She removed her hand from her arm and backed away, the woman's cries pursuing her. Leaning against a shop doorway, shivering, Alice noted to her astonishment that she still had her bag.

"You all right?" a gruff but friendly voice said. She nodded weakly, struggling to stay upright as someone placed a blanket around her and handed her a cup of tea. She drank it greedily, hoping to clear the dust from her throat.

She recalled the figure slumped at the table, the companion of the woman she had led from the building.

"We have to go back to the restaurant; there are still people inside."

She led a firewoman up the street and indicated the building from which she had fled but it was obvious no one had survived the conflagration inside.

"You'd better leave it to me." The firewoman spoke without hope or enthusiasm.

Her words filled Alice with anger. She could have been one of those slumped over their table, overcome by the smoke. She had relied on the judgement of someone claiming to love her who, with his false sense of bravado, had left her to die in the flames.

She waited as another Denis inched up the street and the firewomen jumped down from its deck and unfurled the hoses. When the flames were subdued, the blackened timbers, the gaping windows, the smouldering rubble made clear that no one could have survived the inferno to which the bomb had given rise. Waiting with others to have her cuts and bruises treated, Alice considered the reasons for Malcolm's conduct. Why had he refused to leave until the danger was acute? Why had he fled, leaving her to her fate? She could not conceive of any explanation that would justify such behaviour, especially by someone who had professed to love her. The war's legacy? Some trauma revisited? She neither knew nor cared. Her love for him had died in the blaze. He had fled, leaving her to face the flames on her own, concerned only to save his own skin.

~

She declined offers to find her a taxi, not wanting to add to the burden of the tired but uncomplaining nurses, the wardens sifting the wreckage, the firewomen in their trousers and peaked caps and the policemen who restrained the crowds. She knew how fortunate she had been to escape unscathed but, though the effort had distressed and fatigued her, she gave no thought to going home. No one there was expecting her or knew of the dangers that she had faced. She didn't want to have to explain her situation to anyone. She needed time on her own, time to wander haphazardly in the night air, finding a taxi when she had found words to describe her experience and had adjusted to the loss of a relationship that had meant so much to her.

Expressing her gratitude to everybody, she set off down the road, taking to the back streets to avoid the crowds of souvenir hunters who had flocked to the scene, pausing when she reached Trafalgar Square, before making her way down Whitehall, its long avenue ominously dark, its great buildings silent and impenetrable. Behind their blacked-out windows, thousands toiled, lubricating the machinery of the war that dominated the nation, supplying the men in the line with armaments, weapons, supplies and food. The street was empty. She had left the crowds far behind. She heard footsteps, distant at first then closer, their presence intimidating. She slowed, thinking that she might be mistaken until, sure that she was being followed, she quickened her pace. The footsteps accelerated, drawing nearer in spite of her efforts. She began to run, forcing her tired limbs forward, fearful of finding Malcolm behind her, still more afraid to find a stranger there.

She was thirty yards from the river, on the point of crossing the road, when she felt a hand on her shoulder and a familiar voice said, "Alice, it's me."

"What do you want?" she demanded, without breaking step, shaking herself free of restraint.

"I want to explain my behaviour," he said, his voice breaking.

She recognised the voice. It belonged in the past. It was the voice of a man she had loved who had gone, his reputation consumed by the fire, and in his place stood another man with the same voice whose words couldn't be trusted and whose actions had done great harm.

She crossed the road, ignoring his pleas, and walked east along the Embankment. Beyond the bridge, Cleopatra's long finger pointed at the darkening sky and clouds jostled the moon. Over the parapet, the water glistened in the moonlight, rocking the boats by the jetty, bearing the flotsam it had swept from the shore as it made its way to the sea. In the middle of the river, barges tied together like cattle waited patiently for tugs and on the opposite bank, tall cranes stooped over the water. She halted by the wall, her hands on the cold stone, before turning to confront Malcolm, fear and anger on her face.

She said, "I think it would be better for us both if you left me alone."

"I thought you were dead. When the fire took hold, I decided all hope was gone."

"I was fortunate. Others died in the flames."

Malcolm was barely recognisable. He appeared to have shrunk, to have shrivelled up inside his uniform. He wore the mask of someone old and afflicted over a face she used to know well. Gone was the proud defiance, the bold, cynical gaze, replaced by the look of a pitiful creature, pleading evident in its eyes. It was as if he had been stripped of his uniform, badges and epaulets by the explosion, and stood before her, a civilian like her, for the first time.

He said, "I am so sorry…I can't tell you…"

"What you did was unforgivable."

She gazed at him defiantly, unwilling to hear the excuses he intended to utter. Beneath her hostility lay a confusion of emotions: a reluctance to forgive, a desire for revenge but also a yearning to restore to his former place in her affections the man who but a short time ago she had loved. She knew it was impossible to turn back the clock. Nothing he might say or do would induce her to forgive him for what he had done. Her love had been destroyed by the fire.

"How could you leave me to be consumed by the flames, when you professed to love me? What came over you? You insisted we stay when our lives were in danger and then, when the bombs fell nearby, you ran away."

"You're right…It was unforgivable… I left you to die… It was madness …I don't know what came over me. The bombs were so close. The noise, the smell, the fire brought it all back. I was convinced I was my old, robust self and that my mind and body had healed. But I was mistaken. I wasn't over it. Not in the least…I panicked and ran away…how could I have been such a coward?"

"Over what?" Alice stared into his face, trying to determine his expression in the shadows.

"Over what happened in the line."

He knew he was beyond redemption in her eyes but wanted her to understand that his actions were not without reason. He needed her to recognise that, in the circumstances of the bombing, he had not been responsible for his precipitate behaviour.

"There was a time when I was brave. When the preparations were done, the barrage had lifted and we were told to advance, I was rarely afraid. I was immune to shrapnel and bullets, even when men fell all around me. I grieved for them, regretting their passing, but went on fighting, as if every death – and, God knows, there were many - was evidence of my invulnerability. I wrote stirring letters of regret to soldiers' families… brave, courageous soldier…much loved by the men…died performing his duty… single bullet to the head…died without pain…and felt like a god, convinced that I'd be spared or would die quickly and painlessly. It was a form of madness, induced by the conflict, that couldn't possibly go on."

When Alice said nothing, he continued: "We'd gone back into the line near Givenchy. A mining area. The soft soil was tailor-made for tunnelling and both sides were digging and detonating for all they were worth. We'd done fatigues several times, bringing up props and explosives, carrying the spoil back to the rear. One day, the Boche exploded a mine. It blew a crater thirty feet deep in our line. Large sections disappeared completely. I was inspecting a sap at the time. The chore saved my life. The trench collapsed and everyone in it was buried. The explosion threw me into the air, showering me with earth and debris. I lost consciousness. I don't know for how long. But when I came to, I had been buried alive. I had a pocket of air to sustain me but I was covered in earth and my legs were pinned by timbers so I couldn't move. There was no way back to the surface without help. I heard troops above me, searching for survivors. I could hear their voices. Some of their words were distinct but when I called out, nobody answered and, after a while, they gave up. They didn't think anyone was still left alive."

He began to sob, his shoulders shaking. He leaned against the wall for support, brushing the tears away from his eyes.

"I can't describe how it felt to be left to die. The bodies around me were still. I was the only one left alive. Then, they came back and started digging again. I heard one of them say... he must be here somewhere... let's see if we can find him and bury him properly. They dug round me, stopping and starting. Each time they rested, I thought they were about to give up. Then a shovel came through the soil. I could reach out and touch it. There was daylight. I was able to make myself heard. The men had resurrected me. Their loyalty had prevented me from being buried alive."

Alice could barely comprehend what she'd heard. She had thought that she knew him but she hadn't known him at all. He had concealed everything from her, putting on a brave face, pretending to be someone he wasn't. Had he not realised that he would carry this legacy with him for ever? Had he thought that he could go back as if nothing had happened? He'd done enough, surely? He'd no business going up the line.

"Why did you insist on going back?" she asked, a look of bewilderment on her face. "Even when we met and you could barely walk, you were fretting to go back. No one would have thought any the worse of you if you'd chosen to go somewhere back from the line."

His face assumed a stubborn expression. "I couldn't abandon the men – not after what they'd done for me."

Which men did he mean? Those who had rescued him? Would they still be there? Would he go back to his battalion or would they send him elsewhere? She thought his loyalty misguided but said nothing, wanting to respect his feelings, the sentiments that had driven him on.

"Why didn't you tell me any of this before? Why did you allow me to go on thinking that you were unscathed?"

"It was difficult in hospital. I couldn't stop trembling. I felt the damp earth pressing down on me; the taste of the debris was still in my mouth. I used to wake up in the night, struggling to cast off the blankets, reliving my burial, convinced that I'd never see daylight again. Then, when the memories faded and I gained control of my body, I convinced myself that I was over it and that nothing like that would happen to me again."

"You believed in your immortality again?"

He looked sheepish. "I suppose I did?"

"Well, you weren't over it. That was wishful thinking. You don't know yourself in the least. That experience will live with you for ever. Something so awful is bound to endure."

"The doctors declared I was GS again."

Alice made no effort to conceal her contempt. They were nothing but recruiting officers for an army hungry for men. Perhaps they had relied on his enthusiasm, his view that he was ready for more?

"You're suffering from shock. Few doctors recognise the condition but I don't suppose they've ever been in the line. You probably said nothing of your experience or of the fears to which it gave rise. You allowed your determination to prove yourself whole to prevail at the expense of your health. Think of the men who saved your life. What good would you be to them in your present condition? Don't they deserve more than you are able to give?"

"I didn't know how I felt then."

"Put a stop to this nonsense. Be frank with your superiors. Explain to them what you've been through and why you're not fit to go back. If you won't tell them, I'll spell it out to them. I'll tell them that you're not fit to serve and that they're to find you something else for you."

"I need more time."

"Time's got nothing to do with it. You've suffered a trauma you'll never forget. How could you, after all you've been through? You mustn't place yourself in danger again or fool yourself into thinking that you're fit to return."

Malcolm's face was in shadow but the reflection of the moonlight on the water revealed that his haggard features had acquired a new hope. Now his fears were out in the open he believed there might be a chance that Alice would forgive his neglect of her welfare, his cowardice in the face of the fire.

"So now you see why I behaved as I did. There was a reason for it. I know it doesn't excuse my behaviour or mitigate your distress but I couldn't help myself when I ran away. It was a legacy of the war."

Alice said, "I understand only too well."

His heart leapt at her words. If she understood his behaviour, she would surely forgive him and revive the affection that had once been theirs.

"I'm grateful you've told me everything. It makes your behaviour explicable." Alice placed her hand on his arm, touching him for the first time since he had abandoned her . "But it doesn't make any difference. You must see that surely? I can't forgive what you did. Not now, anyway. How could I? You left me to die in a blazing restaurant. You didn't come back to find me. You abandoned me… now, when the danger's past, you've come back. I was sure I was going to die. Blind panic freed me from that place. The fact that there's an explanation for what you did makes no difference. It happened – for whatever reason – and I'll never be able to forgive you, however hard I try. You've destroyed everything we shared."

He reached for her, intending to take her into his arms. She allowed him to hold her but when he attempted to kiss her, she turned her face away. She remained unyielding until he released her and returned his arms to his side.

"Try to forgive me," he said. "I only want to do the right thing".

"It's impossible," she said, shaking her head, her eyes staring into his with a startling frankness. "You're not the man I thought you were. You've never been honest with me. You misled me about your experiences in the line and concealed your marriage from me. You've been careless with my affections. How can I love you when I can't rely on you? Your behaviour has torn us apart."

She was at pains to be frank with him, as he never had with her. When the shock of the bombing and its aftermath were gone, their impact would live on. It would be impossible to truly forgive him for what he'd done. Yet, even as she acknowledged her loss, she was forced to admit her part in their demise. Why had he come to her at the Fellowship if not to solicit her help? His uniform had blinded her to his frailty. She had allowed herself to be drawn into supporting his return to the war.

"Go back to your war if I can't convince you that you've done enough."

"I came back to find you…"

"It was too late by then."

"They told me you'd escaped…and that you had saved somebody else."

"I did what I could…"

"I wanted to apologise for my conduct…"

He thought his words inadequate and ignoble but could think of no others. It would have been better if he had perished in the flames. He had no business going back into the line. The struggle would overwhelm him and yet it was what he had to do. He wasn't doing it for the men that he had left behind. Nor was he trying to impress Alice or to regain her sympathy.

He was doing it for himself. Shell shock or whatever weasel words might be employed to excuse his conduct were not good enough. He had seen the the ill-concealed contempt and the pitying stares reserved for others with that condition and knew it would be more than he could bear.

"Please try to forgive me."

"Not yet…it's too soon. You've no right to ask. Give me time to get over it. Perhaps when the war's over? Who knows?"

"I want to leave with your blessing."

"I want only the best for you, but forgive you…how can I… what happened tonight will live with me for ever. I'll always bear its scars."

What did it matter whether or not she forgave him? He would never forgive himself, whatever she said to console him. His safety was all she cared about now. His attitude placed him in danger. She wondered if his superiors would seek to protect him. Wasn't a man determined to prove himself in the line a person under sentence of death?

She watched the chill waters coruscate the grey stones of the wall. Free of the clouds that had concealed it, the moon cast a silver cloak over the tide. The thick trunks of the railway bridge reared up in the darkness, immoveable and enduring, the rumble of the trains a reminder of its purpose. The inbound brought back the wounded, the stricken casualties of the battle raging in Flanders; the outbound conveyed fresh drafts to the killing grounds. Tomorrow, Malcolm would be on the leave train and she might never set eyes on him again.

She said, "Rest assured that you go with my blessing and all the love that I still have to give. Perhaps, some day, we'll put this behind us, you'll be free of your marriage and able to make a fresh start?"

"You'll say nothing to anyone?"

She gave her assent without hesitation.

"Will you come to the leave train?"

She shook her head, knowing that she lacked the strength to watch him depart.

He asked her to remember him as he was, before the bombing and the scene in the restaurant tore them apart. With all the conviction she could muster, she assured him she would, though she knew that the link between them was broken.

She said, "Forget about me for the rest of the war."

"No letters?"

"Write if you want to but I won't reply."

Though she spoke assuredly, her heart was breaking. She was grateful that the darkness concealed her distress. She hoped he wouldn't notice the tears that stole down her cheeks or the trembling hands that wiped them away. She wanted to build a wall between them and cower behind it. Their only hope was that they might meet as strangers, long after the war, discovering each other again, their past safely behind them. She shivered in spite of her coat. The nervous energy that had sustained her through the perils of the evening had deserted her. It was time to go.

They parted by the bridge, shaking hands formally, like acquaintances meeting in the street. They voiced their goodbyes, vowed to meet after the war, sealing their commitment with a perfunctory kiss. She waited at the foot of the steps. He waved when he reached the top. She responded with a cursory flutter of the hand, wishing now that they weren't parting, that she had agreed to go to the train. She trudged along the Embankment, shoulders hunched as the wind swept off the river, searching in vain for a cab. The moonlight had given way to a shy dawn, the river had ceased to lap at the walls and the city was stirring from its eventful night. She thought of the tasks that she had to do at the Fellowship, the work she had neglected in favour of Malcolm. His departure was a signal. She felt she was being steered in new directions and the prospect excited her.

A taxi took her to Hammersmith Bridge. She watched the sun rise over the river, painting the rooftops of Barnes in a rough, golden hue. The factories in Hammersmith were at work, the sounds reminding her that the requirements of the war were unceasing, that factory, office and farm struggled to meet its demands. When she reached the door of the house, she listened apprehensively for sounds from within. She turned the key and stepped inside, placing her shoes on the mat with studied care. Her mother, in nightdress and dressing gown, her unpinned hair covering her shoulders was standing at the top of the stairs, a tray of tea in her hand. She looked down at Alice, curiosity and concern in her eyes, noting her dishevelled state, the torn coat, the bruise on her face. Not trusting herself to comment on what had happened, Alice said nothing, preferring to wait until she had rested.

"You look as though you've been in the wars."

"Malcolm and I were caught up in the bombing but I'm unharmed."

"Is Malcolm alright?"

"He's gone to pack for the train."

"He leaves later today?"

"Three o'clock."

Louise didn't ask if she was going to the train. Some people made a point of seeing them off. Others preferred to take their leave in a less public place. They had no doubt decided what they wanted to do.

"Is that Alice?"

Bennett's hoarse voice came from the bedroom.

"I'm so glad that you're back. The bombing alarmed us. We didn't know where you were."

"It did a lot of damage but Malcolm and I were unhurt. It ruined our last evening together but otherwise we suffered no harm."

"I'm glad to hear it. We're not safe in our beds anymore."

CHAPTER 25

Stickler for the regulations though he was, Colonel Beaumont-Dart was always prepared to disregard them in the battalion's interest. Fearing they were about to spend a second Christmas in the trenches, he lobbied to have their orders changed. The compromise agreed found the battalion in brigade reserve near Neuve Chapelle on Christmas Eve, occupying a deserted village behind the line with two whole days at its disposal before going up, time enough to enjoy the Christmas Day denied to them the previous year. The sector had been a quiet one for several weeks, a far cry from the previous months' hostilities.

Shortly before Christmas, Michael was promoted to orderly room lance-corporal. He regarded his promotion as a mixed blessing. Whilst it meant that he often had the opportunity to snatch a few hours' sleep on the makeshift bed in the CO's dugout and could take a turn at warming himself at its evil-smelling stove, it meant also that he often spent the night staggering along the trembling duckboards or wading through the icy water of the trenches in search of company commanders, colliding with grumpy sentries at every traverse or would find himself despatched to some distant trouble spot to find out what was 'brewing'. He thought his duties to be inspired by his persistent failure to apply for a commission.

His determination to remain a private had been prompted by his parent's opposition to his enlistment. He felt no one could doubt his sincerity if he remained in the ranks for the duration of the war. Now after eighteen months in the line, he realised that the time had come to do more and that in choosing to seek a commission he would have the support and understanding of his parents. Facilitated by Alice, who remained his confidant, there had sprung up between him and his parents a degree of mutual respect and understanding absent when he had first enlisted. He wrote to them frequently, despatching carefully crafted letters, designed to inform but not alarm them and eagerly awaited their replies. He marvelled at the continuity of their world, which, for all the changes wrought by the war, was essentially the life that he had left behind and contrasted it with the hazardous and topsy-turvy world that he inhabited. He didn't resent their unchanging ways, drawing comfort from them, and encouraged their interest in his activities, even as he excluded from his letters anything likely to concern them. He felt, in the light of his experience and their ignorance of the nature of the war, that he was the parent and they were the children and that any advice that he received from them, and there was much of it, might be safely ignored.

His reluctance to leave the battalion had diminished as many of his friends, young men who, like him, had responded instinctively to Lord Kitchener's beckoning finger, had gone: dead, missing, wounded, captured or transferred elsewhere. So great had been the casualties that it was now customary to hold back a tenth of the battalion's strength during any action and it was difficult to keep up with the rash of drafts. Sometimes, when he found himself alone beneath the stars, staring into no-man's land, his febrile mind conjured up the presence of his lost comrades. They marched past the wall of sandbags as if taking up their former places in the trenches or paraded on the denuded plateau over which he watched in spectral ranks, sloping arms or forming fours in response to inaudible commands. He recalled the many faces, struggling to put names to them, before busying himself with his duties, fearing for his sanity if he dwelt too long upon their absence.

The colonel shared his dismay at the loss of so many officers and men. 'B' company's CO was dead, killed supervising repairs to a trench wall when a German "48" had put down a shell in the midst of his working party. Captain Reynolds, 'A' company's CO was gone, badly wounded, convalescing somewhere in England. An exemplary officer, a tall, young man with a terse voice, a brisk manner and the habit of command, he had been the apple of the colonel's eye. It had been an inglorious end for a promising young officer and the colonel felt his absence keenly. He always made a point of receiving the news of casualties with a stern, impassive face that kept his thoughts well-hidden, but when he thought that he was dead the mask had slipped. His face had crumpled, his voice had broken and he had turned away, taking several minutes to resume his gruff, old ways. Later they had found him slumped across the dug-out table, the candle beside him burned down, his eyes red from exhaustion, an empty whisky bottle on the floor beside him.

The colonel always found new officers a challenge. Their training was brief, their experience limited and their approach to command varied between infuriating caution and rash initiatives that placed the men in danger. He consoled himself with the thought that the longer they survived, the more useful they became, but all too often their tenure was brief and he and his subordinates found themselves assimilating further new recruits. However, asked to assess his officers old and new, the colonel would have admitted without hesitation that none had taxed his patience or that of his company commander as much as Lieutenant Jenkins.

Jenkins was the youngest and least capable of four sons, all of whom had rushed to enlist and three of whom had died during the course of the conflict. The fear that her youngest son might go the way of his brothers had crazed Jenkins's mother. She was a vigorous and well-connected widow, determined to ensure that her remaining son survived.

She seemed to have the capacity to bend everyone to her will except him. In spite of her efforts, he insisted on joining the infantry as his brothers had done and survived some of the most hazardous campaigns of the war, not by any show of competence but by sheer good fortune. Urged on by his general, the colonel had responded to a particularly provocative letter from Jenkins's mother by assuring her that her son would come to no harm. This was plausible as their sector was quiet and the battalion's duties consisted of little more than trench maintenance, sentry duty, wiring and reconnaissance. However, it was clear that the battalion's good fortune had run its course and that their next spell in the line would take a further toll on their numbers. Whilst the colonel had no wish to favour any officer, he was mindful of his rash promise to Jenkins's mother as they prepared to go up.

Twenty four years of age, short and plump, Jenkins combined a cherubic face with a voice that rose sharply when he was agitated. He was conspicuously deficient in the physical requirements of an officer. His vision was poor. How he had managed to pass his physical was a mystery to everyone. He was clumsy, finding it impossible to tie knots or fit things together, and was always falling over things in the cramped conditions of the billets. The merest hint of a strafe threw him into confusion. Yet, he was not disliked or dismissed. There was a dogged persistence about him, an indifference to danger that commanded respect and a willingness to put up with any inconvenience. He accepted the troglodyte conditions of the trenches as if they were the only life that he had ever known. "My God, what next?" the CO was often heard to declare when informed of another of his mishaps but blessed as he was with his presence, there was little he could do to protect him other than to transfer Sergeant Fox to his platoon with instructions to do his utmost to keep him out of harm's way until he could engineer his transfer elsewhere.

The battalion reached its new billets on December 23 after six days in Brigade reserve, destined to spend the two days of Christmas there before going forward. The men marched the ten miles from the railhead, leaving their packs to be brought up on ASC lorries, striding along the uneven roads in the biting wind with their rifles and equipment, the officers' horses breathing like dragons in the chill air. The sound of tramping feet echoed across the threadbare fields. By the side of the road lay abandoned carts and limbers, burnt-out lorries, the bloated remains of horses, ice-filled shell craters and the splintered trunks of trees. The only signs of life were the parting troops, their shouts of encouragement and the irreverent messages passing up and down the columns. They assured the battalion that their time in the ruined village would be uneventful even though the waiting billets lay within the range of the German guns.

Lieutenant Jenkins was not amongst the marching columns. He, Michael and the quartermaster were scavenging in the nearby villages for the Christmas lunch. They visited as many of the farms as they could, spending a largely futile day in search of milk, poultry and fresh vegetables. They had almost despaired of finding anything when they spotted some turkeys in a farmyard. Their owner, a churlish French farmer, viewed them with immense suspicion before agreeing to sell his flock for what Michael regarded as an outrageous price. Mission accomplished, Jenkins rushed back to the village to ensure that his men had been properly housed.

Michael had hoped that Christmas Eve would be uneventful, an opportunity to talk, rest, smoke and write letters. Instead, he spent the night transporting ammunition, sandbags, barbed wire and duckboards to the forward positions. Shadowy figures stumbled over each other in the darkness as they hastened down the communication trenches with their burdens, waiting all the while for the lights to go up and a strafe to begin. For all the assurances of the departing battalion, the troops in the trenches opposite were a treacherous lot, given to unexpected forays and short bombardments intended to cause disruption and confusion. Michael only hoped that they would be left in peace to enjoy the festivities. When he returned to the village, dawn was already breaking over the German lines. He fell asleep with the sound of the Christmas preparations ringing in his ears.

It was anticipated that lunch would last the whole afternoon, the men eating first, followed by the officers, concluding with the cooks and servants. The first sitting began at midday. The men sat in groups in the bright sunlight, availing themselves of whatever seating they could find: kitbags, ammunition boxes, bags of hay. They were as excited and as exuberant as a group of school children on an outing. Enthusiastic voices echoed down the street; snatches of Christmas carols mingled with raucous laughter. Knowing that they were going up for ten days the following night, the men were determined to enjoy themselves, to avail themselves of the battalion's generosity whilst they had the chance.

The colonel moved amongst them, watching with quiet satisfaction as they tucked into their food, jostled for a second helping, smiled appreciatively. They deserved a treat, he thought, after the rigours of recent months. The irony of the trenches was that the hardship, the uncertainty, the absence of family and friends, the prospect of death contrived to elevate the simplest of pleasures. Those who survived the hostilities would relive this unexceptional lunch for the rest of their days. He also recognised their willingness to savour every moment was unlikely to survive the peace. Freed of adversity, they would all, himself included, become the ungrateful crew they were before the war, weighed down by everyday concerns, unmindful of their conspicuous good fortune.

At two o' clock, the officers sat down at an oak table in the large farmhouse that stood at the end of the village and served as battalion headquarters and officers' mess. The colonel sat at the head of the table, flanked by the adjutant and the regimental medical officer. Each place was designated with knives, forks, spoons and napkin, place card and a handwritten menu. Michael's mouth began to water when he smelt the food. He had volunteered to wait on the officers. It meant that he ate with the cooks and servants but obtained the officers' seven courses including Scotch woodcock and toast, roast turkey and sausages, Christmas pudding and mince pies and a selection of fine wines. He willed everyone to eat faster so those waiting on them could begin their feast. He directed the waiters as if he were a transport officer at a busy crossroads, determined to ensure that everyone received their fair share of the food and that it was served hot. The conversation never flagged as the food was devoured, each course heightening its intensity. Even Jenkins, usually so shy and reticent in the presence of his fellow-officers, was flushed and voluble, laughing readily as his companions joked at his expense.

The colonel kept a watchful eye on the proceedings, noting that Michael in his quiet way had taken over the logistics. Though he said little, his affable expression betrayed his pleasure that the menu over which he had laboured for so long had been the subject of many appreciative comments. When he rose to speak, he was conscious of how many new faces gazed up at him and how many of those present previously were missing. The changes made him wary, conscious of the need to engage with everyone but to keep his distance, to take note of events, but pass on unperturbed. What was his message to be as he proposed the toasts? Carry on? Do your duty? Never once look back? It was simple enough advice, and probably right, but difficult to implement. What of the future? He smiled sardonically. Did they have a future or would the conflict consume them all? Their fate was in the hands of God and the High Command and their conduct of the war had failed to impress him.

"Nice to see the old man looking so jolly," muttered Aspinall, the transport officer, as the colonel sat down. "The casualties of the last strafe had seemed to knock the stuffing out of him."

"Hardly surprising, was it?" the quartermaster said. "But don't you worry about him, he's indestructible. He'll see us all out."

"He's started drinking again," said Aspinall, lowering his voice and looking pointedly down the table.

"Wouldn't you, if you had his responsibilities?"

The quartermaster was not about to be drawn into any discussion of the colonel's deficiencies. In his eyes, the CO was beyond reproach. He patted his ample stomach, looked across the table at Lieutenant Jenkins and said with satisfaction, "The turkey was the final touch."

Jenkins gazed round the room, examining every officer in turn, proud to be one of them. He knew that he could be a liability, that his life was a constant struggle to do what others found easy, but he felt that he had at last proved equal to the challenge of being an officer, that he had been accepted by his company and battalion, and that, perhaps, in the army's impersonal embrace, he had found a home.

"When's the carol singing?" asked the quartermaster, glancing at his watch. He had been put out when the battalion had been occupied on Christmas Eve. He was looking forward to the singing, believing falsely that he had a pleasing bass voice.

The colonel and the medical officer were deep in conversation at the end of the table. Michael caught snatches of it as he moved in and out of the room. The RMO was a grizzled, little man with iron-grey hair and piercing, blue eyes. He was the CO's eyes and ears amongst the men. The two of them were laying bets as to how many men would report sick on Boxing Day.

The RMO's prognosis was gloomy. He believed that the mix of volunteers, attested men and conscripts had changed for the worst.

He said, "I've never seen such an astonishing variety of narrow and misshapen chests as I have in this last draft. Where are they getting these people from? Few of them are fit enough to do fatigues, let alone undertake long route marches or fight the enemy."

"They're certainly shorter than they used to be," the colonel said, though he was unconcerned. He saw the line as a great leveller. It didn't matter who you were or what you had done, when you were under fire. There was no way of knowing who would do well. He was constantly surprised by who prevailed and who failed miserably. It was the lack of numbers that concerned him the most. In spite of the War Office reducing the entry height by five inches, the battalion was still under strength, numbering five hundred and forty at the last count, three hundred less than when he had first commanded it.

He said, "I'm in favour of anything that increases the numbers."

The RMO shook his head; "You'll have to change the conditions in the trenches then. Sore feet, trench fever, influenza and colds are the real enemy. They exact a fearsome toll at this time of year."

"How many will parade sick tomorrow?"

"In 'A' company? Fifteen, at least," the RMO said, definitively.

"Good God, that's more than ten percent and they're about to go back in the line. Are you sure?"

"Certain, but if you don't believe me, you can always risk a little wager on it."

The CO was not to be intimidated, though he knew the RMO was rarely wrong about these things. He felt that his battalion was being unfairly criticised and that he should support his men.

"Five shillings?"

"Fifteen or less, you win; more than fifteen, I win," the MO countered.

The Colonel looked at him suspiciously. "I expect you to treat their plaintive cries with your usual cynicism?"

The RMO said, "The brave and diligent are rarely ill. I learnt that long ago."

The CO wondered how he was going to pay up if he lost, as he surely would. His young and wayward wife had stopped writing to him again, a sure sign that she had spent all of their money. It was incredible how much she spent. Where did it all go? She had never adjusted to his army pay. The Christmas lunch had been a last act of defiance, an assertion of financial independence before he sank beneath a sea of debts. She was expecting to become a widow, he was sure of it. Well, he was going to disappoint her.

Michael wondered if he was going to survive the war. He felt strangely confident that he would. He had no wish for a Blighty like so many of the others. He wanted to see the war through, to experience every aspect of it. He never ceased to be surprised how quickly he forgot its dangers. Today, as on so many days, the hazards of the line seemed a distant, hazy dream.

He had just summoned the servants to clear away the plates when the bombardment started. There was no mistaking the enemy's intentions. They were ranging their guns. The first salvo fell short of the street; the second passed over their heads, kicking up huge clouds of earth and dust in the fields behind the houses and the third fell squarely on the patch of ground where, barely an hour previously, the men had sat in groups, devouring their lunch.

There was little panic in the dining room, only cries of outrage, curses at the inconvenience and shouts of disbelief that the enemy should have chosen such a time to demonstrate its malevolence.

Michael's preoccupation was the Christmas lunch. Surely after all their hard work, after watching others stuff themselves for the best part of four hours, he was not about to be denied his feast? He consoled himself with the thought that the cooks hadn't eaten and that, reputedly, they never missed a meal.

The colonel's thoughts were with the men. They had to be dispersed quickly, secreted in the basements and other shelters where they would be safe. He wondered what had prompted the enemy to strike. The men in the forward positions would know soon enough. He began to shout orders, his face red with anger, his fury at the enemy's aggression matched only by the thought that his determination to indulge the men might have placed their lives in danger.

"What a time to choose," the RMO said through gritted teeth, as he jammed his helmet on, wrestled with the strap. He didn't doubt he was going to have his hands full for the rest of the day. He wished he'd eaten less, desisted from the wine, as he headed for the door.

"Two can play at this game," the colonel said. "Ruin our Christmas and we will surely ruin yours." He said this in the certain knowledge that behind the village on a gentle slope were ranged the British guns, a motley collection, but sufficient to exact a toll on the artillery that had them in their sights. He knew that as soon as the German shells passed over the forward observation posts, the British artillery would reply in kind.

Then he realised what they were up to. This was no ordinary bombardment designed to interrupt their afternoon. It was a gas attack. Planned many hours previously, before the wind had changed, the Germans had decided to unleash it now the wind had turned half circle. It was blowing in the right direction and was strong enough to convey the gas beyond the trenches but too weak to disperse it. That was the trouble with gas. Rarely were the conditions right for its use. You had to exploit the opportunity whenever you could. It might not come again for some considerable time. At least it wasn't mustard gas, the newest and most deadly effluvium in the German repertoire, he concluded, as dense clouds of dark, green vapour advanced down the street. They would deal with it well enough in their respirators, if everybody had sufficient time to shroud themselves against the deadly fumes.

The room has already begun to empty. Gas! The Colonel's cry was taken up. Respirators appeared by magic, everyone aware that one whiff of gas would suffice to induce the splitting headache and sharp pain in the lungs that was the prelude to drowning. They stared at each other with large, oval eyes from their imperfect sanctuaries, heads swivelling slowly to extend their field of vision, their movements laboured and clumsy as if performing some exacting mime, and colliding with each other in the confines of the house.

The colonel took one last, lingering glance at the chaotic scene and prepared to slip his mask over his head. He had put it off as long as he dared. He loathed wearing it, hated being sealed in his own muffled, odourless world. Then he caught sight of Jenkins. He was standing in the corner of the room, helpless, unsure whether to flee to his billet and the mask that he had left there or whether to announce his mistake and seek help from others. What could they do to help him when he had no mask? He seemed transfixed by the hooded figures around him. Meanwhile, outside the window, fanned by the breeze, the dark, green cloud was stealing up on them.

He was on the point of dashing out of the house when the colonel restrained him.

"Don't be such a bloody fool. You can't risk being caught out there without a mask. Wait here, until we kit you out."

A search of the building confirmed that every mask was spoken for. Jenkins's mask would have to be collected from his billet. His panic mounting, he stood by the window, watching the gas cloud advance towards them. It dispersed neither right nor left. It seemed to have him in its sights, to sense his vulnerability.

"You'll be all right here," the colonel insisted, with more confidence than he felt. "We'll block the doors and windows; seal ourselves in until the gas disperses." Mindful of Jenkins's mother, her plaintive letters to the general, the colonel prepared to offer up his mask to Jenkins but Sergeant Fox was too quick for him.

"Sir, I'll look after him; he's my responsibility."

He had told the colonel he would keep an eye on Jenkins and meant to keep his word. He removed the mask that he had just put on and thrust it into Jenkins's hands. "Here, take this, I'll get by without it."

Jenkins hesitated, a look of horror on his face, torn between his terror of the advancing gas and his unwillingness to place the sergeant's life in jeopardy.

"Go on, take it," the sergeant insisted, shaking the helmet like a rat.

Jenkins's hands were trembling so much that he had difficulty pulling the mask over his head. He kept shooting anguished glances at the colonel's face but if the colonel took him for a fool, he gave no sign of it. His thoughts were with the sergeant, the burden he had assumed on his behalf and how to make him safe.

Michael helped Jenkins put on the mask, jamming it over his face unceremoniously, leaving the hapless figure to adjust the box, begin his laboured breathing. Others, focused on the sergeant's plight, were shedding tunics and even trousers; soaking them in wine and water to make them pliable, they attempted to draught proof the mess, to secure it from the gas.

Outside, the afternoon sun had disappeared, obscured by the dense, green cloud. The wind that had carried it beyond the line for which it was intended had faltered, depositing the cloud upon the village so that the opposite side of the street, the abandoned estaminet, the church with its brazen steeple, had been reduced to distant, ill-formed shapes. There was no sign of movement on the street, no shadowy figures, no sound from any living thing, merely an awed hush, a tense expectancy, a longing for release. From beyond the village came the drumming of the guns as the

British artillery expressed its indignation. Before the trenches, the German troops swarmed forward, hoping to benefit from their unexpected malice.

Soon, every nook and cranny in the house was firmly closed. A broken window had been sealed with planks and table cloth; a table jammed against the chimney breast, served to mask the gaping hole, where once a fire had burned. The sergeant had retreated up the stairs. There on the uppermost floor, his helpers resumed their makeshift carpentry, sealing up the doors and windows as best they could, fighting to preserve the stale but healthy air.

Jenkins refused to leave the sergeant's side. He mimicked every move and gesture of the older man as if by faithful replication it was possible to undo the damage he had wrought. Watching him through the goggles of his mask, Michael was convinced that, at the first approach of gas, he would attempt to save the sergeant's life by offering him his hood. The colonel thought it also. He motioned Michael to keep an eye on him, to prevent him doing anything that would put his life at risk.

The RMO produced a set of rags and indicated to the sergeant that he was to urinate on them. When that was done, he bound the sodden rags over the sergeant's mouth and nose with a short piece of cord, so tightly that the sergeant could hardly breathe, and urged him to lie down in the corner of the room. The others then covered him with the sacks that they had gathered up at the RMO's instigation. The sergeant was to remain concealed until the gas was gone.

The colonel, a strange, masked figure, seemed as calm as ever as he checked the arrangements. He doubted the measures they had taken would fail but you never knew. Gas was unpredictable, at the mercy of the elements, a hazard to the perpetrator and the victim in equal measure. He had seen its consequences at first hand, had glimpsed its victims coughing up their greenish froth, had observed the yellowing skins, the protruding tongues, the fearful spasms that signified the end and never wanted to see their like again. It was the only death he really feared and yet he felt he should have overruled the sergeant, that it should be him beneath the sacks, with a rag around his mouth and nostrils, rather than the man that he had charged with Jenkins's welfare.

The house began to fill with gas. The crude precautions, swiftly taken, had not sufficed to keep it out. The house had taken on the same ghastly silence as the street outside. Now no one moved or spoke. They stood motionless or leaned against the walls, watching the fog thicken, taking comfort from each other's presence, each sealed in his own, private world. Occasionally, they glanced at the sealed door that led up the stairs, waiting on the coughing, and the cries of anguish that would indicate that the gas had claimed its victim. By the time a surplus mask arrived, the gas was circulating freely throughout the house and closing the front door no longer served any useful purpose.

Inside the sealed room, the light was fading but the air had failed to take on the green hue outside the window and there was no evidence of distress from the muffled figure in the corner, save for the occasional cough, a choking sound from beneath the sacks. The sergeant lay motionless, intent on doing nothing that would accelerate his breathing, conscious only of a raging thirst and a cracking headache. He prayed earnestly that his luck would hold or that if the air grew hostile, they would get the mask to him in time.

There was no sign of the cloud retreating. The gas was seeping through the cracks and apertures of the upper room as if it knew of the potential victim there and was determined to pursue him. The colonel signalled by knocking on the door that the time had come to act. By means of signs and muffled shouts, it was agreed that Jenkins would open the door, that Michael would rush out for the mask and that, having discarded the sacks and cast off the rags around his mouth, the sergeant would don the vital headgear, assisted by the colonel.

The door swung back, Michael appeared; the helmet was thrust into his outstretched hand. He stumbled back into the room. Jenkins slammed the door behind him. As he neared the pile of sacks, the sergeant rose up to greet him, the urine stained rags still clasped to his mouth. The colonel reached out for the mask and thrust it to his face, almost trapping his hand. The wadding dropped to the floor and the kneeling figure fell back, letting out his breath in a great sigh. For a moment he laid writhing and coughing on the ground. Then he rose shakily to his feet, the mask firmly in place. A muffled cheer went up from the anxious group around him.

They remained inside the house until the gas had cleared. Outside the sky darkened, the wind picked up again and it began to rain. The colonel moved amongst them anxiously, intent on ensuring that no one removed his helmet in spite of the discomfort, until he was sure that it was safe to do so. He kept Jenkins in his sights throughout their vigil. He didn't reproach him publicly or indicate by words or signs his disapproval but his scrutiny betrayed a deep suspicion, a caution in his presence, as if he could not quite believe that he had been spared the onerous task of writing a letter of condolence to Jenkins' anxious mother or submitting an apology to the general for failing to protect him.

Surprisingly, the casualties were few. However, in the scramble to protect the troops, the battalion had neglected its animals. The makeshift stables at the back of the house were strewn with dead horses. They lay in tortured postures, many of them torn and bleeding from their efforts to escape their tethers. The sight of them sickened Michael. Innocent bystanders that they were, they had not deserved such an awful fate.

The next day Jenkins started to act strangely. He refused to parade or to attend to his duties. He lay under his blankets, refusing to move or speak, staring into space. The RMO examined him, pronounced him fit and well and asked the colonel to have a word with him.

The colonel, pale and weary after their ordeal, ushered everyone out of the orderly room, closed the door firmly and addressed Jenkins for the first time since the gas attack. Their meeting was a brief one and no one ever discovered what passed between them but shortly afterwards Jenkins was back on his feet again, as keen as ever. Nonetheless, two weeks later, to no one's great surprise, he was transferred to another battalion. His folly in misplacing his gas mask was never openly discussed in the colonel's presence and remained known only to those who witnessed it.

"You got rid of him pretty damn quick," the RMO commented when he heard the news of Jenkins's departure. He was still aggrieved that Jenkins's resurrection had cost him five shillings. The colonel kept his counsel. He had never mentioned Jenkins' circumstances to anyone but, having convinced himself that Jenkins's days were numbered, he had wanted to be certain that he wouldn't be the one to communicate the news of his demise to his next of kin.

He adopted the house that had been their refuge as his HQ in spite of its unpropitious beginnings. His office there acquired a battered desk, a swivel chair and an old sofa with springs sticking through its cushions. Soon, the desk was piled with papers demanding his attention. Michael found him there when he sought him out, gazing at his correspondence with anger and frustration.

"Where does it all come from?" the colonel demanded. "How am I supposed to find the time to deal with all this stuff?"

His antipathy to paperwork was a legend throughout the division. He was incapable of managing the avalanche of orders that descended on his battalion and unable to bring himself to reply to the innumerable requests for information that issued from division and brigade.

"Is it important?" he asked brusquely when Michael looked at him expectantly. "What do you want? Still hoping for your Christmas lunch, I suppose?"

Michael's grimace indicated that the absence of the Christmas lunch that the others had so enjoyed rankled with him still. It was something he would hold against the Germans for the remainder of his days.

He said, "Sir, I just wanted to tell you that I've decided to apply for a commission."

He leaned forward, hoping to lay the papers, newly signed by his CO, on the colonel's desk but seeing the heap of papers there, he hastily withdrew them.

"No need to put them in the pile," the colonel said, "They could be there a while. Give them to me. I'll sign them right away and you can take them to the adjutant. What's brought this on so suddenly?" he asked as he flourished his pen. "I thought you were committed to the ranks. Some men are, you know. They prefer it, God knows why, to the officer's mess."

"I think I'm ready, sir."

"You're certainly needed. Anyway, if it's what you want to do, you can be sure of my support." He gave Michael a quizzical look. There was more to this than met the eye, he was sure of it, but knowing that certain things are best unsaid, he didn't press Michael for his reasons. He was very young, but so many of them were. He would make a good officer if he applied himself. He certainly knew how to keep his head in a tight spot. That was no small thing. He just hoped that he would survive longer than the others.

Disappointed by his taciturnity, Michael saluted smartly and turned to leave the room. Then as he neared the door, the colonel said softly, "You'll keep your respirator with you, won't you, when you're an officer?"

"Yes, sir," Michael answered promptly.

The colonel resumed frowning at his papers before Michael had the opportunity to catch his eye.

PART V

April, 1918

CHAPTER 26

Louise had watched the telegraph boy in his dark, blue suit and pill box hat in the early months of the war. He was an angel of death, omnipotent and feared, who flitted from house to house. It had been different then. Robert had been in America; Michael was at boarding school. She had no reason to fear the telegrams that he delivered, the messages they contained. Now the telegraph boy with his shock of red hair and his spindly legs was gone, swallowed up by the war and telegrams and letters could come at any time, delivered by girls or old men. She watched and waited, like any mother whose son was in the line. She occasionally sat by the bedroom window, gazing out across the street and common, waiting for the post, welcoming the letters that told of Michael's adventures or the field postcards with their deletions that signified that he was well. Unread books lay beside her, long abandoned sewing, unfinished letters and the diary that she had written since the war began. She was convinced that Michael would survive as long as he was present in her thoughts. Bennett sometimes took up her position if he had time on his hands. It was during one such vigil that news of Michael came.

He was sitting by the window idly turning the pages of a magazine, lost to his thoughts, when he saw a figure in the street, saw her stand her bicycle against the wall, place her hand upon the garden gate. When the straw hat passed beneath the window, he craned forward, hoping that the approaching figure was the product of a tired mind but there was no mistaking the footsteps in the porch, the rap of the knocker. He raced down the stairs, stumbling in his haste, to intercept the tidings that she brought.

A young woman stood on the doorstep. He recognised her at once. Her mother owned the flower stall in the village; she helped out at the weekends. He had been there only yesterday, buying the flowers that adorned the dining room. She stood before him nervously; a slender figure in navy blue tunic and shirt, black stockings and boots, a straw hat with a blue band and GPO badge balanced on her head. She dug into the pouch at her waist and thrust an orange envelope into his outstretched hand. She began to speak, thought better of it and retreated down the path. Bennett noted her downcast eyes, her indecent haste to leave as he closed the door. The unopened letter in his hand, he retreated to the study.

Louise was standing in the hall, drying her hands on a towel. She allowed it to fall to the floor as he approached her, making no attempt to retrieve it. Her face was pale, drained of its usual colour, her eyes wary and alert. She followed every motion of his hand, poised to snatch the envelope he held, to extract the words that it contained.

"It might not be what you think it is," Bennett said, without conviction, clinging tightly to the envelope, ignoring her outstretched hand.

"Open it," she said, her voice rising.

Her words had a force difficult to ignore, but he could still not bring himself to open the envelope. He wanted to retain his fragile hopes as long as possible. If the envelope remained intact, there were grounds for optimism.

He led her, hands trembling, into the study until, standing in front of the fireplace, he tore apart the flimsy paper and read:

B 104-83

Sir,

I regret to have to inform you that a report has been received from the War Office to the effect that S4765, Second Lieutenant Michael Bennett, was posted as missing on the 12 Day of April, 1918,

I am, sir
Your obedient servant

The study was silent, perfectly still, as if everyone in the world held their breath. Nothing moved or stirred. There was a new chill in the air; spring had reverted to winter and storm clouds filled the sky, threatening rain or snow. The leaves on the trees outside the study window hung irresolutely, waiting on the breeze. Bennett read the letter again, mouthing the words silently. They were familiar enough. Others had shown him the same sorrowful tidings but only now did he begin to understand their impact. Only when they concerned his son, was their meaning clear.

"What does it say?" Louise demanded but there was no need to ask or read the message for herself. Its contents were evident in Bennett's eyes, in his inability to speak. She watched him read the words repeatedly hoping further scrutiny might change the tidings they conveyed.

"He's been posted missing."

"Missing?" She mouthed the word contemptuously. "I thought you were going to say he was dead." She shook her head defiantly. "He's missing. They don't know where he is. He might be lost or wounded. He might have been taken prisoner. We'll have to wait for further news."

Bennett handed her the letter, wanting her to see the typed phases, the spaces where Michael's name, rank and number had been inserted. They meant that the battlefield had swallowed him up, that he had been destroyed beyond recognition by artillery fire or lay unburied somewhere, exposed to the elements until his remains became unidentifiable and were placed in a mass grave with others who had shared his fate. It was the outcome he had most feared: a death that meant that his body remained uncommitted to God, except in their hearts.

When she had finished reading the telegram, he reached for her hand, wanting to hold her, to bury her sorrow in his embrace, but she held back, fearing that by touching him she would acquiesce in Michael's death.

She said, "We can't be sure he's dead, can we? We'll have to contact the War Office and write to his battalion to find out what they know. Why are they so vague? Don't they recognise we hang on their every word?"

"I'm sure they've told us everything they know. Thousands of men are listed missing every month. It simply means that their deaths have gone unrecorded, that they've been swallowed up by the battlefield."

"But how many of them will reappear when the fighting's over? How do we know that he hasn't been captured or isn't lying in a hospital somewhere, unable to contact us?"

Bennett felt a dark fury well up inside him. He was angry at the world, for the scale of the injustice and the folly that had torn his son from him. He was angry at Michael for defying him, for enlisting so enthusiastically for a conflict they opposed. He was angry at Louise for hoping when there were few grounds for optimism; above all, he was angry at his inability to influence events or to return his son to their midst.

"He's gone," he said violently, "there's no point in pretending otherwise. Ambiguity is unavoidable in a conflict on this scale. I can't bear it. No one should be listed missing or have to die without the rites and ceremony that are due to them."

He slumped into the armchair, cradling his head in his hands.

Louise could see that he was crying whilst trying not to show it. He held back the storm successfully at first and then his grief prevailed. Sobs shook his body; he turned and twisted in his seat, his face contorted with pain. He was aware of Louise falling down on her knees, of her arms enveloping him, of feeling her cold tears on his cheek but had little idea how long they remained there or what words they exchanged. Eventually, they stood upright, brushed each other down, smiling wanly, drawing comfort from each other's presence. Neither of them touched the telegram that lay beside them on the floor.

When Bennett had composed himself, Louise said tentatively, "You'll try to find out what's happened to him, won't you, for my peace of mind, if for no other reason? I know it probably won't make any difference; I'm sure they've told us all they know but I couldn't bear it if we never knew what had become of him."

Though she chose her words with care, Bennett knew her hopes were undiminished. They were an opiate, a refuge, a way to postpone still greater pain and he wanted to destroy them, to reduce her to his circumstances but dare not for fear of adding to their grief.

He said without conviction, "I'll do what I can. But now we have to talk to Alice; Robert has to know as well. Where's Alice? Why isn't she here?."

Louise found his urge to inform the others premature, almost indecent; she wanted him to make enquiries, before leaping to conclusions. She recognised his urgency for what it was. His resort to bustle and activity was an effort to dilute his grief. When his activities were exhausted, his distress would issue unrestrained. Meanwhile, she could only envy his manic energy, his desire to orchestrate their mourning.

She said, "I tried to stop him going. I did everything I could."

"His mind was made up. He was determined to serve his country. That's the phrase they use, isn't it, to describe this mindless sacrifice of the nation's youth?"

He had sought to utilise his parental authority; he had begged, cajoled and bullied to no avail. It had been as if the whole of Michael's life had been a preparation for the day that he enlisted. He had always been different from the others though his rebellion had never been overt; it had lain below the surface, awaiting an issue worthy of the struggle to break free.

"I tried to get him back after he'd enlisted," Louise stated, though she didn't understand why she felt compelled to reveal her defiance after so long. "I wrote to the War Office and told them that he was under age."

"What happened?"

"They never even replied."

"You can't have been alone in your desire to save your son."

Louise rose to her feet, crossed the room and stood before the window, craning her neck to see above the hedge that shielded the front garden from the street. Bennett was reminded of her hours of vigilance, her efforts to avoid the news that they'd just received.

He said, "We dispatched Michael with our blessing. That was what we agreed to do when we felt we had no choice. We certainly didn't say we wouldn't support him or would try to get him back."

"You never really tried to stop him."

When Bennett started to protest, Louise said quickly, "Oh, yes, you appealed to his ideals; you cited our long tradition of opposition to war but you never forbade him to go, never required him to defy you..."

"It wouldn't have done any good. We talked about it at great length. His mind was made up."

"He was only a schoolboy. You could have made him wait until he was old enough."

To Bennett's consternation, Louise seemed intent on rehearsing the old, fruitless arguments as if Michael's future still hung in the balance.

"I couldn't bear to think of him leaving without our blessing. That was the alternative. Imagine how he'd have felt, risking his life at the front, knowing we'd rejected him. Surely, it must always be the case that we support our children in their endeavours? That's what parents do, isn't it? That's what it means to be a parent."

Louise bowed her head in acquiescence. Everything he said was true and yet she couldn't rid herself of a feeling of guilt over her son's fate. Nor could she stop believing that they had conspired unwittingly to expose him to danger.

She said, "We tried to bring our children up as individuals, as people who could think and act for themselves. The risk we always took was that when they went their separate ways, they would act in defiance of our wishes."

Bennett joined her at the window. She consented to take his outstretched hand and rested her head on his shoulder. Together, they watched the rain drip from the trees, the flowers swaying in silent synchronicity, the blackbirds searching busily upon the lawn for the worms they craved. She knew that he was right, that reluctant acquiescence had been preferable to being estranged from Michael. She still had his letters and the memory of him first appearing in his uniform, immensely proud of it and but embarrassed to wear it in their home.

"We mustn't blame ourselves for what's happened."

Bennett spoke as though she had left the room and he was sifting his thoughts, attempting to make sense of everything, imagining a future without his younger son.

"Events have taken the course we feared. We'll have to bear our loss like all the other families who have drawn their curtains and turned their backs on the world. Our duty's to preserve his memory, support the others in their grief.."

"Poor Alice. Whatever will she do without her little brother? There were times I thought she made a better mother than I did. He used to follow her everywhere, hanging on her every word, and she never neglected him or let him down. Whatever she was doing, she would always find the time to play with him."

"You were always admirable, the rock to which he clung."

"But in the end I couldn't save him."

"We've lost him to the war."

"We mustn't talk as though he's dead. He's posted missing. That leaves grounds for hope. We have to write to everyone who knew him, contact those who served with him in the belief that somebody can throw some light on his whereabouts. Until the evidence of his death is irrefutable, we have to go on hoping there's a chance that he'll return."

Bennett struggled to conceal his scepticism even as he agreed wholeheartedly with Louise's sentiments. He wanted to be optimistic for her sake but knew too much about the war's ravages to believe that his son might have been spared the fate of countless others. When the battle of the Somme had been at its height, he had seen whole streets with their curtains drawn in mourning. Few of the Quaker families that he knew, for all their pacifism, had been immune from grief. He thought of Michael's future. What had it held in store for him? He had achieved nothing noteworthy at school, showing none of Robert's effortless scholarship, nothing of Alice's uneven flair. His passion for games had been unmatched by any great ability. He had been neither prominent nor popular amongst his fellow pupils. Yet, he had felt that his passage through life would not go unnoticed. He had possessed an assuredness, a determination, remarkable in someone of his age, openness to new ideas, and an appetite for risk. He might have had the political career that eluded his father. Perhaps he had been born to be a soldier and some quirk of nature had placed him in their midst? The tragedy was that they would never know what fate had held in store for him. His promise would always remain unfulfilled.

He said, "I'll write to the War Office, though I'm sure they've told us everything they know. I'll also write to his battalion, to his CO, to find out what he has to say."

"What about Alice and Robert? What will you say to them? It would be better if you gave them grounds for hope rather than expose them to your pessimism?"

"They'll have to read the telegram, decide matters for themselves. That's all that they can do."

"You'll be gentle with them, won't you? You can be so brusque at times. What's this going to do to Robert when he nothing to distract him from his gloomy ruminations?"

"It'll certainly put paid to any thoughts he might have of giving up the struggle."

The reminder of Robert's predicament, the knowledge that he and Alice had to be informed of Michael's fate brought their introspection to an end. The time had come to part, to respond to the news of Michael's loss in their different, separate ways. Louise hoped that their grief would bring them closer but knew there was a danger that it might force them apart. She was determined to preserve her fragile optimism, to urge Bennett to make enquiries. He wanted to nurse his grief. She found it difficult to predict how Alice and Robert would respond. She knew that if Bennett's enquiries yielded nothing, they would all be cast adrift.

Bennett said, "The others aren't to know about my investigation. Let's keep it to ourselves until we have some news for them."

Louise agreed, knowing that his actions would suffice to keep her hopes alive. For now, that was all she required.

CHAPTER 27

Robert had a slate on which he had marked the days of his sentence. He had divided each month into strokes. Each day gone was a line passed through. The method was clumsy and uncertain and he counted the remaining days with obsessive care, unsure of the position. Yet no amount of laxity or repetition could mask the fact that the day of release was drawing nearer. Ten days before his departure, he gave up counting, concealed his chalk in a vain attempt to curb his apprehension and was called to task at his daily cell inspection. He grew fearful that excuses might be found to detain him longer, that a spiteful warder might delay his departure. When his release approached, he enjoyed a brief celebrity amongst his fellow prisoners. Imprisonment was only made tolerable by the prospect of release, by the certain knowledge that normal life would eventually resume. Spurred on by this insight, he attempted to raise others' spirits, determined to be helpful and encouraging in his final days.

The day before release he was locked up in his cell. There he waited nervously for the medical examination that was a condition of release whilst other prisoners filed past his door to exercise, their muffled footsteps adding to his trepidation, his anxiety to leave.

He had disliked doctors since he was a child. He associated their scrutiny with unpleasant remedies and harsh regimes. He disliked their cursory examinations, obscure questions and needless air of mystery. It was an uninviting process to which army and prison doctors brought a new malevolence and a fierce scepticism that ran counter to their vows.

Two hours passed before they came for him. He lined up with the other dischargees in the centre of the prison hall. There was an air of subdued excitement amongst the prisoners, a collective awe at the first evidence that release was near. Gone were the complicit looks, the hurried, whispered words of other gatherings. Everyone waited stiffly and unmoving, on their best behaviour, afraid that they might jeopardise their freedom by a careless word or gesture.

When the warder shouted, "Caps, off," a dozen hands reached up in unison. The prison doctor strolled towards them. He was in no hurry; he didn't share their sense of urgency. He was a small man with narrow shoulders and long arms. The prisoners towered above him, shifting uncomfortably beneath his scrutiny. He halted and scrutinised the first prisoner with a cold, superior stare.

"Who are these men?" he demanded suddenly, as his eyes swept down the waiting line.

"Dischargees, sir," replied the warder. If the question was unexpected, he gave no sign of it. His face was inscrutable as he waited patiently.

The doctor regarded the prisoners with unconcealed distaste. "Right, they'll do," he said, turning on his heel. "Go on, dismiss them. They're no use to me." He strode toward the door without a further word, his demeanour indicating that men about to leave the prison's jurisdiction were no longer his concern.

Robert's encounter with the prison chaplain lasted little longer, though the two of them had met before. The chaplain was an earnest young man with a fresh faced complexion that contrasted sharply with the pasty, furrowed faces of the prisoners. New to his job, he was eager and diligent and anxious to bridge the chasm between the authorities and their charges. He was also overwhelmed by the extent of his new responsibilities.

His regular visits always took the same form: the nervous tap on the door, the key scraping in the lock, the strained, expectant air, the hurried words of consolation, the covert glances at his watch, the vague promises and undertakings and the final, spluttering retreat.

His latest visit was little different from its predecessors. He appeared suddenly, anxious to do his duty, to represent as best he could the neglected, caring side of prison rule. Robert, wary of his interest, was grateful to receive a visitor, especially one permitted to speak freely. The chaplain was the only visitor who ever knocked before entering his cell, a courtesy he appreciated greatly.

They stood as far apart as the tiny cell permitted and looked at each other expectantly. Both men felt the need for valedictory words but neither of them could quite find phrases equal to the situation.

When Robert greeted him enthusiastically, the chaplain said, "The moment you've been waiting for, eh? Well, I hope you've learnt your lesson and that we won't be seeing you here again."

Robert preferred not to think beyond the moment of release, knowing that in a matter of days he might face the same, unenviable choice and, if he remained an absolutist, would soon be back in prison.

"I thought, perhaps, you might decide to enlist after all? The need for men has never been greater."

Robert shook his head. He had not the least intention of giving in after all this time. The only things he had to look forward to when he returned to the barracks were visits from his family and an opportunity to talk freely to them whilst he remained there.

"The law requires you to fight for your country," the chaplain said without enthusiasm.

"I'll continue to follow the dictates of my conscience."

The chaplain regarded Robert with still, sad eyes and Robert sensed a lack of confidence, a degree of uncertainty behind the proprietary air. He was encouraged by the thought that his presence might have given the chaplain cause to question the war's validity.

"You'll still hold out, in spite of all you've been through?"

The chaplain noted the bloodshot eyes, the poorly-shaven face, and shaking hands. No one need remind him that men like Robert suffered. The objectors had destroyed his brittle equilibrium. He tried to conduct a thorough, caring ministry but the harshness of prison life, the weight of regulation and the confusion of objectives were too great. He was only too aware of the unsatisfactory compromise represented by his presence.

He said, "Can I ask you something? You've lived amongst the prison population now for many months. I know it's difficult to strike up a friendship in the conditions here or to have a conversation with your fellow prisoners but you must have formed some views about them. Would you regard them as wicked people? Should they be cared for even as they're punished?"

Robert looked at his troubled face. The question was unexpected, still more the doubt that it betrayed. He said, "You no doubt joined the prison service in that belief and you were right to do so, if you want my view."

"I try to be a good influence, to divert them from a life of crime but so many of them come back time and time again."

"You mustn't blame yourself for that. The whole weight of the system is against you and the numbers are too great. You can only hope to influence a handful at best. Teaching's much the same. You persist in the belief that a few of your students will heed your words and be influenced by them."

"But is there an alternative to this, something likely to reform as well as punish prisoners? That's what I can't decide."

"That depends on your view of human nature. I happen to think that we're all capable of change. Much depends on the circumstances in which we find ourselves, the challenges we face. The problem with the prison regime is that no one is prepared to risk a measure of generosity. There's little virtue in the rule of silence or any sense in starving and degrading prisoners. The ability to live an ordered and untainted life after prison surely requires a degree of pride and self-respect?"

The chaplain nodded gratefully. Those had been his views when he joined the prison service but now he wasn't so sure. He never knew what prisoners really thought. Conscious of his power, they rarely spoke the truth. The prospect of privileges, probation or freedom encouraged them to lie. How many of those who professed remorse or expressed a determination to change their ways could really be believed? He found himself amidst a twilight world in which truth remained elusive and honesty disguised.

"Well, good luck," the chaplain said when he could stay no longer. He mustered a watery smile, extending his hand in farewell. Robert grasped it eagerly, conscious that it was his first physical contact with another human being since his imprisonment. Even his sister's embrace eluded him, separated as they always were by a wire mesh. The other woman whom he longed to hold was an ocean away, banished from his thoughts.

"I hope we meet again," the chaplain added. "Not here, of course," he added swiftly, "but somewhere we can talk freely."

"I'd like that too," Robert said as the chaplain retreated, leaving him to wonder at the confusion his unguarded words betrayed. They were likely to meet again in circumstances little different from those they knew so well.

He slept badly that night, exhilarated at the prospect of release, chilled in spite of every effort to keep warm. As he lay awake in the darkness, shifting uncomfortably on the boards and blankets, a mouse scuttled somewhere in the darkness, vainly seeking crumbs of food on the cold, stone floor. Outside the narrow window, the moonlight bathed the flagstones of the courtyard in a watery glow. At dawn the cell door swung ajar without ceremony and a warder, all bustle and purpose, hastened forward, issuing commands as if his life depended on it. Robert gathered together his few belongings: sheets, pillow-slip, towel, dish cloth, brush, comb and books and followed the warder down the corridor to the desk where another man, waiting patiently, relieved him of his bundle. Clutching card and number, he joined the queue of prisoners waiting to be locked in the tiny cells in which their sentences had first begun. Memories of his arrest, trial and sentencing came flooding back with unexpected vigour. The sky was brightening by the time that he had shed his clothes. He placed them by the door of his cell and stood naked in the narrow room, rubbing his limbs in an effort to keep warm, whilst a warder painstakingly checked his garments until satisfied that everything was present. "Why so many checks?" thought Robert, as he started to dress again. "Do they think we're going steal our prison clothes, abscond with them as souvenirs, in memory of our stay?" As he withdrew his own clothes from the bundle placed before him, the warder itemised each garment, oblivious to Robert's nakedness. Teeth chattering, Robert willed him to make haste. His clothing was followed by his personal effects and money. "Thank you," Robert said when the list had been completed but the irony was wasted on his guardian. The warder smiled begrudgingly, gave his list one final check and handed over the receipt book for Robert's signature.

Breakfast took its customary form. Robert thrust the unappetising meal aside, resolved to wait for better fare in the world outside until, nervous at the prospect of delay, he began to wolf it down. He was led out of the cell to the bench that he had occupied on the day of his admission. The prison government, resolved at last, was now anxious to be rid of him.

Other prisoners waited silently, avoiding each others' eyes, preoccupied with what awaited them. They showed none of the exuberance Robert had anticipated, none of the excitement he felt.

When they had signed the big discharge book, they marched in line through the empty exercise yard. It felt strange to ignore its contours, to march across the circles they followed so meticulously on their daily round. They waited impatiently at the main gate whilst a warder with a flat, disinterested voice called out every name in turn from the paper in his hand, before stepping through the little doorway in the great, iron-studded gate into the street outside.

The street was narrow, cobbled, flanked by terraced cottages; a line of chimneys smoked vigorously, sending curling exhalations into the morning air. It was time to leave for work and a procession of clerks and workmen straggled to the station and the workmen's trains, heads bent, briefcases, sandwich boxes and tool kits tucked beneath their arms. A milkman ran from house to house, bottles, full and empty, in his hands whilst his horse edged forward, keeping pace with him, nosing the bag of oats suspended from its neck.

Outside the gate, the prisoners dispersed to the groups of relatives who waited patiently around the walls, clutching the meal voucher thrust into their hands as they left the gatehouse. Few of them looked back. Those with no one to greet them hastened up the road, anxious to put behind them as quickly as they could the scene of their disgrace. Others chattered excitedly, starlings flocking together with others of their kind, preparatory to taking flight. Robert sought in vain a face he recognised but saw no one he knew. He savoured the scene before his eyes, its space, light and bustle and breathed in the welcome air, its flavour sharp and clear. As he did so, two policemen stepped forward. He hadn't noticed them before.

"Robert Bennett?" asked the sergeant, the taller of the two. His tone was pleasant, undemanding, with no hint of malice.

"That's me," said Robert cautiously. He looked at each of them in turn.

When the sergeant reached into the pocket of his tunic and produced a piece of paper with a flourish, Robert said, "I'm about to be arrested again, aren't I? Even as I step outside the gate, you're waiting for me with your warrant."

"Not yet," the sergeant said, his friendly tone persisting, "but you're expected at the barracks. Whether you go back in there," he gestured at the gate through which Robert had passed with such enthusiasm, "is entirely up to you."

"What about my family?" Robert asked, mindful of the groups dispersing rapidly, each with their grateful prisoner. "They'll be waiting for me. I must talk to them."

"Don't worry about them. You'll have an opportunity to see them later but for now you have to come with us."

The sergeant placed his hand on Robert's arm and steered him up the street. His companion took the other side. They began to march in step until, observing Robert's clumsiness, and noting how short of breath he was, they slowed their pace to his, knowing he wasn't their prisoner yet but would be very soon.

When Robert said, "Will I be able to go home for a few hours?" the sergeant shook his head. The cycle of arrest, trial and sentence had begun again.

CHAPTER 28

It was difficult to accept Michael's death when the only evidence was a terse, unhelpful message. When he had been away so long, his absence meant nothing. A body, a burial and a service were required to convince her of his passing. Without funeral rites, it was easy to forget his death, to wait expectantly on the post and to look forward to him coming home. Her mother's behaviour was an added burden. Alice could see no virtue in ill-founded optimism, in preserving the belief that Michael might come back. Her mother rummaged through his possessions: toys, letters, school books, clothes, the adolescent clutter that filled his room, relishing their presence, whilst for her each sighting was a signal for grief and pain. She wanted to put his things aside, have some breathing space, but knew that any changes would provoke an unseemly confrontation with her mother and that she was doomed to see reminders of her brother's absence everywhere.

She rose early on the day of her visit to Robert, made some breakfast for her parents and prepared to leave. She struggled over what to wear, wanting to avoid anything funereal but feeling that she should wear something that would indicate their loss. Eventually, she compromised, choosing sombre colours in marked contrast to her wardrobe of recent months. She had just finished dressing and was making her way downstairs when the front door opened. She assumed it was her father returning from his morning walk and didn't look up until a familiar voice said loudly, "Well, hello."

There, on the doorstep, stood Michael. He removed his cap and sloughed off his kitbag as she gazed at him open-mouthed, ran his fingers through his hair and said, "What are you standing there for? Aren't you going to welcome me? It's taken days to get here. I deserve a greeting surely?"

"Oh, Michael," was all she could bring herself to say as she ran down the hallway and threw herself into his arms.

She repeated his name as she hugged him fiercely, wanting to be held, needing to reassure herself that her brother's presence was not some phantom conjured up by her fevered mind. Then, when he was certain that he was destined to spend the rest of his life in her arms, she struggled to be free of his grasp. She looked him up and down, unable to believe her eyes, before giving a shriek and rushing back into his arms, clinging to him so tightly that he could hardly breathe. He had dreamed all the way across of a warm welcome but hadn't imagined for a moment that his presence would occasion both joy and consternation.

"We received a telegram to say that you were missing. We thought that you were dead, but you're not dead, you're here. It's really you. I can't believe it. You've come back to us in spite of everything."

"Missing?" He looked at her bewilderment. "I'm not missing. I never was. I simply went on leave as I was entitled to."

He fumbled in his pocket, produced his leave pass and waved it in the air, insisting that she look at it, as if it were the only proof of his existence, but she refused to read it. She no longer believed in telegrams or official papers; they plunged you into dark despair without good reason. It was sufficient that he stood before her, available to touch and see again, her brother in the flesh.

"I've been given seven days' leave. The pass came through whilst I was in the line. I couldn't believe my luck. It was touch and go but we held them off. This was my reward. I was delayed. The train left without me. I had to find a lift. I spent the night on an open wagon. I took the first ship in the morning, jumped off the train at Victoria, ran down the platform and found a taxi - no easy matter when the leave train's in. I have four days of freedom left."

Alice smiled broadly, even as the tears ran down her cheeks. "Four minutes, four days, who cares? The fact is that you're alive when we thought that you were dead."

"Well, here I am," he said consolingly, "you can put your fears aside. We can forget about the war and catch up on everything that's happened whilst I've been away."

He recalled how he had felt when he was told that he was going home on leave. The prospect of release had frightened him. He might have been part of a new draft going over for the first time. The shells had seemed louder, the machine gun fire more rapid, the trenches too shallow to keep him safe from harm. You heard about it all the time: men dying in the line from a sniper's bullet when they were going home on leave or becoming the luckless victim of an unheralded barrage deep behind the lines. He had heard of someone dying in a road accident on his way to the depot having survived two years of the war. Though rarely superstitious, he had been racked with nerves throughout the journey home. He had only felt safe when he saw the cliffs at Dover.

Then, over Alice's shoulder, he caught a glimpse of his mother. She had come to see what all the fuss was about. She stood there motionless, tears streaming down her face, wanting to utter words of welcome, to replicate her daughter's excitement but unable to move or speak. She felt that a huge burden had been lifted from her shoulders and that her life, so rudely interrupted, had resumed its course. She stood and watched him, praying that her son, so unexpectedly returned to her, would not be stolen from her. Only when he stretched out his hands to greet her was she able to say, "I was certain that you hadn't been taken from us. They said all hope was gone, but even as I grieved, I felt sure that you'd come back."

"It's true," Alice said, dancing from one foot to the other, "she was convinced that you were safe. The rest of us…" her voice trailed off; she found it impossible to list the alternatives in Michael's presence.

"Well, here I am," he said, smiling weakly, noting as he did so that his mother looked more fragile than she had ever done before.

Her hair was greyer, her face more lined than he recalled. She was no longer upright, her head held high, her face serene. He had often thought about her on parade when the drill sergeant had urged them to stand up straight, chin in, chest out, thumbs down the seams of their trousers, knowing she would have approved of the sentiments. In his absence her shoulders had rounded and he discerned the beginnings of a stoop. Intimations of old age, the strictures of the war? There had certainly been a reckoning, a calling to account. He felt protective towards her, resolved to spare her further grief and pain. He had never thought when he had courted danger that he had a responsibility to others to ensure his safety, a duty to those who cared for him, to survive the war. It was not a burden that he welcomed but there was no avoiding it. He would remain vigilant on their behalf after he went back.

"So, you are," she said, smiling as he kissed her on the cheek and took her trembling hand in his. "So, you are, and you look so well."

"I need a bath, a shave, a hot meal and a good night's sleep, that's for sure.

"I'm sure you do," she said, her mind already contemplating the larder's meagre contents, "but you're unscathed. You look so grown up as well, in your officer's uniform. I sent a boy off to the war and now…"

"Where's father? Michael asked.

The prospect of meeting his father again filled him with apprehension. He wanted to to make his peace with him. There had never been any overt hostility between them. After the shock of his enlistment, his father had been vocal in his support and proud of his achievements but behind the generous words had lurked a look of disappointment impossible to conceal from someone who hung upon his every word. He hoped that they could meet again as equals, two men who having disagreed, were reconciled at last.

"He's out walking," Alice said, "he'll be back at any minute."

Michael smiled, pleased that his father hadn't changed his ritual during his long absence. He said eagerly, "I could go and meet him."

Louise recoiled at the idea, her hands fluttering in protest.

"Oh, no, that would never do. Imagine his surprise, if he were to see you walking up the street when he's convinced that you've been killed. He didn't doubt it when he saw the telegram. He wasn't sceptical like me. It wouldn't be right to meet him in public. It would be a huge shock..." She paused to collect herself before continuing, "...I know you're desperate to see him but it's better it happens here."

"All right, I'll wait for him."

Michael bent down to remove his boots, worn and caked with mud. He unbuttoned his tunic, loosened his shirt and said, "I feel as though I've been in these things for ever, that they're welded to my skin. I can't wait to wear something comfortable again, something that feels like mine, and isn't occupied by something that has no right to he there."

As if to emphasise the point, he scratched his shoulder savagely, sighing with relief.

"A bath then?" his mother said.

"Absolutely," Michael answered, "deep and hot until all the lice surrender."

"Would that the Germans would do the same," Alice said, as he lifted his pack.

"Hot baths for them as well," Michael answered gaily, making for the stairs.

He was halfway up when he heard the front door open. Alice and his mother stood paralysed, bursting with their news, but wanting Michael to announce himself, to watch his father's face. Bennett didn't look up at first. He stared at each of them in turn, wondering what had happened, why the gloomy countenances he had left behind had been transformed.

"Father, I'm home again, alive and well."

Bennett stood open-mouthed. He might have seen a ghost rather than his younger son, robust and weathered by the elements, standing on the stairs. He said, "I can't believe it. Is it really you?" He repeated the question several times, shaking his head in disbelief. "There's been a mix-up, hasn't there? You were never missing?" He grinned broadly at the thought of their good fortune. Then his face clouded over. He looked at Michael sternly. "This visit has been authorised, hasn't it? You haven't done anything wrong?"

"Deserted?" Michael gasped. "Of course, I haven't deserted."

"He's home on leave. He has the papers with him."

"I didn't doubt it for a minute. It's just a shock, that's all. I'm still trying to take it in. I was convinced that you were..." Bennett couldn't say the word to Michael's face. He began to sob, his countenance dissolving before he pulled himself together sharply and said, "Well, this is cause for celebration. Carry on, do what you have to do and by the time you come down stairs again, we'll have something ready for you. Unless you want to sleep, of course, you must be tired after your long journey."

"Oh, no," Michael said, "I won't be long upstairs and then we'll celebrate. I have waited on this moment for so long, I'm not about to put it off by taking to my bed."

"I can't believe it," Bennett said again as Michael disappeared. He said it partly to himself, as if saying it repeatedly was the only way to make it true. "He's come back to us, unharmed, after all this time."

The rest of the morning was chaotic. Michael was a magnet. His parents and his sister followed him everywhere, afraid that he might disappear, anxious to spend every moment in his presence, plying him with questions, talking over each other in their excitement until his head was reeling and he didn't know who to answer or what to say. Love them though he did, he needed time alone. He was also in a state of shock. He hadn't anticipated coming home again. It had been a dream, unrealistic and elusive, always out of reach. Now he was amongst them, he was unsure how to take advantage of their presence. He needed a period of solitude; he had never been alone since the day he had enlisted.

Eventually, everyone calmed down, noting that for all his enthusiasm, Michael looked lost and tired. When he thought that he was unobserved, his ready smile vanished and his shoulders sagged. He gazed about him anxiously, unsure where he was. They feared their welcome might have been too much for him but how could they restrain themselves? They had thought he was dead. What were they to do but drink in his presence greedily?

Conscious of how late she was, Alice departed for the prison, her excitement mounting at the prospect of informing Robert of Michael's resurrection. A few hours previously, she had been wondering how to break the news of his demise to him. Now she could hardly wait to share her good tidings with him.

Bennett and Michael went walking in the village but soon took to the byways to avoid the neighbours and well-wishers, preferring to be alone and unmolested. Michael marched; it seemed to be the only form of walking he knew, strolling only when he saw his father's difficulty in keeping up. Bennett used a stick, a cane with an ornate handle he treasured greatly, but previously an affectation, a means to occupy his hands, he leaned upon it heavily when he stopped to catch his breath. As they promenaded, there sprung up between them a new intimacy, a pleasure in each other's presence that reminded Michael of his childhood, that had no need of words, whose appeal lay in the mutual recognition that time spent together was full of moments to be cherished.

Bennett was circumspect. He curbed his curiosity, reasoning that if Michael wanted to talk about his experiences, he would chose to do so but that it was not for him to question him or dwell upon the recent past. Michael said nothing at first, content to absorb the sights and sounds of the village, welcoming its tranquillity. Here, briefly, it was possible to forget about the war and everything that he had witnessed there. They found a bench beside the pond and watched the wildfowl that populated its waters: diving ducks; geese, honking noisily; skittish moorhens; the heron, battleship grey, gawkish, that waded in the shallows; swans, cruising serenely, confident in their command.

"Such activity," Michael remarked, as the heron took flight, its wings beating magisterially. How long it had been since he had seen a tree with leaves or waters occupied by wildlife? What a pleasure it was to exchange the battlefield for somewhere where nature was free to go about its business.

"I can't tell you how ghastly it all is."

"Are you sorry you enlisted?"

"No, I still regard it as my duty and will see it through. But it's very hard and you're right to campaign for peace, even though your protests are in vain."

"They told us you were missing," Bennett said, shaking his head in disbelief. He still marvelled at how such a brutal message had been overturned so swiftly.

"Well, in a sense, I was, or, at least, I'd been mislaid. There must have been a roll-call after I'd departed and no one told the CO that I'd had permission to leave."

"Do you think he'll know by now?"

"I'm sure it's all in order. There are so many of us coming and going, it's hard to keep track, especially when the front shifts, as it has...and then, there are the casualties, with such a weight of numbers, keeping track of them is no small task."

"Killed, missing presumed killed, missing. They use so many gradations to announce the deaths. Then, there are the newspapers. They employ another language. Their favourite word is 'sacrificed'. They speak of 'our glorious dead'. I never knew the English language offered so many variations on the word for death."

"Not enough it seems to me, for all those whom I've known and lost."

"Here, the German offensive has changed everything," said Bennett. He was sitting on the bench, gazing out across the pond, his stick planted firmly in the soil, his hands clasped together on its handle. "Last year when the waste and futility of Ypres was at its height, there was a mounting tide against the war and some sympathy for the objectors, some slight belief that they might be right to insist that the Government should sue for peace. Now all that is gone. Our backs are to the wall. Doubts, we're told, are a luxury we can't afford. The nation is united in its adversity and believes it must go on. Certainly, there are grounds for hope. The Americans are arriving in France; fresh troops are available, new resources in abundance. It seems that the recent German offensive has failed, that its army is exhausted. Our blockade of Germany has taken its toll on civilian morale. Who knows that we might gain a victory of sorts though many more will lose their lives before it comes to pass?"

"Where does this leave Robert?"

"Where indeed? He'll brook no compromise. Alternative service isn't for him. His struggle's with himself. It's not a struggle like yours. He isn't risking life and limb. But his health is poor. He finds it difficult to remain cheerful. They release him for several days and then arrest him again and the whole cycle of solitary confinement, the rule of silence, the pointless prison work resumes once more"

"I wish I could see him before I go back."

"Two visits, one person each time is all he's allowed, at two weekly intervals. He follows your progress with keen interest. Alice'll tell him that you're back with your family again. That'll mean a lot to him. He worries about you constantly."

"I've nothing but respect for the route he's chosen."

"Even now?"

"Especially now," said Michael.

CHAPTER 29

Michael had looked forward to being with his family again but now he couldn't settle at anything. There seemed to be nothing to hold on to, no issues to address, nothing to divert him from the thoughts of how his comrades were faring. It seemed to his careless eye that his family had changed little in his absence and that, after the shock of his arrival and the anxiety preceding it, the rhythm of their daily life had resumed.

"What did you expect?" Alice asked, vexed by his insensitivity. "Parades, bands to play? They thought you were dead. They lack the words to say how much your presence means to them."

"Of course, I understand how they feel," he asserted, mortified that the sister of whom he was so fond should consider him uncaring. "I know how much they must have grieved when the telegram came. The whole thing must have been appalling. Yet, because my life has been stood on its head by the war, I had expected life at home to have changed also."

"How could it not be different when so many men have gone to war and those left behind wait for news of them?" But even as she spoke, she recognised her words were wasted, and that for someone out of the line only a matter of days, their world must seem as if it hadn't changed at all.

"I don't belong here," Michael said, confiding in her when his parents no longer hovered round him, watching him intently. "I don't feel that I've any part to play in the civilian world. I don't understand its ways any more."

Alice concluded that he had become a creature of the conflict, that without its routines and emergencies, its lulls and crises, there was really nothing, just a descent from the rush of danger that left him prey to recollections and the exhumation of painful memories better left at rest.

"Let's do something," she said, "something that'll get you out of the house and stop you brooding. The minute you go back, you'll think of all the things you should have done and said. Let's think of them now and get on with them in the time remaining to us."

His first thought had been to visit Robert, to see the conditions he endured. They had never been close owing to the difference in their ages and temperaments and yet he felt that they had much in common. Letters had passed between them in spite of the censorship. His letters had been full of the detail of military life, saying little of the conflict and its purpose, the army's insatiable appetite for men and munitions, the prodigious losses. Robert's letters had been painfully crafted treatises in which he wrestled with his boredom. Their correspondence had given rise to a mutual respect that had surprised them both.

He found his father's attitude to Robert's stance a curious one and was unsettled by it. He had expected to find him partisan, willing to do anything to help his son, but now that Robert was back from France, Bennett affected a curious detachment, as though his son's destiny was in his own hands. If he saw that Robert had backed himself into a corner and was obliged to go on with his protest whatever the consequences for his health and sanity, he gave no sign of it, creating the impression that opposition to the war was a matter of broad principle, unrelated to any member of his family.

"He has doubts; most certainly," Bennett said when they discussed the matter, "but he's not alone in that. Many Friends are uncertain about how best to behave, even now, after three years of war."

"How can that be? You told me Friends had always fought for civil and religious liberty, that it was their birthright. The Society's duty couldn't be plainer: it should do everything possible to secure the release of those in prison on grounds of conscience."

They were walking through the village, enjoying the spring sunshine. Bennett was delighted to be seen with his son, proud to have him at his side, alive and well after his recent fears for his life, and yet felt compelled to restrain his joy, in public at least, lest he give anyone the impression that his views on the war had changed. When he tipped his hat to a neighbour, she looked approvingly at Michael, as if to say, "well, that's more like it". Michael was wearing his uniform, cleansed and deloused, and the sheen on his boots was a tribute to his mother's labours. He walked stiffly, his back upright. Whatever the drawbacks of military training, Bennett thought, as he walked by his side, it gave a young man a good posture, a back that, ramrod straight, was in sharp contrast to his own ungainly stoop.

Bennett said, "It's more complicated than you might think. So many Friends have gone to prison that the Society's in danger of appearing to be pleading for its own."

"What's wrong with that?" Michael demanded, puzzling over his father's retort. His was a world of tribal loyalties. He saw no reason for reticence on behalf of family and friends.

"The Society's never gone out of its way to demand special treatment for its own. That's not the way that it's done."

"Even when they're suffering at the hands of the authorities, when some of them are in a very poor state of health? Alice is very concerned about Robert's condition."

"We all are; he's in our prayers constantly. Not a day goes by but that I don't hope for a change of heart on the part of the Government, such that he and others like him no longer have to suffer."

Bennett had visited several prisons as a chaplain and was only too aware how quickly hard labour prisoners were debilitated by solitary confinement. He knew that Robert was ill equipped to withstand the rigours of imprisonment, that denied stimulus or distraction, he was likely to turn his restless intellect against himself. Even so, he could not resist the brutal thought that, if Robert had been more pious, he might have coped more easily.

He said, "Some Friends have said that prison should be regarded as an unrivalled opportunity to influence the views of others in favour of peace."

Seeing Michael's look of incredulity, he added hastily. "Not that I would go that far. Those who regard hard labour as an opportunity to do anything constructive clearly have no inkling what's involved."

"They're also forgetting the rule of silence," said Michael, recalling the frustration evidenced by Robert's letters. "What's being done to help him or is he just going to be left where he is?"

"I intend to propose a compromise at the next Meeting for Sufferings. Robert won't be abandoned but nor will we ask that Friends be treated differently from other objectors. Instead, I'll urge a repeal of the Military Service Act."

This semantic solution appeared to please Bennett but Michael was unimpressed. Struggling to keep the scorn from his voice, he said, "You might as well call for an end to the war, for all the good it will do."

"You're probably right," Bennett said, appearing old and rather frail in Michael's eyes. "What else can we do? I visit prisons because I feel I can do nothing politically. It's too late for anything like that. All I can try to do is alleviate the sufferings of others until such time as events move in their favour."

"And I'm sure that they're grateful for your help," Michael said, trying his best to appear encouraging, even as he marvelled at his father's unchanging nature and the unreal world in which he dwelt.

Later that day, he announced that he was going to visit Holcombe in the Third London General Hospital in Wandsworth. Alice, seeing an opportunity to spend some time alone with him, suggested that she should go with him. They agreed that they would go the following day, whereupon Bennett volunteered to drive there in the car he owned but rarely used. When they demurred at the prospect of being driven to the hospital by their father, he insisted, saying that he was contemplating donating the vehicle to the ambulance service and that it might be his last opportunity to drive it. They agreed that he and Louise would take them to the hospital and that Alice and Michael would return home by train, a journey made easier by the temporary railway station that had been built in front of the hospital so that the wounded could be brought up to the door.

Alice was troubled by the news of the vehicle's impending departure, not because she had any great liking for it but because of what it said about her father's state of mind. It was his only indulgence in an otherwise abstemious life. He garaged it in a workshop in the village where a local mechanic fussed over it. He cleaned and polished it, consulted a library of manuals on every aspect of its maintenance and chose his driving clothes with an eye to the latest styles. Even Louise, notoriously indifferent to matters of fashion, had a wardrobe of clothes that she kept 'for the car'. Alice wondered if his plans meant that they were short of money. She could never remember money being of any concern to them. There had always been sufficient for their needs. Perhaps the wealth that they had taken for granted had diminished as a result of the war. None of them, except Michael with his modest army pay, could boast of a regular income. They had simply assumed that the uncomplaining Bennett would provide for them for the duration of the war.

The hospital was a Gothic Victorian building. Its extensive grounds housed huts built of corrugated iron and roofed with asbestos that were linked to the main building by long, covered walkways. Further additions beyond the hospital grounds meant that the hospital had eighteen hundred beds. Alice and Michael entered through the main doorway beneath the central tower with its statue of Saint George and the Dragon, passed through the double doors beyond the reception desk and filed down the long hallway, glimpsing room after room, crammed with beds with barely space between them, each populated by a figure in striped pyjamas. Some patients sat upright, reading or talking. Others lay immobile and silent. Attendants bustled around them: nurses in their hats, uniforms and aprons, VADs sporting Red Cross armlets and jaunty caps, elderly porters guiding trolleys bearing patients on their way to theatre or pushing men in wheelchairs through doors thrown open to the gardens. It was visiting time and there were friends and relatives everywhere. Some were grateful, almost joyful at the progress of their loved ones. Others, reluctant witnesses to grief and pain, gathered round the beds in protective clusters. A woman stood beside a mound of bedclothes adjacent to the door, dabbing at her tears, whilst two small children scrambled at her feet, untouched by her distress. Alice could only marvel at the scale of the casualties, even as she speculated as to the dreadful wounds concealed beneath the crisp white sheets and the fate awaiting those whose minds and bodies had changed beyond repair. She could not help but notice other wards where the bustle was less evident, where curtains ringed the beds and an ominous silence hung in the air, and be grateful that Michael was not among the ashen figures that populated them.

They established after many enquiries that Holcombe was housed elsewhere. They reached the hut that was his home only to discover that his bed was empty, its blankets neatly folded, its pillows newly plumped. Two letters, roughly opened, lay scattered on the sheets. The soldier in the next bed, his head swathed in bandages, his leg in traction, said in muffled voice, "You'll find him in the gardens. He won't be here much longer, now that he can walk again." He seemed to consider this possibility for himself and then, concluding it was hopeless, fell back on to his pillow, watching the visitors with his single, discernible eye as they turned to leave.

The garden with its manicured lawns, tall hedges and ordered flower beds, each with their dashes of colour, could not have been more different from the sombre buildings that surrounded it. The gardeners were long gone but someone was still making an effort to keep everything in order and though the flower beds had a wearied look about them, they were largely free of weeds. The paths between them were populated with benches, most of which were occupied by soldiers in blue suits. At certain vantage points, there were clusters of wheelchairs, neatly parked, set to face the sun, some empty, others occupied by men smoking cigarettes or talking quietly, grateful to be outdoors after so long in the wards.

"Where's Holcombe?" Michael asked, conscious that visiting time would soon be over and that there would be no chance to come back. He could barely control his excitement at the prospect of seeing his friend again.

He had explained to Alice that he and Holcombe had trained together and that Holcombe had been badly wounded on their first encounter with the enemy. There had been no sign of him when the survivors returned to the trench nor had he been amongst the wounded brought in by the bearers. He had assumed he was dead, his remains concealed in no-man's land, perhaps never to be recovered. Their friendship had exhibited an intensity only possible amidst the dangers of the trenches. They had been thrown together in the random way of the army and their circumstances had contrived to make them inseparable. The belief that Holcombe had died had been devastating. Even the knowledge that he had survived, brought in belatedly by the battalion that had relieved them, had done little to mitigate his absence. For months, Michael had conducted fractured conversations with him, drawing on the memory of his presence to make sense of his circumstances. He had written to him as he made his way through the hospital system, never receiving a reply beyond a brief acknowledgement. He had vowed to visit him when he could but now the moment was upon him, he feared he might be at a loss for words. It had been so long since they had spoken to each other and they had gone their separate ways.

"Perhaps, he's with his family somewhere?" Alice volunteered as they peered at the animated faces in the gardens. She held a photograph that Michael had given her, showing him and Holcombe together, proudly wearing their new uniforms, shy before the camera. She thought the soldiers in the garden a rudely cheerful lot, grateful for a chance to leave the crowded wards and the misfortune they contained. Many of them called out to her or waved, glad of the distraction of a visitor. She was the object of many admiring glances and pointed comments.

"I'm the man you're looking for," one soldier offered hopefully as she compared him with her photograph of Holcombe. "Can't you see the likeness?"

"I could take you out tonight," another claimed, "if you'll push my wheelchair."

"I'd love to but I'm not available," Alice said, rewarding her admirer with a dazzling smile, "My brother keeps his eye on me, I never get away."

"He can come as well."

They found Holcombe tucked away in a secluded corner of the garden. He was sitting on a bench, his face inclined towards the sun, legs crossed, arms folded neatly on his lap as if posing for a photograph. He stared rudely at Michael, unable to believe his eyes and then spoke rapidly to his companion, a man in a wheelchair who had his back to them. He began to wave, only curbing his enthusiasm when they stood before them.

"Michael, it's you?" he said as Michael rushed up to him, halting before his chair, arms outstretched. "I'm so glad to see you; I'm forever wondering what you're up to."

"It's been nearly two years."

Michael's words betrayed a certain unease. He had often asked himself as the casualties mounted how long his luck would hold. He added, shaking Holcombe's hand vigorously, "You're looking well. I never thought I'd see you again, if I'm honest."

"Half an hour was all I managed in the end. Wasn't much, was it? Not after all that training, all that fuss...."

"You went over the top like you were supposed to. We never had a chance."

"When I say 'fix'?" Holcombe asked, his eyes expectant.

"You don't fix..."

The words brought it flooding back. For Michael, they had signalled the start of a perilous adventure; but for Holcombe, they had heralded a cursory encounter with the enemy. Later, there had been times when to go on living had seemed to require too great an effort, when all the care and attention he had received in hospital had merely led to more pain but somehow he had come through it and soon he would be returning to his family, ready to start a new life.

Michael said, "I sent the letter, the one you gave me for your mother. I always wondered what it said..."

Holcombe smiled gratefully but made no effort to enlighten him.

He said, "Mine never got there. I expect they burnt it along with my uniform - what was left of it."

Michael looked Holcombe up and down, drinking in his presence, as though he might disappear, never to be seen again.

"Were you there when they brought me in?" Holcombe asked.

Alice watched him carefully. She wasn't sure that he should be revisiting the details of his demise.

"No, I wasn't," Michael said, "but I followed your progress as best I could. I wrote to you often but wasn't surprised when you didn't reply."

"I've kept the letters," Holcombe said, a note of satisfaction in his voice.. "I'm not much of a letter writer but I like reading them." He looked away, lost to his recollections. "You mustn't stop, either. Not while the war continues and you're in the thick of it."

"I'll write whenever the opportunity arises."

"We're all pleased when you do that," Alice said.

Michael looked up in surprise, as if he had forgotten she was there.

He said to Holcombe, "I still talk to you, as if you're there. It was a habit I got into when I knew you were alive. It's because we spent so much time together. It helped when things were bad, to imagine that you were at my side."

Holcombe looked surprised. "You weren't scared when you were with me."

"I was always scared after that first time."

"I wouldn't have been much use to you. I was too terrified to help anyone, though strangely, on the day that we went over, once we were out of the trench and going forward. I felt strong, Funny that? Even when the lads were falling all around me and there was only noise and confusion, I was confident that I'd be spared. I should have known better!"

"It wasn't to be," Michael said, "but there again, you're alive and you'll never have to go back."

"Unlike you," Holcombe said, watching him with concern.

He said, "You remember Captain Reynolds, don't you?"

The officer in the wheelchair spun round dextrously at the mention of his name.

Michael gazed at his former CO in wonderment. His first instinct was to salute him as in the old days. His heels came together and his back straightened of their own accord. The Captain had liked them to 'chuck up' a good one, thought it important to put on a decent show. Some officers weren't bothered about the formalities but he had insisted that the little things mattered, that they were part and parcel of being a soldier. Michael had not expected to find him, a wounded officer, here, amongst the men.

"I'm just passing through," the Captain said with a friendly smile, "I'm on my way to Roehampton. They've parked me here - until a bed comes free." He looked Michael up and down. It felt like an inspection. Michael fingered the buttons on his tunic, grateful he had polished them that morning and said proudly, "I'm an officer now."

The Captain said, "Congratulations. You deserved it." He turned to the others and said, "Not before time." He made no further comment on the matter, leaving Alice to ponder on his words.

Holcombe said proudly, "I come here whenever I can."

"It's a nice spot," the Captain said.

Holcombe contemplated the fields beyond the gardens, sporting huts like the ones they had visited when they were trying to find him.

He said, "When I first arrived, they were playing fields. I used to look out of the window and pretend I was at school again."

"I was there when the bearers brought you in," the captain said, "you're a lucky man."

"He was always that," said Michael.

Holcombe's face darkened as he remembered his early days in hospital: slipping in and out of consciousness, the endless, searing pain. He recalled the doctors in their blood-stained coats clustered round his bed, the cold table on which they cut him open, the nurses who put water to his lips. Though his memories of those awful days were fading, a single, careless word, a well-meant observation could still return him to that painful world.

"Where's home?" said Alice, to distract him from his recollections. His accent, broad and unfamiliar, offered her few clues.

He told her that he came from Lancashire but had been working in London when he enlisted. He said that the War Office didn't look favourably on casualties being treated close to home for fear of encouraging visits by families and friends.

Holcombe and Michael soon plunged back into their old relationship as if it had never been rudely interrupted by the conflict. Exchanging notes and places, they relived their experiences and retold many of the anecdotes they shared. Holcombe had none of Michael's ability to capture time, places and events in words but he was quick to add a stripe of colour to the scenes that Michael painted vividly. Alice felt she was intruding and decided she would walk around the grounds until their reminiscences were over. When she announced her intentions, Michael looked meaningfully at the captain. He sat unmoving in his wheelchair regarding them with benign interest but making no effort to join their discussions.

"Would you like to come with me?" asked Alice.

He nodded eagerly, preparing to propel himself forward.

"No need for that, I'll push you." Alice said. The two of them set off, forgotten by the others, their conversation taking on a new intensity as they departed.

"I don't think we exist," Alice said as they trundled down the path, skirting round the benches, the soldiers exercising. Some walked swiftly, others barely moved; their progress slow and painful, they required sticks and crutches or leaned heavily on their companions as they inched forward.

Captain Reynolds said, "Holcombe had no idea that you were coming. Apart from me, he's met no one from the battalion since he came back to England."

"He must have been very glad to see you then when you turned up."

"Mixed feelings, I'd imagine. I was his commanding officer. However well we get to know each other in the line, there's still a great divide between the officers and men."

"Even here, in England?"

"Under fire, we're equals but when the danger's past, the old class divides emerge."

"Well, he's thriving now. He seems quite recovered from his wounds. He must be pleased at that."

"Oh, I'm sure he is," Captain Reynolds said. "He's made a startling recovery. When they brought him in, I was sure that he'd get no further than the clearing station. He must have gone through hell, before he reached his present state. It changes you, all that pain and anguish. When you recover, nothing's quite the same."

"What'll happen to him now?"

He turned in his wheelchair, looking at her as best he could over his shoulder. The movement seemed to cause him pain for he winced and turned away, hiding his expression.

"That's the thing, isn't it? You want to be free of pain, to be out of the ward and independent again. Then, you ask yourself: what happens after that? What if I'm fit enough to go back into the line? Will they send me back? Have I done enough?"

"Is that what'll happen to you?" Alice said, looking down at him. They swerved to avoid two soldiers, deep in conversation, had who strayed across their path.

"I doubt it," Captain Reynolds said, laughing out loud. "I wouldn't be much use to them."

Alice couldn't help but notice, even though he had his back to her, that there was an edge to his mirth.

"Here, they're likely to discharge you. It's different in the clearing stations and the base hospitals. For some, the MO's daily inspection's a matter of life and death. You're in trouble if he decides you're fit,. It was different for me. I was too ill to care what they did to me but others lay there hoping theirs was a Blighty or, if it wasn't, that they'd have a few more days until they were shipped out to convalescence, before going back into the line."

They reached a junction on the path and halted to let a soldier in a wheelchair pass. He turned the wheels of his chair with great determination, a fierce expression on his face, frustrated at his lack of progress, the weakness in his arms.

"Go right, it takes us to the lawns."

He began to fumble in his pocket for his cigarettes and the blanket covering him caught in the wheel of the chair and tumbled to the ground. Alice halted to untangle it and gasped in horror and surprise. The captain was an amputee. One of his legs was gone above the knee. He was perched precariously on a cushioned seat, his stump thrust out in front of him. Neatly dressed in a blue jacket and red tie, it had been impossible to tell that his leg had fallen victim to the surgeon's knife.

"Oh, I'm so sorry," Alice said. She replaced the blanket hastily, averting her eyes without meaning to, "I'd really no idea. Here's me asking if you're going back. How stupid of me! I didn't know...that you were..."

"An amputee?" He supplied the missing word without hesitation. "Don't be embarrassed. How were you to know I'd lost a leg?"

He had seemed so relaxed, so at ease with his circumstances, his smiling features supporting the pretence that he was whole. Even now, with the extent of his wounds revealed, he appeared more concerned to alleviate Alice's consternation than to portray himself in a favourable light.

He said, "Your reaction doesn't surprise me. It happens all the time. Even here, where so many are maimed and disfigured by the war, amputations still have the power to shock."

His voice was gentle and considerate, as though she were the patient and he was a visitor putting her at ease. He said, "I'm slowly getting used to being an amputee. It's what life holds in store for me. Shock, distaste and pity are what I'll face from friends and strangers. I've witnessed them already but I refuse to be ashamed of my condition or cloaked in bitterness. There are many here far worse off than me."

Alice wanted to tear the blanket away, expose his wound again, hoping to convince him that she was not repulsed by his condition and nor would others be, but even as she smiled encouragingly, lit his cigarette for him, she knew it was too soon for that.

When she went to push the wheelchair again, he put his hand on hers, restraining her. She looked at him expectantly, waiting for instructions but he remained silent, gazing up at her with his intense, blue eyes. He regarded her without embarrassment, wondering whether he could trust her, if she was the confidant he had been waiting for throughout his convalescence.

His mind made up at last, he said, "Let's go on then," and she took his brief command to be a sign of confidence in her. In spite of her clumsiness, her ill-concealed surprise, she felt that she had passed some kind of test and had qualified to be his friend.

When they reached the corner of the garden that he had recommended, they halted before a statue of a young girl holding aloft a torch. Water burbled from it into the pool below with its lilies and goldfish. They sat facing each other, he in his chair, Alice on a bench, her back resting against the metal plaque acknowledging its donor. She kicked off her shoes. The gesture of familiarity seemed to comfort him, prompting him to speak.

He said, "You're very much as I imagined you'd be, when I read Michael's letters."

Michael's letters had been a surprise to everyone. When he was away at school he had shown no inclination to write to his family nor had he been much given to studying. His passions had been the sports ground and the gym; the classroom had been something he endured. At the front, he had written frequently: heartfelt and perceptive letters, principally to Alice, as if only she of all his relatives was capable of appreciating the changes the line had wrought in him. Water building up behind a dam, his thoughts had been waiting only to be free of school and family before bursting forth.

He said, "I was his CO. I read every word he wrote. He was drafted into my platoon, a raw recruit, even by the standards of the day. I had to censor his letters. He was one of the most diligent correspondents. Few wrote more letters than he did. They were largely to you, as I recall. Such letters: frank, insightful; astonishing for somebody so young. Then when I became a company commander, it became someone else's job."

Alice looked at him in astonishment. Was there no end to the surprises this man was capable of springing on her? Now he was speaking to her as if he already knew her, as if their relationship had long preceded the visit she had made.

"Why were they so memorable?"

"No one else who wrote home felt they had to justify their presence. Everybody else was a hero to their family - but not Michael. He felt that he'd let you down. Even when he risked his life, he longed for your approval."

Alice was quick to protest, even as she recalled Michael's doubts. "We respected his decision. We made that very clear to him."

"He still wondered if he'd done the right thing. That was why he wrote to you so often."

"How very disconcerting," Alice said. "We've only just met and yet you know so much about me."

Her comment made him afraid that he had trespassed on her privacy.

"Well, in a manner of speaking, I feel I know all your family, but especially you. When you first arrived, I didn't turn round to greet you. Did you notice that? I wanted to hear your voice before I saw your face. I thought about you often when I was in the base hospital, wondering what you were like and whether we would meet."

"He didn't show you any of my letters, did he?" Alice asked, thoroughly alarmed.

They had been unusually frank, as if Michael had been a friend and confidant her own age. His earnestness, the thought that each letter that he wrote to her might be his last, had unhinged her at times. She had never known where he was. The captain and the other censors had made certain of that. She had read the bland announcements in the newspapers, the ground gained and lost at such expense, the false claims of victory and had wondered at his whereabouts. She had been so much closer to him than the rest of the family. She had helped to bring him up, looking after him when their mother was distracted, missing him intensely when went away.

"Good heavens, no," the captain said, "that would have been terrible. No, the little I know about you and your family is the result of what he wrote, his answers to your questions and his reaction to your comments. He once showed me your photograph though and asked me to admire you, which I did, of course. He carried it with him everywhere. But then,

I read a lot of letters, and wrote many too, so what I think I know is probably incorrect."

"You haven't had an easy time of it, have you, and yet you seem so positive, so full of life, in spite of everything? I admire that, if you don't mind me saying so."

"Everybody feels sorry for me and I find it very hard to bear. Most of those I fought with are long gone. They lie in graveyards next to the field hospitals in France or are buried in mass graves on the battlefield. I've survived the conflict. It's a gift denied to others, unwittingly received. I may be infirm, an object of pity, but I still have a life to live, and that's the point. It probably won't be the life that I'd have chosen but it's still an opportunity, one denied to so many others I've known, and I mean to make the most of it. That was the promise that I made to myself in hospital, when the pain was at its worst, and I intend to keep to it, however difficult it might prove."

"I'm sure you will," said Alice, "victory seems to be within your grasp already."

He laughed and then his mirth subsided and he became serious again, recalling the events that had led to his convalescence.

He told Alice he was not consistently good spirited and that he was trying to impress her, not with his looks, demeanour or gaiety, as he might have done once, but with his courage. He told her how he had suffered as a result of the gas gangrene that had affected his wounds, how even three hourly irrigations had failed to save his leg and that when, weeks after the amputation, the pain had become tolerable, he had sank into a torpor, a sea of misery and foreboding from which nothing could shake him. It was only when it had become possible to leave the ward, to go outside for the first time, that his depression had lifted and he had begun to address the issues that faced him and to acknowledge that he was fortunate to be alive.

He said, "When you suffer trauma and wrestle with its consequences, you realise that though your life has changed irretrievably, nothing else has changed. The world hasn't ceased to rotate around the sun, night still follows day, everyone still gets on with their lives and nobody is greatly concerned about you."

"That's how it always is," said Alice, "but it must make your condition hard to bear."

"What's the point of envy or regret? They won't restore my missing limb, heal my wounds more quickly or make me whole again. What I have is what I am. I never saw that clearly before but now I know I have to play the cards that I've been dealt."

Alice marvelled at his frankness, his willingness to confide in her after so short an acquaintance. Taken aback though she was by the sudden intimacy, she found that she was drawn to him and was keen to hear his story.

She said, "I'm not sure many people in your position see things with such clarity."

"It isn't all bad news. I'm going to Roehampton to get an artificial leg. It's touch and go but if my stump's long enough, and it might be, I might be walking in a few week's time."

She looked him up and down, emboldened by his frankness. He was an attractive man, dark, curly hair, parted neatly, a nose prominent and proud, eyes that followed hers unceasingly as if seeking the truth concealed there and lips, which pursing thoughtfully as he expressed his views, she felt she might have liked to kiss in other circumstances. His suit, meant for somebody larger, hung about him loosely, but she didn't doubt he'd fill it up before too long.

He said, "I was training to become a doctor at the outbreak of the war. I was late to the profession. Joining the infantry was the quickest way of getting to the front. I wanted to be an officer, felt ready for command. I hadn't the least inkling what lay in store for me. None of us had in those days. We were infected with a curious blindness, a collective failure of the imagination; we lacked the ability to anticipate what it was going to be like. Now we know. Those of us still alive know only to well."

They began a final circuit of the garden. The day was warm, the flower beds alive with insects. The trees cast shadows across the lawns and paths so that those strolling along their lengths passed from light into dark and back again in a matter of yards. It seemed so remote from the war, yet Alice recognised that there were other parts of the establishment where patients suffered fearfully. She was also aware of certain figures in the garden who showed no sign of injury but were silent and listless or animate and wild-eyed and were accompanied by nurses.

"Who are those people?" she asked her companion.

"They're from the neurological unit around the back. Many of the patients there have lost their minds. What they've seen and done has exacted a fearsome toll. They're encouraged to mingle with us but some of them can't be persuaded to leave the ward. They take fright readily and are easily intimidated. We found someone lost in the garden two days ago. He was in sight of the building in which he lived but he couldn't find his way back to it. What will become of such people? Outwardly, they look normal, but some of them are damaged beyond repair. There are so many of them, each with different needs and issues, waiting on someone to return them to the world they left behind when they crossed to France."

Michael and Holcombe were still talking when they rejoined them but less animatedly than before. They broke off when they caught sight of them, as if their reminiscences had run their course. It's often the case, Alice thought, that two people, inseparable in certain circumstances become strangers in others. She was struck again by Michael's good health, his restless energy, so different from those around him. She wondered how Robert would have fared in the army. Not well, she decided, though he didn't lack courage or fortitude. The war had left no mark on Michael. He looked more youthful and fresh-faced than on the day of his departure. It was almost an affront to those whom he visited. When she had said as much to the captain, he had said that he had known many men who thrived on war but most of them were gone.

"How long are you home for?" he asked Michael.

"Two more days."

"Will you be going to the train?"

"Oh, yes," Alice said, mindful of the other time when she had declined to go to the station.

The captain neither urged Michael to enjoy his leave whilst it lasted or commiserated with him on his imminent departure. Who knew what he was going back to? He might be thrown back into the line as soon as he arrived or spend weeks or even months in reserve or training. That was how it worked. Some anonymous staff officer with his maps and dispositions decided arbitrarily whether you would live or die.

He swivelled in his chair, a sudden motion that Alice found heart-stopping. He said to Michael, "I'm hoping your sister will come and see me again. I don't get many visitors, certainly no one so delightful. I'd love it if she visited me again."

Alice said, "How could I not return after such flattery?"

She attempted to engage with Holcombe as they made their way back to the main building but her heart wasn't in it. The captain had sucked all the air out of her, leaving her incapable of small talk. He was clearly alone. If he'd had a wife or fiancé before the war, she was no longer by his side. She wondered if he would ever find someone to love him and take care of him or whether his disability would prove an insurmountable obstacle.

That would be the cruellest loss of all. She decided that she would visit him again and become his friend. The shell-shocked soldiers with their staring eyes and helpless ways, wandering through the gardens, made her think of Malcolm. She wondered what had become of him. Perhaps she had been too hasty in her judgement, too anxious to be free of the man who had let her down so badly? She hoped that time would weave its magic and that a war that had separated them so cruelly would make him whole again.

CHAPTER 30

Robert was devastated by the length of his new sentence. Two years was thought to be the longest hard labour sentence endurable. What had sustained him through several shorter sentences had been the prospect of release. This time, his sentence was continuous and the prospect of remission slight. He felt that the authorities were determined to destroy the absolutists and could not pretend he retained sufficient strength to resist their efforts.

Wandsworth prison's weathered walls only heightened his misgivings. The prison looked impregnable, its footprint vast, its star-shaped keep exhibiting a forbidding permanence. The authorities confined him in the darkest corner, excluded from the sunlight by an outer wall. Each night, when the cell door closed on him, he lay unmoving and when morning came roused himself reluctantly, feeling none of the restlessness or the fever he had known before. He found it easy to sink into the torpor that had characterised the final days of his previous sentence.

Even in his isolation, he began to notice changes. The dreary prison round persisted. The diet was meagre. He still slept on bare boards and laboured over his mailbags, intent on his rewards. But it soon became clear that the discipline he had known before had dissipated. Its absence was noticeable in the march to the chapel, in the strolls around the exercise yard and in the stifling workshops. The cell inspections lacked the rigour of previous intrusions. Though orders still rained down on him, they were delivered without their former zeal. Subject to a more benign regime than he had known before, he began to ponder on its true extent and to wonder at its causes.

His first discovery was that the rules in respect of conscientious objectors had changed. Henceforth, they were to be accorded the privileges of rule 243A. These had been introduced in 1911 by the Home Secretary, Winston Churchill to ameliorate the conditions affecting the suffragettes subject to recurring sentences. Its aim was to accord a selection of first division privileges to third division prisoners.

Two daily exercise periods were introduced. Prisoners were allowed to walk in groups and to converse freely. They were permitted to wear their own clothes or supplement prison clothing with their own garments. Books could be received from outside and four were permitted in a cell. Monthly visits were held in private rooms under supervision instead of on either side of double bars or gratings. Those whose health had been broken by the conditions were promised release.

Though scarcely generous, the new regulations were like a breath of fresh air, dispersing the stale odours of the prison cells. They mitigated the long period of isolation that had heralded each new sentence, giving hope to those despairing newcomers whose lips still bore the taste of freedom. They were especially welcome when implemented by a regime inclined to be benign.

Wandsworth was not one prison but two, one wing being a detention barracks under the control of a military governor, the other housing five hundred and sixty prisoners of whom one hundred were conscientious objectors. When Robert began associating with the other inmates, he realised that the conditions were ripe for mutiny. The authorities had neither considered the impact of placing so many objectors under one roof nor the effect of new if limited prerogatives on prisoners long deprived of liberty. The first few days of his sentence were punctuated by sudden choruses of *The Red Flag* and other revolutionary songs. Some prisoners held protest meetings or disturbed the whole prison at night by banging cell doors with stools and bed boards. The military prisoners were a particular target of their barbs. Their drills were accompanied by cat calls and incitement to rebellion. They were an indication of how quickly the tide had turned.

One day, Robert found himself amidst a protest meeting in the dining hall. There, standing on a table, his face flushed, his hands waving angrily, was Levine, a companion of his abduction to France, whose rhetoric he still remembered. Gone were the wry observations, the penetrating questions, the insistent reasoning. They had given way to a revolutionary doctrine as uncompromising as it was embracing. Here was an ardent socialist, violently opposed to the war on political grounds, who, wearing his true colours, professed the view that won or lost, the war would pave the way for revolution.

Robert had little sympathy for the disruptive tactics of Levine and others. They seemed calculated to return them to the harsh restrictions of the past. He also found them confusing. There seemed little purpose in prolonged resistance to conscription if the resistance was violent in nature. "What's the point of making trouble?" he asked. "You'll only discredit the cause that we espouse."

"Your cause isn't mine," Levine said, his face twisting in derision. "You haven't really got a cause beyond a plaintive cry to end the war." He was buoyed up by his new prominence after years of obscurity. He was determined to prevail against the prison authorities, seeing it as a first step along the winding road to revolution.

He said, "Their will's weakening every day. They'll release us, if we make sufficient trouble. We were mistaken to acquiesce in our punishment. The non-violence you favour is a straitjacket in a violent world."

"Even if we're united, our numbers are too small to be of consequence."

"Our numbers are unimportant if we're firm in our resolve."

Levine was immeasurably excited by the news from Russia. He viewed the industrial unrest on Clydeside as a promising development. Revolution was in the air. History had delivered the opportunity for violent change. Unfortunately, he languished in prison and each day deprived of freedom was an agonising setback. Robert neither shared his views as to the prospects for revolution nor felt it was an outcome that would serve any useful purpose. He desired only an end to the war, the prospect of release from prison and the opportunity to play a part in the country's reconstruction.

Frustrated by his continuing imprisonment, Levine turned his ire on Robert. He condemned him for his pacifism and when Robert pointed out that the circumstances of backward Russia would not be easily replicated in the other warring nations, his objections were brushed aside.

"Words are all you have to offer," Levine shouted, pushing past him in the corridor. "The time for words is past. We have to plan and organise, prepare for revolution."

He never tired of pointing out that the Bolsheviks were few in number. The war would be their recruiting sergeant. Their duty was to prepare themselves for leadership so that when the time was ripe they could direct the proletariat to socialism.

Robert knew of no disciplined cohort inside or outside prison. The few socialists that he had encountered held widely differing views, were ill-organised and had few links to the people they aspired to lead. Moreover, he could see no evidence that the Government was on the run. The tide of the war was turning in the Allies' favour, the spirit of the people was unbroken and the army was still resolved to defeat the Germans, supported by a Government that was convinced that victory was the only certain route to peace.

His father's visit confirmed him in his views. Bennett told him that other prisons had been reluctant to recognise the claims of Rule 243A. Though political pressure had secured the release of certain notables whose health was crumbling, there was still no prospect of liberty for the mass of objectors. He said the attitude of the governor was the key to conditions in the prison and the intermittent leniency of the staff there reflected the confusion in his mind.

The governor was a tall man, thin and angular. His pale, troubled face and stooping figure were unmistakeable as he swept from cell to cell. He had a brittle confidence, an air of authority that, coupled with a rapid turn of speech, served to mask a raft of doubts, uncertainties made all the greater by the band of conscientious objectors within his jurisdiction

Unlike many prison governors, he was not a former soldier. Nor had he risen through the ranks of the prison service. He was educated, a lover of music and literature, a man whose route to the office of prison governor had led him through the byways of the Home Office. He was an experiment his sponsors were unlikely to repeat. He owed his tenure to the influence of his former colleagues and the diligence of his subordinates.

The real governor was the chief warder, John Harding, a man whose unthinking application of the rules prevented their dilution and stifled any innovation by his staff. The governor allowed him a free hand whilst he continued to be a remote and ineffective administrator, promulgating rules and procedures as though still behind a Whitehall desk.

The influx of objectors destroyed this harmony. They seemed to strike a long neglected chord in the governor's mind. He resolved to treat them differently from other prisoners in the third division. His motives were unclear. He was not inclined to radicalism. He supported the vigorous prosecution of the war. He seemed to regard the objectors as kindred spirits and wished to recognise their status. Robert suspected that he was anxious to differentiate himself from his subordinates.

The Governor told a former colleague from the Home Office who had ventured to suggest that he might be losing control of his prisoners that whilst the objectors might be cowards or shirkers they were still gentlemen. He said, "They're not common criminals, not the kind we're used to, and should be treated differently from other prisoners."

The problem was that the prison regulations were incapable of distinguishing between prisoners of the same division. Moreover, the ranks of the objectors included activists of every kind, some of whom sought to sow discontent amongst the other prisoners. When the prison staff tried to limit their activities, it proved difficult without the active support of the governor.

The governor's intervention compounded their difficulties. Gone was the haughty detachment, the imperial wave with which he had dismissed so many problems. Gone were the hasty inspections, the hurried footsteps on the landing. He examined cells and workshops. He appeared unexpectedly in the kitchen, laundry and bakery. He greeted prisoners by name and encouraged them to voice their views. Suggestions for improvement rained down upon the heads of his staff until it seemed no aspect of prison life was safe from his zeal. It would not have mattered if the rules had been more flexible and the chief warder had been less intent on pleasing his superior. The governor's every impulse was implemented to the letter and only bemusement and confusion slowed the rate of change.

The orderly room became the flashpoint. Here, every morning after chapel, the governor heard applications from prisoners and adjudicated on reports of misdemeanours. It soon became evident to both warders and prisoners that a new era had begun. Hitherto, trial before the governor had been calculated to tax the nerves of any prisoner. There, he stood alone in the narrow dock, flanked by high railings, accompanied by the principal warder from his hall. Facing him were the governor, the chief warder, the reports and applications officer and the clerk. The ritual never varied. The charge was read formally, the warder offered his evidence, the prisoner was asked for his comments and the governor read out the sentence, entering his decision in the punishment book.

The punishments embraced diet, confinement, loss of remission and deprivation of mattress. The trials were held in the confident belief that the governor could be relied upon to exploit this repertoire of punishments, whatever the evidence and the circumstances. The belief that the governor would come down in favour of the accuser underlay the entire system of control. Without this guarantee, any warder could be readily exposed as a tyrant.

The first sign of change was the governor's willingness to challenge his warders' testimony. Hitherto, a warder's statement had been beyond question. The realisation that they might be challenged prompted the bolder prisoners to speak up in their defence. The hearings began to resemble a court of law, their outcomes no longer certain. The warders became more circumspect in their accusations. Offences began to go unreported. Prisoners behaved wilfully. Only the governor's unpredictability kept it in check. If compelling logic lay behind his judgements, his reasoning escaped his audience. Where he saw decisiveness and clarity, they saw impulse and indecision.

The unrest dragged on for weeks, Levine and his allies failing to bring matters to a head. For many of the prisoners, there was a more vital struggle under way: the struggle to survive. Many of them had been subject to the cruel cycle of deprivation and release for more than two years. They were worn down by solitary confinement, lack of food, insomnia and illness. Many of them wanted only to experience a day free from sores, disease and distress. Like the population at large, their attitude to their condition was one of dogged resignation coupled with a desperate longing for the war to end.

For Robert, there was the added burden of widespread disillusionment with the pacifist cause. He was haunted by the knowledge that his time might have been spent more productively. Had it not been for his opposition to conscription, he might have preserved sufficient freedom to perform useful work. Whatever meaning his stand had for him, he was not foolish enough to believe that it had symbolic value. He had watched others accept alternative service only to decline the work schemes intended to occupy them. He had heard of those who had refused to work in prison. Such intransigence struck him as absurd. It was a gesture more meaningful to the objector than to the cause he represented. As for socialism, it was a religion without a deity, a recipe for conflict and struggle, a beckoning star to which the weary traveller drew no nearer however tortuous his journey.

Only the prospect of an end to the war with its promise of release persuaded him to continue his opposition with good heart. He had little inkling as he persevered that the conclusion of the war would add to his burdens, testing him in ways that the conflict had failed to engineer.

PART VI

November 1918

CHAPTER 31

They gathered in the chapel, eager for the governor's words. His uncertain links with the outside world were their only source of news; without them there was only bold conjecture, unsubstantiated rumour and the wild imaginings of prisoners prohibited from speaking to each other. Now, as they waited for the governor, the discipline of row and block, of file and queue broke down irretrievably. There was an unseemly scramble for the seats at the front of the chapel. The frowning chaplain looked on disapprovingly as the prisoners pushed and shoved each other or talked excitedly, without restraint, even as the disconcerted warders attempted to assert the rule of silence by which they set such store. Some of the sick and the infirm were present from the hospital. They sat at the back, supported by their friends. Late arrivals clustered in the aisles. When the governor entered the warders had to clear a way for him so that he could reach the pulpit unimpeded by the crowd of prisoners waiting on his words.

Every eye upon him, he strode the length of the chapel, looking neither right nor left, conscious only of the expectant hush that had descended on his audience. His expression betrayed no sign of excitement, no hint of the contents of the speech to come but, as he neared the pulpit, his eyes shone with anticipation and his usual measured steps gave way to quick, ungainly skips. He announced the armistice in solemn, ponderous tones. He spoke of a sweeping victory, the collapse of German arms, a triumph for freedom and democracy. Delighted as he was, Robert wondered at his choice of words. Peace, most certainly, who hadn't longed for that after four, long years? But victory? What had been gained from a conflict so unendurable? Then his doubts and reservations were swept aside by his relief. The carnage was over: that was all that mattered. Freedom in its many guises had raised a beckoning hand. He trembled at the prospect of a life renewed, marvelled at the richness of its promise. Would release come quickly? Home in time for Christmas? He recalled the words of 1914, echoed by the crowds, so many casualties ago.

The governor called for silence. The chatter subsided, the coughs and shuffles ceased. A hush descended on the crowd of prisoners. Eyes focused on the pulpit, the self-important figure there, waiting for the bell to toll. They were good at silences, thought Robert; silence was their stock in trade. Alone in their cells, they were silent. At work, nothing could be heard but the sound of needles, thread and sacking. In the exercise yard, the only words heard outright were the admonitions of the warders, the sudden, sharp commands. When the bell rang, the governor urged them to remember the many who had fallen. Heads dipped obediently at his sombre words. Robert thought of Michael, his parents' deep despair, the merciful reprieve. Why had so many died? What had it all been for? Their sacrifice was indisputable, their willingness to die a matter for awe and consternation besides which his own suffering was paltry, without significance. Yet, stripped of its unthinking chauvinism, its tragic grandeur and its pathos, the loss of life made no sense at all. He noted the hint of reprimand in the governor's words as he addressed the objectors, the threat of the reprisals still to come. What right to freedom had they who'd failed to heed their country's summons? The irony of pacifism, thought Robert as he returned the governor's gaze, was that those who had survived, those who would depart the prison whole in mind and body, would remain condemned for ever for having dared to stand in opposition to a war which had prompted untold suffering.

When the clock struck eleven, the chapel erupted, the prisoners' joy drowning out the governor's words. The chaplain, who had risen to give his benediction sat down hastily and watched, a bemused, expression on his face, as the prisoners surrounded the pulpit, spilled into the aisles and clambered over the pews, shaking hands, thumping backs, embracing each other in their joy at the demise of the war. Groups of them burst into song, *God Save The King* and *Land Of Hope And Glory*, competing with the songs favoured by marching soldiers, *Tipperary* and *The Bells Of Hell* and popular music hall songs such as *Flighty* and *A Broken Doll*, each chorus ending with loud, enthusiastic cheering. The warders, abandoning their attempts at stern-faced supervision, joined in the euphoria, sliding from their high stools, disappearing into the throng, sharing in the prisoners' joy. One of them was picked up and thrust aloft as though he were a hero. Others lost their caps and jackets to their enthusiastic wards. The throng of prisoners overflowed into the yard and Robert found himself carried along, singing and laughing as he staggered towards the door. He felt as though he were free already, as if the balance of his sentence had been cancelled and that the day that he longed for since the time of his arrest had come to pass at last.

Soon, the prison keep reverberated with the crash of the maroons in Hyde Park, the rise and fall of the 'all clear' that issued from Trafalgar Square and the peel of the church bells throughout the city. Every building visible above the prison wall had sprouted Union Jacks and bunting and swaying figures hung from office windows or swarmed over the trams and buses arrested by the crowds. Robert heard the bands that, hastily convened, struck up rousing choruses and anthems as they marched along the streets and imagined the policemen struggling to maintain order before abandoning all pretence at supervision and joining the festivities. He thought of the soldiers, the new recruits, the combatants home on leave, the wounded, gathering to express their joy at being spared the fate suffered by so many of their comrades and paced up and down his cell for hours, pausing only to stretch his limbs, restored to vitality by thoughts of liberty.

That night the city discarded the cloak of darkness that it had thrown across its shoulders and the night sky glowed with the light of the street lamps, brightly lit shops and restaurants and the glow of bonfires. After its victory chimes at three o' clock, Big Ben struck hourly for the first time in four years. As the crowds before Buckingham Palace called for the King, Robert wondered when the prison gates would be thrown back and how long it would be before he was back with his family. The prospect of release filled him with joy. He experienced no sense of vindication; nor was he unduly proud of his behaviour. His stance hadn't been born of stubbornness or the desire to prove a point. He had embarked on his resistance to conscription, had determined to behave in accordance with his sincerely held convictions, because he was a pacifist and wished to play no part in the prosecution of the war. He had maintained his stance in the face of threats, inducements and reprisals. Sentenced to death, he had still persisted, propelled by his determination to remain loyal to his beliefs. Now, after he had given up hope, had resigned himself to indefinite imprisonment, the conscript armies had been torn apart, the carnage had been halted and his reward for remaining resolute was likely to be life and liberty.

It was inevitable that Levine, with his dour pragmatism and jaundiced eye, should be the first to warn him that release from prison after the war was over, would be no small matter for the authorities to engineer, even if they were minded to do so. Robert noted with surprise when they spoke at exercise, a newly relaxed affair in which prisoners conversed openly with whomsoever they pleased, that Levine exhibited none of the others' excitement at the end of the war. He seemed strangely disappointed by the governor's tidings as if only the prolongation of the war or a catastrophic defeat could be relied upon to precipitate the social and economic changes that he voiced with such vigour.

"You would have had us lose the war, would you?" Robert asked with astonishment. "Only when denied victory would the country have embraced the changes that you long for?"

Levine was not about to go as far as that in the midst of the celebrations but he had little appetite for the high spirits that prevailed within the prison. He saw in Robert's attitude a foolish optimism and didn't hesitate to tell him so when Robert began to speculate as to when they might be released and what conditions were likely to govern their departure.

They had completed their third circuit of the exercise yard and were about to form up in lines to go back to the cells when he said, "You surely don't imagine the Government is likely to release us soon? I see every prospect that we'll still be here next year, required to complete our sentences in spite of the peace."

"Do you think so?"

Robert stopped abruptly and was urged to keep on walking by the warder supervising them. He recognised that any delay in their release would be entirely in keeping with the spirit of vindictiveness that had prompted their imprisonment. It had occurred to him also that he might be required to complete his sentence but he had decided to ignore the possibility on the grounds that victory was likely to usher in a new spirit of generosity on the Government's part.

"I most certainly do," Levine said. Robert's unbridled optimism flew in the face of his harsh view of the world. "The Cabinet's hardly likely to fall over itself to get us out of here, is it? Their first priority is to get the troops home. How long is that going to take with a large, conscript army in the field?"

"But we aren't part of the army. We're very few in number. What could be simpler than to allow us to go home?"

"We were deemed to have enlisted, have you forgotten that? Think about the numbers under arms. There'll need to be elaborate rules to govern their demobilisation. Who will get precedence? Some might have to wait for months to see their families. If it's announced that we're to be freed before them, somebody's going to say 'that isn't fair', why should they get priority when they wouldn't fight; let them wait till the end, it's no more than they deserve."

"You think we might have to remain here until the whole of the wartime army has been disbanded?"

Levine thought it likely that they would be positioned at the end of the queue and it troubled him greatly, not because he longed for home and hearth like Robert, but because there was work to be done. The return of so many soldiers, embittered by the war, facing an uncertain future, was music to his ears. He wanted to be amongst them, stirring them up, fomenting unrest, helping them to recognise that they had been cruelly used. There were already rumours that the troops in France were unhappy with the speed of the demobilisation, the clumsy timetable to which they had been subjected, and were preparing to take matters into their own hands.

He said, "I think it very likely and we must resist it. Salute the dead, by all means, but let's not cloak their death in false glory, not those of my class anyway, those who had no stake in victory before the war began. We must take this opportunity to change the country they're returning to. Only when that's been done to everyone's satisfaction, can we truly speak of victory."

Although it was announced on the day of the Armistice that all recruitment under the Military Service Acts had been suspended, that call-up notices were cancelled and that the cases before the Tribunals were to cease, there was no news about the fate of the conscientous objectors. Robert told himself to be patient, vowing to live from day to day, in the certain knowledge that release would come soon and the prospect of an end to his sentence brought nourishment to a spirit starved of hope. What did another week or month matter, when the end would come soon? He blamed the delay on bureaucracy, on unintentional neglect rather than malevolence but when the weeks stretched into months, he began to lose faith.

"Why are they doing this," he asked Alice on one of her visits, 'haven't we suffered enough?

"Apparently not," she said, struggling to find words of reassurance.

She avoided speaking of Michael's impending demobilisation, the plans to celebrate his return, noting the delay in Robert's release was prompting a frustration and a bitterness she hadn't seen before.

He had suffered fits of rage before, resulting from slights and indignities magnified beyond endurance by isolation and boredom. It was something that afflicted every prisoner at some time or other. But this time it was different. He had no need of an insult or a snub, real or imagined, to ignite his wrath. The target of his anger was himself. Even as his mind declared its resistance to indefinite captivity, his body, weakened by malnutrition and inactivity, prepared to surrender. He knew that a year of his sentence remained and that only the onset of madness or illness was likely to prompt his release. This knowledge was an invitation to connive in his destruction.

He was not the only prisoner vexed by the authorities' intransigence. Others objected more strongly. Some were late arrivals, not yet worn down by the prison regime. Others had enjoyed the comparative freedom of alternative service under the Home Office scheme, only to return disillusioned to the confines of prison. Unlike Robert, they retained their vigour; their faculties were unimpaired and they were determined to secure their release. The end of the war had prompted a passion for freedom in everyone. Whatever their agenda, their plans on release, they found it intolerable to remain in prison. Everyone wanted to be a part of the peace, to participate, in their separate ways, in the construction of the 'land fit for heroes' that alone could justify the sacrifice of the nation's young.

Their repertoire was limited at first to defiant meetings, cell disturbances and the flouting of the petty regulations that impinged upon them. These occasioned some satisfaction, creating the impression that something was being done, but their impact was no more striking than they had been in the past. Then, unexpectedly, a leader emerged from the ranks of the objectors, someone with the capacity and determination to organise resistance that, in its nature and scale, was more effective than anything that had gone before. Then the struggle for freedom began in earnest and the views that Robert had nurtured for so long were put to the test.

CHAPTER 32

"Well, what do you think?" Tom Reynolds stretched out his legs. They extended stiffly over the end of the wheelchair, clothed in smart, blue trousers. Two shiny, black boots emerged from beneath his turn-ups. He gazed at his limbs proudly as if they were both his flesh and blood, although one of them was a skilled artifice created to his specifications by a craftsman in the workshop at the nearby Roehampton Hospital.

"Never mind what I think," said Alice, sharing his delight in spite of her attempt to appear severely practicable, as was her habit in the face of Tom's persistent, good humour. "What I think is neither here nor there. Can you walk, that's what I want to know? Will it help you to get around on your own?"

"Oh, yes," he said as if that could be taken for granted and required no demonstration of expertise on his behalf.

"Go on then, show me, let's see what you can do."

They were walking in the grounds of the Queen Mary's Convalescent Auxiliary Hospital, to which Tom had been transferred from the London Military Hospital. He had been fitted with a prosthetic leg and would remain in hospital with nineteen other officers until he had mastered its use. His case had been touch and go, owing to the length of his stump, but he had refused to take no for an answer. He had grown to love the three-storey house, with its entrance porch, tall chimneys, range of outbuildings and extensive grounds. Most of all, he appreciated the fact that it was within walking distance of Alice's home in Barnes. He had promised her that one day he would walk to Barnes on his new limb to see her and to meet her family.

She stood back from the chair, casting him adrift. She looked him up and down, smiling encouragingly though he needed no inducement to display his expertise. She knew that in her absence, he practiced relentlessly, ignoring the pain and the sores that resulted from his labours. She said, "I want to see you walk. That's what it's for, after all. The rest is mere words."

He gave her a pained look as if she had no right to doubt him, stopped the chair, applied the brake and prepared to lift himself up whilst Alice hovered round him anxiously. Her misgivings were not without foundation. There had been several false starts with other limbs and at least one occasion when Tom had collapsed in a painful heap at her feet, having brushed aside her efforts to support him.

"Right then, this time."

He stood upright, hovering uncertainly, before taking a hesitant step forward. Rocking dangerously, he attempted another one and another until soon he was ten steps away from the chair, still standing upright, if swaying dangerously, his face red, his chest rising and falling from his exertions, before preparing to plunge on.

"That's enough, for now," said Alice firmly, hastening forward with the chair. To her immense relief, he fell back into it without protest, wincing as he did so. "Did that hurt?" she enquired anxiously when he was seated again.

"Well, it did a bit," he said, smiling ruefully. He didn't tell her that he had spent much of the morning practicing for her arrival and that his stump was sore.

"That means it hurt a lot," said Alice, "I know how your mind works when you're talking to me about your progress."

"I'm not sure I know any longer. Sometimes, I think it doesn't work at all, beyond revisiting the past and thinking how things might have been if I'd been less fortunate."

"That's exactly how it works," Alice said triumphantly, "unfailing optimism in all circumstances. That's your signature thought. Others you push aside as so much baggage."

"How would you have me be? You've seen the others; you write about them all the time. You administer to them with that diligence I so admire. We can't let our problems get us down. That might be alright in other circumstances but in hospital, giving in to pessimism can be fatal, as you know, and it can't be right when others have it so much worse."

"I'm not criticising you," said Alice hastily.

She paused to watch a Red Cross lorry trundle up the drive. It disappeared between the two conifers that guarded the house.

"I just wish you would let your guard down sometimes when you're in my presence. I want to know you as you really are."

"That's no small thing to ask of any man. I'm more frank with you than with anybody else. I think you ought to know that."

"I do know that," Alice said. She patted him on the shoulder as she prepared to push him up the path. "I've known it for some time."

There was no need to push him in his chair. He was perfectly capable of propelling himself on any surface or gradient but it was something she had done on her early visits and the habit lingered. It made her feel connected to him, as if they were touching, even though they weren't, and she found she needed that in spite of her twice weekly visits, their lengthy conversations.

It was four months since the war had ended and their lives had changed profoundly. She worked with former soldiers whose minds and bodies had been shattered by the war. She didn't nurse them or treat them. She lacked the skills or aptitude for that and the training required for knowledge and competence in such a complex field would have taken too long to acquire. With her father's help, she had set up a small charity dedicated to returning wounded soldiers to their families and communities. She wrote about their needs extensively in an effort to raise money and led a group of volunteers who worked with hospitals and families to meet the needs of patients discharged from treatment. She also urged the Government to do more for those returning soldiers for whom the war had been a step too far. Tom was her inspiration both by word and deed. She took her problems to him, solicited his advice in her twice weekly visits and all the while, nurtured his recovery, as he sought mobility and independence, by virtue of her presence. Neither of them spoke of their mutual affection, dependence and regard. It was their best kept secret, revealed only in sly looks when the other was distracted, brief, fond gestures when together, the smiles that they exchanged on meeting and departing.

It took the intervention of third parties to make them aware how close they had become and to realise that decisions were required of them if their lives were not to diverge irretrievably.

CHAPTER 33

It was Alice's fortnightly visit to the prison. She had been absent for several weeks, conceding to her parents the visits that were hers by right. The meeting was their first in a private room, one of those newly set aside for visitors. Now there was nothing separating them, no desks, screens or tables. They sat in stiff-backed chairs facing each other, forbidden to embrace or shake hands. No objects of any kind were allowed to pass between them. An impassive warder watched over them, standing at Robert's shoulder, feet astride, hands clasped behind his back, pretending to ignore every word.

"I've some news from America." Alice said, taking up her place.

Robert looked at her with misgivings. He could think of no news from that quarter that might be welcome. Alice had written to Mary as agreed and her letter had been followed by months of silence. Then, when the war ended, the letters had resumed, infrequently at first and then more often until it seemed that one came every week, always from the same address, written in Mary's neat hand. Alice had begged him to let her open them, to find out what was going on, but he had been resolute. He and Mary had been apart for three years. How could it be in her interest to have more to do with him?

"Have you opened one of my letters," he asked more in sorrow than anger, "when we agreed that you wouldn't?"

"The letter I opened was addressed to me."

"She's written to you also?" Robert looked at his sister in amazement. Three years on and Mary was still trying to contact him. Would she never give up?

"She replied to my letter - eventually," Alice said, "the one that you urged me to send on your behalf. I wasn't expecting it, I must admit. After I'd passed on your message, I was certain that she had left the scene for good."

"If you're not careful, you'll start up the whole cycle again."

"Is it such a bad thing for the two of you to remain in touch?"

"What happened was a long time ago and was very painful for us both. I've always felt the least that I could do for Mary after the mess that I created was to leave her free to start a new life."

"Even if that wasn't what she wanted?" Alice persisted

"She was very young and I misled her. I'm trying to do the right thing - belatedly, I know," Robert said, wondering why Alice had taken sides against him.

"She asked me to pass on a message," Alice said, a determined look on her face.

Robert looked at his sister despairingly. He had never seen her looking so well. There was a gaiety about her that he hadn't seen in a long time, an energy he could only envy, given his despair. It made him realise how good life could be if he were ever fortunate enough to put prison behind him. Meanwhile, there was the stone in his shoe that was Swarthmore and the unfortunate events that had happened there.

"How much has she told you? I don't suppose she told you how she misled me, how she copied other peoples' work, how she tried to use our friendship to improve her grades and how she attempted to intimidate me into giving her credits that she hadn't earned."

"Yes," said Alice, looking him full in the face, "she told me that, and more besides."

"What else did she say?".

"She told me her side of the story or, as she put it, the plain, unvarnished truth."

There was a determination in Alice's eyes that Robert didn't care for, a warning of unpalatable truths that she intended to deliver.

"Was she ashamed of what she did?"

"Did you regret your part in it?"

"Of course," Robert said, without hesitation, "how could I not? I meant her no harm."

"She freely admits the damage she did and regrets it hugely...as for what she did and why she did it...well, it all depends on the interpretation you choose to put on it. She had her reasons, as I'm sure you realise, for confronting you."

Alice pulled her chair up closer to his. The warder watched suspiciously as it scraped on the floor. "Anyway," she continued, interrupting Robert as he started to speak, "the rights and wrongs of what happened are for some other day. Suffice it to say that she was very young and the reasons for what she did were more complicated than you might think."

She glanced at the clock on the wall, conscious of its relentless progress, and hoped that twenty minutes would be enough for everything she had to say.

Robert said, a vexed look on his face. "It's extraordinary, isn't it, that after all this time, she hasn't given up? That can't be healthy, can it?" He looked at Alice expectantly but she declined to be drawn. "She's obsessed with something that happened three years ago. You mustn't encourage her. That would be wrong. She has to move on, as we all have to do after a setback. That's what I've tried to do, though it hasn't been easy, when I spend so much time alone. She needs to build a new life for herself, free from Swarthmore and all that happened there. Leaving college without a degree isn't the end of the world."

He wanted to tell Alice of the agonies he'd suffered, the nights when his insomnia had been unbearable and he could think of nothing but his time with Mary, time truncated by the need to meet his obligations to her, the college and his profession. How many times had he relived those hours by the shore, over almost before they had begun, wrapped in her arms, the sound of the waves on the rocks greeting them each time they parted? Then, there was the guilt at having taken up with one of his students, at not having had the foresight to see where it might lead and the regret at his sudden departure, when what had been beautiful had become a conflict beyond his capacity to resolve. He wanted to say all that and more but there wasn't time and he knew it would serve no useful purpose when he was trying to forget someone who was unobtainable, whom he had hurt greatly, to whom he could never make amends.

Alice leaned forward, confronting him in a way he hadn't anticipated. His was a sister who hung on his every word not one who defied him or took sides against him. Taken aback by her determination to prevail, he sat back in his chair, arms folded across his chest, asking himself if his sister wouldn't support him, who would?

Choosing her words with care, Alice said, "You see, in her case, it isn't that simple. You may have found it possible to make a clean break with the past but for her it's more complicated. Events have conspired to deny her that choice."

"I don't see why," Robert asserted, believing himself to be on firm ground. "She's far younger than me. Whatever I did wrong and I acted very badly - I freely admit it - I've paid my dues. I abandoned the teaching post I worked so hard to earn. I left the college to spare her any embarrassment and and came back to this." He surveyed his surroundings with disdain. "What more could I do? I'm sure she'll get over it if she's left alone."

Alice looked at him despairingly. "Oh, Robert, she's been writing to you all this time to tell you that you have a child, that you're a father with a beautiful daughter whom you've never met."

"I have a daughter?" Robert stared at Alice in disbelief, his eyes full of alarm. "Mary's a mother and the child's mine? How can that be when I've been back in England almost three years?"

"She was born in September 1916," Alice said excitedly, free to share with her brother the secret that had been hers for so long.

"Mary sent me a copy of the birth certificate. I didn't ask to see it. She volunteered it. She didn't want there to be any doubt in your mind. I've seen a photograph of your daughter. Such a lovely little girl. No one could be in any doubt that she's yours."

Robert gazed at his sister in amazement. He lurched forward, his chair sliding beneath him. Only the warder's restraining hand kept him upright. He looked down at Robert, a bemused expression on his face.

"This can't be. It's impossible," Robert said loudly, even as the memories of his New Year weekend with Mary flooded his mind.

He recalled the hotel on the shore: the smirking girl in the gift shop who had sold them the ring; the white lies he had told to secure them a room; Mary's face concealed beneath a broad hat; the hurried entrance, the climb up the stairs with the luggage; their embarrassment as they removed their clothes in the twilight; the passion he thought would never end. How often had he relived those hours? He remembered her naked by the window, watching the waves as they dashed over the shingle. He had been surprised by her lack of inhibition, her appetite, her desire to please. He had struggled to put those hours behind him. He had despised her for her deception, blamed her for his downfall. It had made no difference. He had longed for her presence for three years, clinging to her memory, the things she had done and said, aching for her in spite of their discord and, for all that time they had shared a child, a daughter whose existence had been unknown to him, whose face he had never seen.

He said quickly, "The photograph? Do you have it with you?" He held his hand out abruptly, noting, as he waited for Alice to delve into her bag, that it shook perceptibly.

Alice said, a little smugly, "Yes, I do. I also have the letter that came with it - if they'll let you read it." She looked across at the warder expectantly.

"The letter can wait," Robert said. "I want to see the child. Hold up her picture so that I can look at it."

The warder intervened, bent on preventing anything passing between them.

"What d'you think you're doing? You can't give him anything. That's not allowed. You were told that when you came in."

Ignoring his protests, Alice held up the photograph. Robert peered at it anxiously but was not close enough to see it clearly.

Alice rose from her seat. The warder's eyes filled with alarm.

She said, "I want to show him the photograph. It's his daughter. He's never seen her, though she's almost three years old. What do you think? A quick look and then he'll return it to me."

"You can't give him anything," the warder repeated with little conviction. Sensing he was about to give way, Alice rewarded him with her most fetching smile.

"All right," he said after a token show of resistance. He held out his hand for the photograph. "I'll give it to him."

Alice handed over the photograph. It swayed tantalisingly before Robert's face. He wanted to snatch it from the warder's grasp. It was his daughter's photograph. It belonged to him.

"You can't keep it, though," the warder said, holding back the portrait until Robert acquiesced.

Robert said, "I know but let me take a good look at it. I might not get another chance."

The warder kept the photograph at arm's length as though it were contaminated. Robert seized it eagerly and held it up to the light, drinking in every detail of the small figure peeping out from under bonnet and crinolines, a contented smile on her face.

"What's her name?" he asked without looking up.

There was a tenderness, a solicitude in his voice that Alice hadn't heard before. His detachment, his cherished scepticism, his preoccupation with his circumstances had been stripped away. If he doubted her provenance, there was no sign of it. He seemed captivated by the photograph, unable to tear his eyes away from the happy bundle it portrayed.

"Rosamunde. A pretty name, don't you think?" Alice asked. "One you might have chosen, had you been there?"

He sat back in his chair, a startled look on his face. He said, "Schubert: the A Minor String Quartet. We heard it together. She was captivated by it and learnt it to play it on the piano. She played it for me whilst we were away."

"You have to give it back now," the warder said in an effort to assert himself. He had almost forgotten his instructions, caught up as he was in the drama unfolding before him.

Robert made no effort to release the photograph from his grasp.

"Her mother calls her Rosie," Alice said.

Robert repeated the name, still gazing at the photograph. Knowing his daughter's name seemed to cast her features in a new light. "So that's why there were so many letters?"

"She wanted to share the good news with you."

"Of course, she wanted me to know that I had obligations, as well…"

"That's uncharitable," Alice said sharply, "though you do and I'm sure that you'll discharge them when the time comes. But that wasn't why she wrote to you. She was very clear about that. She was conscious of the fact that you were in prison. I think she felt responsible for that."

"It was my choice; no one forced me to come back."

"She was desperate for you to know that you had a daughter so that you would have a reason to be strong. She longs for you to meet Rosie, to spend time with her, on your release."

The warder held out his hand, looking at Robert expectantly, a frown on his face. Robert parted with the photograph reluctantly, bestowing on it one last, lingering glance. The warder gave it to Alice but not before he had looked at it himself, registering his approval with a faint smile. He started to speak and then thought better of it, lapsing into silence, a disapproving frown on his face. Alice returned it to her bag and said, "I have others you can see later."

She hoped that she had done the right thing. After all, what could Robert do about seeing his daughter? He was still in prison, the date of his release still unresolved. His daughter was on another continent, growing up without him. It would only add to his frustration, heighten his sense of loss at being in prison. Then, when she saw the smile on his face, heard him repeat Rosie's name not once but several times, her doubts took flight. Mary had been right to persist. The knowledge that he had a daughter waiting on his presence would give him a reason to endure his sentence in good heart.

She said, "You'll go and see her as soon as you're able to?"

There was a sudden look of anxiety on Robert's face. Alice was reminded of a bear, a sorry creature she had seen once at a fairground, its keeper poking it repeatedly through the bars of its cage with a pointed stick in the hope of making it dance. He couldn't wait to see her. He was desperate to do so but at the same time he feared complications, an opening of wounds that had barely healed.

He said, "Mary and I didn't part on good terms."

"She said you ran away."

He looked shame-faced. "I did in a manner of speaking."

"That's how it seemed to her, anyway. This is an opportunity to make amends, to be a father to your daughter, to help her mother to care of her."

"She'll have found somebody else by now."

Alice shook her head, "If she has, she's never mentioned it." She added warily, "She shows every sign of being a remarkable young woman."

"She was always that."

"It's no small matter to find a husband when you already have a daughter."

"Yes," he said eagerly, as if the thought had just occurred to him, "we have a daughter, no matter what happens to us. But what can I do about seeing her - or her mother, for that matter - when I'm stuck here? I have to get out. I have to regain my freedom. Why not, the war's over? Haven't I suffered enough? Why shouldn't I have an opportunity to see my daughter now that I know about her?"

To diminish his mounting anger, Alice said, "The first thing you have to do is to write to Mary. I'll do the same. Tell her how much you welcomed the news of your daughter's arrival and how keen you are to see her."

Robert looked troubled. "Yes, I will," he said eagerly, "but what'll I say about her letters, the fact that I never allowed you to open them or attempted to reply to any of them?"

"Tell her the truth. Tell her that you had her interests at heart. I'm sure she'll understand."

"It was foolish of me," Robert said, "spiteful even, but after everything that happened, I thought it for the best. Why am I so naive in matters of the heart?" He asked the question of himself but Alice answered for him.

"Your head's in the clouds. You don't see what's under your nose. I doubt you'd have stayed in Pennsylvania much longer,. It's never been in your nature to sit on the sidelines. Oh, I know you're a scholar and happiest at your books but only up to a point. You're like your father. You want to be involved in things. You would have finished up in here eventually."

Robert couldn't disagree. Much as he had enjoyed his months at Swarthmore and in spite of his affection for Mary, his absence from the momentous events taking place in France had blighted his teaching, making him long to be home.

He said, "Had I not left so abruptly, I might have avoided going to France."

"There's that, of course," Alice said, nodding in agreement, "but you would still have opposed conscription and ended up in prison. You're a person with strong views - like everyone in our family. We were brought up to express our beliefs, regardless of the consequences. A mixed blessing, in my view - but there you are. You were never going to join the army or undertake alternative service. I've always known that."

The warder stirred, his eyes on the clock. He said to Alice, "You have to go now," asserting himself as best he could. He seemed reluctant to have her depart in spite of his words. Above the door a bell rang and the fingers on the clock announced the hour.

"You'll visit her as soon as you can?" Alice said, anxious now their meeting was drawing to a close. "I can promise that on your behalf? The other things can take care of themselves. What's important is that you see your daughter at the earliest opportunity."

"But when that will be?" Robert looked at the warder speculatively, as though the decision were his.

Alice said, "She was very young when she met you, don't forget that. She wanted to impress you and was afraid of failing her course." She recalled when she had been studying for her degree and had turned to Robert for help. "You can be a harsh taskmaster. Your students admire you but fear you as well."

"I want them to do well."

"You can't expect everyone to be clever or to match your dedication. Most people aren't capable of that or don't want to make the effort its requires. They want to be good enough, that's the extent of their ambitions. Mary always struggled. The more she tried, the more you demanded, not just from her but from the whole class. What she achieved was never good enough. Then she feared that she would fail her course and lose you. That's why she copied someone else's work. It wasn't her idea. Her friend was trying to help her. Nor was it just any work. It was work you were certain to admire. She realised that she had overreached herself but by then it was too late. When you found out what she'd done, you were outraged. You felt betrayed. You never asked her why she'd done it. No wonder she tried to restrain you...."

"She threatened to ruin my career."

"Your glittering career?"

"The one that I worked so hard for..."

"Did you really think that this young woman who had fallen in love with you was going to denounce you? She looked to you to find a solution, something that would save her from ignominy and keep your integrity intact."

"How was I supposed to do that?"

Robert stared at his feet, unable to look Alice in the eye.

"I panicked - I realise that now. There must have been some way, a diplomatic illness or something...a different course for her...who knows... but I'll make it up to her, I promise. I'll become a devoted father and encourage her to find love elsewhere."

"I don't think she wants to find love elsewhere. I think she wants to find it with you. But that's for later. Focus on your daughter. Events will take their course. What Mary chooses to do with her life is a matter for her. She's a mother and has responsibilities she didn't have before."

The warder held the door ajar for Alice, his impatience mounting. He felt that he had indulged Alice, charming though she might be.

His actions filled Robert with a sense of urgency he could barely control. He said fiercely, "I must get out of here as soon as I can. I've been here long enough."

"Be on your best behaviour," Alice said, knowing that the prison had become a hotbed of unrest. "Don't do anything that makes you conspicuous or brings you up before the governor. Be helpful and cooperative - above all, be patient - release will come soon enough."

"Then I'll go and see Rosie and make up for lost time."

Alice smiled encouragingly, knowing she had lit a fuse. She only hoped that it would burn slowly and that the authorities would move quickly to procure Robert's release. She said, not knowing whether it would be helpful or not, "I'll send you the photograph with my next letter."

"No, don't do that," Robert said, thoroughly alarmed, "they might confiscate it and then we'll have nothing."

"There are other photographs."

"Will you bring some with you the next time?"

"Father will be here next. He knows nothing about Rosie."

"He knows about Mary. I wrote to him. I felt it was the least I could do. Will you tell him about Rosie?"

"No, that's for you to do. I wouldn't do it yet. Wait until you're home and tell him the whole story then. The photographs and letters, will be waiting for you when you get out."

"But when will that be?" Robert said as the door closed behind her and he was alone again.

CHAPTER 34

Though the prison chapel was plain and shabby with none of the touches of a parish church, Robert was unmindful of its shortcomings. He delighted in the space afforded by its vaulted roof, the lines of pews like soldiers on parade, the tall windows with their shock of daylight. The organ's deep resonances, the loud, uneven choir heightened his exhilaration. He loved to sing loudly after the endless silence of his cell. He always croaked at first, chest rising emptily, before his voice escaped, revelling in its unexpected freedom. He sang heartily, prayed fervently and drank in the words of the lesson, leaving the short services uplifted.

It was through the medium of the chapel, the journeys to and from its services, that he encountered others who had shared his experiences in France. He met Castlereagh in the doorway of the chapel. He encountered Clapham, former journalist and trenchant critic of war, when queuing for his seat and Hicks caught his eye on account of his notable singing, his efforts dwarfing others' tuneless offerings. However, it was only in the yard that they had the opportunity to speak. There Robert and Levine resumed their relationship with their former comrades.

From the first, it was evident that their experiences of the last two years had differed greatly from theirs, with consequences for both their health and points of view.

"Goodness, what's happened to you?" Castlereagh asked when he and Robert first spoke. Robert had been notable for his robust, good health. The figure before him was emaciated, incapable of looking him in the eye and struggled to speak. The prison's long silences had destroyed in him the art of conversation.

"You're a bag of bones," he said, labouring the point. "Look at you. You can barely stand. Prison hasn't been kind to you."

"That's for sure," Robert said, wincing at the other's scrutiny, his obvious surprise.

He hated being reminded of his condition. It only made him feel worse. That was why Alice was such a welcome visitor. If his condition gave her cause for concern, she kept her worries to herself. She was always cheerful, anxious to support him. He had no tolerance for anyone who expressed dismay.

"I've been in and out of here for almost three years. Each bout of solitary confinement was worst than the last. You'd think that you'd get used to it, but you don't. Knowing what to expect only makes it drearier. But I haven't capitulated," he added quickly, "I still have my wits about me. That's no small thing."

"You rejected the Home Office Scheme then?" said Castlereagh. "I'm not surprised. You always were a stubborn chap."

"I felt I had no alternative after what took place in France."

"You're looking well," Robert said, comparing Castlereagh's appearance and demeanour with his own deficiencies.

"Oh, I've been holidaying on Dartmoor."

Castlereagh gave a short laugh as he recalled the efforts there to make them work.

"Fresh air, lots of exercise and reasonable food. We were sent back here when we refused to work. Not a great success, I have to say, the Home Office scheme."

"It kept you out of here."

"Yes, that's true."

"I'm delighted to see you again."

Robert soon recognised that their relationship in France had been too intense, too claustrophobic to transplant to another, wider universe. Their paths had diverged and now their views and intentions differed. Castlereagh had been persuaded into alternative service. He said that, at the time, anything had seemed better than the dreary prison round but forced to undertake a series of pointless tasks, derided and bullied, his spirit had rebelled. He had found it intolerable to suffer the indignity of forced labour. It made it seem as if the old, familiar world of master and servant had been inverted in favour of a new world wholly ignorant of his provenance.

The others were more sanguine about their circumstances. Hicks regarded resistance to conscription as a mistake, believing the circumstances of the moment had swayed his judgement. Not only had the music hall he loved changed but the army had sought to entertain the troops under its command and many of his old colleagues had responded to its call. He had been trapped by his views, compelled to carry on with his resistance to conscription even though his heart was no longer in it. Now he worried that he would never work again and wondered whether the talents he had once exhibited still remained with him. Clapham had continued to write: tracts, articles and features on aspects of the war, trenchant and funny pieces about prison life, anything that sprung to mind, even when the opportunities to put pen to paper were limited, his efforts often lost and his work rarely read or published. "The point is to make the effort, keep my skills intact," he said to Robert, "so that when the day of freedom comes, I can continue with my work."

Castlereagh assumed the leadership of the prison protests. He seemed to do it effortlessly, his boundless energy and obvious charisma, elevating him in the eyes of everyone involved. Robert wondered if he had become a socialist as he began to dominate the group of socialists who were the core of the resistance.

"No, I haven't," Castlereagh protested but his scepticism seemed no barrier to his adopting socialist views. Robert concluded that his politics were a moveable feast and all that mattered was his prominence.

"The death sentence was the turning point for me," said Castlereagh when Robert questioned him about his views. "That was when the price of pacifism was revealed. I realised it was insufficient to turn the other cheek, that when your opposition's stifled, you merely help your enemies. You have to fight for your beliefs. We don't live in a reasonable world and it'll be no different in the future."

"What beliefs do you intend to fight for?"

Robert concluded that Castlereagh had few objectives beyond his release. There was nothing wrong with that. He was no less anxious to be free, especially since Alice's disclosure, but Castlereagh's selfishness troubled him. He wanted to believe that his imprisonment had served some useful purpose and that his freedom, when it came, would bring new meaning to his life. Castlereagh, to whom he had been so close, seemed to want nothing from the future but his own advancement.

"One of the first things I'll do when I get out of here will be to claim my inheritance," Castlereagh said.

"If your father was disinclined to favour you before the war, I see little prospect of it happening now."

"So many family members died in the war. Brothers, cousins and nephews. To a man, they rushed to serve. Now nearly all of them are gone."

"He'll become a politician, I'd stake my life on it," said Clapham. "You can see it in him now."

"No one's going to vote for someone who opposed conscription."

Castlereagh joined with the socialists and was to be heard promoting their philosophy. The socialists were the largest, most cohesive group and had their counterparts, their supporters in the world outside. He devoted himself to dominating their committee. He shunted Levine and other potential rivals aside. Robert could only marvel at the speed with which Levine became his follower and confidant. Under Castlereagh's direction, the prison protests became an organised and persistent effort to subvert the authorities, the vehicle of his implacable determination to be free.

The exercise yard was an unchallenged opportunity to converse freely. The prisoners demanded two hours of exercise at any one time and the freedom to do as they pleased. When their demands were ignored, they refused to return to their cells. Conditions in the workshops were no less fraught. Castlereagh and his lieutenants organised several work strikes and when they were punished for their recalcitrance, urged a ban on work throughout the prison. Robert was amongst the few who declined to heed their call.

"Why won't you join us?" Levine demanded as he attempted to recruit those who had failed to respond. The struggle had caused him to behave like a man possessed. It was the first time in a lifetime of dissent that he had possessed any power and influence and he meant to make the most of it.

They were in the yard, talking freely, watched over by resentful warders who no longer felt they had the power to intervene. Robert likened the prisoners to a herd of animals. The warders were hyenas, circling the herd, alert for signs of weakness amongst its number, the opportunity to isolate a victim and bring it to its knees.

He said, "No good will come of this. You'll only make things worse."

"This time will be different," Levine said, revelling in his power. "There's a growing sense of grievance amongst the prisoners that didn't exist before."

Robert wanted to be left alone until he had the opportunity to leave the prison. He aspired to spend more time with his family, to visit his daughter, seek the peace of mind that had evaded him for three years before finding a way back into the community, assuming a role and purpose there that he lacked at present.

He said, "I'm going to abide by the regulations as long as they're in force."

Levine was quick to object. "That isn't good enough. Why do you think we're able to talk freely? Why are we still in the yard though our time's up? You've benefited from our protests and yet refuse to help us. What do you hope to achieve by your acquiescence?"

"Concessions freely offered I'll accept but I won't agitate for change. I volunteered to come here out of opposition to conscription and I'm resigned to remaining here until they set me free."

"They'll see you rot first," Levine said, turning on his heel.

He stomped across the yard to where the others gathered, looking back to give an angry wave. He reminded Robert of every officer and warder who had attempted to coerce him: the bemusement, the anger at his obduracy, the stifled violence, the contemptuous dismissal. Now the pain of rejection was made worse by knowing that his stubbornness had cost him a friend and ally.

He clashed with Castlereagh in the workshop before the work ban reached its height. It was Castlereagh's job to collect their work. He had persuaded the incumbent to stand aside so that he could monitor the progress of the strike and control the flow of information between one group and another.

"Still working, eh?" he said to Robert as he gathered up the empty baskets. Robert smiled weakly. He had no wish to be provocative but he was not inclined to give up working as long as the rules remained in place and the warders cared to implement them.

"You know the chairman of the No-Conscription Fellowship refused to work before he was released?"

Castlereagh spoke in a stage whisper so that everyone could hear. The supervising warder stirred restlessly, gave him a angry glance but made no attempt to intervene.

"He declared that prison work was unacceptable as long as he was subject to the provisions of the Military Service Act."

"He was released on grounds of ill-health after certain people, including my sister, lobbied on his behalf."

He had followed the case with interest, plying Alice with questions, wondering how ill you had to be before you qualified for early release. He had found the news curiously dispiriting. It was as though Clifford Allen's illness, the departure resulting from it, had amounted to betrayal. Alice reassured him that he had been ill before he entered prison and would not have been there but for his prominence.

"Why don't you follow his example?" urged Castlereagh. "If your sister were here, she'd urge you to stop working."

"You've no idea what she'd say."

Robert had assumed an importance in Castlereagh's eyes quite beyond his status. He represented the past, the behaviour that Castlereagh affected to despise. Hoping to avoid a confrontation, he said, "It's not Friends' custom to conspire to break the law."

"You broke it when you declined to enlist."

"It was an act of conscience. I spoke only for myself."

Castlereagh began to cough. The atmosphere in the workshops tore at his throat. It was one of the reasons why he had abandoned work in favour of the collection of the baskets from the line of stalls. He also resented the pointlessness of the tasks. It made him angry to see men labouring in the hope of an extra cup of cocoa or a piece of bread.

"Hasn't prison taught you anything?" he asked as he fought for breath. "You'll achieve nothing if you isolate yourself from others. You challenged the Government's authority when you declined to enlist and it won't release you unless you challenge it again."

"My circumstances have changed. I have a three year old daughter, whom I've never seen. She's my priority. I'm not prepared to do anything likely to delay my release."

"We're intent on getting out of here as soon as possible."

"What you're doing isn't going to work."

Robert recalled Alice's words: the need to avoid controversy, the necessity for good behaviour. He had thought her advice timely. He dare not risk prolonging his sentence by some careless act. He thought it better to allow events to unfold. It was consistent with the stance he had taken in the past.

"I hope that you succeed but I won't be amongst the beneficiaries. My daughter is all that matters to me now."

Castlereagh was dismissive, concluding in a voice loud enough for everyone to hear, "You've grown so used to suffering that you conspire with your tormentors. If you're going to leave here, you'll have to fight for freedom."

Robert watched him go, glad to see the back of him. He was attempting to make an example of him. It wasn't an act of friendship or concern, it was a means to intimidate the others. He recalled his father's words, unwelcome at the time, his opposition to any special pleading. Well, he wasn't wavering. Nor was he seeking special treatment. His goal was to see his daughter as soon as possible.

He defied the strike, even as its supporters increased, but it was with a heavy heart. He wondered if Castlereagh was right and compliance had become an impulse, servility a habit.

He waited for Castlereagh to confront him again, determined when the time came, to defend his actions with greater vigour than before but Castlereagh was careful to avoid another clash. Their dispute had served its purpose. Robert was isolated, his views discredited. He was unlikely to inspire others to conform. Meanwhile, Castlereagh promised the destruction of the prison system that had them in its grasp. The devotion of his followers added to his prominence. It fostered the impression that the widespread and spontaneous unrest was largely his creation, convincing the authorities that they had no alternative but to negotiate with him.

The governor began by attempting to be conciliatory, only to discover his offer of concessions meant nothing without the promise of release. He had failed to recognise that for men deprived of their rights, a taste of freedom was intoxicating. He was to be seen pacing his office, hands clenched tightly, a look of anguish on his face. He was reluctant to return to the old regime but felt he had to act before the prison's governance collapsed. Leniency gave way to rigid discipline, a dominion made all the more unpalatable by the enthusiasm with which the warders applied the many sanctions. Prisoner after prisoner came up before the governor to have their privileges removed, their diets reduced and their freedom curtailed. Meanwhile, the work strike hardened until Robert, deprived of materials, was compelled to join in. The prisoners sat down without warning in the corridors. They held impromptu concerts, broke up furniture, refused to return to their cells. When a fire started in the kitchens, ten of them took refuge on the roof and refused to come down, agreeing to descend only when promised a full amnesty. It was all too much for the governor. He demanded that his harassed staff applied the full panoply of prison regulations against the mutineers, only to recognise that his hands were tied. His portfolio of threats and punishments was designed to deal with awkward individuals. He was powerless to act when the mass of prisoners defied his rule.

He responded by imprisoning Castlereagh and his comrades in the basement dungeons. Robert was included in their number, as were certain other conscientious objectors who had been in France. Unused and neglected, the dungeons were dank and cold. Water cascaded down the walls; the air was chill and lifeless, heavy on the faces of the prisoners as they lay there in the darkness. The only sound, aside from the echoing voices of the inmates, was the squeaking of the rats that scuttled in the darkness, resentful of the strangers in their midst. The governor swore that the prisoners would remain entombed until they promised to end their agitation, certain that they would capitulate after a few days. He was equally confident that the disturbances would end without their pernicious influence. He was wrong on both counts. The prisoners in the dungeons did not give in and the mutiny grew worse and, as Robert had predicted, violent clashes took place between the prisoners and warders. When it seemed that the disturbances could hardly grow worse, Castlereagh announced that he and his companions were going on hunger strike until promised their release.

CHAPTER 35

"Miss Bennett, may I have a word with you?"

Alice halted, surprised to hear her name. Having seen Tom back to his room after their stroll round the grounds, she had been about to leave the hospital building. The wheelchair had hardly been necessary. It was a convenient way to convey him to the bench from which they started out but after that it wasn't needed. He was more than capable of making his own way around the gardens, albeit slowly and sometimes painfully. Since his first hesitant steps, his progress had been rapid and he would soon make way for another officer from the long list of those awaiting artificial limbs.

She turned to see Stephanie Brown, the ward sister looking at her expectantly, a trifle nervously, suggesting that she wanted to say something to her that she might not want to hear. She was a young, buxom, rather careworn woman with long dark hair wedged carefully beneath her cap and the large cross upon her apron gave her ample bosom a startling prominence. The officers were very fond of her, in spite of her strictness, and her implacable determination to get them up and about. She was their commanding officer, mother, nurse and counsellor, a mirror on the lives of everyone.

When Alice said, "Of course," she pointed to her office and held the door ajar. Alice stepped inside. The room was bare but welcoming: a desk, overflowing with papers; a filing cabinet; three chairs; paintings of the hospital grounds; photographs of groups of officers and individuals, some signed, and vases of flowers, daffodils and tulips by the window that overlooked the grounds.

"I wanted to have a word with you about Captain Reynolds."

The ward sister looked Alice squarely in the eye as she spoke. It was the same bold look with which she addressed the officers in her care. No nonsense, matter of fact, but betraying an underlying sympathy, a degree of understanding that won the heart of every officer entrusted to her custody.

"I suppose he'll be leaving shortly," Alice said, as she took her place in the chair that had been offered to her and arranged her skirts. She removed the hat that she had just put on and placed it on the filing cabinet, taking care not to displace any of the photographs arranged upon its surface.

"Yes, he will," the ward sister said. "He's made good progress and deservedly so. With your encouragement, he's worked very hard on his mobility. He'll need to be looked after at first, of course, but in due course, I've no doubt he'll become entirely independent."

"Another of your successes," said Alice, a look of admiration on her face.

"And yours," the ward sister said. After a moment's hesitation, she added, "That's what I want to talk to you about."

"Oh, he's all prepared to leave. He's going to stay with his widowed sister for a few months until he's decided his future. He was training to be a doctor before he enlisted and will probably go back to doing that in due course."

"What about you? What role do you intend to play in his life?"

The ward sister's stare had taken on a new intensity, a combination of mild scepticism and earnest enquiry. She began to toy with the pins that held her hair in place but her eyes never left Alice's face.

"Well, I'll do all I can to help him. It'll be difficult for him, at first. It's not just a question of mobility. He'll have to adjust to a life that will be quite limited compared with the one he led before. There'll also be the attitude of others to his disability, no small thing to live with, even when so many others are in the same position. Then there's the legacy of the war, the memories, the pain and suffering. He'll have to overcome all these things before he's whole again."

"He's very fortunate to have so understanding a friend. He wouldn't have made such progress without your help." The ward sister leaned forward in her chair, a plaintive look in her eyes. "I'm not sure you understand this. He doesn't only see you as a friend. He's very fond of you. His life centres on your visits. He talks about you all the time. The effort that he's made has been for you. In short, I think he has expectations of you that you might not want to meet."

"Romantic expectations?"

"He feels that when he's fully mobile and has resumed his career, that he would like to marry you. Moreover, he feels that you might also be drawn to the idea."

Alice fell back into her chair, astonished at the other's revelations. She was surprised both at their nature and at the extent to which Tom had revealed his thoughts to someone else. Nothing overt of that kind had ever passed between them. She had felt sorry for him and had wanted to help him. She had admired his strength and courage and felt it deserved to be rewarded but as for anything romantic, she hadn't given the matter any thought at all. Only now did she recognise that her actions could have been misinterpreted, that in attempting to help him with such solicitude, she might have confused him.

She said, "Oh, I didn't mean to mislead him. I felt sorry for him from the moment we met. How could it be otherwise after what he'd been through?"

Sister Brown considered this for a moment before saying in a confidential voice, "I wouldn't blame you; it's easily done. In my profession, it's an occupational hazard. You have to be attentive and caring and yet somehow contrive to keep your distance."

She remembered the matron, so rigid in her opposition to fraternisation, in the base hospital in Calais where she had first encountered the tidal wave of casualties from the salient at Ypres. The men that she had encountered there with their dreadful wounds and traumas had broken her heart. There had been so many of them, so many individual tragedies, requiring her skills and devotion. The fact that the numbers were so great had been her salvation. The demands on her time and energies had been so unending that every time she stopped working she wanted only to eat, wash and sleep. That had protected her from individual cases, preventing her from getting involved with anyone inside or outside the hospital. She still remembered the casualties; they would live with her always: the suffering and pleading in their eyes, their gratitude for every little favour that helped to make them comfortable. Now, her heart was hardened. She still cared enormously but felt that she could no longer love. She had worked so hard to prevent it for so long. In her own way, she was also a casualty of the war and would likely spend the balance of her life alone.

"He's not to blame," she added needlessly, for it had never crossed Alice's mind that he might also be responsible for the situation that had grown up between them. "These men are very vulnerable. They have a lot of time on their hands, no matter how hard we try to keep them occupied. Many of them are disfigured and wonder whether any woman will find them attractive. And you are a good looking, sensitive, young woman. What man wouldn't delight in your devotion? Especially, someone," her voice trailed off, "who has lost so much."

"I've grown very fond of him," Alice said.

It was true. She looked forward to their encounters no less than he did and made every effort to be attractive to him. She looked down at the dress that she was wearing, its colour especially chosen to set off her complexion; the shawl, embroidered by her mother, that she had slipped around her shoulders; the hat from her favourite milliner, its brim angled to accentuate her large, green eyes. Eyes which regarded him without restraint, revealing her affection and admiration. She allowed her hand to linger on his tunic needlessly when she helped him to walk. She let go of his hand reluctantly when they met or parted. She didn't hesitate to kiss him lightly on the cheek when his efforts at mobility merited reward. In helping him to plan and organise his future, she had been mindful of the need to go on seeing him when he was discharged. And all the time, she had told herself that she was being kind, that she was doing all these things for him, because he deserved her help. Now, for the first time, she wondered at her motives. What it possible that she was doing them for herself as well?

"There's something else," Sister Brown said, looking even more uncomfortable than she had before.

She stood up from her chair, her starched uniform crackling faintly as she moved towards the window, gazed out on the conifers that guarded the drive, unfailing sentries through the seasons. Figures populated the garden: officers with their orderlies taking exercise with sticks and wheelchairs, earnest in their efforts as she had instructed them to be. They were her boys, all of them, back from the war, passing through. She must never forget that. She must remain conscious of the length of the waiting lists, of how easily limbs posted to the unsupervised were subject to neglect or misuse. The war might be over but her task was only just beginning. The war's consequences would live on for a generation, touching every household in the land.

Alice looked at her expectantly, and not a little fearfully. She felt that the ground had opened up and that she stood on the rim of a crater looking down, until the light gave way to darkness and vague shadows.

Sister Brown said, "You must forgive me for saying this."

She continued to gaze out of the window so that Alice could only see a pale reflection of her face. "But I'm a nurse and you're not and I'm always conscious of these things. Captain Reynolds is an amputee. You only see him wearing the limb that's been crafted for him. If you were ever to be closer, you would be reminded of his true condition daily and might not care for it."

Alice thought back to that day at the military hospital when they had met for the first time. She recalled how the rug had fallen from his chair and how shocked she had been to see him sitting on his stump and how she had revealed her consternation in spite of her efforts at restraint. Sister was right. If they were together, that was how it would be every day. That was the man whom she would lie next to at night, the man who would father her children. Did she mind? Did his disability matter to her now she knew and cared for him? It was a question she had never asked before She had allowed his uniform and artificial limb to fool her into thinking he was whole.

She said, "I hadn't really thought of it that way."

"Well, you must ask yourself before he leaves this place what he means to you and let the answer govern your responses to his interest in you. For him, the question's vital. One day, some woman, close to him, it might not be you, is going to have to ask herself whether his condition matters to her. For him, and for her also, life would be impossible with someone less than wholly reconciled to what the war has done to him."

"I can see that," Alice said as the sister looked her up and down, wanting to satisfy herself that her words had been received in the spirit meant.

"You see, he's been with us for two months. He's become one of our boys. He's been through so much since he came out. We wouldn't want to see him hurt; not now his recovery has progressed so far."

"No, we wouldn't," Alice said and for a moment, she thought that she was going to weep. She pulled herself together so that when she came to leave she was brisk efficiency, effusive in her thanks for sister's timely advice, full of assurance that she would do the right thing. But what was the right thing? Was she to go backwards or forwards? If backwards, how was she to maintain their friendship and leave no room for ambiguity? Was that what she wanted? What did she really think about this man whose rehabilitation had dominated her thoughts since she had first encountered him?

Sister Brown saw her to the door. She held it ajar and stood aside to let Alice past. When Alice stopped to shake her hand, she accepted readily and then stepped forward and hugged her tightly before ushering her out, embarrassed at her gesture. She said, "I hope I haven't intruded. I thought it better that you knew how the land lay."

"Oh, no," said Alice, shaking her head. "I'm glad you mentioned it."

The sister said, "I know I can rely on you to do the right thing by the captain."

Alice started down the path. By the time she turned to wave goodbye, the door was closed, the sister gone. She looked up at the tall windows and saw a figure waving from behind the glass. Whilst she had been in the sister's office, Tom had been waiting patiently at the window. How many times, unknown to her, had he followed her progress to the gate and into the road? She lengthened her stride, deciding that she would walk to Barnes, wanting to be alone with her thoughts, hoping that the journey would help her shape the future for them both.

CHAPTER 36

They had been thrown into the dungeons in their prison clothes and their thin flannel suits were ill-suited to the conditions. They were no proof against the water that ran down the walls and gathered in pools on the rough, stone floor. Nor did they provide any protection against the intense cold or the lack of light that reduced them to insects doomed to grope their way across the floor. They were dependent for illumination on the pale light from the stairway when the dungeon door flew open and the reluctant warders appeared carrying their drinking water and the food that everyone but Robert had declined to eat.

"Absolutely not," he said, when Castlereagh first proposed the idea of a hunger strike, "you can't ask people to risk their lives in such a wilful way."

"You risked your life when you went to France. You were prepared to die for your beliefs then. How's this any different?"

Robert was defiant. The whole idea made him angry beyond reason. He felt it was something that Castlereagh was trying to impose on everyone for his own purposes and that it would be a victory for the authorities, a self-inflicted degradation.

He said, "I didn't elect to go to France. There was nothing I could do to prevent it except to change my mind and that wasn't something I contemplated. None of us did. I'm no less keen than you to see the back of this place but I won't go to any lengths to achieve it. A hunger strike will serve no purpose other than to harm those undertaking it. I'd rather endure the rest of my sentence than secure my freedom by threatening suicide."

He recalled his mother's action in support of the suffragettes and her opposition to the hunger strikes. He said, "We were wholly committed to extending the franchise - even my father came round to it - but none of us supported the threat of self-destruction. That was our view then - and it's mine now, desperate as I am to be free."

Castlereagh was infuriated by Robert's obduracy. He saw their protest as the only means to gain release. The others deferred to his leadership because he was persuasive and because they saw no prospect of securing their freedom by other means.

He tried everything he knew to persuade Robert to join their protest but when Robert remained unmoved by his pleas, he railed against him, accusing him of cowardice.

"You'll be quick enough to avail yourself of any gains we make. I can't see you volunteering to stay here because you disapproved of our methods. If we prevail, I've absolutely no doubt that you'll follow us out of the door as soon as possible."

His voice was all the more intimidating for being disembodied. The all-pervading darkness had reduced him to a shadow. Robert could only sense his angry face and his accusatory gestures. Unable to see them for himself, he imagined them to be worse than they were.

When Castlereagh persisted, he began to see him as another bullying warder and his resistance hardened. Everybody seemed to be in his thrall, willing to accede to his wishes whatever their misgivings whilst it seemed he was no longer allowed to decide anything for himself. Whatever he chose to do, it was forbidden or somebody took offence. The others were conciliatory, anxious to prevent a harmful breech in their unanimity, but Robert didn't doubt that when they experienced the humiliation of forced feeding, a process he regarded as akin to torture, they were bound to resent the presence of someone who continued to eat normally.

It wasn't certain at first that the authorities would attempt to force the prisoners to eat and Robert was horrified when their intentions became clear. He tried to persuade his comrades to desist, insisting that no good would come of their suffering, but Castlereagh made sure he had little opportunity to make known his views. So when none of those fed forcibly felt able to give up their hunger strike for fear of letting down the others, the dreadful process continued unabated, each prisoner suffering its indignities, with Robert forced to observe their experiences.

Twice daily, the dungeon door opened and a welcome stream of daylight cascaded down the steps to the floor of the keep. The prisoners aroused themselves from a twilight state that was neither sleep nor consciousness. Then a doctor in a white coat descended the stairs, followed by a warder clutching a chair and a group of warders carrying the wedge, tube and liquid food that the process required. Last, and most humiliatingly for Robert, a warder appeared with his meal tray. He placed it in front of him, before retreating up the stairs to watch the proceedings from the doorway, leaving Robert to decide when to eat. Robert couldn't bring himself to eat whilst the others were being forced fed. He waited until the forced feeding was over and then, when the warders were leaving, he would gulp down his food shamefacedly, hand his tray to the waiting warder and gratefully resume his place in the darkness, hoping that his actions would pass without comment from the others.

He could hardly bear to watch as one prisoner after another was seated in the chair. The doctor, helped by two of the warders, held the prisoner down before inserting the wedge with its hole into the prisoner's mouth, forcibly if necessary. Then, when the gagging prisoner's mouth was open, a tube was inserted through the hole and threaded down into his stomach. The writhing prisoner was then fed milk or other, liquid food of the doctor's choosing, until the doctor decided that he had enough, whereupon the tube was extracted, the wedge removed and the prisoner hauled from the chair.

The first time Robert saw this process he was horrified. Whilst some of his comrades dealt with it better than others - Castlereagh made a point of demonstrating his insouciance – they were all left prostrate on the floor, secure in the knowledge that in a few hours time, the humiliating and painful process would be repeated.

The second time Robert observed the procedure, he was unable to restrain himself. When the doctor was packing up his instruments, he confronted him angrily, barring his way to the top of the stairs.

"How can you do this? You're a doctor, not a prison warder. You're supposed to take care of people, not torture them or make them suffer."

The warders gathered round, preparing to restrain him but the doctor, hearing his accusations, showed no sign of consternation or regret. He was the short man with greying hair and glasses that slipped down his nose who inspected the prisoners on their arrival and release. He brought the same brusque manner and uncaring attitude to all his activities together with the absolute certainty that whatever he chose to do or prescribe was for the best.

He looked up at Robert, who towered over him, and said resolutely, "My job is to keep these people alive and well. If they try to starve themselves to death in order to make some point to the authorities, I'm here to prevent them from doing so. They're obliged to eat and drink. Those are the regulations. How they chose to do it is entirely up to them. There's no need to go on hunger strike, as your own behaviour demonstrates."

The final barb was particularly telling and when Robert stood aside to allow him to pass, it was all he could do to restrain himself from striking the complacent figure before him. He knew how painful and undignified the process was and yet he carried on doing it as if it were all in a day's work. The prisoners had chosen not to eat. He didn't agree with their decision but that was the choice they had made and they were prepared to live with the consequences. No one had the right to make them eat against their will or use such brutal means. That a doctor should take it upon himself to intervene only added to his sense of outrage.

"What do you want me to do?" the doctor called over his shoulder as he mounted the stairs. "Let them die? Are those the views of a Christian man?" he said, before the door closed and the dungeon was plunged into darkness again. Robert was grateful for its anonymity. He didn't want the others to see his confusion. He asked each of them in turn if they were all right and when Hicks answered with a hideous croak, hastened to his side, to see what he could do to help him.

Hicks was not well. His face when viewed in the half-light of the open door had evidenced a deathly pallor. The corpulent figure that Robert had first encountered in France had been reduced to an emaciated and pitiable shell. His voice, once so rich in tone was little more than a whisper. Even in the silence of the dungeon, Robert had to concentrate hard to catch his words.

"I'm not sure I can do this any more," he asserted. Of those subject to forcible feeding, he struggled the most. Even the thought of having a tube thrust down his throat was sufficient to panic him. "It's my voice," he croaked, "they'll damage my vocal chords if they carry on doing this. What'll I do for a living if I can't sing? I have nothing else."

Robert wisely kept his counsel. He believed they would all struggle to find gainful employment when they secured their freedom. Alice had already told him of local authorities whose advertising for teachers excluded conscientious objectors. He said, "If you want to stop, you must. Nothing's to be gained by damaging your health."

Castlereagh prevailed on Hicks to continue, even though he trembled at the sound of footsteps on the stairs and gazed in horror as his turn approached to take the chair. Castlereagh made no further efforts to persuade Robert to join in, confining himself to barbed asides at his selfishness, his determination to go his own way.

One night when the rats that shared their quarters were particularly active, Clapham, whose sardonic asides they had all come to value, said grimly, "They're here for the food. When we were in France, the rats were so well-fed they didn't bother us. Here, it's different; we're all starving. They're scuttling around in the false hope that they'll find something to eat."

"Well, they know where to look," Castlereagh said pointedly. There was a venom in his voice that Robert knew only to well. He was only surprised to hear it on the lips of someone from whom he had drawn so much strength in the past and to whom he had offered so much. It was a tribute to how far apart they had grown.

How long the strike would have persisted and what it might have achieved was never put to the test. Taylor, another of Robert's former comrades, another hunger striker, in a different prison, intent on securing his freedom, became gravely ill and the likelihood of his death panicked the authorities. Fearing that his demise might prove to be the first of many and aware of the increasing public revulsion at the methods used to keep the starving prisoners alive, they resolved to release all the objectors on hunger strike. Without warning, the door of the dungeons were thrown back; the cold, half-starved prisoners were returned to their cells without explanation and at the next meal time, the bread and porridge that was the fare of third division prisoners was delivered to their cells. They remained there until the next morning whereupon they were handed their civilian clothes and their belongings before being ushered to the prison gate and the freedom they had sought.

Castlereagh was triumphant, both at the prospect of freedom and in the way it had been gained. He was convinced that it would never have happened without his leadership. He conveniently overlooked the fact that another man, gravely weakened by three years of captivity, had paid for their early release with his life and that there been a public outcry. He was disappointed that he didn't have the opportunity to remind Robert how he had been, for Robert, not having been on hunger strike, was returned to his cell. When the gate opened for the release of his comrades, he turned again to his mailbags, doomed to serve his sentence in its entirety, along with other objectors who had complied with the regulations.

CHAPTER 37

John Harding, the chief warder, regarded any variation in the prison routine as a sign of failure. He liked to avoid surprises and to begin every day knowing what it held in store for him. He viewed the prisoners as an undifferentiated mass and rarely involved himself in individual cases, believing the prison population was best governed by unchanging rules that permitted the warders no discretion. Individual initiative had the potential for inconsistency or favouritism. Prisoners who broke the rules deserved the severest punishment. Those attempting subversion were guilty of sedition.

When, following widespread disorder, the governor was replaced by Major Blake, a military man and strict disciplinarian, the chief warder made it his job to remove any lingering suggestion that the objectors deserved special treatment. Someone who had declined to serve his country was no less a criminal than a thief. Following the release of the hunger strikers, he expected a new cohort of malcontents to reveal their presence and determined to destroy any resistance to his rule. His cropped head, earnest face and peevish eyes were inescapable. He encouraged staff with scores to settle to eradicate the tolerance that had made life bearable. He introduced a new rigidity, resulting in an emptiness and bleakness only too familiar to those who had suffered three years of confinement.

He could hardly fail to notice that a number of objectors kept themselves apart and viewed their behaviour with suspicion and resentment. They were not obvious troublemakers but neither were they cowed or intimidated by their treatment. He likened them to worms boring into timber, apparently immobile but capable of great destruction if allowed to go unchecked. Though they were no stronger, no less prone to ill-health or depression than the others, their faces were alert, their backs unbowed and they were outspoken in defence of their rights. He longed for them to challenge him, to pay in full the price of their dissent. Making an example of them would intimidate the others, nipping in the bud the rebellion he feared.

Knowing that the prison had become a powder keg, Robert attempted to keep his head down. He told himself that his sentence was drawing to a close but attempts to draw comfort from his circumstances failed to change his attitude. Castlereagh's release mocked the quiet resistance that had sustained him for so long. The notion that his opposition had served no useful purpose was too awful to contemplate. There was also the question of his daughter. He longed to feel her arms around his neck, to play games with her and read to her before she went to bed. Back in solitary confinement, excluded from any contact with other prisoners, his resentment at his circumstances increased with each day that passed, becoming a volatile and lethal mixture, at odds with the magnanimity that was his objective.

His animosity was undiminished by the end of solitary confinement. Contact with the surly warders served to stoke his anger further. Why had turning the other cheek resulted in him faring worse than others? He thought it typical of his wretched luck that he should fall foul of the chief warder in an incident that, though trivial to those who witnessed it, marked him out as a trouble-maker.

He was threading rope mats in the workshop, choking on the dust, twisting the stubborn fibres around the frames that hung down from the walls, communicating with others by means of nods and whispered phrases when, without warning, one of the uncertain structures collapsed.

"Who did that?" their supervisor shouted. "What fool broke the frame?"

Every accident was treated with suspicion. Bored prisoners were not above throwing a spanner into the works to break the monotony but the ageing structure had collapsed when Robert was reaching up to change a mat.

"Nobody did anything," he retorted quickly, sinking back into his place, amid a cloud of dust. "It collapsed of its own accord."

"Well, don't just sit there, pick up the mats and put the frame back up against the wall," the warder shouted, "and then get back to work."

Everyone had stopped working. The disruption was too good a chance for idleness to miss. Some of the prisoners began to talk amongst themselves, regarding the confusion an opportunity for a few asides before the mindless discipline that governed every aspect of their lives descended once again.

"It'll fall down again," Robert said impatiently, addressing no one in particular. "The hinge's broken - shorn right through. It'll have to be replaced."

The warder was in no mood for explanations. His concern was to get everyone back to work again, to reimpose the silence that was the litmus test of his supervision.

He urged Robert to stand up and right the frame.

The other prisoners made little effort to hide their delight at the warder's discomfort. Someone needed to be on report for this, of that he was certain. He turned vengefully to Robert. Nearest to the frame at the time of its collapse, he was the obvious culprit. He was also insisting that it wasn't his fault.

The chief warder appeared in their midst, drawn by the commotion. He was not in the best of moods. He had been roundly criticised by the Governor at their daily meeting. The objectors were causing unrest in the prison again and they were divided over what to do about it. Both feared another hunger strike and were anxious to avoid it. They also wanted to prevent any further crumbling of the prison's discipline, no small task when so many prisoners hungered for release. The governor was minded to to apply the rules without discrimination. The chief warder wanted to pick off the dissidents, find reasons to isolate them and confine them to punishment cells where they could do no harm.

"What's going on here?" he demanded, standing in the doorway, feet astride, a squat, ominous figure amidst the clouds of dust. His presence was enough to silence everyone. He peered at each of the prisoners in turn before his peevish eyes came to rest on Robert standing by the frame.

"Why's he standing there like that?"

Responding to his scrutiny, Robert lowered the frame back on to the ground and looked at the warder expectantly.

The warder wasn't a complicated man. He believed in cause and effect. It wasn't an accident or the result of wear and tear that a frame had fallen off the wall. Someone had displaced it and as Robert was the nearest at the time, it was almost certainly his doing.

He looked the chief warder in the eye, pointed at Robert with a sweep of his arm and said, "He pulled the frame down."

There was a murmur of dissent from the other prisoners. Few were surprised that the rickety structure had given way. None of the frames could be relied upon to stay upright. They didn't care why the frame had collapsed. It was sufficient someone had been accused unfairly.

The signs of insubordination were too much for the chief warder. He fixed Robert with a malevolent stare and said, "Is that true? You pulled the frame down?"

"Of course not, it fell down of its own accord."

He offered to hand over the bolt that he picked up but the chief warder was not interested in establishing the truth. He was more concerned with the note of defiance in Robert's voice. This was not a man who had been humbled by prison; nor was prepared to accord him the deference he expected. It was right that he should be punished, whatever part he had played in the collapse of the frame.

He said, "Put him on report. It'll teach him to be more careful with the prison's property. The rest of you, get back to work. I want to hear nothing further from you."

The Robert of old, resigned to his circumstances, would have picked up his needle and resumed his work. But after Castlereagh's departure, he was not prepared to allow the injustice of his punishment to pass uncontested.

When the chief warder turned to leave, Robert said loudly, "This isn't right. I've explained to you what happened. I had nothing to do with it."

He turned to the warder, who was on the point of returning to his stool to resume his vigil. "Tell him what happened. You know it was an accident. Why don't you speak the truth?"

The warder gazed at Robert, unsure what to do. Robert was on his corridor. He gazed through the peephole of his cell every night as he padded along the corridor in his slippers. He was usually reluctant to defend himself. Now the look of defiance in his eyes made him hesitate to challenge him outright.

The chief warder turned to Robert with all the assurance of someone who knows that the system is weighted in his favour. "You'll have your say when I put you on report. We'll see what the governor thinks about the matter. For now," he said, turning on his heel, "all of you get on with your work. If you want cocoa tonight, you've got a lot of sacks to sew."

The admiring glances of his fellow-prisoners made Robert a marked man. He managed to avoid any further brushes with the chief warder but other warders, taking their cue from their superior, bore down on him. He tried to remain unperturbed, to betray no evidence of weakness but his bitterness mounted. For three years, he had relied upon turning the other cheek; it was the riposte to provocation learnt at his mother's knee. Now as his anger mounted, he was compelled to acknowledge a new side to his character, a shadow long ignored, disquieting in its strength.

He clashed twice with other prisoners. Both were minor incidents, born of constant supervision, frequent amongst men who were bored and harassed. It was not unusual to harbour deep resentment; the cells were full of hurt and brooding men. What was remarkable was the depth and suddenness of his anger. It flared up without warning and was uncontrollable. He wanted to strike his tormentors, to hurl them to the ground and though the conditions of imprisonment: the lack of exercise, the meagre rations, had greatly weakened him, he believed he was a match for anybody present. He delighted in the surprise and fear his anger prompted. It was intoxicating to feel that he was capable of dominating others, that after years of acquiescence, he might be one of that handful of prisoners whom others feared and respected. Noticing the change, the warders competed to provoke him. They wanted him to abandon all restraint and their actions reinforced his rancour, forcing to the surface what was worst in him.

Mindful of the dangers, Robert attempted to recover his composure but, the more he struggled to contain himself, the more embittered he became. He prayed fervently, hoping to revive that inner strength that had withstood the threat of execution and had supported him in prison. He turned his anger on himself, believing he was guilty of persistent arrogance, of abandoning the principles that had sustained him for so long. He sought in vain the optimism of his early months in prison, the belief that there was a controlling hand, a source of comfort in distress, a signpost to what was right or wrong. But, whenever he felt confident of controlling the demons that possessed him, an unexpected setback, a sharp rebuff would fuel his wrath. He began to fear that further rioting would see him at its head.

New riots weren't long in coming. They were spontaneous outbreaks of frustration prompted by the new restrictions. The response of the authorities was different from before. The chief warder had prevailed in his contest with the governor. There was no blanket confrontation, no overt show of power. The chief warder picked off the individuals he had identified as troublemakers and isolated them. There was scant time to organise effective opposition when potential leaders were denied the opportunity to foster discontent.

Robert listened every night to the litany of protest: the shouts, the choruses, the clatter of pots and pans, the breaking glass and played his part with gusto. He broke his stool into pieces against the cell wall and shattered the glass in the spy hole in his door but even as he expressed his frustration, he felt a sense of hopelessness. His actions brought release no nearer and added nothing to the quality of his meagre life.

The exercise yard was the scene of the final confrontation. Exercise had been the subject of dispute ever since the governor had resolved to limit it to a single hour. There had also been efforts to restore the silence that had prevailed previously. The prisoners were determined to talk freely and to retain the extra hour conceded to them months before. Threats and warnings had issued from both sides but there were hopes of compromise until the chief warder chose to intervene.

His timing could hardly have been worse. He chose a luminous morning, when the sun darted between billowing, white clouds, throwing shadows on the yard. A stiff breeze ruffled the hair of the prisoners as they walked in circles round the yard, freeing their lungs of the stale air of the cells. Birds swooped and fell above the keep. Smoke from nearby chimneys stained the mottled sky. It was a morning when, for prisoners freed of the dank, oppressive cells that were their habitat, the air was to be relished like wine. Free to stretch their limbs, the sun warm on their backs; able to hold conversations with each other, the endless wait for freedom suddenly seemed bearable. Then, as they delighted in their circumstances, unmindful of the tedious work awaiting them, the whistles blew and the warders began to shepherd them into lines, shouting and pushing, determined to lead them back to their cells whilst they had the advantage of surprise. Had the chief warder not chosen at that moment to reveal his presence, they might have prevailed, but suddenly his squat, unwelcome figure was amongst them, directing operations.

Someone close to Robert, sighting him, shouted loudly, "It's Harding, the bastard's come to get us in."

"Stay where you are, don't move" cried another louder, more subversive voice, anxious to arrest the slow drift to the cells.

Suspicious faces followed the chief warder as he strode across the yard. His bustling, self-importance made him seem larger than usual. He reminded Robert of the bullfrogs with their ability to inflate their bodies in the face of danger that had so fascinated him as a child. Now, as the chief warder neared their group, other voices took to warning of his presence, until it became a slogan, a war-cry, signifying their resistance to their loss of freedom. The prisoners broke ranks, halted, impervious to the warders' anger, determined to remain in the yard for the two hours they regarded as their due.

The chief warder was furious. His eyes burned with a fierce resentment; anger coloured his distorted features; He glanced around, hoping to find a means of decapitating the protest but the faces that gazed back at him were impassive, unafraid to meet his eye, happy to make known their willingness to defy his orders. He looked at everyone in turn, hoping for a face he found familiar, an object worthy of his ire. He had assured the governor that the protests were diminishing and that a few arrests would restore their authority over every aspect of the prison's governance. He failed to recognise that his intervention had been badly timed or that the prisoners wanted to prolong the uplift of the spirits occasioned by the heady morning. He believed he was a victim of a scheme to humiliate him and such a scheme must have a leader, an opponent whom he might identify and punish.

"Who shouted?" he demanded of those nearest to him, his voice rising dangerously. "Come on, own up, who was it?"

His demand met with a wall of silence. There had been many voices raised at the prospect of confinement. Who was to distinguish between them or identify which voice was the well-spring of defiance? The warders hated angry confrontations. They preferred to wield their power in the privacy of the cells where the prisoners were outnumbered and hidden from the watchful eyes of their companions. The prisoners neither knew nor cared who had spoken up. They knew only that safety was to be found in numbers and the maintenance of a resentful silence when accusations were abroad.

Disconcerted by their animosity, the chief warder stood rooted to the spot, arms folded across his chest, not trusting himself to speak or move, aware of the dangers involved in confronting a large group of prisoners but knowing that he was too vulnerable to ridicule, to depart the stage defeated.

He addressed the warders nearest to him. "You saw nothing? Nothing at all?"

The heads around him shook unhelpfully, anxious to deflect his wrath, unwilling to do anything to cause unwanted prominence.

He pushed his way through the ranks of prisoners. Some fell back to make way for him. Others held their ground. There would be a victim;

he would find somebody, all were sure of it. They only hoped it wouldn't be them.

He turned to the warders again. It needed only one of them to nominate a victim; the governor, the process of trial and retribution, would do the rest.

He fixed his gaze on one of them, a shifty, weasel-faced man who had served him well. Giving him a knowing look, he demanded, "Who was it? Did you see him? Who started this defiance? Point him out to me."

The warder had no idea who had spoken up. He attempted a non-committal answer, pointing at the group of prisoners immediately before him, their faces indistinguishable to someone who rarely spoke to them.

Suddenly, the nearest prisoners had become the guilty group. The chief warder thought to punish all of them but decided against it on the grounds that the governor wouldn't welcome a further sign of mass rebellion. It would be better to nominate an individual, to have him suffer the reprisals all of them deserved.

He pushed his way towards them, beckoning the warder to follow him. He stepped forward with obvious reluctance and the other warders formed a circle pushing outwards to clear a path for him. They halted abruptly in front of the cluster of prisoners that included Robert.

"Was it one of them?"

The chief warder raised his arm as if about to cast a spell. The prisoners watched him warily, moving closer together in an effort to achieve the anonymity they sought. Robert's height, his closely cropped red hair, conspired to make him prominent. He was reminded of his school days, the mischief of that time. Whenever there was trouble, he would be the one who had been spotted, leading to reproaches from his mother, his father's stern rebukes.

Now he composed his face, affecting an innocence he didn't feel, for he had called out excitedly, no less than others caught up in the fervour, urging his fellow prisoners to resist any attempt to lead them to their cells.

The warder hesitated, torn between making a name for himself and admitting the truth. He wished he hadn't responded to the chief warder's pleas, hadn't attempted to court his favour by feigning knowledge of an incident shrouded in confusion. He scanned the sea of faces in the hope of inspiration but the prisoners' faces revealed nothing. No one dared to look him in the eye or even risk a glance in his direction, whilst the outcome hung in the balance.

"Point him out, will you?"

The warder shook his head, his voice, barely a whisper and said, "I'm not sure."

The chief warder walked between the prisoners, subjecting them to his fiercest scrutiny in the hope that somebody would admit by a look of guilt or stern defiance that he had played a part. But no was about to admit his actions. Their expressions of studied innocence were set in stone.

He stopped in front of Robert and a look of recognition passed across his face. He recalled an incident, a report that he had prompted. The details escaped him but Robert was an acknowledged troublemaker, he was sure of it; he was certain to have been involved.

"Was it him?" he said, turning to the warder, pointing a stubby finger at Robert, hoping that his look of certainty would solicit a positive response.

The warder was reluctant to commit himself. He was not a malicious or ambitious man. Some residual belief in fairness that had survived the prison system held him back at first, but the chief warder's scrutiny demanded a response.

"We'll stay here all day, if necessary, until we identify the culprit."

Robert looked him squarely in the eye, determined to do nothing to compromise his innocence.

The chief warder had him firmly in his sights. He turned to the warder, repeated his terse question, this time with greater vehemence and urged him to speak out.

Robert recognised what was coming next. It mattered little that the confrontation would not have taken place had the chief warder not appeared amongst them. It didn't appear to concern him that the protest had no leader or originator. He had chosen to see it as something more than a spontaneous protest at the loss of an important privilege. A cleverer man would have allowed the prisoners to return to their cells. They would have been unable to collaborate or to organise their opposition to the changes now in progress there. But he was bent on finding a culprit and was not about to be diverted from his task.

Responding to the weight of expectations placed upon him, the warder blurted out, "It was him. He was one of them," and, extending his arm, nominated Robert as the instigator of all that had happened in the yard.

Robert regarded him with dismay. But when the chief warder planted himself in front of him, arms waving, feet astride, his face close to Robert's and demanded to know if he had urged the prisoners to defy their instructions, he couldn't bring himself to lie outright. It was true. He had protested vehemently at the unfairness of it all. He indicated that his voice had been one of many attempting to preserve a privilege that was rightly theirs but the warder had no interest in the details. He had the victim that he had sought.

When he gave the signal, hands reached out for Robert, tore him from the crowd. He waited vainly for other prisoners to admit that they had called out also and were no less guilty of subversion but they made no move to help him They edged away, keen to avoid any guilt by association, as he was frogmarched to his cell. It suited them that someone should be blamed for the rebellion. Had Castlereagh and his friends been present, the outcome might have been different. They had achieved a degree of solidarity. Those remaining lacked their determination to prevail. Capable of nothing more than an angry muttering, they watched as Robert was led away. As for the real culprit, if any single cry could be held responsible for the confrontation, he kept determinedly silent, one of the many prisoners whose hold on health and sanity was so precarious that he dare not risk exposure. In failing to support Robert, or share his culpability, he had elected to survive the harsh conditions of the prison as best he could.

CHAPTER 38

Robert paced his cell, thinking of the high ideals that had driven him to oppose conscription. How was it he, an exemplary prisoner, languished in his cell when others, more strident in their opposition, had regained their freedom?

He thought of his daughter, almost three years old, whom he had never seen, growing up without her father, and the pain of her absence, the possibility that he might never see her, weighed upon his mind.

He paced his cell distractedly, three paces one end to the other, and, with each step his anger mounted: disgust at his naivety, distaste for those who persecuted him, frustration at his helplessness. He began to toss the contents of his cell aside with the speculative air of a petulant child. With every step he took, he grew more animated. Blood rushed to his face; he started to perspire; his laboured breathing filled the tiny cell; he began to feel alive again. He took the unfinished mailbags and tore at them, determined that his fingers would never sew another stitch. He picked up one of the pots from the shelf and began to strike at the unyielding stones. He imagined that they trembled and that a greater effort to dislodge them would bring them crashing down. He reached for the stool, the books, other implements, employing each of them until the deliberate rhythm of his early blows gave way to a new and frenzied pounding and harsh cries of exultation issued from his lips.

A voice called out, "What's happening in there?"

When a malevolent eye appeared at the spy hole, he poked at it with the leg of the stool.

"Open up," another voice said excitedly.

Further shouts, urgent now, boots racing down the corridor, keys rattling, goaded him to greater efforts. The door was loosening on its hinges. The walls were buckling beneath his blows. The whole edifice was under threat. He alone had the power to bring the building down and win their freedom.

The cell door flew back. Two warders entered and attempted to control him. The first, a slight, nervous man hung back, hoping that his presence might suffice to curb Robert's frenzied efforts. His companion, larger and more confident, plunged forward recklessly. Robert was too quick for him. He thrust the man aside. Others crowded forward. Robert glimpsed the man whose false accusations had led to his arrest. He swung the stool aloft. It hovered in the air, the warders clawing at his arm, before falling on the unprotected head of his accuser.

Then the others were upon him, anxious to protect their fallen comrade. Robert hurled them aside, intent on striking further blows. His demonic energy enabled him to dominate the tiny space. They forced him to the ground by weight of numbers. He fought back fiercely: punching, kicking, biting until exhausted. When they had overpowered him, they straitjacketed him, twisting his arms painfully behind his back. He lay prostrate and helpless on the ground. Contorted, sweating faces loomed above him. Boots struck him in the ribs. Someone spat into his face. His violent struggle had run its course; he was at the mercy of his captors.

They bundled him along the landing. His legs buckled beneath him as he attempted the stairs. He lurched from side to side, his sight obscured by the blood that trickled down his face but as he staggered forward, his anger spent, his concern lay not with his condition but with the battered victim. His last glimpse had been of a prostrate figure, limbs twisted awkwardly, surrounded by his anxious comrades, a pool of blood forming by his head. His body had evidenced no signs of life.

"I've killed him," Robert thought.

His blows, born of frustration and anger, had ended someone's life. His actions had swept aside three years of restraint. His pity for his victim was matched by the scale of his defeat. By failing to master his anger, he had betrayed the very cause he claimed to represent.

When he hesitated on the landing; a violent blow sent him spiralling down the stairs. He came to rest on the next level, bruised and bewildered but retaining sufficient presence of mind to maintain his balance as further blows rained down on him. Every warder wanted to register their outrage at what he had happened to their comrade. The door of the punishment cell was ajar. He was thrown forward and a leg, entangling his, brought him crashing to the ground. When the door closed, he attempted to free himself from the jacket. He rolled on the floor, twisting and turning, but the fabric held fast. Exhausted, he dragged himself upright, seeking a comfortable position in the corner of the room and attempted to take stock of his position.

The cell was tall and narrow. In the ceiling was a skylight peppered with spy holes. The walls were upholstered with cushions and the floor, which housed a large drain, was strewn with matting. The room was devoid of furniture and the blank door sealed tightly. The only sound was his laboured breathing. It seemed to issue from a stranger, present but invisible. His arms remained pinned. From his bruised thigh and cracked ribs came a dull, persistent ache. Slumped in the corner of the cell in a twilight world of remorse and self-pity, he was conscious of a raging thirst, stabbing pangs of hunger and a deep desire for news of the havoc he had wrought.

He was dozing fitfully when the door of his cell swung ajar and a warder shouted, "On your feet."

He reached for Robert's shoulder and, grasping it tightly, attempted to pull him upright. Too heavy for him, Robert fell back on to the floor. Other warders crowded round him as he struggled to stand, alert for signs of violence until, convinced he was emasculated, they ushered the prison doctor into his cell. It was their first encounter since the hunger strike. Robert recalled his ill-concealed distaste for the objectors, his unremitting efforts to make them eat.

"Bennett isn't it?" the doctor said, as if there was room for doubt. He rolled the name across his tongue. He peered at Robert with no great show of interest before backing towards the door and saying, "Let him out of the jacket, will you? I want a better look at him?"

A warder began to fumble with the buckles of the straitjacket, his eyes trained on Robert's face. They believe I'm dangerous, Robert thought, and the idea accorded him some satisfaction. Then he recalled his victim, bleeding on the floor of his cell, and a look of anguish appeared on his face. Freed from the jacket, he raised his arms. They were stiff and painful. A sharp pain in his back forced him to stoop.

The doctor regarded Robert suspiciously as he slowly straightened, ignoring his attempts to restore his circulation. He peered at the cut above his eye, the dried blood on his cheek and said, "What else's wrong with you?"

Whilst Robert catalogued his aches and pains, the doctor prodded him perfunctorily and said, "You look all right to me. You haven't broken anything."

"More's the pity," said the warder who had freed him. "What now? Shall we leave him like this?"

"No, put the jacket back on. Keep him trussed up. You can't tell with these people. They're capable of anything."

"Why are you doing this?"

The doctor turned on Robert angrily.

"You're a violent criminal. You'll stay tied up till I decide otherwise and that," he added with some satisfaction, "may be for some considerable time." He turned on his heel, almost forgetting the faded, brown medical bag that stood by the door.

When the warders advanced on him with the jacket, Robert made no effort to resist. They bound his arms again, more tightly than before, as if the doctor's brief inspection had given them licence to add to his discomfort, and delivered further, well-aimed blows.

As they went to close the door, he called out after them, "What's happened to the warder? Is he all right?"

The warder by the door looked at him contemptuously.

"What do you think? Of course, he isn't all right." He started towards Robert, intent on striking him, thought better of it and said, "We'll hang you for this, pacifist. You can depend on it."

"Is he dead?"

Robert blurted out the question but by the time the warder answered him, the sealed door had closed, masking his reply.

"Is he?" Robert shouted, struggling to his feet, his shrill cry failing to penetrate the padded walls.

He leaned against the wall. How could he have been so foolish? Why had he acted with such scant regard for the consequences? He would be tried, found guilty and hanged like any murderer.

He imagined the condemned cell with its false wall and trapdoor. He anticipated the silent escort with their solemn faces; the fussing padre with crucifix and bible; the public silent at the gate, the tolling bell and was gripped with fear. He had betrayed the cause he believed in, had let his family down, by ending another sacred life, not in circumstances that made it unavoidable, but because he had lost control. No judge would find cause for mercy in his circumstances and even if he did, according to the conscience by which he had set such store, he was still a murderer.

He lay on the floor throughout the night, shifting from side to side in an effort to get comfortable. Eventually, he sat against the wall, head lolling on his chest, hoping for oblivion but the pain of his bruises prevented it. He feigned sleep so that the faces at the spy holes were convinced that he was resting but his mind whirled unceasingly and the torture of his thoughts was unremitting. The next day they brought him a pound of bread and a jug of water. A prisoner fed him as he crouched there like there a fledgling, gulping down his food, drawing on the water greedily. Light streamed through the open door but when the cell door closed there was no way of knowing whether it was night or day. The prisoner feeding him declined to look him in the eye. He was older than the others, one of the few permitted to undertake menial tasks, unsupervised. Robert wondered how long he had been in prison and what crime he had committed.

When Robert asked repeatedly, "Is he dead? Have I killed him?" he said he knew nothing of his victim's fate.

He said he didn't concern himself with prison business so no one bothered him or held him to account. It was how he had endured his sentence, why he was confident that he would make it to the end. When Robert pressed him, he said in the unused voice of the habitually silent, "They took him away on a stretcher. Who knows what happened after that?"

He visited Robert regularly. The ritual was always the same. A warder unlocked the door, glanced at Robert with unconcealed distaste and stood aside, arms folded, whilst the prisoner entered with his food and water. Sometimes, the warder remained there, following the proceedings with perfunctory interest, but was usually content to leave them to their own devices whilst he visited other cells along the corridor. The prisoner was an elderly man, slightly built, his wrinkled face bleached by a lack of air and sunshine, a purple birthmark on his cheek, dark gaps between his teeth. His features were drained of all expression, a blank and aged canvas. He usually let Robert speak, as if to himself, offering no response. Only his eyes, watchful and alert, revealed that he was more than just a cipher reduced to silent acquiescence by the regulations. They regarded Robert with perfect clarity, missing nothing, suggesting he had come to terms with his condition. Robert felt he ought to imitate his quiet dignity, whilst knowing it was too late for that.

One visit, after he had eaten and drank from the jug of water, the prisoner had emptied his bucket, swept the bare cell and adjusted his jacket, Robert asked him how long he had been in prison.

The old man said, "I don't think about how long I've been here or how long I've got to go - it serves no useful purpose. I live from day to day. What else is there to do in here?"

When the doctor reappeared, Robert asked to be released from his straitjacket and he raised no objection, satisfied that there had been no repetition of his earlier behaviour. The warders too were no longer intent on doing him harm at every opportunity. They didn't repeat their dire threats or speak of the reprisals that would result from his assault. He didn't know what to make of their attitude. It might mean that his victim had survived intact and that the crisis was past or it might be an indication that they were happy to allow the courts to do their work, safe in the knowledge that Robert would suffer greatly for his crime.

"Tell me what I've done," Robert asked each time he received a visitor. "Put an end to my uncertainty," but it did no good. The warders had conspired against him. No one offered news as to his victim's fate and a vestige of pride, a desire to remain unbowed, prevented him from pleading for the information they were reluctant to divulge.

"You'll have to wait," the old man said, amidst one of their exchanges, "they're doing it deliberately. It's a form of torture. They do it all the time. You'll find out what happened when you return you to your cell. Meanwhile, enjoy your ignorance whilst you have the chance. There's probably worse to come."

CHAPTER 39

Malcolm wrote to Alice many times after returning to the front but though she read his letters she never replied to them. He said his return to the line had been short-lived. His nerve had failed him again and the army, showing a degree of generosity accorded only to officers, moved him out of harm's way. She was delighted that he was safe but doubted he was grateful, wedded as he was to his conception of what it meant to be an officer.

He wrote little of his activities in the line, confining his comments to his role on the divisional staff. Though he discharged his new responsibilities with vigour, his accomplishments appeared to accord him scant satisfaction. Eventually, he was transferred to Fourth Army staff where he played a part in planning the offensive that was to prove so decisive in August 1918, earning promotion to the rank of major.

His letters were matter-of-fact and whilst he asked after Alice's activities, he never referred to the circumstances of his departure, the relationship that had consumed them or the marriage that had been its undoing. Nor did he ask after her family, though the fates of Robert and Michael were uppermost in her mind. Several months after the end of the war, she was surprised to receive a letter from him that spoke of his enduring affection for her, informed her of his impending divorce and asked if they might meet. Coming soon after the conversation with Sister Brown about Tom's feelings for her, the request threw Alice into confusion. She had tried to forget about Malcolm, had been unmoved by his letters and had made every effort to put their relationship behind her. She felt that any meeting would only add to her difficulties at a time when she sought clarity but when he pressed her, she agreed to hear what he had to say. Only when she had dealt with her dormant feelings for him would she be free to address her affections for Tom, a matter that she regarded as urgent in the light of the sister's comments.

They agreed to go for a walk in Richmond Park. Malcolm collected her in his new car, knocking on the front door of the house but declining to enter or to meet her parents. He looked more congenial out of uniform. His face was thinner, more contoured and his moustache was gone, making him seem younger. He still spoke in clipped military phrases and held himself upright as if expecting an inspection but the eyes that raked her face had abandoned their old tension in favour of a lively interest. When he led her to the car and held the door ajar, he took her arm, as if fearing that she might take fright or change her mind and, as they drove to the park with the roof folded back, he kept stealing glances at her. Alice felt she was with a stranger, someone whose presence was novel and unexpected, and became wary as the park drew nearer.

They entered the park on a crisp spring day. The sun shone intermittently, a stiff breeze blew in their faces and the ground bore traces of frost. Alice marvelled at how quickly the park had returned to normal. The drilling soldiers were gone; the route marches with their bands and officers on horseback were over; the wild cavalry charges had ceased; the trees were free of would-be snipers and the tent city had been struck so that the deer roamed freely, undisturbed by the voices of recruits at their field craft. Only the hospital that had been the home of the South African wounded remained. Now civilian traffic made its way slowly along the perimeter road whilst visitors walking their dogs, courting couples, and families with tribes of children occupied the paths.

They parked the car at Pen Ponds and set off up the hill to the plantation. The wind threatened Alice's hat, though she had secured it with a scarf, and the sun's rays warmed her cheek. Malcolm strode out purposefully and it was all that Alice could do to keep up with him.

"It's five years, since I was last here," she said, as she quickened her step. "What changes there have been in that time."

"I'm glad to see the park's recovered from the Army's outrageous behaviour. There's no sign of its presence."

"Did you come here?" she said, moved by the thought that he might have trained on her doorstep, that somewhere in the park's maelstrom, he had been learning his craft.

"I came here before they sent me to Surrey. It rained every day. My tent leaked. When I complained, they said, wait until you're in a trench."

"I love this time of year. The park looks as if it's been holding its breath all winter. I only hope the country will prove as resilient now the war's over."

"The country's doing alright. 'A land fit for heroes', it isn't, but most of the soldiers are home, the economy's booming and there's every prospect of an enduring peace."

"Robert's still in prison." Alice said, giving vent to the frustration she felt on his behalf.

His situation was a blight on her existence. He had been forgotten. Even his supporters had given up hope. "The logic appears to be that the objectors can't be released until the last soldier's demobilised. That's so vindictive, isn't it?"

Malcolm acknowledged her words but said nothing further, unwilling to be drawn on the subject. Whilst he had every sympathy for Robert's predicament, he knew he would never prove capable of matching Alice's passion.

"How long have you been home?" Alice asked, stopping to watch a squirrel bound up a tree at the first sign of their presence. It paused halfway up, watching her through its paws, before continuing its climb.

She was surprised when he said several months. His letter had given the impression that he was newly back. Clearly, he had given the matter some thought before writing to her again. She didn't know what to make of that.

She said, with that directness he both admired and feared, "Why did you ask to see me again? It's almost two years since you returned to the front?"

"Not quite, but far too long."

"You're a major now?"

"I'm no longer in the army, so I'm not anything."

"Many men still to use their rank."

"Plain mister for me. I've had enough of all that. I want to put the whole wretched experience behind me."

"You did well in the end."

"I went back into the line but it didn't work. I was willing to risk my life. I thought death might be the best outcome at times. But I was reckless with men's lives. People noticed that I'd stopped caring. The noise was my undoing. Barrages day and night until I couldn't stand it any more. They found me sitting in a dugout with my head in my hands, incapable of speech or movement, whilst the guns blazed all about us. That was when they decided to pull me back. My collapse probably saved my life; the casualties were heavy after that. I doubt I'd have been spared."

"It was no more than you deserved. You'd done more than enough by then."

"I tried to distinguish myself in other ways, but I never forgave myself for how I behaved towards you. That'll be on my conscience for the rest of my days."

Alice looked him full in the face and said, "Well, it shouldn't be. If you've come to ask my forgiveness, there was no need to. What happened that day was beyond our control. It seems a long time ago. I forgave you after you left. You didn't do it deliberately and as you can see, I'm none the worse for it."

He returned her scrutiny, searching her face for evidence of her forgiveness. He had never seen her looking more attractive. Her face had a serenity, a quiet self-confidence it had lacked before. Her eyes sought his when she spoke, remarkable in their frankness and her figure, fuller than it had been, had lost its sparseness so that she appeared to glide when she walked, with none of the abrupt, hurried movements of the past.

"I wish you'd written to me to that effect. I interpreted your silence as a sign of contempt, an unwillingness to forgive what I'd done."

"Is that why you went back?" Alice asked, appalled that her silence might have placed him in harm's way. She had wanted time to put the whole sorry episode behind her, to learn to live with her dashed hopes.

"I thought it was where I belonged but I wasn't up to it."

"Even after what had happened here?"

"I thought it might be different in the line."

Alice looked at him doubtfully. It had seemed obvious to her that his war was over but she knew that wanting her forgiveness was not the whole story and that there was more to come.

She started up the hill. She wanted to stand on the ridge by Pembroke Lodge, to take in the view over the county with its clusters of trees, its winding river, its ribbon roads and diminutive figures but Malcolm remained where he was, unwilling to move.

He said, "I still love you and want to return to you. I'm confident that we can put the past behind us and move forward together. That's been my hope for the last two years; it's why I continued to write to you, even though you never replied."

"I said I wouldn't write."

It wasn't her finest hour, Alice could see that now, but after all that had happened, it was surely understandable that she would try to forget?

She said, "Those were my last words to you before you departed, though in the end I didn't stick to them."

"What happened?"

"I went to the leave train."

"I didn't see you there."

He recalled the impatient locomotive, expelling steam noisily; the struggle to find a place at the window; the crowd of women on the platform, the tearful faces and fluttering handkerchiefs as the train departed. He had searched in vain for Alice but there had been no sign of her.

"I didn't make any effort to find you."

"Then why did you go?"

"I wanted to be there; I thought it was the right thing to do. As for not writing, well, it seemed for the best after everything that had happened and after a while, it didn't seem appropriate to revive a correspondence I had allowed to die..."

"You said you wouldn't write so I have no cause for complaint but I continued to love you, without reward, and still love you, even after all this time."

He recalled how he had waited expectantly for the post, as though each letter written to her, offered the chance of a breakthrough. They hadn't been love letters. His credentials were too weak and he was too proud to risk making a fool of himself. After repeated disappointments he had reconciled himself to her silence, telling himself that he would stay in touch with her whatever happened, in the hope that one day they might meet and that she would be sufficiently moved by his presence to return to him. Now as he looked at her closely, he saw that she had changed. She was not the hesitant young woman of the past. She seemed more content, more certain of herself than she had been before and he saw in her demeanour fresh grounds for hope. His determination to seize the moment was such that it never occurred to him that her thoughts might be elsewhere and that, during his long absence, she had found someone else.

"Is that what you wanted to tell me? That you still love me?" Alice asked, as they walked past the plantation with its densely packed trees, its magnolia showing the first signs of bloom, the rhododendrons green but dormant, the dribbling stream. When Pembroke Lodge came into sight. Alice looked on it with affection and awe. She had always wanted to live there. To her it seemed to occupy the perfect location, with its views over the county and its carefully tended gardens, their ordered flower beds so at odds with the parkland that surrounded them.

Malcolm said, "I loved you then and love you still. You mustn't allow my behaviour to make you think otherwise."

Alice said, "I've always believed actions spoke louder than words." When he started to protest, she urged him to hear her out.

"I'm not talking about what happened on the night of the bombing. Your behaviour that night was a huge shock but I understand why it happened and time has lessened its impact. I'm talking about the fact that you were married to someone else when we were together and only revealed it to me when you felt you had to. The significance of that deceit has not diminished. I thought it might, but it hasn't. What might have been excusable at the height of the war, when we didn't know whether we would meet again, seems monstrous now. Our relationship, for all its excitement, was little more than a lie."

He wanted to say that she was making too much of it and that the war had given rise to all kinds of precipitate and unlikely liaisons. He remembered soldiers going into battle with the words of unfaithful wives ringing in their ears; men who had children they were never likely to see; fathers whose offspring were ill or who had died in their absence. Many had carried with them the memory of some truncated love affair and hoped that they would survive to renew the affection that they had found.

He said "I'll be divorced in a few months' time. Then, I'll be free to love whom I please."

"I hope you're not doing it on my account?"

For reasons that were only clear later, she seemed unable to enthuse about the prospect of him becoming free. She was not sure she believed him and felt he was taking her for granted, expecting her to rush into his arms as soon as his declaration was made.

She said, "If you're still married, this meeting's premature. You would have done better to wait until your marriage had come to a close."

"Don't you believe me?" he asked, his face colouring in the light of her scepticism. He began to protest, "You can see the papers if you want to. We're quite far on with the process."

"I don't doubt it," Alice said dismissively, "but that isn't really the issue."

"Once it was the only issue between us..."

"A lot has happened since then."

"You don't care for me anymore, do you? You've found somebody else?"

"What did you expect? I haven't seen you for two years and then you turn up, full of earnest intentions and elaborate plans for our future."

But there was no holding him back. Even as she tried to take stock, his words assailed her. He said, "I didn't mean to take you by surprise. That was never my intention. I intended to be cautious, to understand your circumstances, but I couldn't restrain myself, after waiting so long."

Alice said, "My life hasn't stood still whilst you've been gone."

She didn't doubt his sincerity. It wasn't that. Nor did she have any wish to embarrass or hurt him but when he kept pressing her, urging on her decisions she wasn't ready to take, she thought it best she spoke the truth.

She turned to face him, her eyes seeking his and said, "I don't feel I love you any more. I may have done once - I'm no longer sure - the war was a heady time but a lot has happened since then."

"My feelings towards you haven't changed."

She said, "I'm delighted you've survived and pleased to see you looking so well. I hope we can be friends but I've no intention of becoming your wife. It's too late for that. You must see that, surely?"

"No, you're right," he said, changing direction abruptly, "it's simply too soon. I shouldn't have confronted you. He took Alice's arm, gazed at her earnestly. "Yes, it's better we wait a while, before jumping to conclusions. Let's see more of each other before we decide anything. Time will tell if we can pick up where we left off." He could not help concluding in defiance of his own caution, "Though I have no doubt that we'll love each other again."

Alice felt she had little choice but to be blunt when he continued to press her, forcing her to make choices.

She said, "No, I'm quite clear about how I feel about you and how I want to proceed. Meeting again, except as friends, would cause us needless distress."

"You've met somebody else, haven't you? That's it? I should have known."

He grew agitated at the thought of her in the arms of somebody else. It was what he had feared when she hadn't answered his letters, why he had rushed back to her when his divorce was under way, even though his wife was doing everything she could to delay it, urging him to spend the time with the children she had denied to him previously.

He said, "There's somebody else and you can't bring yourself to tell me about him. Well, don't spare my feelings. Don't hold back on my account. Tell me the truth."

Alice remained silent, hating to be confronted, loath to declare her intentions when her future with Tom was anything but clear.

She made her way to the ridge from which she could look down on the winding river with its scattering of boats, brightly coloured like ribbons, its waters glistening in the sunlight, merging with the horizon to form an untroubled sea. Malcolm stood restlessly beside her, as she drank in the view, loath to interrupt her appreciation of what was before her but anxious to find out what had happened in his absence.

When he could stand the silence no longer, he said, "You have, haven't you? I'm too late. You're an attractive woman. I've been away a long time." He began to scold himself, saying, "I shouldn't be surprised. We parted on the worst possible terms. It was inevitable that you'd turn to somebody else."

Alice said, "Your letters weren't exactly affectionate, were they? Never once did you ask after my family, say that you loved me or begged my forgiveness for what you'd done."

"I didn't know what to write. You said you didn't want to hear from me again until after the war. I tried to comply with your wishes but found it impossible. I felt I had to do something that kept us in touch. If you'd replied, even once, my tone would have been different. Then, you would have seen how I felt."

"Why were you surprised when I kept my word?"

She felt that he was trying to bully her into a commitment she wasn't ready to make. She failed to see that in talking over her, in trying to retain the initiative, he was seeking to put off the moment when she spoke the words he feared.

She said, "It's impossible to carry on where we left off. You must see that, surely?"

"Why can't we put the past behind us and move forward together? It was what you wanted once. Is that not possible again?"

Alice shook her head. Two conversations were going on in her head simultaneously: one with Malcolm, all too present, and another with Tom, absent, but uppermost in her thoughts.

She said, "Yes, there's somebody else. I should have warned you. It's early days but I feel I'm committed to him. My feelings for him have reached a point that precludes anyone else."

"I thought as much. I've left it too late."

He spoke with grim satisfaction, even as his eyes scanned hers for signs of uncertainty, for a hint she hadn't meant what she said. He was aware that he had done his case little justice, that he had rushed into things, abandoning the restraint that he had intended. Seeing her again after so long, realising that he wanted her no less than before, the circumspection he had planned had melted away.

When she started to apologise, he knew that there was no way back.

"I'm very sorry if I've disappointed you."

Alice paused to watch the crows that swooped and fell above the house, calling loudly to each other before quieting and gathering again in the trees that were their home.

"Why do they do that?" she demanded as they came to rest. "Why do they suddenly take flight without reason and return to the same place as before?"

It seemed to her that her life was like that. Sudden launches into the air, a flurry of activity only to finish up where she had started from with little to show for her efforts. With Tom she felt it might be different; with him she was grounded in a way that she had never been before. They were edging forward slowly, feeling their way, preparing for a life that they might share. It would never have the fireworks that she had known with Malcolm but that was no matter for regret. There had been no communion there, no progress, just a flurry of activity brought on by the war, before they plunged to earth, locked together, destroying everything they cherished.

"Who is he?" he asked, his voice low and insistent, urging her to speak yet fearing her words. "Where did you meet him? Has he come back from the war?"

Alice could see no virtue in giving him the instruments with which to heighten his pain but he was intent on knowing. Reluctantly, she admitted that Tom was a wounded officer whom she had met in hospital when she had gone there with her brother.

"Badly wounded?" he asked.

Unwilling to be drawn on the nature of Tom's wounds, she conceded only that he was in hospital and would be leaving soon.

"Which hospital?"

When she replied, "Queen Mary's," he looked at her knowingly.

"I suppose you feel sorry for him?"

"There's more to it than that."

"Wounds you can see and touch invoke sympathy but trauma, the other consequence of the war, has to be borne alone. There's nobody to help your recovery, no one to erase your nightmares or help make you whole again."

When Alice began to protest, speaking of the work she was undertaking on behalf of those traumatised by the conflict, he was unmoved.

He said bitterly. "Oh, yes, what happened to me has a name now. There are hospitals to which the shell-shocked can go and psychiatrists who treat them as best they can. But, for such people, recovery lies in their own hands. Some prove capable of putting their lives back together. Others are less fortunate and retain their nightmares for ever. Even for the lucky few - and I'm one of those - there are still consequences, as we know to our cost."

"I didn't appreciate what you were going through when we met but you didn't tell me - or even hint at it. You spoke only of doing your duty," Alice said, reluctant to be grouped with the insensitive and the uncaring. "Only now do I understand what you suffered and why you acted in the way that you did."

When she saw the hope in his eyes, she said, "It doesn't change anything, though. That was never really the issue. You misled me. Even now, I am discovering things about you that were hidden previously. How can I love someone I can't trust, who never tells me the whole story? Anyway, it all seems a long time ago."

"For me, it seems like yesterday."

"But it isn't. Two years have gone by. Can you not recognise that everything was changed by the war? Try to see our encounter for what it was: a wartime liaison, a love affair, wonderful at the time but not something that we can replicate, something likely to endure."

"A butterfly that lived for a day?"

Alice leaned forward and gave him a kiss on the cheek. She said, "Yes, something like that," her words indicating that it was time to go. If Malcolm had further questions, he kept them to himself and she was grateful for the opportunity to order her thoughts. She had spoken of Tom with more confidence than she felt. She only had Sister Brown's word that he was fond of her. He was a long way from achieving the physical independence he craved. Her feelings for him, despite her brave words, were unclear. Was she, as Malcolm had suggested, moved only by sympathy for him? How could she be sure that she loved him and could live happily as his wife?

The sun was setting when they returned to the car, bestowing a becoming pink glow on the clouds. The park was emptying, its visitors conceding the clearings, paths and fields to the wildlife for which they were home. There was always a sadness about the park at dusk, Alice thought, a sense of disappointment that another day was over. She realised that she might never see Malcolm again. He would reassure her. He would make promises. She would concede the possibility of meeting him, knowing that it was unlikely to happen. His fond letters would never be written or those that she received would fail to prompt a reply. She was surprised, after so much concern about meeting him, how resolute she had been. Perhaps, if Tom hadn't existed, she would have found it more difficult but she felt they had reached a level of understanding that was hard to find and that she would disappoint him, and betray her own feelings, if she allowed herself to be diverted by Malcolm.

She admired the car again as she climbed into it but the engine wouldn't start and had to be cranked. She waited patiently whilst Malcolm wrestled with the handle, his face reddening. She said what a perfect day it had been for the park and how pleased she had been that Malcolm had seen it at its best. He told her that he was practicing law and that a multitude of cases were coming his way. She spoke of the charity that she had founded and the work that it was doing on behalf of war victims. He asked if he had inspired it and she admitted that his behaviour had played a part. She confirmed that her parents were well and told him of Michael's ambitions to stay in the army. He was horrified at the thought of anyone embarking on a military career, saying that volunteering had been something that he had felt obliged to do at the time and that every day he thanked God for the certainty of never having to do it again.

"In time, that's how you'll feel about us," Alice predicted with more confidence than she felt. "Our affair was right at the time and we'd do it again, even knowing what we know now, but the world has changed, our circumstances are different and it can never be replicated."

"Oh, I think it can. I really do," Malcolm said, taking his hand off the wheel so that the car swerved violently, startling a dray horse by the side of the road.

"Isn't it better to look back on our time together with great fondness and be grateful it happened? It would be a pity to cloak it in disappointment and bitterness, when it once meant so much to us."

When he said, "Well yes, it would," she thought she might have convinced him that it was truly over and that something else, a friendship they might treasure, could be put in its place.

It was almost dark by the time they reached the house. Malcolm halted the car at the kerb abruptly, so that she was thrown forward, and jumped out to open the door for her, offering her his hand as she swept up her skirts. When he attempted to kiss her, she did nothing to prevent it, knowing that it was for the last time.

"Well, goodbye then," she said with a crispness that belied her confusion. "I'm glad that you wrote to me again and that we decided to meet. I'm sorry if I've disappointed you..."

He smiled and said, "Yes, we must do it again," but his mind was made up. There would be no further meetings, no more painful encounters. Her message had been clear. She had found somebody else and when Alice said, "Yes, we must," he recognised her words were not an invitation but a conclusion whose meaning he acknowledged with a brief nod of his head.

"I would have loved you if you'd been honest with me," she whispered, as she watched him climb back into the car, hoping that it would start the first time so that he would be saved the embarrassment of having to crank the engine again. When it reached the end of the road, its indicator saluting as it turned, she felt sure that she had done the right thing and her thoughts turned back to Tom, all that had happened between them, and where it might lead.

CHAPTER 40

Though Alice was early, Tom's possessions were already packed. His trunk, strapped and labelled, stood to attention by the front door and his bed had been stripped and prepared for somebody else. He was seated by the window that overlooked the driveway, wearing a dark flannel suit with knife edge creases in its trousers, a shirt with a crisp white collar, a brightly coloured silk tie and from the breast pocket of his waistcoat hung a watch on a gold chain, ticking surreptitiously. He sat with his legs out stiffly in front of him, as was his habit.

When Alice entered the room, he rose to greet her with practiced ease, giving her the impression that the move had been rehearsed in anticipation of her arrival. When she kissed him on the cheek, a trace of cologne rose up to greet her. She stepped back, looked at him approvingly, and said, "You're looking smart."

He grinned broadly, relishing the compliment and said, "But, of course. Then I'm not collected from hospital every day. Still less am I collected by a beautiful woman in a large car."

Alice laughed gaily. "What a flatterer you are. It works every time. As for the car, well, it's my father's, the one he couldn't part with during the war, and the driver is here because my father doesn't trust me to drive it and thought I might need someone to help with the luggage."

"There isn't much of it, as you can see," Tom said, gesturing towards the door through which she had just passed.

"There seems quite a lot to me," Alice said, wondering if the trunk would fit on the back of the car.

"The army's good at luggage, providing it's properly labelled. Mine's been to so many hospitals and I haven't lost anything," Tom said in wonderment. "It always get's there in the end."

"They lost my brother."

"Oh, I'd forgotten about that," Tom said, his eyes widening.

"We'll try to keep up the good work. I only hope it'll all go in the car."

"Oh, it will," Tom said confidently, "luggage shrinks to fit the space available. I've always thought that."

He became more sombre, ran his fingers through his hair, a nervous gesture she had come to recognise as such, and sat down suddenly, one leg bent beneath him, the other stretched out stiffly.

He said with a frown,"I wonder if we might have a word before we leave, just the two of us, here, perhaps, where no one will disturb us."

"Of course," Alice said, noting that the benign expression that had greeted her arrival had given way to something more earnest. "If you'll wait a minute, I'll go out to the car and ask the driver to wait. I'm sure he won't mind."

He watched her depart with unconcealed admiration, grateful that he had made such an effort to enhance his appearance. Sister had inspected him when he thought that he was ready and had given him a vote of approval. He would miss her and the staff. They had looked after him so well, solicitous and attentive, without being overbearing, always ready to raise his spirits when he was intimidated by the challenges he faced.

When Alice returned, she assumed a stern expression and said with mock severity, "You haven't been talking to Sister Brown again, have you? You know that's a recipe for trouble."

"The matchmaker, you mean?" Tom said, laughing aloud. "I've tried to avoid discussing my personal affairs with her since you warned me about her." He pointed vaguely in the direction of sister's office and said, "Medical matters only, wasn't that what you said? Well, it wasn't easy. I can tell you. She can be quite persistent, as you know."

"She's lovely, but such a romantic," Alice said affectionately. "What's more, you're her favourite. That's very clear. I can't think why," she added, feigning surprise, "but that's how it is. There again, if she hadn't interfered..."

"Well, yes," Tom said, clearing his throat nervously, "that's what I wanted to talk to you about. I think she might have misled you."

"Misled me?"

Alice's stomach gave a sudden lurch. She had been hoping to hear something positive, something likely to resolve the issues she had been considering at length since Sister Brown had first taken her on one side.

She had been aware, following their meeting, that she had taken Tom's affections for granted, believing the interpretation that the sister had put on his words was the right one and that she was free to plan for the future in spite of his saying nothing to confirm her aspirations. For all she knew, there might be somebody else in his life or he might not care for her greatly. After all, she still knew little about him. The only member of his family whom she had met was his sister, a rather tired, put-upon war widow with three young children to care for who was glad of any help she could get. It was to her crowded home that she was taking him. There he was going to stay until he found a home of his own, somewhere convenient for the medical school he planned to attend.

She sat down more heavily than she had intended in the chair by the window, looking out on the park with a fierce intensity, unable to return his gaze. She watched an ambulance turn into the drive and wondered who was inside it and what condition they were in. The sun, high in the sky, bisected the room, warming her face, casting Tom's in shadow, varnishing the dark, wooden floor. Tom watched her carefully, adding to her consternation, as he struggled to find the words that he wanted to utter. A clock behind his head struck the hour, startling her and she found herself counting the chimes. From elsewhere in the house came the sound of voices, footsteps and the rattle of a trolley bound for the wards. A balding man holding a newspaper stuck his head round the door, said "Oh, excuse me," and went out again, concluding from their expressions that they wished to be alone.

"Well," Alice said, when she could stand the silence no longer, "what was it that you wanted to say?"

"I was hoping to talk to you about what's to become of us."

"I think I knew that," Alice said gently, hoping to coax from him the words that he was reluctant to utter and that she wanted to hear.

She said, "I'd been meaning to talk to you also, but the time never seemed right. It hardly seemed necessary when we were getting on so well."

He said eagerly, "We do get on well, don't we?

The thought seemed to encourage him, as if it hadn't occurred to him before. He sat upright in his seat, adjusted the cushions and prepared to speak.

"If Sister Brown hadn't intervened," Alice thought, "events would have taken their course." Now, there was a danger that they were about to confront certain issues before they ready to do so, before their feelings for each other were plain. She recognised there had been grounds for confusion. Sister had been right about that. Meeting as they had in a hospital, patient and visitor, the way ahead had been anything but clear. Now, as Tom prepared to say something formative, she realised that she cared for him greatly and hoped that he had something more to declare than his gratitude for what she had done for him.

He said, with some misgivings, "I'm aware that a certain affection has grown up between us. You were very kind to me at a time when I was in need of care and attention and after each visit, I felt we'd grown closer. But what did this affection mean? I kept asking myself. You're a kind and considerate person but what were your intentions towards me?"

Alice smiled and said, "Isn't that what I'm supposed to ask you?"

He acknowledged the observation with a wary smile.

"You see, I really don't know. You may feel nothing, of course, beyond a desire to help me back on my feet but I thought I'd better be frank about my feelings towards you so that you'd have an opportunity to consider them before we meet again."

"His disability confuses everything," Alice concluded. If he had been about to leave hospital unimpaired, the problem would not have arisen. As it is, he believes that I feel sorry for him. There was a danger, unless she was forthright about her feelings for him, that nothing that she might say or do would convince him that she felt anything for him other than pity.

"Can I ask you something?" she said, leaning forward in her chair so that she was near enough to him to reach out and touch him, even as she resisted any sudden display of affection for fear that it would only serve to confuse matters at a time when the need for clarity had never been greater.

"What is it?"

"Do you feel sorry for yourself, sorry for everything that the war has done to you and the condition in which you find yourself now?"

His fingers drummed on the arm of the chair as he considered her question. Then, he said, with all the dignity that he could muster, "Oh, you don't beat about the bush, do you?" After thinking further - to Alice it seemed like an age - he added, "No, I don't. After my operations, when

I first realised what had happened to me, I thought a normal life might be impossible. Gradually, I began to recover and realised, as the pain subsided, that a new life was perfectly feasible. I recognised it wouldn't be like the old life with its infinite choices, the arrogant belief that anything was possible; I saw it would be more limited in scope, more difficult than anything I had attempted before, but that it could still be a good life. I had survived the war when hundreds of thousands had been less fortunate. I had lost a limb, certainly. I would have to learn to walk again. I would have to adjust to the attitude of others to my disability but my mind was unimpaired and I would still be able to earn a good living if I applied myself diligently. But I had imagined that this new life, whatever its merits, would be spent largely alone. I didn't anticipate that anyone would want to marry me or wouldn't be disconcerted by my reduced state."

"Do you think that now?" Alice asked, her voice little more than a whisper. How could he think that, how could he imagine that he was disadvantaged when she had been drawn to him from the first?

She looked at him intently, searching his face for clues as to what he might say next but the face that she studied was impassive; his eyes were cast down and she saw no grounds for encouragement there, no sign that there might be a meeting of minds.

"No, I don't. I can see I've been foolish, even negative, with regard to others. Of course, it's not out of the question that somebody will love me in spite of my wounds. Why do I think this? Well..."

He paused, unsure whether to continue, now the moment of decision was upon him. Then, taking a deep breath, he plunged on, the words he had held back for so long tumbling forth.

He said, "When I realised that we'd become very close, that you had a certain affection for me, it gave me grounds for hope, hope that others would have regard for me also and that some day I'd find someone I cared for, as much as I care for you, so that I could ask her to marry me and she would agree with enthusiasm to be my wife."

"Has it ever occurred to you," Alice asked, "that your affection for me might be reciprocated, that I might care for you no less than you care for me, and that I might be the person whom you've described?"

"I've longed for that since the day we met but convinced myself it was impossible. I thought you felt sorry for me and wanted to aid my recovery. I anticipated that we would become friends when I left here but no more than that. Why would you choose me when you had the world at your feet?"

"The world at my feet? I don't know about that?" Alice said, with a shrug. "My point is: why would I feel sorry for you when you don't feel sorry for yourself? A man sunk in misery has few attractions to me, or to most people I'd imagine, but you're a fighter, that was clear from the start. I wanted to help you because I admired and respected you - not because I felt sorry for you. Your determination to overcome your difficulties was obvious. You didn't need me to give you a push."

"Admiration and respect are fine things but love - that's harder to find. Sister warned me not to confuse friendship and love, not to assume that you wanted me because of your willingness to aid my recovery."

"Sister has much to answer for," Alice said, but she spoke without malice.

What Sister Brown had done, in an effort to protect one of her 'boys' from harm, was to warn them about the difficulties they faced. Tom had been cautioned, as she had been advised to take care, and her intervention had been timely and proper. Without it, she might have been thoughtless or hurt Tom without meaning to. As it was, Sister had prompted each of them to examine their feelings and to consider the consequences of their behaviour. Tom, fearing that he had only her sympathy and admiration, had kept his feelings concealed. Confused by the circumstances of their meeting and the nature of his condition, she had failed to understood how she felt. Neither of them need have had any great cause for concern. Their affection had blossomed not because of the circumstances in which they found themselves but in spite of them. There was no further need to hold back.

Alice rose from her chair and held out both her arms. Tom lurched to his feet, a manoeuvre he now had to perfection, and they clung to each other, a little shakily at first and then with more certainty, confident that together they could face the world, whatever others might say and whatever difficulties might be put in their way. Arm in arm, they made for the door of the hospital, Tom striding out down the corridor, Alice clinging on to his arm whilst Sister MacDonald watched covertly from the door of the ward, convinced at last, that her 'boy' would be fine, before bidding them both goodbye.

The trunk was safely secured on the back of the car. The back doors were ajar, the silver door handles reflecting the light; the mirrors and the headlights gleamed, having been lovingly polished by the driver whilst he waited for their appearance. He greeted them with a smile. Tom escorted Alice to her seat, standing beside her proudly as she ducked inside the car. She thanked him for his courtesy before he closed the door with exaggerated care. Climbing into the car unaided, Tom took up his position next to her and reached for her hand, clasping it tightly as the car made its way down the drive.

CHAPTER 41

"I'm not sure about this," Robert said, "it could go horribly wrong."

"You'll have the best people acting for you. You need have no concerns about that. Eminent people are queuing up to defend you. I've been agreeably surprised by the enthusiasm shown for your cause."

When he named some of the QCs who had come forward to represent him, Robert was impressed. His father was certainly well-connected. He recalled his appearance in the camp three years previously and the hope that it had brought to everyone. He smiled and said, "You always prevail when you have a mind to."

It had taken him a week to establish his victim's condition, a week during which malevolent warders had made every effort to convince him he was a murderer. The pretence had only collapsed when it became known that the victim had recovered sufficiently from his beating to go back to work. Robert found it hard to forgive his tormentors but recognised that he had only himself to blame. Thereafter, there had been a battle for jurisdiction over his crime. Encouraged by his father, Robert had insisted on taking his case to trial on the grounds that whilst his guilt was obvious, it was likely that would be granted bail and might receive a shorter sentence when the nature of his treatment was revealed. The governor, already under pressure for opening the dungeons, preferred to deal with Robert's actions in the privacy of the prison. Thanks to Bennett's vigorous lobbying, the matter was now out of his hands. Robert could be released on bail in a matter of days, free to prepare for his trial and able to defend as best he could the actions he so regretted.

"You do realise," Robert said, speaking softly in an effort to avoid being overheard, "that, at the time, I would happily have murdered him."

Bennett whispered, "You mustn't say things like that. There were mitigating circumstances. Your previous conduct was beyond reproach, in spite of provocations too many to mention. That's your best prospect of a nominal sentence. Moreover, it's an opportunity to turn the spotlight on the prison authorities and their behaviour toward you and other objectors. Your evidence will be meat and drink to those pressing for prison reform."

Robert looked at his father with misgivings. He wasn't sure he had the stomach for the fight. He had weathered the uncertainty better than he had feared, drawing on his experience in France to combat any despair. Nonetheless, the situation had taken its toll. He had been convinced that he was a murderer and that he would hang for his crime. Only when the warders had lost interest in him, resorting to the tyranny that was their way, had he been convinced he would survive.

He said, "I can't tell you how angry I am with myself. If there's one thing worse than being betrayed by a friend, it's betraying yourself."

"You haven't betrayed yourself," his father countered, "I won't have you saying that. After all you went through, something unfortunate was bound to occur."

Robert marvelled at his choice of words. 'Something unfortunate' was not quite how he saw it but if his father was dismayed by his actions, he had never said so outright. When he had learnt of his predicament, he had leapt into action and the impartiality he had laboured to maintain throughout the war had given way to fiercely partisan lobbying on his behalf, urged on by Michael, newly returned from France.

Bennett said, "You've always been hard on yourself. Look at what you've achieved. You set your face against conscription and held out against every attempt, including the death sentence, to force you to change your mind."

"I suppose I did," Robert said, encouraged by the thought of what he had endured, "there was certainly no lack of effort to intimidate me."

"You resisted the parade ground bullies. Subjected to field punishment, sentenced to death and reprieved, you never wavered. You declined alternative service, when many took it up and regretted it, and were subject to years of consecutive sentences. Then, when the war ended, your sentence was prolonged without good reason and when you declined to go on hunger strike, those who did were released. Finally, you were falsely accused of inciting a mutiny. If all that isn't cause for loss of control, I don't know what is…"

"What would have happened if I hadn't been restrained?"

"We all have murder in our hearts at times."

"But we don't act on it - we control our emotions - at least, those of us who promote non-violence and seek to live in that belief."

"When you resisted conscription, you did what you thought was appropriate - as Michael did when he enlisted. You both searched your consciences and came to different conclusions, as was your right. The path you chose proved to be more difficult than we anticipated. No one could have foreseen that pacifism would prompt such animosity. It's a matter for regret that you failed to live up to your principles but it doesn't mean that they were the wrong ones. It means only that on one occasion you let yourself down. Eventually you'll look back on what you endured with amazement and forget all your shortcomings."

"Well, I hope you're right because now I'm full of remorse and believe I betrayed everything in one careless moment."

"You're fallible, like the rest of us," Bennett said, determined to resist Robert's mawkishness. "It doesn't mean you lived a lie."

"There was another reason for my anger."

"What was that?" Bennett's deep-set eyes scrutinised his son. It was a look that always made him uncomfortable, the prelude to a judgement best avoided.

"It's to do with my reasons for coming back from America."

"I still have the letter you wrote to me. What more's there to say?"

He rested his elbows on the table, his chin on his fists. Of all the challenges posed by the war, Robert's revelations regarding the events at Swarthmore had been the hardest to bear. At first, he had thought that his son had lied to him and had never intended to fight conscription. Then, he had thought the opposite: that by coming back when he did, Robert had been seeking to atone for his behaviour, a view reinforced when his college principal, an old friend of the family, had told him of his efforts to prevent Robert leaving. Now, it turned out that there was more. He waited on Robert's words with misgivings. It seemed that these days he rarely encountered his children without some revelation, some unwelcome news to consider.

"You'll recall," Robert said, "that I wrote to you about my reasons for coming back from America and my involvement with Mary, a student I taught there."

"We were greatly upset by that letter, as you might imagine. We wished you'd been more frank with us when you came back."

"I was always going to come back. I could never have sat out the whole of the war in America."

"Our concern was somewhat different. We feared that you were trying to make amends for everything that had happened at Swarthmore by opposing conscription."

"Do you think that now?"

Bennett shook his head, "No, I believe you did what you felt to be right at the time and have nothing but admiration for your stand. Dr Hull, your Principal, wrote to me some months ago. He told me of his conversations with you, your determination to come back. He didn't share your view that the college's reputation was at risk and that you had to leave for its sake."

"He conceded that my rightful place was with my family, opposing conscription, doing what I could to mitigate the consequences of the war."

"Nobody doubted your sincerity."

"Several months after I left, Mary gave birth to a baby girl."

"You left knowing she was pregnant?"

Robert threw his hands up in horror, "No, of course not. I had no idea. If I'd known, I would have stayed and done what I could do to help."

"And you're the father?" Bennett asked reluctantly

"Undoubtedly," Robert said. "Look at the photographs, talk to Alice, there can be no doubt that Rosamund's my daughter, born though she was three years ago."

He was excited now, his face flushed and animate, his reservations giving way to pride. Whatever the circumstances, he had a daughter and intended to see her as soon as he could.

Bennett looked at him in bewilderment. Robert had never seen such confusion on his face: distress that his son had a daughter born out of wedlock, pride that he had a grandchild, something he had wanted for so long, and which had been denied to him by the war.

"I have a granddaughter?" Bennett repeated the question several times, weighing up Robert's answers, "and for three years none of us knew?"

"I didn't even have a photograph of her," Robert replied. "Nothing. It was as if she didn't exist."

"Well, she does," Bennett said delightedly. He rose from his seat, sat down again, looking about him, wanting to share his good fortune with somebody. Then, his smiled faded. He turned to Robert, his voice, quiet and insistent and said, "You must have resented being here when you heard the news?"

"I promised myself that as soon as I was released, I'd visit her in Pennsylvania. Well, here I am, still waiting to be free."

"Have you written to her mother?"

"I've apologised profusely for ignoring her letters. I've also told her of my delight that we have a daughter and have spoken of my earnest wish to see them both soon."

"All those letters, week after week, whisked away by Alice before any of us could read them...or even see who they were from."

"Alice was only doing what I asked. Another of my misjudgements. Mary's very young. I felt that I would serve her best if I removed myself from her life. That way she would have the time and freedom to find someone else. Of course, as we discovered, her letters were an attempt to tell me that I had a daughter."

"How old is Mary?"

"Twenty three."

Bennett looked relieved she was no younger. "Did she know you were in prison?"

"She had heard about it from Alice. She thought news of Rosie would lift my spirits and, of course, it did but it was also my undoing. It heightened my anger and frustration at still being here, although the war was over.

"The release of the hunger strikers must have been the last straw?" Bennett reflected sadly. "No wonder you fought back when they accused you unfairly." His face contorted angrily, before assuming its usual demeanour. The insight into his feelings, though fleeting, helped

Robert understand the nature of his response. How many parents would have heard the news of his fatherhood without criticising him for his selfishness or would have learnt of his violence without judging him? He was fortunate to have a father who, for all his rectitude, invariably supported his children.

But Bennett also came with news and, conscious of how little time was left, decided he had better speak up. "You are aware," he asked, changing the subject abruptly, "that Michael has decided to join the regular army? He said that he would write to you to that effect. Has he done so or is his letter still to come?"

"He's written," Robert confirmed. "I was quite shocked. I had no idea that he was intending to go back."

"None of us did," Bennett said with regret. "Then you know Michael, he always keeps things to himself." When Robert agreed, his reward was a look that suggested that he was no less guilty of the same crime.

Robert looked fondly at the tall, emaciated figure who had visited him often, knowing that behind his stern countenance lay an unwavering affection for his family. He had always loved his father unreservedly even as he struggled to meet his expectations. He recognised him for the tortured figure he was. His father's life had been a struggle to achieve the standards he had set himself. At times, when he fell victim to his rectitude, forced to share with him a burden that ran counter to his nature, he had resisted his views. Now he understood better how fortunate he was to have such a father and recognised that he would have had it no other way. The last three years's difficulties were not to be laid at his door. They were entirely of his own making. His father had observed his actions, had given them his blessing when appropriate, but the decisions had been his alone. He thought of Michael and wondered what his father thought of his decision to go back. His enlistment had been such a blow and now he had joined the army, flying in the face of the family's traditions.

"I wasn't in the least surprised," Bennett said, "not after he came home on leave. It was clear that he was comfortable in the army, in spite of the war."

"Why was that, do you think? We hardly encouraged it."

"Perhaps, we did in a way?" Bennett smiled, rather sadly Robert thought, as he offered his view. "We question everything. We always have. It's a habit with us. The army's different. Its lack of ambiguity appeals to Michael. He prefers to give and follow orders, to lead and be led. He finds our deliberations a strain. I used to think that was on account of his age but now I realise it's his nature. He doesn't like complications or introspection."

"There's something to be said for that. I've had enough introspection in the last three years to last me a lifetime."

"I hope you won't be joining the army."

Robert laughed out loud, causing the warder observing them to frown and move closer.

"Did you try to talk him out of it?"

"Not in the least. Nor strangely, did your mother. She was reconciled to his going back into the army as soon as she saw that he had survived the war. We both reasoned, after everything he had seen and done, that he was more than capable of making up his own mind with regard to such matters."

It was then that Bennett grasped just how much Robert had missed as a result of three years in prison. It was not merely that his life had stood still, reduced to a twilight of boredom and idleness by the prison regime even as the outside world had been shaken to its core, but also that, for all that time, he had been denied responsibility for his own actions, subject as he was to the will of vigilant warders and the oppressive regulations that were their provenance. It was little wonder that he had endeavoured to break free. The alternative had been capitulation, a surrender of his true self.

He looked around the grey, ill-lit meeting room. The era of individual meeting rooms had flowered briefly only to wither and die under the new governor's wilfulness. It was bare of everything other than the long desk that bisected it, the tall mesh that ran its length, the line of chairs on either side of it around which the prisoners and visitors clustered. He had imagined that prisoners subject to the rule of silence would be garrulous when given the opportunity to speak but most of them had little to say. What did they have to talk about? Their lives were dull and repetitive. They had nothing to describe or explain. Most of them listened desultorily to their visitors' monologues, asking few questions, reluctant to acquaint themselves with other, more meaningful lives. Robert had told him that many of them preferred to avoid visitors because being reminded of the challenges and pleasures of life outside prison was simply too painful. They thought it better to follow the mindless regime to the letter, to live its restricted and meaningless life, undisturbed by thoughts of what others were doing. At least Robert still had his wits about him. He was as aware and as curious as ever, still interested in the fortunes of his family even though his knowledge was a mixed blessing when there were no outlets for insight or imagination, little access to pen or paper and his comrades were his own dark thoughts.

Bennett said, "Did Michael ever tell you how he earned him his DCM?"

"No, but Alice did," Robert said, surprised at the question. "She thought it an act of great bravery that might have cost him his life."

"Did she tell you any of the details?" Bennett persisted.

"Not really, but then I didn't ask. Though I was curious, I didn't think it appropriate at the time."

"Well, I'll tell you now," Bennett said, drawing his chair up to the table, "not to be gratuitous but because I think it's relevant to your situation. He and his comrades stormed a machine gun post, a sap forward of the line. He killed its two occupants. He didn't attempt to disarm them or take them prisoner. He stabbed both of them to death. When I asked him if he had any regrets he replied, "No, none whatsoever." He claimed - quite rightly, I'm sure - that there was nothing else he could have done if he and his companions were to escape with their lives. He pointed out that the ground in front of the sap was littered with the bodies of his comrades. To this day, he feels not a shred of remorse for what he did and few, hearing his story, would dream of condemning him. I certainly wouldn't, would you?"

Robert was silent for a moment. He regarded his father with still, sad eyes. He had been moved by Michael's story when he first heard it and was moved by it still. He said suddenly, "What would you do if the Hun was at the door, threatening to rape your wife and sisters, or to kill your parents and children?"

When his father looked at him blankly, he smiled slightly, gave a shrug and said, "That's the question the military representative asked at the tribunal whenever he was faced with someone who declined to enlist on grounds of conscience."

"What did you say?" Bennett demanded, a strange light in his eyes. The light of battle perhaps, a willingness to defend himself and his views, honed over a lifetime of dissidence. He had often told Robert that if it hadn't been for his age he would have been standing in his shoes and Robert believed it was true. He would have been even more intractable, even less willing to serve.

"I don't remember exactly. Some glib retort, no doubt, some circumlocution intended to demonstrate my wit. The truth was that I didn't have an answer then and I don't have one now. Perhaps, there isn't one. Who knows what they'll do when the time comes?"

"There's no point to the question," Bennett said indignantly, "I wouldn't have answered it. No man has the right to sit in judgement over your conscience, believing he knows better than you what's the right thing to do."

"You're probably right," Robert said. "Where I stand now, after three years of this," he looked at the prisoners and visitors staring at each other through the gauze, "is that there are circumstances that are right for pacifism and there are those that aren't."

He placed his hands together on the desk, clasping them tightly as if concealing a coin and said, "It might seem that my views have been unswerving for the last three years but that's far from the case. My years in prison have been plagued with doubts. I was never inclined to give up or compromise, as some did, but I've often asked myself whether, knowing what I knew then, I would do the same thing again."

"And would you?" Bennett asked, a look of anxiety on his face. He couldn't bear the thought that at some point Robert had experienced a change of heart that had rendered his suffering in vain.

To his immense relief, Robert said, "I made certain choices and have lived with their consequences, much as I hated them. No, I have no regrets, any more than Michael regrets going to war on behalf of King and Country. My only regret is that I let myself down."

"But you'll forgive yourself in due course?"

It was a question rather than a statement and an urgent one. The room was beginning to clear, the visitors were rising from their seats and the warders were beginning to marshal the prisoners prior to returning them to their cells.

Robert was slow to reply. His father watched him anxiously, fearing that he had added self-abnegation to the burden that three years of imprisonment had placed on his shoulders. He longed to tell him how much he loved and admired him, how proud he was of his stand and how, for all his fine words, he would never have possessed the strength and determination to do what Robert had done. But he couldn't say it. The words stuck fast in his throat. He wondered if he should write them down, put them in one of the two letters Robert was permitted to receive from his family each month, but knew that he would remain silent, admiring him from afar, as he did with all his children, leaving Robert to fend for himself, as he must, if he was to survive a new sentence without mishap or loss.

Bennett rose clumsily from the table, his eyes focused on Robert's face, waiting expectantly on his words, Robert said, "I've always tried to do what I believed to be right and, in spite of my obvious failings, I'd do it all over again."

"It won't come to that. We'll make sure of it. One day the tide will turn and your opposition to conscription will be seen for what it was: the response of a man determined to follow his convictions whatever the consequences for his safety and health."

"You mustn't worry," Robert said. "I'll get to the end of this, in spite of the trial, with my mind and body intact and I'll go to America, as soon as I can. I'll meet my daughter - and her mother - take up my rightful place in the world and attempt to be a force for good and when I see Michael, I'll wish him well in his new life and thank him for all that he did for me, our family and the country we cherish - even though it wasn't what I chose to do. I'll suffer the consequences of my shortcomings as best as I can but when that's done, I'll put them behind me and start again."

With that he allowed the warder to lead him away, failing to notice the tears in his father's eyes. With a brief wave of his hand and a whispered farewell, he joined the queue of prisoners as they filed through the door at the end of the hall and made his way back to the cell that had been his home for three years, leaving his father to watch his departure and count the days to the release that he hoped to engineer for his son, whom he had always loved and respected so much.

Made in the USA
Charleston, SC
14 March 2016